The Abolitionist's Daughter

DIANE C. McPHAIL

JOHN SCOGNAMIGLIO BOOKS
KENSINGTON BOOKS
www.kensingtonbooks.com

Although based on historical fact, this is a work of fiction, and all characters and narrative are fiction.

JOHN SCOGNAMIGLIO BOOKS are published by

Kensington Publishing Corp.
119 West 40th Street
New York, NY 10018

First Kensington Hardcover Edition: May 2019

ISBN-13: 978-1-4967-2032-0 (ebook)
ISBN-10: 1-4967-2032-6 (ebook)

ISBN-13: 978-1-4967-2031-3
ISBN-10: 1-4967-2031-8
First Kensington Trade Paperback Edition: September 2020

10 9 8 7 6 5 4 3 2 1

Printed in the United States of America

PRAISE FOR
THE ABOLITIONIST'S DAUGHTER

"Diane McPhail excavates a nearly forgotten corner of American history and brings it to full, beating life. This is a fascinating and heartfelt look at the kinds of stories that don't always make it into the history books."
—Louis Bayard, author of *Courting Mr. Lincoln*

"A contender, a deeply felt, thoroughly researched story . . . as good as it deserves to be."
—Jacquelyn Mitchard, *New York Times* bestselling author

"Complex, vivid, and emotionally engaging. This is a story of harsh realities written with a tenderness that shines through and honors the account of one woman's struggle to overcome her society's rules and her circumstances in the face of inconceivable devastation. I couldn't put it down."
—Carol E. Anderson, author of *You Can't Buy Love Like That*

"What an impressive book this is! Diane McPhail works a spell on the reader, transporting us to Mississippi in the nineteenth century, introducing us to a family torn apart by the time and place in which they live. She tells a dark tale, yet it's laced with lyricism and compassion. This is a powerful, imaginative, captivating book—I'd say, even urgent, considering the time we find ourselves in now."
—Judy Goldman, author of *Together*

"A tender, sparkling debut that bears gentle witness to the abominations of slavery and oppression while heralding the grace, power, and necessity of righting wrongs and choosing love. McPhail is full of talent and heart."
—Ethel Rohan, author of *The Weight of Him*

"*The Abolitionist's Daughter* brings to light the tragic yet inevitable entanglements of slavery, as ultimately manifested in the Civil War. The complications of race, division, and hate in this epic novel are still with us today and necessary to contemplate; *The Abolitionist's Daughter* is *Gone with the Wind* for the twenty-first century."
—Brian Railsback

"What a gripping, wise, and richly imagined novel this is. This is historical fiction at its best—a beautifully written, compulsive read that resonates with the moral complexities of our own time."
—Abigail DeWitt, author of *News of Our Loved Ones*

In memory of my mother, Loree Dunlap Cox

ACKNOWLEDGMENTS

Let me begin with gratitude to all the unknown people and family of Webster County for keeping alive the stories surrounding the history of what has been known as the Edwards-Gray feud, though the violence between the two families did not continue beyond the initial violence. I am thankful to those family members and local citizens who have continued to tell the story and contribute to the newspapers. I am especially indebted to Ralph Dunlap and to Sarah McCain Saxon for introducing me to the genealogy of the Edwards family. The staff of Mississippi State University Library Archives provided invaluable help in preserving and making available the historical papers and crucial inventories of Judge Edward Edwards. I offer my deepest gratitude to Gene Bridges, whose wisdom guided me through the intricacies of family and trauma and who will recognize himself in these pages.

From the beginning of this endeavor I have been supported and encouraged by members of my writing groups: Highlands Writers, Duke Writers Workshop, Table Rock Writers, Sweetwater Novel 6 and Critique Group, Abroad Writers, and Yale Writers' Workshop. I am especially indebted to my esteemed teachers and mentors: To Madeleine L'Engle, I owe the realization that, indeed, I could write and trust the work to know more than I do. To Brian Railsback, the moment of commitment to this particular story. To Darnell Arnault, the years of patient sustenance of my skills as a writer. To Jane Smiley, refinement of research skill that led me to the crucial role on the Civil War of the extremes of climate change and weather at the end of the Little Ice Age. To Jacquelyn Mitchard, as my working editor, the ongoing push to never settle for less. To Ethel Rohan, the encouragement to reach ever further and to believe the furthest point attainable. To Judy Goldman, a million thanks for her keen eye and tenacity to detail. To Marian Thurm, gratitude for her amazing generosity of spirit and skill. To Louis Bayard, the validation that I belong. I am especially grateful to Jotham Burello and to the Yale Writers' Workshop for providing me with that last step over the threshold into a waiting and wider experience than I might have imagined. And especially to Jotham, for providing the opportunity to meet the perfect literary agent for this project.

From our first introduction and intriguing conversation, my agent, Mark Gottlieb of Trident Media Group, has offered deep insight into the underlying themes of this work and steadfast support. His enthusiasm provided the connection to my editor and publisher, John Scognamiglio of Kensington Publishing Corporation, who has been a pleasure to work with and unfailingly supportive.

Many thanks to those patient souls who took the time to read and respond to early versions of this manuscript, and to provide me with invaluable reader responses. Their questions and observations helped to form the novel as it is: David Sharp, Nancy Bolton Beck, Karen Barnett, Jim and Martha Yelverton, Jim Rollins, Theodora Ziolkowski, and Rawson Gordon. Later readers of the final manuscript have been equally generous in the gift of time and support: Carol Anderson, Corabel Shofner, Jody Franco, Alan Hlad, Louis Bayard, Ethel Rohan, and Brian Railsback.

Finally, this book would not have been possible without my husband, Ray, who believed in me and to whom I am forever grateful.

Book One: Marriage

1859–1861

CHAPTER 1

Heat hung fierce for spring over the town of Greensboro, Mississippi, the late sunlight flickering in dusty rays. A breeze that might have otherwise refreshed only added to the oppressive atmosphere, diving in gusts to trouble the crinolined skirts of the ladies along the boardwalk. Except for the few accompanied by personal slaves, the women struggled with their parcels as they clutched their bonnets close against a dry haze of dust unfurled in the wake of passing carts. Nailed to the livery stable, a slave auction notice snapped in the gritty air. At the sound two women halted on the boardwalk. Emily Matthews pressed a gloved finger to still the paper. A cluster of men nearby suspended their conversation to stare. Ignoring them, Emily jerked away from Ginny's restraining grip and tore the poster from its nail.

"You best drop that thing, Miss Emily. Here, give it to me." Fierce determination drove Ginny's half whisper.

"Leave me be, Ginny." Emily thrust the paper in crumpled folds deep into her pockets. "Papa must see this. Holbert Conklin is selling Nathan."

"People's watching you, Miss Emily. Leave it now. You gone get somebody killed." Emily shook herself free of Ginny, grabbed at her hoops, and stepped down onto the dirt of the street.

In spite of sullen glances her direction, Emily shouldered through the dwindling afternoon crowd and negotiated her way through the fine buggies, plodding mules with clattering wagons, and the ever-present dung of Main Street. Ginny funneled behind her, eyes down, but missing nothing. Opposite the courthouse, Emily clasped the edge of her gray bonnet, squinting. She brandished the crumpled paper up at her father where he watched for her from his office, as he did every Friday. His hair and beard glowed white in the sunlit window, his eyes intense under the thick brows. He saw me, Emily thought, as she stepped onto the courthouse lawn. By the time the two women mounted the steps, Judge Matthews was locking the heavy front door, one arm loaded with law books. Emily restrained herself, but barely, as he ducked under her bonnet to kiss her cheek and smooth a loose strand of hair over her ear. He smiled and nodded to Ginny.

Emily thrust the notice at him. "This is a travesty, Papa. You must do something." Though his antislavery stance took a heavy toll on them both in a town like Greensboro, she counted on that foundation.

He shook the rumpled paper flat. Ginny clutched the unstable law books, as Emily peered over her father's sleeve, her hand fisted against his arm. He retrieved his spectacles from a pocket, flicked them open, and adjusted them on his nose, where they magnified the intensity of his almost-brown eyes.

TO BE SOLD & LET, By Public Auction,
On Monday the 7th of March, 1859
For Sale, THE THREE FOLLOWING SLAVES:
Nathan, a 30-year-old buck and excellent hand of Good Character
with some training as a household servant

He got no further as Emily jabbed at the words. "Nathan has a wife and two children," she said. "I see them when I call on Virginia. Conklin's going to tear that family apart. He cares nothing for family, including his own. He's a despicable man, Papa. And cruel." She glanced at Ginny. "Virginia never speaks of it, but I see her bruises. The ones she can't cover and more than ordinary life accounts for."

Judge Matthews folded the notice and retrieved his books. "Thank you, Ginny."

The judge knew Conklin well—an unwelcome, perhaps even dangerous, cohort of his son, Jeremiah. Silence enveloped the three as they jolted over the rutted road home. First father, then daughter commenced to speak, but stopped, their utterances incomplete.

"He is a vile man, Papa," Emily said, as he helped her from the buggy. Evil was the word she wanted to use. "Can you stop him?"

He hefted the law books from the wagon and held a hand to Ginny. "I'll do what I can."

Jessie pulled the ripped dress around her frail torso and shivered. Morning was moving toward the horizon. She stood on the unpainted porch, her eyes blank, not seeing her children's red ball in the dusty yard, the pile of rocks she hauled up from the creek yesterday to line the front walkway, nor the broom abandoned in panic. Jessie did not see her own shoe on the sagging step, caught there as she fled Holbert Conklin.

Her dark eyes saw nothing before her, her mind seeing only what had befallen her in the cabin behind: the heavy white hands, freckled like dirty snow; a straggling lock of reddish hair over the icy eyes that burned into her naked flesh; and her own hand gripping the post of the bed Nathan had built her from scrap. Today she would lose him, perhaps forever. He would never need to know this thing that had happened.

She spun back into the cabin with its single room, closed the door, wrenched the coarse sheet from the bed, and piled it on the floor. Heaving, she collapsed onto the violated fabric of her rough mattress. As her body quieted, she rose. She stripped off her torn dress, dipped the barest edge of it in the water bucket by the door, and wiped the blood from her legs. Removing her other shift from its peg, she pulled it hard over her thin body and threw the damp remains of her dress on top of the mounded sheet.

Out back, she gathered an armload of fallen branches, ignoring the sharp twigs digging into her flesh. She stacked them, one by one, on the banked coals from the night before and blew into the fireplace, coughing from the dust and ashes. A flame sputtered. As the kindling caught, Jessie shifted on her haunches, but without relief from the pain. She held the wet edge of the ruined dress over the flame. When it was dry enough, Jessie laid it on the growing fire. With her teeth, she tore the edge of the sheet, ripped it down its length, and fed the two halves into the flames.

When the last of the fabric caught, Jessie stood. Holding the bedpost, she gazed around the cabin. Blood stained the ticking of the corn shuck mattress. With rag and lye soap, Jessie scrubbed the stains in narrowing circles. She took clean water and reversed the spirals, rinsing away the soap. But not the stain, not all of it.

Outside, Jessie dropped the rag in the dirt and started up the lane toward Auntie Clara's. A cluster of children, including her own, too young for the field, played in the early dawn around the old woman's cabin. As Jessie came into the yard, Auntie Clara shushed a boy's wails and brushed dirt from his knees.

"Auntie, I needs your help." Jessie looked down at the boy, who stopped crying and ran. "I needs a bedcover."

CHAPTER 2

At 7:28 on Monday morning, a violent knock shook Judge Matthews's front door. Ginny heard it from the house kitchen, which had been added as an L to the main farmhouse for convenience. She slipped the flowered china cup back into the dishwater and wiped the soapsuds on her apron. Through the window, Ginny recognized Holbert Conklin's overseer, a man whose name circulated through the quarters amid tales of unbridled cruelty. Behind him, four slaves huddled in the curve of the drive: a broad, clean-shaven man, a woman hardly larger than a pubescent girl, and two small children, a boy and a girl. In the dirt beside them lay two half-empty croker sacks.

"Go tell the judge I've come for Mr. Conklin's money," McCabe said when Ginny opened the door. He spit a stream of dark tobacco juice down the steps.

Ginny studied the little group. The man, a strapping buck, clasped his right arm in the other elbow. He leaned, bracing himself almost imperceptibly, against the tiny woman. The girl clung to her mother's leg, and the little boy rubbed at his nose. Ginny nodded to McCabe and disappeared, shutting the door behind her.

McCabe spit off the porch again, swiping at his unkempt mustache with a dirty handkerchief, his back was to the door. When the judge opened it, he did not turn around. Judge Matthews stepped out even with him. Neither man greeted the other.

"Well, Judge. There's your goods. You got the cash?"

"I do." Judge Matthews handed him a stack of bills, which McCabe stuffed into his pants pocket, the wad of money folding in on itself. He wiped at his mustache again before thrusting the soiled handkerchief into his pocket on top of the bills.

"Man's a drunk," McCabe said. "Fell off his goddamned porch on a binge last night."

Now, just how would a slave get liquor? Judge Matthews thought.

McCabe handed over the documents of sale. "May not be much of a bargain. But he's yours."

McCabe never looked at the judge, nor at the human merchandise he left in a wake of dust. When the wagon rounded the end of the drive, Judge Matthews started down the steps. Ginny rushed past him toward the band of frightened slaves.

"What you do to yourself?" Ginny assessed the man, who towered over the little cluster, his arm akimbo, cradled in his other like a baby. The swollen flesh of his left eye glistened like ripe eggplant. The boy swiped at his nose with the ragged sleeve of his shirt, eyes wide and bloodshot. *Shame is an awful thing*, Ginny thought. She laid her hand on the child's woolly head and pulled him against her long leg.

"Ginny, get this man to the back porch and send someone for Dr. Slate." Judge Matthews turned to the tiny woman. "Have you and your children been fed this morning?"

The woman shook her head.

"You'll be all right now. Ginny will see to your needs." Judge Matthews studied her face, shook his head, and returned to the house.

Ginny patted the girl's short cornrows as she led the family around back. "Come on now, what's y'all's names?" The children stared up at this strange woman, almost as tall as their father.

"Nathan," the man said. "This here's Jessie. And Lavinia and Joseph."

At the rear of the house Ginny indicated a bench at the long pine table on the porch. "Jessie, put your arms 'round your young'uns while I fetch you some victuals."

Ginny stepped into the kitchen, where Samantha, in a sullen huff, was cleaning up from breakfast. Her ample body threatened to escape her dress as her hair had its kerchief. Perhaps everything about her wanted escape. Ginny ignored her foul mood.

"How many biscuits we got left?"

"Umm, six," Samantha counted. "We got six, but one done broke cross the middle."

"Never mind about that," Ginny said. "Got us some hungry young'uns out here. They don't give a hoot which way a biscuit's broke." Ginny considered Samantha's feelings about that broken biscuit. She was new to the household, bought from a place where slaves had eaten with gourds from a common trough. But apparently sufficient to round out her ample body.

Samantha slapped butter on the leftover biscuits, jamming bits of smoked pork into them, licking her fingers. One of the biscuits fell to the floor. She wiped it on her apron and walked outside to set the plate down hard on the table. Ginny eyed her sideways as she brought out a jar of apple butter.

"All right now, y'all eat," Ginny said.

All four sat motionless, looking at the food and then up at the two women. Samantha grunted and vanished back into the house.

"What you waiting for?" said Ginny. "Eat."

Jessie picked up a biscuit. Ginny slathered apple butter on

another and handed it to the little girl. She studied the child's surprise as the tart sweetness of this unfamiliar brown stuff touched her lips.

"You need some help?" Ginny said to Nathan.

"I be all right," he said. "Happens I'm left-handed. Mighty good victuals, mighty good. Ain't it good, Jessie?"

Jessie nodded. Ginny held a spoonful of apple butter out to her. Jessie glanced at Nathan for approval and he gave her a small smile. Ginny spread the biscuit.

"You like apple butter, Jessie?" she said.

"Never had none. Served it before. I been a house gal, but never had nothing except molasses myself. Has you, Nathan?"

"Had a little honey once," he said, grinning. Jessie bit into the biscuit.

Rapid hoofbeats clipped the air.

"That'd be Dr. Slate," Ginny said, rising.

Taking the reins, Benjamin motioned the doctor toward the porch. Charles Slate, ash-brown hair disheveled, mounted the steps two at a time. "Understand you have a patient here," he said to Ginny. His dark hazel eyes rested on Nathan. "What's your name?" Slate gave Jessie a penetrating side glance.

"Nathan, sir."

"Well, Nathan, finish your breakfast while I speak to the judge." He beckoned to Ginny. "Get me some lint for bandages. I'll need a good bit. And linen for a sling. Give that man a shot of whiskey. No, several." He looked around for a likely place to examine the injury. "And make me some fresh coffee. Where's your master, Ginny?"

In his study Judge Matthews looked up from his conversation with Emily as Slate knocked on the doorframe and entered without pausing. He straightened and stepped forward.

"Dr. Slate, this is my daughter, Emily," Judge Matthews said, half blocking the space between them. Extending her hand, Emily curtsied to the doctor and took her father's arm. He kissed her cheek and nodded toward the door. Though slow to withdraw her hand, she obeyed her father's silent bidding and exited. Charles stared after her, taking in the hay-colored hair, the narrow waist, and swaying hoops. The judge cleared his throat and said, "You see my new man?"

"Yes, sir. Looks right ashen." Slate swiveled, his eyes on the empty door where Emily had parted. "What happened?"

Judge Matthews stepped across the carpet and stood with his back to the door, as if to shield even the vanished shadow of his daughter from Charles's gaze. He focused on the issue at hand. "Man was posted for auction this morning. Without his family." He cleared his throat. "I made Conklin an offer for the lot of them, and McCabe delivered them earlier. Obviously not in the condition the man would have been for auction."

"First glance, I'd say he's likely to have a bad break. Woman doesn't look so good, either."

"McCabe claimed the man fell off his porch drunk in the night."

"I reckon it's a possibility, Judge. But I expect Conklin keeps tight control over there. So McCabe claimed he's a drunkard? Feat for a slave to get his hands on enough liquor for that."

"That's what he said. I find it unlikely. I'd say Conklin's control on alcohol might be selective." The judge returned to his desk and straightened some papers. "Convenient timing. Conklin wasn't keen on selling the woman and children. My offer was fair and for the lot only."

"Buck looks strong. Eye will heal, I warrant. Shame about the arm. If it's broken, it might be two, three months that he'll be no good to you around here." Charles hesitated. "Don't know as I'd trust Conklin, Judge Matthews. But he's a friend of Jeremiah, isn't he? Be that as it may, the man has a vicious streak. I hear tales and I've seen enough evidence myself. Shame he had to rough up a good nigger to get at you."

Judge Matthews's face hardened. "Yes, a good Negro man. See what you can do."

"Well, let me go see what we're looking at here," Charles said. "Are you coming, sir? You may want to know the condition of your merchandise."

"That would be wise." Judge Matthews stared after him, shut the drawer of his desk, and locked it, pocketing the key.

Out on the porch, Charles straddled a bench. He took Nathan's injured arm in his hands, his hold strong and precise, fingers deft. Charles studied the man as he manipulated the arm slightly, one way and then the other. The slave's face was taut, the mahogany color drained. As Charles rotated the arm another fraction, a constricted groan escaped the man's throat, though his expression did not change. Charles supported the arm in one hand and with the other pulled down the lower lid of Nathan's uninjured eye. What should have been a robust rose was the color of putty. He pulled open the man's lower lip. The same deep gray. Charles palpated the swollen, purple flesh of Nathan's arm, avoiding the open wounds, which appeared superficial. Midway of shoulder and elbow, he probed. As another deep groan surfaced, Jessie's head jerked up in alarm.

"Arm's broke bad," Charles said. "Ginny, I'll need—no, wait. Put a big pot of water to boil. And go fetch Benjamin."

Charles scraped back his chair and motioned to the judge. The two men kept their eyes on the ground as they strode to the rear fence. The judge waited. Charles spit and cracked his knuckles.

"Well, Judge, here it is," Charles said. "I can do nothing, put him in a sling, and it will heal maimed, somewhat useless, and likely painful from here on out. I can amputate. Don't need to expound on that one. Or I can set it, splint, and starch it. It'll take a couple of hours to do and overnight to dry. Healing, if it can, will take a good eight weeks or more. Can't be gotten wet or the lint'll come undone. Like washing the starch out of a petticoat. And I can't guarantee the arm'll be good afterward. Don't know how much more investment you want to make here."

"There's no decision to be made, Charles. Set the man's arm and splint it. Let me know when you're finished."

The judge strode back to the house. At least the doctor was competent and apparently cared, despite his derogatory language—and the questionable amount of time his horse spent tied in front of the brothel. The judge nodded to the slaves as he passed through the porch. He was displeased to see Emily standing in the shadows with Ginny and Samantha. Benjamin had joined the group and nodded back.

"Benjamin," Charles said, entering the porch. He hesitated when he, too, spied Emily, then proceeded briskly. "I need a piece of wood the length of this man's upper arm and a piece of leather strapping. Then I want you to carve me out another piece to fit around the back when I close it up with the bandages and starch. Come here and get the feel of this arm up and down. Whittle me out a piece as close to fit as you can. And not so thin the wood might be apt to break."

"Ginny," Charles said, "show this family whatever cabin they'll be occupying. And get back quick now. I need you."

Judge Matthews nodded and held out his hand for his daughter to come into the house with him.

"Yes, sir," Ginny said. "Come on, young'uns, and bring your mama with you. Hop to it, now." She herded mother and children through the tree-lined path to the quarters and into the first of three vacant cabins. "They's bedding already here," Ginny said. "You may want to lay it over the fence, air it out in the sun a bit. The well's thataway and outhouse yonder. Cooking shed between here and the big house. You need anything, you find me or Benjamin. Right now, you see to the bedding and send these childrens up the lane to Auntie Mag, last cabin this row. Make them some friends here. Maybe even learn them some letters."

The door creaked as Ginny left the woman and her children alone. Jessie sat on the mattress. The children curled themselves over her knees, one on each side, heads in her lap, tapping their fingers on one another's arms.

CHAPTER 3

Days passed in the way days tend to do. Emily worried some over Nathan's arm, but contented herself with having kept a family together. The heat clung to everything with an unrelenting dampness. Seeking some relief from the stifling afternoon, Emily entered the library to find Ginny engrossed in one of the many books collected there, by both the judge and her mother, who by all accounts had been an avid reader. Emily loved to come upon Ginny reading and felt a surge of gratitude to her father for including Ginny in their household tutoring, for setting up a school for all his slaves in spite of their education being illegal. Emily tilted the corner of the book to see the title: *Jane Eyre*, one of her childhood favorites. She identified with the orphan girl and remembered weeping inconsolably at the death of Jane's only friend, Helen.

"What do you think of it, Ginny?"

"I think I wished I knew a woman that strong." Ginny laid the book aside and picked up the feather duster. "I think I wished I was one."

"Yes, I wish the same. Now leave that, Ginny. Take some time to read."

"No, ma'am. I'm gone finish up this here library right now. I gots a heap to get done today."

Emily studied Ginny's back for a moment. "Ginny," she said, "there is something I keep wondering about and maybe now is the time to ask. You studied with me, with my tutor. You spent most of your life in this house. Why do you not speak correctly?"

Ginny took several swipes at a high shelf before answering. She lowered the duster and turned. "Yes, Miss Emily, I have studied and I have learned almost everything that you have, though I began somewhat later than you did. Was that correct enough?" She turned and pushed the duster into the back of a shelf.

"Yes, of course, Ginny. I know you can speak as well as I do, and yet you persist in speaking the slave dialect."

"And do you know what speaking as well as I know how to, as well as you do, speaking better than lots of white folks around here, would make me? An 'uppity nigger,' that's what. Do you know what happens to 'uppity niggers' around here, especially women? Rape? Lashings? Things you couldn't protect me from in spite of owning me."

"I'm sorry, Ginny. I didn't mean—" Emily stumbled on her words. "What I mean is your education makes you special. You shouldn't waste it."

Ginny pulled the duster through her other hand and shook her head. "No, Miss Emily, I ain't special. I tell you who special. Them black folk breaking they backs out there in the sun trying to make a life for themselves out of leftovers, they the folk who special." Ginny straightened to her full height and laid the duster beside the closed book. "Education does not make a person special," she said, her face clear and open. "Courage and fortitude and perseverance, self-denial, and any number of other admirable qualities, like Jane Eyre, like your papa going up against slavery—those things make a person special. And as to dialect, I don't know what that is. I do know this. What I am speaking so correctly now is 'white' dialect. It sets me apart from my own and I choose not to be set apart. What we speak is a language, black language, slave language, one forged out of the most impossible conditions: seized from all parts of Africa, speaking hundreds of different languages, unable to understand even one another, chained up by slavers speaking multiple other languages. And out of that, Miss Emily, these tortured people made a way to communicate with one another and with their enslavers. That is history you have not studied in your books. And those are my people whose language I will not dishonor by failing to speak it. You asked me plain out, Miss Emily, and I answer you plain out. And I ain't saying nothing about that subject again."

Ginny returned *Jane Eyre* to the shelf, picked up the duster, and left Emily alone in the room full of books.

CHAPTER 4

At the edge of the swirling dancers, Emily buried her hands deep in the pockets of her green gown, her fingers worrying at some dry seeds she had picked up somewhere along the way. Around her the dancers circled, clapped, changed partners, tapped their feet as the fiddler wove his spell. Emily did not dance, though she wanted to, longed to, even, and found her toes tapping under her hoops whenever there was music. As a young girl, occupied with the grief of her motherless upbringing, she had deemed herself clumsy. Her father tried to teach her the steps, but she never found them natural—too much counting and concentration on left and right. Nor was Emily at ease in conversation, except in her family; even there she often kept her thoughts to herself. Social events were a self-conscious agony to her. However, her widowed father insisted on attending, hoping somehow that social exposure would make up the deficit.

Now Emily lifted her gaze to the gangly fellow who pranced through the line of dancers with one of the Sutton girls on his arm. Here was her younger brother, Jeremiah, all mouth and legs, same as on his horse or in the field, and even at his studies, prone to blurting out whatever came to mind. He moved incessantly, prone even in sleep to toss and jerk. Perhaps juggling his mother's death like an endlessly burning coal. Emily turned away from the current of dancers, seeking refuge by the door, ajar to the cool night air.

At the door, Emily's elder brother, Will, was speaking intently with Michael Lambert, who smiled and nodded to her. She knew Mr. Lambert as kind, a quiet man, one of a pair of old bachelor brothers working their homestead together. Emily returned the nod, but hesitated, unwilling either to be drawn into conversation or to turn back toward the undertow of dancers.

Emily sensed Will's brooding. Bereft since the death of his wife, Fran, and their infant boy, he had never recovered himself. Lately, however, Belinda Slate, the doctor's sister and a school friend of Emily's, had charmed him with her excess of senseless exuberance. Her lighthearted, effusive babble had raised Will's spirits, given him hope. In that momentary hope, he had posted a letter proposing marriage on her graduation, only to be answered by an inexplicable silence. Now he brooded incessantly. Emily nodded again at Mr. Lambert and returned her attention to Jeremiah, cavorting down the line again, so forward, so lacking limits.

From behind her, a man spoke. "A special evening, Miss Matthews. Leaving so soon?"

Emily startled. The voice had laughter in it, quiet like a whispered secret in her ear. She turned. Stylishly dressed in a double-breasted black frock coat, the man stood mid-height, tan and muscled like a man of the field, yet somehow not. Emily knew she should recognize him, but no name came to her aid.

"Charles," he said, relieving her. "Charles Slate, Miss Matthews. I'm Belinda's older brother."

"Ah, yes, Dr. Slate," she said. "You treated my father's new slave. I do remember. I was distracted. I beg your pardon." She did not offer him her hand, guarded in her pocket, working the little seeds. Belinda's often unflattering gossip about her brother's exploits with women flitted through Emily's mind. But she gave credence only to bits of Belinda's endless tales.

"I've not seen you on the floor tonight, Miss Matthews. Are you saving up your dances for some absent partner, lucky man?"

"No, Dr. Slate, I just—" Emily faltered. "Well, I've no knack for it, you see."

"Well, that can be remedied, much like a chill or a fever. Perhaps you'll allow me to judge the temperature of your dancing?" He held out his hand, but she shrugged, losing hold of the seeds as she flattened her hands in her pockets. "Come now, Miss Matthews, I'm sure there's a cure for this. And equally sure, I might be the one to have it."

Emily raised her eyes, and her hand. Inside something unfamiliar stirred, like pangs of early hunger before breakfast.

"I thank you, Dr. Slate," she said, so softly he had to lean forward to hear over the music and stamping feet. "I am most inept. I shouldn't want to shame you on the floor."

"A highly unlikely outcome, Miss Matthews. Highly unlikely." He took her hand and stepped onto the floor. They were immediately absorbed into the whirling crowd and he guided her skillfully, so that her steps hardly mattered. Emily laughed at her missteps. It was a short venture. The music stopped and he led her back to the bench. "May I fetch a glass of punch and sit beside you here? Watching this crowd is entertainment in itself. It's a marvel how old Widow Jones keeps up with that young Darrell Snow! Dancing him right into the floor, she is. You wait here in the fresh air and don't be dancing off with someone else, now."

Emily sat rolling the seeds at the tips of her fingers until Charles returned with the punch. She drew her right hand from its hiding place and took the cup, careful not to touch his hand as she did. She was grateful for the focus of the cup. She raised her eyes at the laughter that filled the interval between the last note of the fiddle and the first of the banjo beginning another round.

Charles settled beside her on the bench, leaving space for only her hoops between them. He stretched his legs out in front with his back against the wall. Less than gentlemanly, Emily thought. He made no effort to elicit conversation. Under his breath, Charles hummed the tunes, sang a word or two, off-key.

"You're beautiful, you know," he said, without turning his head toward her.

Emily lowered the cup. A dark seed that had stuck to her thumb dropped into the green silk of her lap. She brushed it away, but it caught in the ruffles of her skirt.

Charles rubbed the toes of his seamless riding boots together, then planted them flat on the floor, his hands on his knees. Emily marked the neatness of his striped trousers and the cleanliness of his nails. *Like my father,* she thought.

"Yes, beautiful," Charles said. "Just so you know."

The caller announced, "Last dance." The fiddler struck the pace. Charles stood and bowed ever so slightly.

"Good night, Miss Matthews," he said. "I plan to have you dancing every tune. And don't forget to plant those seeds. I've seen things sprout and grow even after much neglect."

Emily blushed that he had seen, had caught her tension out, but she raised her face and said, "Yes, Dr. Slate. I expect you are correct. Good night."

She sat a few minutes more, then rose when her father came toward her.

"Two Slate courtships with my children?" he said. "Hardly what I envisioned for either of you. However, Belinda seems to have lost interest. Erratic and flighty, that girl, even if she is your friend. I'm grateful that Will has been introduced to Lucinda Morris, who seems thoroughly solid and willing, though he doesn't appear much cheered from the looks of his face tonight." He offered his elbow to escort her home. "Be careful with yourself, Emily. Though he is a good doctor, I have my misgivings about Dr. Slate. I believe he may be a bit too practiced at how to put himself forward."

A week later, Charles Slate dismounted his sorrel and handed the reins to Benjamin, who had stepped out from a nearby shed at the sound of the approaching horse. Benjamin wrapped the reins around his wide hand and smiled at the profusion of flowers arching across the doctor's arm.

"Evening, Dr. Charles."

"Good evening, Benjamin. A very good evening, actually."

Benjamin's throaty chuckle elicited an accompanying laugh from Charles, who mounted the steps two at a time and strode across the porch. The door opened before he could knock. Ginny did not widen the door nor back up to admit him.

"You guarding the tower, Ginny?"

She slapped her leg and stood back. Her narrow face broadened with infectious laughter. Charles joined in, unsure why.

"Lordy, Dr. Charles, you looking like a bride 'bout to jump the broom, all those flowers on your arm!" She slapped her leg again.

"Ah, well, Ginny." He mocked a small curtsy. "If I have my way tonight, perhaps we shall have a bride at this threshold, but going out rather than coming in."

Ginny clapped her long fingers over her mouth. What might have been laughter strangled into a cough when she saw Emily on the landing.

"What sort of foolishness are you two about?" Emily said, descending into the hall. She gazed at Charles with open curiosity and not a little wariness. He was dressed as he had been at the dance, with the addition of a startling green shawl-collared waistcoat. Ginny scrambled to retrieve the flowers as Charles reached to take Emily's extended hand.

"How lovely," Emily said, bending over the loose blossoms.

"From my mother's garden," he said.

"Perhaps they should go into my own mother's vase. Ginny, will you bring some water, please."

"Yes'm. They're right fine, Dr. Charles. Smell *good!*" She emphasized the word. "Quince and daffodil and forsythia. Yes, sir, even got some early foxglove. I'll just put them on the back porch, Miss Emily."

"I will fetch the vase," Emily said. "My father is in the parlor, Charles, no doubt smoking his pipe. You'll find him there. I'll join you in a moment."

Charles was pleased. Now, he would have the time he needed with Emily's father to express his hopes for marriage to her. He found Judge Matthews, as predicted, in front of the fireplace with his pipe. Charles strode across the room and offered his hand.

Though Judge Matthews took the extended hand, he was not pleased to see Charles Slate come courting. True, he wished to see Emily blossom, see her dancing, laughing, talking. See her married. But he had not counted on Charles Slate with his disreputable father and his own questionable reputation, in spite of his medical competence. Nor could the judge imagine his sons would be pleased: neither Will, who managed the plantation and shared his father's steadfast sense of justice; nor Jeremiah, whom nothing pleased, and who lived life much the way he had entered it, angry and restless, with a burden of unnamed guilt.

The judge had concentrated his attentions on Emily in a hovering protection, attempting to heal his own grief by healing hers. He had prayed for a suitable husband, had sensed the growing interest of one or two young men of good families, only to see them reined in by fathers who vehemently opposed the judge's antislavery stance. He had even imagined Michael Lambert for her, though the man was so much older. Instead, here was Charles Slate, wanting to court his daughter—the son of a belligerent drunk, who barely made crop on the small acreage he had inherited from a maiden aunt. Most likely, it was Adeline responsible for how the family managed. She was as much respected as her husband was scorned. Whatever had brought Adeline to Thomas, no one knew. By the time they moved to the small farm outside Greensboro, he had long since taken to drink, and she had somehow committed to making a life for herself and her children, with or without his assistance.

Adeline had done well. She had schooled the boys, sent Belinda to the Yalobusha Female Institute, where Emily met her, and had versed all three in rudimentary social graces. Charles had made a doctor, though he was as wild as the horses he rode, if the abundant rumors and the judge's own suspicions about him were true, even in part. The younger son, Hammond, though slow and not likely to ever earn a dollar, much less a living, was good and kind in the way of simple folk. And a productive farmer to boot, thanks to Adeline's mentoring. Then there was Belinda, full of an unruly kind of sweetness, if not strength. Will had set his heart on that girl. The judge was glad to think that union now improbable.

Yet here was Charles Slate, asking without preamble, but with courtesy, to come courting Emily. Educated and smart. Possibly a better man than the judge gave credit for. Though not landed, his profession as a doctor could secure Emily a livelihood. Charles exhibited a practiced charm the judge did not altogether trust, but which might do Emily good, bring out the cheer that had lain so long in her mother's grave. And who else was there? As Judge Matthews thought about his motherless girl, it struck him how Charles was himself essentially a fatherless son. With quiet foreboding, he gave his permission.

As the courtship progressed, Charles and Emily sometimes strolled in the early evening down to the narrow creek near the house. She loved the soft air, cooling in the golden light, and

Charles's off-tune humming. As they walked, Emily studied him, trying to see in his face what could make him want her. More and more, as the weeks passed, she realized how little she knew him, how intimate a stranger he was to her.

"When did your family come from Ohio?" she asked.

"Oh, I was just a little boy, about three, I reckon. All pretty hard on Mama, I think. Belinda was born soon after we settled here. She was premature and they'd had another little girl who had just died. I don't know what from. My pa inherited some land from a maiden aunt and thought there was more to be had. He didn't have but a few acres in Ohio, just Mama's garden, I think. Spent his time doing handiwork around the town."

"Is he still handy?"

"Not with land. Never was that I can make out. Handy with a bottle." Charles's laugh had a bitter edge. "He was drinking then, Mama says, but not so much. I reckon they both thought some acreage of his own might keep him dry. Thought he might could make a farmer after all."

Emily tried to gauge his expression.

"Well, none of that was true. The plot he inherited wasn't much. And a good deal of the better land around was already taken up in land patents by folks like your father. Folks with slaves to work larger acreage. Well, Pa got him some land, not so much as he wanted, but more than he could work. And not enough to keep him dry." Charles gazed up at the sky. "I doubt that much exists."

He turned abruptly toward the house, leaving Emily staring at his back.

She caught up with him. Charles scuffed at a patch of moss with the toe of his riding boot.

"Now, don't misunderstand me, Emily. Sometimes he was dry, early on."

He took her arm. "But I ought to tell you something good," he said. "See, he could whittle, loved to whittle. Kept his pocketknife real sharp. Little old thing you'd think wouldn't cut butter. But in his hands, it was magic. He made us toys—made us whistles, Hammond and me. Out of little limbs. He'd auger out the sapwood from the center, good and hollow. Then, he'd bore a little hole and hand it to one of us to blow on. Course nothing would come out. He'd slap his knee and laugh. He had a big old, hearty laugh in spite of being a smallish man. Now laughing just puts him in a coughing fit. Well, but then he'd take the twig back and make three or four more holes, blow into it with his fingers flying and out would come a little tune. I never got the hang of it myself, but Hammond did. That's how he started making music. Me, I never could."

"I've noticed." Emily laughed.

Charles tapped at her layered hoops.

"You wear entirely too many petticoats, Miss Matthews."

"Indeed?" She smiled, her face tilted down in embarrassment at his forward familiarity, but with an angled glance at his laughing face.

Chapter 5

Nathan's eye healed. The bone did not. The lesion continued to fester. Nathan bent himself to whatever work he could with his good arm, the left one with which he was adept. He found various ways to adjust, balancing boards between sawhorses, holding them steady with his knee while he sawed. His modified methods allowed him to sand the boards smooth, until they felt like Jessie's firm skin under his good hand.

Nathan was aware how bizarre he seemed, sawing and sanding and building while his other arm withered in its sling, stinking. His hand had given him agony, though in the last few days it had deadened, like a useless gar caught and left unhooked onshore to die. He shied away from Jessie and the little ones, accepting the children's hugs around his knees without bending down in return, touching Jessie's cheek or her shoulder with his body turned half away. He sat on the porch late into the night, hoping Jessie would sleep through his lying down beside her.

And while he sat, Nathan thought. He couldn't divine what had prompted the attack. He was set for the block the next day. Agonized at being separated permanently from his family, but set nonetheless. Why would Conklin jeopardize the value of a slave at auction? Beatings were commonplace enough. To be a slave was to live in a netherworld of fear. Lashings waited in the shadows for anything from a failed runaway attempt to dropping a clean teaspoon on the parlor floor. Nathan cringed at the story of a slave infant, not yet walking, whose crying disturbed the mistress. She beat the child until it stopped; then it was dead. Nathan knew the truth of these tales. He knew of almost no black skin that was not laced with scars of one sort or another. Even the most fortunate showed the mark of at least one branding. Accounts of mistreatment abounded, traveling the countryside from slave to slave. Though filtered and embellished through a hundred lips and ears, whispered from one porch to another, one plantation to another, the names and details shifting, all these stories were nonetheless true. But this one made no sense.

Nathan had recognized the men who came that night, all three of them. He knew their voices and their boots before he felt their blows. The fancy silver belt buckle was as familiar to him as Conklin himself. Nathan knew the mustard plaid vest of Conklin's neighbor. And the distinctive boot design of Conklin's youngest brother. He had polished the dust from them himself when the men rode in from a hunt. The images were as familiar to him as darkness to a blind man. The liquored, sweaty smell of the men had singed his nostrils. They had as well held a lantern to their faces as pull those slitted pillowcases over their heads.

What Nathan remembered now came in fragments: the sound of the belt unsheathed from its loops, the heavy silver buckle catching the glimmer of the kerosene lamp in midair, the blur of clothing and limbs, his knee jerking up as the rifle butt hit his arm, the sound of the bone shattering, the rifle butt slamming into his head.

Then, nothing. Nothing until he opened his eyes, Jessie's face brought clear in a blur of pain, the awful throb above his ear as he reached for her. She held his left hand against her cheek, slick with tears. He heard his name tumbling like clean water over him before they dragged him out into the field, pouring some kind of liquor over him, before he lost consciousness again.

The thought of Jessie, of her warm body, soothing him against the pain, brought Nathan back into the moment. He studied the mounting stack of boards, the saw, the pile of shavings and sawdust on the floor, the angled sun pouring in across the dark dirt floor. Nathan lay down the plane and walked with resolution to the back porch of the big house. He stopped at the steps, where Ginny met him.

"I needs to speak to Master."

"Well, then, come on up," she said.

"No, I'll wait here."

Ginny absorbed the steadiness of this man with his stinking arm in the sawdust-covered sling. She wanted to brush the flecks of wood chip from his hair, but restrained herself and went to fetch Judge Matthews.

The judge was not long. He had expected this visit, dreaded it, come to accept its inevitability. Now Nathan stood before him.

"I gots to let it go, Judge."

"You're sure, Nathan?"

"Yes, sir, I's sure."

"I'll send Benjamin for Dr. Slate. Have you talked to Jessie?"

"No, sir. I don't want it in her remembrance, Judge."

"I expect you'd better come in," Judge Matthews said. "Ginny, set up a cot on the side porch, please. Get a clean sheet and have some lint ready. And a bucket. Put some water on to boil. Get some covers. Whatever else you consider needful."

"Yes, sir," she said. "And, Judge Matthews, you best get that man some whiskey."

"Yes, of course. Get the decanter of brandy from my office. And be generous. I'm going to fetch Benjamin."

The amputation was clean and efficient. Nathan maintained an eerie silence amid the sounds of the surgery: the faint whisper of the knife, the rasp of the saw, the slight gurgle and the rattle of the bucket as the arm slid into it, separated from him forever. When it was over and the flap of stump had been stitched and bandaged thick with the lint, Nathan turned his head to the wall. He focused on the grain of the wood. He heard them remove the bucket. Through the fog of brandy and pain, Nathan heard Jessie's wail.

"Don't take it, Master. Please, don't take it." Jessie's anguished cry broke the stillness.

"Now, Jessie, it ain't him we taking," Ginny intervened.

"No, it ain't him, but sure it's his. It ain't garbage."

"No, it ain't. But it's dead, Jessie. And Nathan gone live. What you wanting done, honey?"

"Bury it. I wants it buried in a little grave," Jessie said. "With a cross on it. And a prayer and singing over it. That's what I want."

"All right, Jessie," Judge Matthews said. "It's little enough to ask. Benjamin, find a good spot and set Lucian to work."

"Yes, sir. And I'll get Samuel started on a box and a marker," Benjamin said. "Nobody finer at carving."

"Come on up, Jessie," the judge said. "Come and see your man."

She lay across him as she had that other night, her warmth around him like a blanket in the chill. Nathan stroked her hair, ran his fingertips around her ear, felt the softness of her wet cheek against his unshaven stubble.

CHAPTER 6

The progressing spring of 1859 was marked with unexpected snow and heavy winds. In spite of the fickle weather, Adeline insisted Charles fetch Emily for Sunday dinners several weeks in a row. In spite of her initial shyness, Emily blossomed in conversation with his mother, a demonstrative affection growing between them that he had never seen before in his family. Charles appreciated the talk around the table, so rare in this house: when might it rain, how the corn was doing, who in town had a new baby, the problem of cutting green firewood in the extended winter. He was studying Emily, when he realized Adeline had addressed him.

"Nathan is mending well?"

Charles nodded. "Well, Mama, it helps that the buck is a healthy nigger to start with and left-handed to boot."

Emily went still at the word her father had taught her to abhor and cringed inside at its unthinking usage. Her fork hovered in midair.

Adeline cleared her throat and took a sip of water. "Would you have another helping of turnips?" she asked Emily. "I knew from the time he was a boy Charles would make a doctor," she said.

"I never weighed any other possibilities. Had no land, no niggers. Sure didn't want to be a lawyer, if that's what you mean." Charles looked at Emily and smiled. It took her a moment to return his smile.

Adeline cleared her throat again. "Yes," she said, "he came to doctoring the way a boy takes a cane and goes to fishing."

"Like iron to a magnet, only I didn't know till I was almost grown that it was medicine calling me. I liked to see things heal. Good thing, I'd say."

"How did you know then, Charles?" It hit Emily again how much about this proposed husband of hers she did not know.

Charles laughed. "Well, we had this old cow one time got caught in a gopher hole, bellowing like mad. Pa and me went running and there she was, stuck as could be. He got her out. Left front leg, it was, and not broken, but scraped up right bad. We got her to the barn, hobbling and mewling and her bag getting full. So, while Pa milked her, I got a bucket and some lye soap and a rag, and I set to cleaning her up." He reached for a second piece of cornbread. "There was a right deep cut and some skin chewed up. I ran and asked Mama could I have her sewing scissors, the little ones she still wears around her neck when she's mending."

Adeline smiled.

"I can remember how Mama's face looked when she got to the barn, all soft and puzzled-like. So, I cut the loose skin away, easy as I could, with her watching. I must have done all right because the cow didn't budge. Pa was finished milking and gone by then. Mama handed me some salve out of her pocket and helped me cut a rag in strips. I wound it around and around, thick so the cow'd have some cushion if she bumped it."

"He changed that bandage every day for more than a week," Adeline said, her smile more at the memory than at Charles. "Kept me washing and drying for sure."

"That was my first doctoring, I guess. And it suited me.

Good thing, since I never had any land to plow. I'll leave the farming to Will. And Jeremiah, of course."

Emily looked across at Adeline, who stood and began to gather the plates. She held up her hand when Emily rose to help, but Emily ignored her, picked up two vegetable bowls, and followed Adeline to the kitchen.

The soft green-gold of evening shone through the canopy of leaves. The heat of the day waned and a cool breeze rose as the sun declined. A few sporadic daffodils persevered erratically between the gnarled roots of the trees. There were so few flowers left at all after Miss Liza's death sixteen years before. Mainly volunteers gone native. Ginny wandered among them, knife in hand, snipping the last blooms. She was oblivious to Emily's approach, caught up in the soft air and the light, in her rare moment of being alone to herself. She straightened, her tall, angular form silhouetted against the horizon.

"Miss Emily. What you doing out here?"

"Wandering, Ginny." Emily realized how infrequently she paid real attention to Ginny's height. It was so familiar. And regal when she noticed. "Just glad the winter's finally decided to give up and get gone."

"You be wishing for it back come many weeks. Hot don't tell what summer gone be like."

Emily laughed and bent to pick up a daffodil that had slipped from Ginny's hands. She pulled its bare stem between her fingers. "Ginny, Dr. Slate wants me to marry him."

"He do now? You say that like it's news." Ginny wiped her brow. "And what is it you want, Miss Emily?"

Surprise flitted across Emily's face. "I don't know." She chewed at a hangnail. "Ginny, do you ever think of marriage?"

"No, I don't." Ginny allowed the knife and the flowers to hang by her side.

"Don't you want a man? Don't you ever wonder?"

"No, I don't wonder, Miss Emily."

Emily watched as Ginny leaned forward and cut another thin daffodil.

"I ain't got to wonder. After Master sold my mama, his boy got hold of me. He was some kind of mean. Worse than mean; he was the devil in flesh. I don't never want no man near me again. Not as I can help. And now I can. Back then I was just a child. And all alone."

Emily put her hand on Ginny's arm and Ginny covered it with her own. *History makes a mockery of us,* Emily thought. All the years of their deep connection and Emily never suspected. Had she been oblivious? So lost in herself. Lost being where she found herself presently. *Finding oneself lost, what paradox,* Emily thought. *I must find myself where I am and stop the fantasy of where I ought to be.*

"I'm so sorry, Ginny."

"You ain't had nothing to do with it. Why you sorry?"

"I'm sorry not to have known, to have been so caught up in my own life."

"Honey, I never told it. Hope I never showed it. And you got some things to be caught in."

"But nothing, Ginny, nothing even close—"

"No, you got your own. We each got our own wilderness to travel. Moses out there forty years. Ain't never seen the Holy Land. But the people did. You can't travel my wilderness and I can't travel yours. Not much I know, Miss Emily. But here's something I believe I do know. You take care of your own crazy place and I take care of mine, and somehow together we make the world a little bit safer place to wander in." Ginny handed Emily another daffodil. "Now," she said, "what you want to do about your life?"

"No one has ever asked me what I want, Ginny. Not like that." Emily pulled the bare stem through her fingers again. "No one asked me did I want to go to the Yalobusha Female

Institute. But I went anyway. No one asked what church I wanted to attend. Or did I even want to. No one asked if I want to get married. But I don't want to wind up a spinster."

"Um-hmm. Nobody asked you nothing? You sure?"

"Oh, they asked did I want the solid yellow silk or the green plaid. Or both. Or did I want empress sleeves on my dress? Or did I want fried chicken or ham at Sunday dinner, or both? But, Ginny, no one has ever asked me what I want about the things that determine my life. I can't imagine how to think about such a question."

Ginny leaned forward to cut another two blooms. *She is like a great, long-legged heron,* Emily thought, *all grace.* Ginny handed the flowers to her.

"You got three choices now," she said. "Just like those three flowers in your hand. You can go right on letting everybody 'round you say what you must do. That's one. You can say you ain't doing it. That's two. Or you can ponder what you want and say it out loud. And that's three."

"Ginny, I don't know how to know what I really want."

"Yes, you do." Ginny tilted her head and studied her young mistress. "And besides that, I ain't sure what your papa thinks about them Slates. While you thinking on things, let me hear what you think about Charles Slate?"

"He's charming. Intelligent, ambitious."

"He good to women?"

"He seems well-mannered." Emily hesitated, tapping a daffodil against her skirt. "Belinda used to hint—no, more than hint—that he was quite a ladies' man. Sometimes she seemed to gloat on it."

"She say that, do she? But you don't believe her?" Ginny stood up tall.

"Belinda's apt to say most anything, if it suits her at the moment. I never give much credence to what Belinda says. One thing one minute and the opposite the next."

"He kind to his sister?"

"She said not, said he was always mean to her. Like Jeremiah with me."

"You seen it yourself?"

"Well, no, Ginny. I've never been around them together."

"So you don't know what's true. And you don't know what you want." Ginny straightened her shoulders. "The difference in me and you is, you can choose. And since you can, you ought to know. And maybe you gone find that what they think you want and what you do want turn out to be the same. And maybe not. And that's all I got to say on that." Ginny stretched. "Now, give me them daffodils so I can get them in some water before I done wasted all my time out here. And you go wander 'round in your head for a while. Won't take you no forty years."

Emily's thoughts were indeed a wilderness and she found herself lost in them. She was all aflutter, as the expression went, with Charles's attentions, and his charm made her laugh. She yearned for laughter. He had even taught her some rudimentary dance steps, and she had learned them quite well in spite of feeling clumsy. He focused on her in a way that not even her father did, though Charles could be sometimes unpredictably abrupt, even somewhat harsh. He was handsome in a slightly off-kilter way, boyish still, though enough older to have his medical practice established. He was a good doctor, if his treatment of Nathan were any example. Yet, she felt discomfited and sometimes invisible in his presence.

Now this choice: not a thing she had ever envisioned. All around her, girls grew up, got married, and had children, often by the dozen. If a woman lived, she grew old. If not, she died, like Emily's mother. Or her husband died and the woman married again. Her children had children, or they died. The woman grieved and went on. Or no suitors appeared and she became a spinster, someone's maiden aunt. What other choice had there ever been?

Emily was young and inexperienced. Except for boarding school, she had never been away from home. The unfamiliar made her anxious: a different home, different people around her, responsibility for a household to manage. Perhaps Ginny was right. Perhaps she might not want to be married. Not to Charles and not to anyone. Was that possible? The life she imagined was the life she had lived: life with Charles as an extension of the life she had experienced. Only she would not be lonely. Except for Ginny and her attentive, but vaguely unknowable father, Emily had been forever lonely. She yearned to be known, to be understood and accepted, to share herself with another. She yearned for everything that seemed to define a normal life: husband, home, children. Yet she carried in her an underlying apprehension of being with a man, of bearing children. The raw physical hunger of Charles's attentions, his blatant dismissal of convention both enflamed her and frightened her. As Emily examined Ginny's question, her stomach constricted; her breathing shallowed; her fear amplified into anxiety that bordered on panic. Emily fought the irrational urge to flee from herself. The reality that she had a choice, must in fact make a choice that would determine the remainder of her life, invaded her body, growing exaggerated and ominous.

Ginny found her behind the shed, counting chickens and sobbing.

"What you doing out here, Miss Emily?"

"Ginny?" Emily looked around like a lost child.

"Honey, why you crying like this?" Ginny reached for her.

"I don't know. I truly don't." Emily shook her head against Ginny's arm. "I'm so afraid that I feel crazy."

"Let's you and me go set down on the bench and have us a talk now, honey. You ain't crazy. But you got reason for your fears. You gone be all right."

"I can't do this, Ginny. I want to, but I can't."

"Be married?"

Emily nodded. "Something is wrong with me, Ginny, something not like other women. I feel all torn up inside. It gets too much and I just go blank. Like when I got my first blood."

"You got cause, Miss Emily. And me to blame. You just don't remember." Ginny hesitated, struggling with what to tell. "I've told you about me; now I'm gone tell you about you. You was there when your mama died."

Emily jerked her head, staring at the precision of Ginny's profile.

"They let me say goodbye to her?"

"No, didn't nobody let you do nothing but me. I was supposed to be watching you, but I wasn't maybe twelve years old myself and I got to playing and let you get away. And when I found you, it wasn't no pretty sight. I'm sorry for that." She reached over and took Emily's hand, but did not turn her head. "And now I don't know what to tell you."

"Just tell me plain."

"Didn't nobody ever know but me and whoever was tending your mama. I don't remember who it was. I found you in there. I reckon you seen the whole thing. Wasn't nobody paying attention except to Miss Liza lying there dead, and that baby crying. And there you was right in the middle of it, them women keening and all that blood."

CHAPTER 7

The courtship was not an extended one. Emily recovered herself. She brightened when Charles came calling, usually bearing flowers from Adeline's garden. He told stories at the table that focused the attention on himself and entertained the family, all except Jeremiah, who became more and more distant from all of them as Charles inserted himself into the family. Emily paid her brother little attention. He had never been kind to her, had in fact been domineering and spiteful, even in childhood. Charles was indifferent to Jeremiah's slights.

"When will you give me an answer?" Charles asked one night as they swayed on the porch swing, its chains creaking.

"When I know myself," Emily said.

"And what will it take for you to know, Miss Emily?"

"Are you mocking me, sir?" She balled her hand.

"Not at all." He pressed his palm into hers, compelling her fingers open. "Soft," he said, rolling her hand over. "You have lovely hands. Hands that have never had to work."

Emily withdrew her hand and slid it into the folds of her wide skirt.

"Nothing to be embarrassed about," Charles said, leaning back, rubbing his palms along his thighs.

Emily looked out across the yard to the night sky. He could not see her face.

"Have you ever had a servant, Charles?"

"You mean slaves? No." He stood and joined his fingers across the back of his head, stretched his elbows. "Emily, I am singularly aware that our lives have been very different. I shouldn't have thought—"

"No, Charles." Emily jumped to her feet. "I've made you misunderstand me." She stopped just short of touching his back. "And yes, our lives have been quite different. But I've given a lot of thought to my inexperience, you see. Your remark about my hands, and spending time with your mother now, have made me keenly aware of how little I have had to do for myself. I feel ashamed, Charles. My question came from a sudden realization as to how different my life might be if my hands were not smooth and soft, if, in fact, I used them to work. Or had to."

"You will never need to work, as long as you are my wife. I can provide for us. And you will have the slaves you need to help you. I will certainly be able to buy you all you require. You need not worry."

"I do not want to buy people, Charles. I want to work, and I want to hire them free."

"We can do that, too. There are always slaves 'to let,' plenty of them."

"But they are still slaves, Charles. Don't you see?"

"Your father owns over a hundred, Emily."

"Yes, but—"

"Yes, but his illegal school for them? His push to set them free? Emily, the liberation of slaves is a fantasy. Manumission was outlawed in Mississippi two years ago. It is not going to happen. Not in our lifetime. And I pray it doesn't." He took her by the shoulders. "The economy of the Southern states depends on slavery. Don't you know that? And the economy of the country depends on the economy of the South. Emancipation will not happen."

"Then, what?"

"Then, you and I will be good to the slaves in our charge, as your father has been. I do not know that we will be able to buy up all that we see mistreated, as your father has done with Nathan and any number of others. But I will treat them all as well as I have Nathan. I will heal the niggers as I do the whites—what, Emily? What else?"

Emily pulled her hands loose and turned her back to him. Charles stood for a moment, sighed, and laid his hands loosely on her sloping shoulders. He leaned his face into her neck and whispered.

"What?"

"I cannot bear that word, Charles."

"Niggers? Ah, is that all? Then I will heal the Negroes as I heal the whites." He hesitated. "It is a cultural familiarity, Emily. I hear it far more frequently than any proper terminology. It's just a matter of habit. If that offends you, I can be more careful in your presence. For you, Emily. I can promise that. In fact, I will promise anything you want to hear in order for you to be mine."

Charles pressed on her shoulders, turned her toward him, waited for her averted face to come of her own accord. "Do you hear me, Emily? I will promise you whatever I need to."

"Yes," she said.

He took her chin in his hand. She lifted her face to his kiss.

On a Friday evening in late May of 1859, Judge Matthews presided over his daughter's marriage to Charles Slate. Ginny adorned the parlor with dogwood branches and forsythia from the edge of the woods. Adeline arrived with an armload of pale-pink saucer magnolias. She handed the flowers to Ginny, but followed her about, rearranging a leaf here, a bloom there. Adeline served as witness for her son, and Will for Emily. In her simple dress, Adeline's earthy dignity pervaded the room. Hammond, handsome and manly, but giddy as a child, stood close by his mother. Thomas Slate was absent, but there was general relief in that. Charles's black frock coat appeared abnormally formal for him, but a new white vest beneath softened his square face, accentuated by his almost-auburn sideburns and neat mustache. Whatever misgivings the judge had, he hid well. In spite of his attempted warnings, Emily had made her choice and, indeed, seemed to blossom. He would hold his tongue.

In the end, Jeremiah failed to attend. Knowing his father's intended gift of acreage to Emily, though it was only a few acres, had somehow enraged him. What did the wife of a doctor need with farmland, however small? Belinda was also absent, even for the marriage of her brother to her closest friend from school. Will's proposal to Belinda had gone unanswered for weeks into months.

Now Will stood at the back of the room and spoke little, carrying his own private sadness. No one else was present except Ginny, who had stitched the wedding dress of gray silk—a suitable color for her new name, Emily announced with a smile.

With the name Emily Slate official, the judge presented her an envelope containing the deed to forty-two acres and a newly finished log house, complete with summer kitchen and outbuildings. In addition, the envelope contained documents conveying to Emily ownership of three slaves: Ginny, who had essentially raised her; Benjamin, whose skills ranged from house service to all aspects of the farm; and his son, Lucian, a sturdy young man of burgeoning intelligence. The three could reliably manage Emily's farm and chores while Charles attended to his medical practice.

When the moment for departure came, Emily cried. How

would her father pass the evenings without her? Alone by the fire in winter and alone in summer rocking on the porch? Her brothers would hardly be at home of an evening to keep their father company as she had done. William would surely marry again, though apparently not to Belinda. Even then he would come and go more than Jeremiah, who would be as erratic as ever. Emily saw that her tears saddened her father. Blinking, she kissed his cheek and caressed the soft white waves of his beard. Emily took Charles's hand, her smile timid and affectionate, as he lifted her into the buckboard, filled with bright quilts she and Ginny had stitched.

The rhythm of the horse's hooves lulled her. She leaned against her husband's arm. Charles was silent. When the horses halted at the new house, he took the quilts, kissed Emily, and told her to wait while he lit the lamps. Arching her neck, she studied the stars. Although she marveled to think, Emily also mistrusted herself for the night and the things to come, of which she had only hints, gleaned from glimpses of farm animals mating, scenes from which someone had inevitably whisked her away. But her body gave her hint enough: the longing to be touched; the way her breath caught at the thought of his skin against hers; the hardening of her nipples and the flush of moist warmth in her privates; a tingling mystery at the thing not known, yet secretly held in the recesses of her body. She gazed into the depths of the sky, marveling at the clarity of the stars. Like cottonwood in the fall, she wafted nowhere and everywhere. Emily startled when Charles put his arm around her. He slipped his other arm beneath her knees, the gray silk of her skirts rustling in the dark, her hoops awry. Her trance held through the jostling in his arms across the porch, through the door, and the other doors beyond.

When Charles laid her on the bed, she had little sense of shifting. She murmured to the sound of the silk as he lifted her skirts, spread her pantaloons, touched her, pressed his lips and tongue to her. Her body rose of its own accord. Charles untied the hoops and dropped them to the floor. The wide ruffles of gray silk billowed over her face, smothering her, and the corset inhibited her breath. She struggled against the fabric and gasped at the sudden pain, the stillness, then a slow undulation in herself, filling her, drawing her with it. He quickened and his pace outstripped her. "Wait," she said, "please wait for me," but he did not. Faster and harder, he went, leaving her. At his peak, she turned her head aside. With his breath, harsh and warm, against her neck, Emily lay still, then pulled herself from beneath the unfamiliar weight of his arm. He was asleep. She struggled out of the dress and the confines of the corset. What to do with them? Everything here was unaccustomed. Lifting the hoops, she dropped her heavy garments in a corner. Charles was spread across the bed, his face buried in the bedding. She lifted a corner of the covers and slid into the space left her, still in her pantaloons and shift.

When morning came, Emily sensed the pale coral-gray light through her lids. Married, she felt herself other, enlarged into a new and unaccustomed life, yet simultaneously diminished, no longer belonging to herself. Now she belonged to this man she did not know. Emily opened her eyes to dispel the feeling and stroked the edge of the wedding ring quilt, remembering her hand and Ginny's as they stitched the pieces together from the her mother's clothing they had found in an old chest. She turned, her lips deliberate on Charles's cheek, feeling the rough chafe of his morning stubble. He stirred. She gave her breath to him. He mumbled something unintelligible and threw his legs over the side of the bed, rubbing at his face. She stretched her hand out to touch his back. After a moment he rose without another word or glance, pulled on his clothes, and went out of the room. She turned her face to the window's light and sighed. This was her new life. With no more to fill her than the old.

Caught in a cobweb, a skein of dust wafted across the morning light. This is my house, she thought. Home felt far removed. A realization of ordinary life flashed into her mind: her newly built house still holding sawdust from construction, the edges of its logs and boards still rough, unsettled, uninhabited somehow. A house like any other, demanding constant attention to keep it comfortable, respectable, clean. And in her, a sudden sense of vigilance toward this man who was now her husband. So unlike her father. Something in that difference had appealed to her, and yet she had assumed that the same kindly attentiveness her father provided would form the foundation of any marriage. That would be a given. And to that familiar comfort, with marriage there would be the excitement of something more dynamic and stimulating, something enticing to her senses. Something alive. Such was her expectation and such it would remain until it could no longer.

The cobweb floated across her vision again. She rose and reached for it, pulling it with gentle care from its attachment to the window frame. So fragile, she thought. So easily destroyed. She held out her open palm and let the cobweb drift into it, settle in the cradle of her hand. So fragile. And yet it holds. She lifted one end and watched the dust moats separate and sparkle in the morning light. She tossed the insubstantial thread into the air and bent to retrieve her discarded garments from the corner. A soft knock at the door diverted her. In the quiet Ginny's welcome face appeared.

"Morning, Mrs. Slate." Ginny smiled and entered with a small tray. "It is Mrs. Slate, I believe?" She set the tray on a side table.

"Yes, Ginny. For better or worse, it is Mrs. Slate." Emily let herself be enveloped in Ginny's arms. Her embrace was firm, solid, stable. Neither woman spoke.

CHAPTER 8

Spring's mantle of fragile green turned heavy as the early heat rolled out across the land. Any shade was welcome. On the porch, Will leaned back on two legs of a cane-bottom chair. The green check of Emily's skirt whispered as she settled into the swing beside Charles.

"I'm going courting," Will said. "Lucinda Morris from Winona."

William had met Lucinda through a law school friend who fancied himself a matchmaker. Their father had been introduced to her and approved in relief. She was a few years older than Will, tall, well-bred, and handsome enough, yet so withdrawn that she said little and rarely looked anyone in the eye. She had the reputation, however, as an adept mistress of a small farm, efficient in the management of her property and slaves. Lucinda's reticence fit Will's restraint, and so he thought that, though it would not be a love match, they might make a harmonious and productive life. He had made two visits to Winona and arrangements for a third.

* * *

Meanwhile Belinda arranged to come home. On a Saturday in the oppressive heat of mid-June, she boarded the train and found her seat. Her legs and back wet with perspiration, she fidgeted throughout the trip. When at last the train slowed, Belinda stood, fanning her face with a limp handkerchief. Gripping the unpolished brass rails, she edged her way toward the car door. The depot appeared and with it Hammond's glad face. Belinda's stomach churned from the lurching train and from her dread of coming home.

"Belinda, you're here. Was school a chore?" Hammond said, even as she descended. "Or did you love the learning? I think I would if I could go to school. Love it, that is. But now you're home and I'm so glad."

Belinda touched his ruddy, clean-shaven cheek. He was more handsome even than Charles, his whole demeanor bringing with it the solid quality of earth. Hammond managed her trunk onto the buckboard, helped her up, and took the reins. He was unnerved by her pallor, her uncharacteristic solemnity, and the looseness with which her dress hung on her.

At home, Belinda studied the modest house, whitewashed frame with a one-story porch along its length. The dogtrot had been enclosed to form a central hall. When Belinda entered, only Adeline was there to welcome her. Her father was off somewhere drunk. Charles was married and gone. Hammond struggled up the stairs, dragging her trunk, and the three of them sat down to supper. But eating was no more possible for Belinda that night than any recent night at school, in spite of the tender chicken and dumplings, boiled thick in salty broth. Nothing enticed her—not the peas nor the greens with ham hock. Not even the cobbler from Hammond's foraged berries. Belinda picked at her plate and excused herself from the table.

"I'm only tired," she said, and closed the door behind her, leaving the remnants of her family at the table.

Hammond helped Adeline clear the dishes. "Leave them be," she said when the plates had been scraped. "They will hold till the morning." She took the lamp and mounted the stairs, Hammond following.

In the dark, Belinda heard Adeline and Hammond mount the stairs and close their doors. The house grew still. The night thinned around her. She stared out at the moonlight for a long time. Then she was on her feet. A slight breeze from the half-open window penetrated the shift she wore, one she had begun to embroider after Will's proposal. Now there were tiny roses on the left shoulder and a few scattered leaves that crossed her meager breast on a vine that went nowhere.

Belinda seized her shawl from the floor and wrapped it around her. The hinge creaked as she opened her door. She stopped, her hand on the porcelain knob. There was no other sound. In the hallway, her fingers guided her through the familiar darkness of home. She crept along the wall to the stairs. Below her the pale moonlight washed the lower step. A cough from Hammond's room startled her. And she froze. There was only the sound of the murmuring creatures of the night. With sharpened caution, she descended into the shallow moonlight.

Sometime past midnight, Hammond woke with his back to the window. He heard it again, some unidentifiable sound. Propped on one elbow, he blinked sleep from his eyes and put a bare foot on the floor.

At the open window, Hammond shivered and almost went back to bed. But as he turned, a low sobbing came from the path near the fence. In the breeze he saw a billow of white fabric. Barefoot, he bolted down the stairs and fumbled with the latch until he realized it was already unbarred.

Far down the path, Hammond could make out a woman, stumbling. He leaped from the porch and down the path, not bothering as the gate clanged shut behind him. Near her, Hammond slowed, wary of frightening her. Her progress was erratic, her hair disheveled, her shawl hanging from one shoulder. She turned her head and seemed to listen. The moonlight caught her profile.

"Belinda?" Hammond whispered. He grasped her arm. "What are you doing out here in the night?" He pushed back the tangles of her thick hair and pulled the shawl around her shoulders.

"I have to see Will."

"It's the middle of the night, Belinda. Come on now. I'll take you home." He took a step toward the house.

"He has to talk to me." Belinda struggled against him. "Let me go."

Hammond did not let go. Her arm was so thin. A memory struck him: a fragile figurine he had shattered as a boy. He had a sudden fear that Belinda would break apart in his hands.

"Talk to me, Belinda. We can talk the sun up if you want."

She allowed him to guide her home. As they neared, Hammond saw his mother's face in the lamplight at the door.

"She took it in her head to go to Will, Mama, all wrought up like you see." He reached for the lamp as Adeline helped Belinda into the house. "Not making sense."

On the davenport, Belinda lay like a child who has cried herself to sleep, her breathing ragged. The moonlight accentuated her pallor. Belinda's face disturbed Adeline, as it always had, in its fragility.

Belinda stirred. "I should have told him yes, Mama, straightaway." She paused. "I just thought—well, I can't say what I thought." Belinda twisted a matt of hair. "I thought he'd be more persistent, more romantic, more—" Belinda hiccupped. "And then—well, then I wrote to him." She raised up on her elbow and pointed her finger. "Yes, I did. I wrote and I said yes, I'd marry him."

Adeline thought how Belinda's fear had come into the world right with her, how agitated she had been as an infant. Belinda had seemed to Adeline like a little bird, liable to fall from the nest before she could fly.

"Why would he turn his back on me?" Belinda said. She continued to twist her hair. "It wasn't three weeks—maybe four—well, I don't know how long when I wrote him." She twisted the hair tighter. "I did, Mama. I did write him. Now all this time and not one word from him."

Hammond started for the kitchen, shuffled his feet, and came back.

"Let me go," he said to Adeline. "Will's a good man and an honest one. He ain't unkind. Come daybreak I'll go talk to him and get it clear. You want that, Belinda?"

She nodded, still pulling at her hair.

A pale fringe of morning lightened the sky. Hammond clutched his coat lapels between his hands, waiting for the slave to fetch William, who appeared with a napkin still in his hands.

"I'm here to speak to you about Belinda."

"Belinda?"

"She set out in the night to come to you. All wrought up. Out of her head, if you take my meaning."

"No, Hammond. I don't follow you at all. What are you saying?"

"Why didn't you answer her letter, Will? She said she wrote she would marry you. And you turn your back without a word and go to courting somebody else? She don't deserve that." Hammond's voice was thick.

"I never heard from her."

"What do you mean you never heard?"

"There was never any letter, Hammond." Will's voice was very calm. "Where is she?"

"Home."

"Tell her I'll be there in an hour."

Before he left the house, Will wrote a brief note of apology to Lucinda Morris, canceling his projected visit to Winona. Will sealed the envelope and handed it to his father to post. The judge looked at the address. He held Will's arm in a brief restraint. "Be careful with yourself, son," he said, then shook his head and let him go. Will took the reins of his chestnut horse and rode away.

And so on the evening of July 6, 1859, Judge Matthews presided over a second Matthews–Slate marriage in his parlor. Belinda wore Emily's dove gray silk, which Ginny had altered to fit Belinda's thin waist. At Belinda's insistence, the dress was reworked and adorned with silver buttons, yellow plaid ruffles edging the wide sleeves, and a sash of yellow silk ribbon for good measure. Adeline was once again witness, along with Charles. Hammond was again as giddy as a child. The house slaves had spent the day preparing a wedding supper to follow the vows. Emily attended to her new sister-in-law until the bridal couple slipped away upstairs.

"They will be happy," Emily whispered to Charles, threading her fingers through his.

"We will all be happy, my dear," he said, "if we can manage it."

Emily looked at him, puzzled. Charles leaned down and kissed her, closing her mouth with his. "Let's you and I be going home," he said.

Dew lay across the fields in a glistening veil that seemed as if it could be lifted and shaken in the breeze, to fall again in a shower of silver light. At the end of a turn row, Will crouched, studying the cotton's mid-summer growth as he crumbled bits of dark earth in his fingers. He heard the crunch of approaching boots and stood. From the perimeter of the field, Judge Matthews strolled toward his son.

"Out early, son."

"Yes, sir." Will brushed the soil from his hands. He stared out at the lustrous web of dew.

Judge Matthews surveyed the sky, gauging the weather. Quiet enveloped the two men, punctuated by the chirping of a titmouse and a wren in flight. Judge Matthews rested his hand on his son's shoulder. Will embraced him, his face hidden in the collar of his father's coat. The two men released one another. Will brushed at his face with his jacket sleeve.

The judge waited.

"I can't believe it all, Father. I—I don't know how this came about. All my hopelessness. And hers, too, apparently. Letter gone astray." He paused. "Speaking of letters, I was thinking of Lucinda. It would have been an arrangement of convenience, for both of us. But still, I wouldn't like to have misled her."

The judge laughed. "Lucinda Morris is a practical woman. And a gracious one. She would have made you a good wife, a very good one. She may yet make a good wife to someone else. But though you respect one another, you would never have had more than a relationship of gratitude. I know that. The kind that comes from years of cooperative sharing. Never like your Fran." He sighed. "And not like Belinda, either."

Will went still.

"I know you think about Fran—same as I do your mother," Judge Matthews said. "And your baby boy buried there with her. I watched part of you die with them." He stopped. "Well, and though you know I have reservations, I've seen some life in you again with Belinda. And your sadness all over again when you thought you had lost her, too. How you closed off. I have not provided a good example for you on that score. Perhaps you will be able to lower your guard a bit now that Belinda is here."

"Perhaps."

"Well, these things have a season of their own. Sometimes, gladness is as slow as grief." The judge took his son by the elbow. "Now, let's see what we can accomplish of some practicality in this season of budding marriage."

"I'd say we were doing all right for the first day," Will laughed.

"Yes, but there are generally quite a few more days than that in a lifetime." Judge Matthews lifted his head to follow the flight of a red-winged blackbird. "So, I have a proposal for you this morning. You will need a home of your own. I intend to build you a house on the knoll just past the turnoff to the upper place. In fact, I have the men starting on it today. Perhaps two stories, four rooms to begin with. A summer kitchen, with basic outbuildings."

"That's very . . ."

"Don't interrupt."

"Yes, sir."

"I think five hundred acres should make you a good beginning, same as the old starter land grants. Belinda can choose someone from the women to tend house and a garden boy. You and I will go over the field hands and make those decisions together. I expect we will be sharing a good many hands since part of my expectation—my condition, actually—is that you continue to oversee my acreage as well. For that, I will pay you two hundred and fifty dollars a year. You will need a barn and stock of your own. We'll look through together and make the choice—some of the older calves and a few good breeders, a bull, a rooster, and some laying hens for Belinda."

"You are very generous."

"No, not generous. I'm both selfish and practical. Selfish enough to want you close by. And practical in that at least that portion of land—and more—will be yours at my death regardless."

"I don't know what to say, Father."

The judge's laugh was deep and full. "Thank you would be acceptable."

"Thank you." Will embraced him, his words smothered in his father's coat, as his tears had been earlier.

"There are conditions, of course, which will be outlined in my will. An update on that is overdue and I have been far too distracted. So many changes lately."

"Yes, sir."

"Your children would inherit the land directly. In the unlikely event of your death before mine, Belinda will retain the house and garden as her own until her death or remarriage, in which case they will revert to Jeremiah. And she will retain at least two servants, if indeed we have them then. The remainder of the land will revert to my estate."

"That's very fair," Will said.

"And should you die before me without children—"

"Father—"

"Don't interrupt. This is reality. Should you die without children—" The red-winged blackbird distracted him again. "In that event, Belinda will still retain the house and the garden acreage under the same conditions and the remainder of the land will again revert to my estate. Technically by Mississippi law, Belinda has the right to inherit from you, but not the right to control. That means her father would have control. I will not see my land in the hands of Thomas Slate. If she remarries or dies, that lifetime inheritance of house, garden, and slaves will also revert to Jeremiah, since Emily has her own. Inheritance by direct lineage only."

"You sound like a lawyer."

"I am. That's how I came to be a judge."

"And talk legal to your eldest son?"

"And talk legal to my eldest son."

Will surveyed the field, where the dew was vanishing in a low mist. "Thank you, Father. I'd like to talk to Belinda, if you don't mind." Will scraped the dirt off his boot with a stick.

"You might wait on the part about your dying young or childless. Save the legalities for another time. I'm not sure how cheerful she would find that on her first wedded morning. Now, go on."

Will broke into a slow lope toward the house. Judge Mat-thews resumed his absorption with the blackbirds in the thicket.

CHAPTER 9

At the end of his morning appointments, Charles came into the dining room, where Emily was fiddling at unnecessary adjustments to a napkin. With his hands behind him and a mischievous smile on his lips, he bent to kiss Emily's cheek.

"Close your eyes," he said.

She did, smiling back. Since his self-absorption in their early union, he had gradually begun to court her physically. Emily cherished surprise moments like this. The somberness in her father's home had robbed her of a sense of play in childhood. She had grown up old. Charles's frolicsome capers, though sometimes outrageous, were a restitution of sorts. Emily hid behind her eyelids and waited.

"Open your mouth."

She felt the skin first, heavy on her lips, without much taste.

"Wider."

The bulging skin slid between her teeth.

"Now," Charles said, "suck it in."

The almost-sweet juice burst onto her tongue, the soft, seedy fruit of the fig. Emily laughed and juice spilled from the corner of her mouth. She reached to wipe at it with the napkin, but Charles's mouth was on hers. Emily tried to stifle her laugh, but failed and sprayed them both with fig and juice. Charles retreated, each of them hanging to the corners of the napkin, the dark juice on her face and in his beard. She swatted the napkin at him and pushed him away, pointing and laughing at his splattered face.

"First fig of the season," Charles said. "Just couldn't let it go to waste!"

Emily swallowed, bending over, until she could get her breath.

"You are the devil's own imp, I declare," she said.

"And you the temptation. You could make a man fall, you could."

Charles kissed her again, this time with an urgent hunger. Emily put her arms around him, responding, then pulled back. "It's dinnertime," she said. "Ginny will be coming any moment."

Charles pinned her against the doorpost, his arms stretched out to the sides. He straddled her skirts between his long legs. She wriggled to get free.

"Not till I have my kiss." Charles took her chin in his hand, bent his mouth to hers.

"Open your eyes," he said. "I want to see you watching me kiss you."

Emily opened her eyes. She saw him watching what she was feeling. She had never felt so naked. He slid his hand down her back, into the pleats of her skirts.

"You wear too many petticoats, Mrs. Slate. I believe I've said that before."

"The better to shield myself from the likes of you, Dr. Slate."

"You will never succeed at that, Mrs. Slate. Now, perhaps you would feed a starving man his dinner."

The back door creaked and slammed. As she ducked out of

his arms, Charles kissed her on the cheek. She reached for a steaming dish in Ginny's hands.

"I am a hungry man," he said to no one in particular. "Give me sustenance to heal a broken world this afternoon."

Ginny turned her back and set the bowl of crowder peas on the edge of the table, hot pot liquor sloshing onto her hand and dripping onto the red-checked cloth. She slid the bowl away from the table's edge and dabbed at the spots with her apron. Emily reached across and touched her hand.

"You all right, Ginny?"

"Yes'm. I be fine." She straightened her back and looked into Emily's face as if to assure herself what she might find there. Wiping at her hand with the apron, she flapped it once as if to clear the air.

"Is there much more to bring? I'll come and help you."

Ginny shook her head and brushed the words aside as if she were shooing a fly.

"No, Miss Emily. I don't need you. You just sit down here with the good doctor while he gather himself up for the afternoon. I be right back."

Ginny knew she risked being too caustic. She bit her cheek as she turned, not daring another look at him. Slave gossip traveled thick and fast, and she'd heard more than she wanted as to where he spent his Thursday afternoons, his horse hitched around the corner from the brothel far longer than warranted for doctoring. The knowledge of it was burdensome, her feelings and loyalties mixed and churning. This was white folks' doings and she was a slave. But Emily had been half hers to rear: her sister-child. It was impossible to reconcile her protective instincts with the limits of her station. What a thought that was: the limits of her station. Yet ever present, even in this household. What if she did divulge what she'd heard? What purpose would it serve? Emily would still be his wife and a wife then burdened as well. Perhaps she was already. How could

Ginny know what Emily might suspect? And how could Ginny be sure her suspicions amounted to any more than suspicion? She couldn't. Nor could she relieve its weight on her by putting it off on Emily. No, she would simply fetch the chicken and the cornbread and bring them to the table. Ask was there anything else they needed and then disappear. Same as he would do right after the meal.

The winds of August 1859 brought a touch of relief from the oppressive heat and a sure hint of fall, especially the evening winds. Emily loved the wind. She always had. She thought of a story Ginny loved to tell about her when she was a toddler. Her mother had been changing her clothes, when she caught sight of the treetops blowing outside the window. As her mother turned to get fresh underthings and a pinafore, Emily had darted down the steps and into the yard, flying naked through the wind, arms outstretched, twirling in the gale.

Emily released herself now to the wind's insistent embrace. She swayed, arms raised, eyes closed, leaning into the force of its magnitude. When the rain came, she stayed, letting its needles penetrate her clothing until she was wet through.

From the house kitchen, Ginny watched and waited. The teakettle sizzled on the stove. A homespun gray wool blanket lay across a chair back. When at last Emily came inside, the heavy indigo of her skirts left a trail of water across the floor. Ginny wrapped her in the blanket and handed her a cup of tea before mopping up the puddles.

"Ginny," Emily said, "I have a baby in me now."

"You sure?"

A faint smile played across Emily's face.

"How sure?" Ginny stood still in front of her, challenging.

"I'm sure, Ginny. Really, I'm a woman now. I'm not a girl anymore."

"I know." Ginny dropped her wet rag onto the side counter.

"Well?" She waited. "How you feel about this baby you got in you?"

"Now, Ginny, what kind of question is that? I expect I feel like any other expectant mother. A bit sick of a morning—"

Ginny interrupted. "I thought so. I been watching. And what else?"

"So glad, Ginny. Really, I'm so happy."

Ginny studied her from the other side of the worktable. "You ain't afraid? You got to be afraid, Miss Emily. You know right down to the bone about birthing. Happy is fine, for sure. Babies do make us happy. Tired, too. Up half the night. You don't know that part yet. But you know the other and you best not be fooling around with me. I been there with you."

A long silence followed. Emily held the teacup to her lips like a shield, set it down, and dropped her head.

"Yes." Her voice was barely a whisper. "Yes." She raised her chin and looked directly at Ginny. "Yes, I'm afraid. But there is no cure for that, Ginny. And I'm not going to die. I'm not. I'm going to love this child, and I'm going to be right there and I'm never going to not be there for her."

"Now, how you know it's her? You got second sight."

Emily rose and let herself be held in Ginny's arms. "No, what I've got is wishful thinking. And courage, if I can muster it."

"You can. You been doing it all your life."

Adeline opened the door to Emily's knock days later and beckoned her in. She put her arms around this young woman who had entered her life with such ease. She pondered how much more comfortable she felt with Emily than with her own daughter. But then, Belinda was a case unto herself. Always had been.

Yet even with Emily, she was aware of her reticence. *Is that what I am,* she thought, *reticent? Well, we both of us are reti-*

cent, in different ways. What does that even mean, anyway: wary, secretive, uncommunicative? And why? I learned to keep my mouth shut, Adeline thought; *open it and something bad was bound to happen.* She shook her head and motioned Emily through the hall and out the back to the kitchen, where she drew the iron kettle from the hearth and poured two cups of tea.

Emily took a sip and smoothed her skirt over her lap. "I hope to lay your first grandchild in your arms in the spring," she said.

Adeline set down the cup, her face unexpectedly grave. The thought of loving another child brought unexpected fear rather than joy, especially as the prospect of war loomed over their lives. "And you are feeling well?" she said.

"I keep cold biscuits by the bed and hardly dare to turn my head until I've had a few bites of a morning. Other than that, I'm fine."

"Well, then. Let us hope this is the first of many," Adeline said.

"Did you come from a large family?" Emily said. "I suddenly realize how little I know about your family. Charles's family, really."

Adeline's laugh had a slightly bitter edge to it. "The better for it, likely." She took a sip of her tea. "It's not such a pretty story, Emily."

"But now it's my family as well, Adeline."

"Families often know little about one another."

"I know what an intelligent woman you are. That much is no secret."

"I taught myself all I know, Emily. And not in the most admirable way. As a child I was sent to do day work for the town doctor—not the most reputable of men, I might add." Memories flooded Adeline—a handful of women with little coughs or headaches that defied the repeated treatment on their frequent visits, their moans through the door of the examining room, the doctor moaning, too. He had moaned a great deal with certain ones. And sometimes with a strange gentleman who appeared irregularly. She had known what the treatment was, same as her father imposed on her mother, only her mother's moans were different, stifled and painful. Adeline shook her head, pulled herself back into the room. "I sneaked books from his house all the time and read and read and read. He never missed those books. I think they were mainly for show. And I listened when he talked. He was articulate in spite of himself. I was just a child who worked in the house. He didn't even know I was there. I was invisible to him."

"It's hard to imagine you as invisible."

"There were plenty of other times I wished I truly were, Emily—at home."

"What was at home, Adeline?"

"What was not at home is more the question."

"What was not at home?"

"Love. Love was not at home. Remember, Emily, you asked." Adeline set down her empty cup. "My pa was mean as a snake. Maybe meaner. He had a temper you didn't want to see. Or hear. One time he beat the wall and broke his hand. It turned all purple and was never right after that." She took a deep breath. "So then he took to using his belt or a stick of kindling from the woodbox or whatever else came to hand. I had a brother never learned to keep his mouth shut, always bruised and having bloody eyes. One day when I was at the doctor's, he died, my brother did. I didn't see him. They had him in the box, nailed shut, when I got home. They said he fell and broke his neck. He may have. He was always falling. So he may have. But I never really knew."

Adeline studied her daughter-in-law. What about this girl made her willing to be vulnerable? Adeline saw the cup trembling in Emily's hand.

"What did you do, Adeline?"

"Kept my mouth shut. Wouldn't you?"

"Yes. Yes, I would."

"I got cagey, Emily. And reticent. Reticent has dignity to it. Cagey sounds like an animal. I felt like an animal sometimes. Like an animal caught in a cage. Some kind of cat maybe. I remember seeing a bobcat caught like that once. No way out. And that's how I felt. No way out. And all I wanted was to get away."

"Is that how you came to marry Thomas?"

"That is exactly how I came to marry Thomas. He came around one day hauling wood and I was sent to let him in. He was a little thing for a grown-up boy. Always small. But he had eyes like that cat. Wide open. Wide open and looking at me. And then he smiled. He had these pretty lips like I wished I had myself. Heavy lips on that skinny face. Nobody ever smiled at me like that. And I was hooked. Like a fish on a string. Just caught and him playing with the line to watch me flipping every which way, fighting to get away. I reckon I was. Only not away from him."

Adeline smiled at Emily then. "So after a while one day when he came to haul some more wood, I helped him get it piled up. We didn't either one of us say anything, but when we got done, he put his arm around my waist and kissed me. I climbed up in the wagon and we drove away."

Without taking her eyes from Adeline's face, Emily set her cup in the saucer.

"I figure I was with child—that would have been Charles—by the time we got a preacher, though it wasn't all that long, maybe just a week or two. I wasn't paying much attention to the time. I was listening at the door of myself—hearing me and him and I loved it. I loved my Thomas, who had saved me from my life and let me out my cage." Adeline stood and took the empty cup from Emily.

"I'm sorry about your brother."

"I had five brothers. There were eleven of us. More than one who died. Only six of us got full grown." Why was she telling all this? What was it in this girl that elicited so much trust? Was it the unprecedented emotion of a first grandchild? The unpredictable dangers of pregnancies and childbirth and children? Adeline hesitated. She would be still now. She would not go further with these revelations, these secrets even her own children had never known.

The silence in the room demanded something to fill it.

"One died because of me."

"Because of you?" Emily leaned forward to the edge of her seat. "You don't have to tell me this, Adeline. But I am willing to hear, if you wish."

"I never talked about it in my life." Adeline faced Emily, her hands braced behind her on the table edge. Yes, this young woman was strong enough to hear her. "Pa was teaching me to stand the wagon. I was afraid and I kept sitting down. He was in a rage. Made me get down and stand there in the field, just stand, holding my skirt up while he hunted for a stick. My brother came running and climbed up in that wagon. He was younger than me, but good with the wagon, and he stood up there and smiled. He flicked the reins and turned around, smiling at me, and the wagon hit a rock. He was still looking at me when he fell, looking like he had a big surprise and couldn't quite decide if it was good. He held on to the reins and they jerked him around and the wheel went over his neck. I couldn't move and I couldn't make a sound, but I couldn't look away. I couldn't stop looking at that body that wasn't my brother anymore. I didn't even know who that was. And the next day, after we buried him, I stood that wagon and I've stood it ever since."

"Oh, Adeline." Emily rose and extended her arms to her mother-in-law. Adeline let herself be held, let herself cry the long-withheld tears.

CHAPTER 10

The cooling winds of late August withdrew their promise. Indian summer dropped its torrid days over the land, the house, the verandahs. Emily lifted a worn palmetto fan from the porch table and offered one to Belinda.

"No, I have my own, thank you." From the pleats of her plaid silk skirt, Belinda produced a folding fan of the latest fashion, its tips ending in silk leaves embellished with dark feathers. Belinda flipped it open, fanned herself, the feathers fluttering in its artificial breeze. Emily attempted to hide her astonishment at such a fan in addition to the extravagant plaid of Belinda's dress. Trade was shaky, as was the future, and Will, always frugal, tended to preserve his resources.

"A gift from Will," Belinda said. "He ordered it from New Orleans because I just fell in love with it in the catalog. He didn't seem to love it like I did, but I begged and then he said he would. But, of course, it is never certain if things will actually arrive these days. Like my letter saying I would marry him, but, of course, that had nothing to do with anything except some devilish vandal, pulling his antics at the expense of my life." Belinda fanned herself, flicking the feathers against her cheek. "And what if I hadn't got so upset I couldn't help myself? We would never have known my letter went missing. It would be the great unsolved mystery of Choctaw County. But it isn't. And what if we'd found it all out after Will was married to that woman from Winona?" She flicked the fan closed, then open again. "But he's not. And now I am married to Will and have my beautiful fan. I hope I never have to use one of those horrid old palmetto fans again. I cannot abide to lay eyes on them."

Emily put her fan aside.

"No, no, Emily." Belinda leaned across, her hand outstretched. "I am so sorry. I didn't mean you. All I have to do is open my mouth and I wind up putting my foot in it. But you know that from school."

"Well, Belinda, I—"

"Don't say that isn't true, Emily. I was always saying something foolish or hurting someone's feelings. Over things I never thought mattered, anyway. Just trifles. But they must matter to some folk." Belinda sat back and fanned at her neck. "Truth is, Emily, you were my only friend I could actually talk to. And then I open my mouth and say something stupid to you."

"Belinda, it is only a palmetto fan—"

"I know. And it shouldn't matter, but it does. It makes me think of Pa when he was all the time trying to get religion. All those tent meetings in the heat! And those old fans going back and forth, back and forth. It's enough to make a girl crazy!"

"How could a revival be—?"

"Well, it was. You haven't ever had to go to the likes of these. But I have. Pa wanting to get born again, so he could be different. And him dragging me with him every time. I reckon he hoped if I could get born again, maybe he could, too. But that didn't work. I did not need to get born again. I needed to get over being born the first time and get on with the living part." Belinda closed her fan again.

A loosened feather from the fan quivered onto Emily's lap. The blue-black iridescence of it shifted as Emily pulled it through her fingers.

Belinda paused. "I hated those meetings, everybody hollering and shouting and the preacher bellowing on about hell." Belinda half rose, then sat again. "I went down front with Pa, more than once. If he went, I went. I certainly did not stay on that bench all by myself. Scared to death sitting there in that forest of folks, waving those fans, all whipped up by the Holy Ghost. Now, isn't that enough to scare a girl? If you don't have hell, you have the ghost. No other choices."

Emily laughed out loud, head thrown back. Belinda too.

"Well, Pa did not get saved, at least not from himself. And neither did I. If being born the first time doesn't work quite right, there is not much chance for the second time or the third or the tenth. My pa loves to talk about me being born, but Mama, she does not. Mama will walk right out of the house when he starts in, even if it is black dark and the moon not up. You know about me being born?"

Emily shook her head. Belinda tucked a perverse loop of curls behind her ear.

"Mama must have been so scared when I got born, what with baby Lillie dead just weeks before from the croup, so I don't blame her all that much. I don't guess Pa was scared. I don't know rightly what he was. Are you sure I never told you this?"

"No, Belinda, you never told me." She took Belinda's hand, so small and thin and slightly rough.

"I was born too soon and Mama gave me up for dead. She could not bear it. So, she just went straight out to grief. I was her newborn grief. But Pa, he wrapped me in hot towels. Put his steaming whiskey mouth on mine and blew. For hours, to hear him tell it. Of course, I don't remember that." Belinda laughed and folded her fan. "But Pa has told me so many times, it seems like I do. He went desperate, I reckon, for me to live.

Without it, he said once, life wouldn't mean much anymore. Without it, I was dead. And I am not. I am here alive with Will."

"Yes, you are here with Will. And me." Emily rubbed her thumb across the top of Belinda's hand.

"Pa doesn't go to meetings anymore. I reckon he gave up, figured he'd settle for hell. He doesn't need to die to be in hell. I'm not right sure there is one, anyway."

"Do you talk to him, Belinda?"

"Sometimes he talks to Charles and Hammond, but he and Mama hardly say a word. He sleeps out in the shed. If I'm around, which isn't much, and the weather is dropping, I take a quilt out to lay over him. Most times, there is one already there, tucked in careful-like. And I know Mama has beat me to it."

Belinda stopped, looked around. She waved her fan, the feathers fluttering in front of her face. "It sure is hot today," Belinda said. "Did that come off my fan?" She pointed to the feather Emily still held.

"We can get some thread and put it back," Emily said.

"No, here, I'll get Will to do it. That will make him happy. He likes to do for me. At least I think he does. Sometimes he's cross with me, but then that farm is very hard on him." Belinda tucked the feather into the pocket of her skirt. "Sure is hot today."

CHAPTER 11

After the early months of sickness, Jessie's tiny body began to round. Ginny noted it, as she had noted the sickness that Jessie struggled to hide. Ginny had an eye for life. After dinner one day, when the dishes were washed and the kitchen cleaned, she spoke.

"Your man taken note on this yet?"

"On what?" Jessie said.

"That baby you carrying?"

"No, he ain't." Jessie bent over some unnecessary task, chipping at an imaginary spot with her broken thumbnail.

"Why you keeping this from your man, Jessie? He done been through hell. He could do with a little good news about now."

Jessie looked up, her expression hard, her eyes glittering. Ginny studied her face. Ginny's embrace was awkward, her tall, lean form bending over the diminutive woman as over a child.

"He gone know it soon enough. Best you tell him now. You don't have to tell him the size of it, if you don't want. But he a man, Jessie. He a black diamond of a man."

"He don't need no more to carry, Ginny."

"Ain't you carrying that empty sleeve with him every day? Ain't you carrying it together, just like you buried that arm together?"

Jessie nodded.

"You hoping he'll believe it's his?"

Jessie shook her head. Ginny held her at arm's length.

"It ain't like he won't carry this then. How you think that man gone feel when he find out you trying to carry this heavy load without him? Won't be long now 'fore he see it for himself, honey. He gone be all right with that? Mayhap he noticed already. You thinking you can spare him?"

"Maybe."

"Then, I expect you best get over that and tell him now. Every day he ain't helping you carry this gone be a day he regret."

Jessie raised her chin and looked away.

"I'll be at your cabin after supper," Ginny said. "Your childrens gone spend the night with Ginny. Now get that broom and go to work on the porch before I has to go tell the judge he done wasted his money on you."

From the parlor door, Emily watched Belinda remove the vase from its shelf. She held it close to her face, as she did everything, refusing to wear spectacles except in secret. Emily had glimpsed her with them only a handful of times at school and suspected her failure to wear them in class contributed to Belinda's struggle with her marks. For several minutes, Emily did not speak.

"It was my mother's," she said, finally.

Startled, Belinda fumbled the vase back into place. Below it, Emily could see the carved face of the fox peaking from the intricate design of wooden leaves on the shelf bracket.

"My father brought it to her from New Orleans, before they were married."

"It is beautiful," Belinda said. She scooped up the green silk ruffles of her skirt. "You must cherish it. Well, of course, you would. I don't know why I said that."

"I do cherish it, Belinda. I have so little of her." Emily reached up, tracing the outline of a glass rose with her fingertip. "Sometimes, I try to remember things, but I know it's mostly just imagination on my part: some expression on her face, her hand picking up a hairbrush, the way she might have threaded a needle. Sometimes my father mentions things, how she loved to paint and sew. But the larger things are only stories of her. Stories that I make into a memory of sorts, memories of stories. Imagination. But then things slide away. Her face is just a tintype. Her expression never changes and her eyes don't blink."

"I can't imagine. Well, actually, I guess I can imagine. Of course, I can. Anyone can imagine anything they want, but it would only be, like you say, imagination. Although I do have a vivid imagination. Oh, Emily, it would be like trying to imagine how turnips taste if you'd never had a bite of them."

"Yes, something like that, I suppose." Emily laughed.

"You never mention it, Emily. Her death, I mean. Were you there?"

"No—I mean, yes. Ginny tells me I was, but I don't remember." Emily fingered the gold locket that held a snip of her mother's hair. "I can't think about it, Belinda. But sometimes, it just comes on me."

She halted, opening the locket, fingered her mother's hair, and snapped the locket shut. "Sometimes I imagine myself there, but it goes into a kind of blankness. It's red and it's dark and it has no horizon. It makes me so afraid. It's something I smell. I'm afraid I will go there and not ever come back."

"Oh, Emily," Belinda said, her hand flapping uselessly in the air between them, "there I go again. I do not understand myself. Really, I don't. How things go popping out of my mouth the way they do. I should be ashamed."

"No, Belinda." Emily laid her hand on the wide plaid of Belinda's empress sleeve. "Please, it's not your fault. It's me. Don't fret."

Belinda turned away. "All right, I won't," she said. "But that is just awful. And what about Will? Was he there?"

Emily stared at Belinda, almost through her. She sighed and rubbed the back of her hand across her forehead.

"No," she said. "He was away at school. We never discuss it. I see it in him, though, and Jeremiah. Especially Jeremiah—the way he gets sometimes and can't be still, as if there is no ground to hold him up."

"You talking about me?" Jeremiah whipped into the room like a horse in a brushfire.

"Belinda was admiring Mama's vase."

"And how exactly did my name come into that?"

"I was telling Belinda how differently each of us miss her."

"Well, I don't miss her. She was gone when I got here. And I don't give a whit for vases and such," he said, jerking it from the shelf. "She ain't in that vase. She ain't anywhere, as I know of."

Jeremiah thrust the vase back onto the shelf, its gilt edge protruding from the rim. He leaned against the wall, arms crossed, one foot propped atop the wide baseboard. As he shifted, his arm shot out for balance. The back of his hand made contact with the vase. It shifted. Jeremiah caught his balance. The vase plummeted in a blur of green and rose and gold. Belinda reached for it, but it was beyond her. Emily watched the pieces fly apart. She saw each piece glide up and out as it hit, saw how whatever space it once contained no longer existed.

Emily picked up a shard of glass. On it remained one almost-intact rose. She studied it, holding it up to the light. She put it in Jeremiah's hand and closed his palm around the jagged sliver.

"No," Emily said, "she wasn't in the vase."

Jessie's baby girl was born in the early days of December 1859. An almost-Christmas baby, she was light as milk coffee, red-faced from crying, with a full head of dark kinky hair, frosted at the ends with a coppery glow. Ginny handed the baby, cut free and cleaned, to her mother. She watched as Jessie studied this strange child who had entered the world through her body.

"Where's Nathan?" Jessie said.

"Outside."

"You best show him this baby, Ginny." Jessie's voice was tired and defeated.

Ginny wrapped the child and walked onto the stoop. Nathan stood with his back to the cabin. He did not turn around. She stood watching until she sensed a bit of give to his shoulders. She crossed in front of him, laid the baby in his elbow, and pulled back a corner of the swaddling. Nathan's eyes went narrow. He stared at the pale, bundled face for endless minutes. The baby opened her eyes and blinked, searching for something beyond him. Nathan did not raise his face, but Ginny saw the grimace, the constricted jaw.

"You got yourself a daughter, Nathan," Ginny said, "if you want her."

Nathan handed the baby back, leaped from the porch, and ran. Ginny watched him go. The darkness swallowed him.

Inside the cabin, Jessie slept. Ginny fixed a little sugar tit, pulled her chair to the hearth, and rocked the baby, crooning. Jessie did not wake.

The hours dragged into morning and then past noon, the sun high overhead, its light unrelenting, before Nathan reappeared. He stood in the door with his head bowed before walking quietly across the room. He reached out his arm for the baby and folded her into the crook of his arm. He lifted his stump to caress the little face.

"Look like this gal wearing a halo," Nathan said, his soft voice breaking.

Awake now, Jessie studied Nathan's face. He came across to the bed, leaned down to his wife, nestling the infant into her arms. He dragged his fingers across the blanket covering Jessie, up her cheek, her forehead. He laced his fingers through the thick crown of her hair and kissed her full on the mouth.

"Yep," he said, "got her a little halo, just like her mama."

The baby's curled fists flailed against her tiny lips. Mouth wide, she burrowed after her mother's scent, rooting insistently. Jessie opened her shift and gave her small breast to the child.

"What name she gone have?" Nathan poked at the fire.

"You say, Nathan," Jessie said.

"All right." He hesitated, scratching his beard. "Knew a white slave from down Louisiana once named Aimee. Said it meant she was loved. This gal gone be Aimee."

Jessie nuzzled the baby's open palm.

"Aimee," she whispered. "She gone be loved."

CHAPTER 12

Winter passed and the infant green of approaching spring colored the earth. As she opened the dining room window to the breeze, Emily felt the baby kick. She pressed her hand against the protruding knob on her abdomen, where a little foot pressed against the limits of her skin. A horse approached at the edge of the field where the dark earth was softened by the emerging cotton. Emily smiled to see Will, out surveying the fields on his old bay with Belinda mounted behind him. Charles was walking up from the office for the noon meal. He raised his hand and shouted out to them.

"You two come sit a piece. And stay to dinner." Charles waved them in. "Ginny's cooking up a feast. And Emily will be glad of the company."

Indeed she was, so restless in the late confinement of her pregnancy. While the men stood talking below the porch, she held her arms open to Belinda.

"Will," Charles said, "come see something I've got in my head to do in the drying shed." The men sauntered off across the yard, their voices retreating with them.

Belinda hung her bonnet aside on the hall tree and Emily, who had been reading the news, set the paper on the table between their chairs. The headlines read: RESIST ANTISLAVERY AGGRESSION, MISSISSIPPI LEGISLATURE URGES STATES. Belinda held the paper close to her face, squinted, then flipped it over and tossed it away. It landed on the floor between them.

"I declare, I can't abide these terrible headlines," Belinda said. "It's our very way of life at stake here, don't you agree? Well, of course, you do. Well, maybe you don't, actually. I forget your father's views. But of course, we will prevail. I declare, all this talk of war is more than I can bear. Will says not to worry, but I do." She ran her finger along the edge of the marble-topped table. "I worry about most everything, really. What if the smokehouse burnt down or the rain won't come when it should, or it comes in a deluge when it oughtn't, which seems to be the case these days. Will says it's silly to worry so, but I don't seem able to help myself."

"Well, Belinda. This talk of secession is disturbing, I grant you. It is a genuine worry for all of us. Though surely the legislature will be wise enough not to go through with such a drastic measure." Through the window, Emily saw the men striding back from the shed. "And, of course, terrible things can happen, regardless. But there are such good things, too. Think about fresh eggs, washed and piled in a basket. Or sunlight through the clothes on the line. Think how sweet Will is to you. And your house that Papa built you. It's such a fine house and you have made it fairly radiant, you and Will. With happiness, I guess you'd say."

Emily could make out the men's voices as they drew nearer.

"Now, that was a bitter draft, brother," she heard Will say.

"Warm your insides, won't it? Make the afternoon go fair." Charles slapped his brother-in-law on the back with a hearty laugh as the men mounted the steps.

Something in Emily hardened. The thought of Charles with

whiskey in the shed at noon stunned her. Charles was rarely bad to drink, but when he did, and even when he didn't, images of her drunken father-in-law flooded Emily's mind. Surely Charles would never come to anything like that, she thought. Certainly not Will. It was not for Will she feared. But an unreasonable fear seized her, nonetheless, more terrible by far and more pervasive than Belinda's imaginary smokehouse blaze.

"Well, ladies, I declare," Charles said, kissing Emily on the cheek. She smelled the whiskey on his breath. "I believe we're in for something special here." Charles smiled at Jessie as she set a steaming bowl of chicken and dumplings on the sideboard. He picked up a piece of fried okra, held it between his teeth for a moment to cool, and slapped Will on the shoulder again as they made their way to the table.

Conversation focused on the weather and how it would or wouldn't work to the benefit of the crops. The bitter conflict over slavery lay unmentioned, like the deadly undertows in the Mississippi River. The meal was comforting and restful in the middle of the day. No one seemed to note at what point Will grew pale and his attention waned. It was Emily, not Belinda, who noticed first.

"Will, are you all right?" Emily half rose from her chair, but Will motioned her back down.

"Just feeling a bit poorly, Emily. It'll pass."

It did not pass. Will tried to rise, but stumbled, his fingers spread across his chest. Charles pushed his chair back and rushed to Will, holding him up. Belinda stood by, her hands waving helpless around her.

"I seem to have taken sick," Will said. He smiled at Emily. "Don't blame your dinner now."

"Might have been that nip you gave me in the shed," Will said, as Charles guided him to the parlor sofa, helped him lie down, and unbuttoned his shirt.

"Send Lucian to my office, Emily. Get my bag and stethoscope." Charles snapped his fingers at his sister. "Belinda, wake up now. Get a cold cloth for his head; no, make it two."

Belinda rallied and returned with the wet cloths. She laid them on Will's forehead and his throat. She took his hand in hers, her fingers shaking, unable to hold still. She knelt beside him and laid her head against his chest.

"Belinda, raise up now," Charles said, tugging at her. "You're in my way. I need to listen to his heart."

Emily handed him his bag. She put her arms around Belinda, pulling her away to give Charles room. Charles listened intently at Will's bared chest.

"His heart is weak and erratic." Charles rummaged in the bag. "I'm giving him some digitalis to strengthen the beat. He should be fine."

"His heart?" Belinda shook free of Emily. She whirled toward Will, then Charles, grasping at his shirt. Her skirts tangled in Charles's way and he stumbled. He took her by the arm and moved her aside.

Charles put the tincture of digitalis to Will's lips. His pallor had increased and some of the tincture spilled from the corner of his mouth when Charles inserted the dropper.

"Goddammit. Give me another dose," Charles said. "Hold his chin back, Emily. Steady, for God's sake. All right. Good, now."

Belinda, whimpering, mopped Will's pallid face with the damp cloths. She flapped them in the air to cool them from his heated skin, over and over. Will reached out for her. She dropped the cloth somewhat askew across his forehead.

"Belinda, are you sick?" Will asked. "Your face is blue. Yours too, Charles. Leave me be. See about Belinda."

In dead silence, Charles and Emily looked at one another.

"We've eaten something tainted. Oh, Belinda—" Will reached for her, but plunged on his side to the floor unconscious. Belinda screamed.

"Damn it, Belinda. Hush now. You're in my way." Charles

pulled her aside. "Ginny, send for my mother. Here, Emily, help me get him to a bed."

Emily stumbled as she tried to lift Will's shoulders. She could barely manage herself and her pregnancy. But together she and Charles lifted Will's shoulders and half dragged him to the back bedroom. With a last heaving effort, they situated him at a sideways slant on the bed, his legs hanging at a grotesque angle to the rest of his body. Charles lifted Will's legs and swiveled him onto the bed. Charles did not look at his wife.

Will stirred, turned on his side, raised to his elbow, and vomited onto the braided rag rug. At the bedside Charles held Will's head until the retching passed. Will lay back, exhausted, staring at Emily where she stood at the foot of the bed. He gave her a wan smile.

Rushing in, Belinda threw herself between Charles and Emily. She stepped in the vomit and, gagging, reeled back, wincing as Charles gripped her arm and pulled her away. Ginny rattled in with a bucket of water, rags, and a mop. She stooped and threw the soiled, braided rug aside. When Ginny finished cleaning and took the rug away, Charles pulled a chair beside the bed and motioned for Belinda to sit. Will opened his eyes and held out his hand to her.

"Why, Belinda, you are an angel," Will said. "A golden yellow angel. Your hair is glowing!" He raised his head slightly, looking at Charles and Emily. "Why, you are all of you angels, glowing all of you. I haven't died and gone to heaven, have I?" He lay back. "No, we wouldn't all have died at once." Will turned his head to the window. "But maybe this is heaven. Everything is glowing. Even the trees and the grass." Will rolled his head back toward the door. "And you, Father. Even you are glowing."

Judge Matthews stood at the threshold, and behind him, Adeline. He entered the room, leaving Adeline in the doorway. He studied the faces of each of them gathered around the bed before approaching his son. Will opened his mouth to speak, but closed it again. The judge took his son's hand. No one spoke. Judge Matthews brushed Will's forehead and motioned Charles from the room.

Down the hall out of earshot, Judge Matthews asked, "What's happening, Charles?"

"It's his heart, I'm afraid." Charles did not hedge as to the seriousness of Will's condition, but insisted that all would be well. He was adamant that the tincture of digitalis would strengthen Will's heart rhythm. From the open door, Emily listened to her husband, wanting to trust his skill, but she could see that her father was far from assured.

"If he fails to improve, I am sending Lucian for my friend, Dr. Ester, in Winona. You wouldn't mind some experienced assistance, would you, Charles?"

Charles's face flushed, but his expressions remained unreadable. "Whatever you wish, Judge," he said. "See what you can do with Belinda, Mama. I'll be in my office. Send someone to get me if there is any change."

In the mid-afternoon Charles returned to check his patient. He decided to administer another dose of digitalis. Adeline held out a restraining hand and cocked her head for him to follow her into the hallway.

"How sure are you of his condition, son?" she said.

"His heart is failing. Of that I am sure."

"And how sure of the wisdom of more digitalis?"

"As I said, Mama, his heart is failing. What else should I do?"

"Too much can cause the heart to fail. He's already hallucinating. I know you know that."

"And too little is too little, Mama. You know that, too."

Adeline rubbed the back of her neck. "If he should die, I don't want there to be any doubts. I need to know you are sure."

"There is no such thing as sure, Mama. You should know

that by now. But yes, if there were such a thing as sure, I would tell you I am sure."

Adeline stood staring at his back as Charles returned to the bedroom. She leaned against the wall, her face in her hand.

Ginny came in the late afternoon to check. Will saw her as yet another haloed angel, come to rescue him from death. His condition remained unchanged until early evening. Judge Matthews beckoned Charles to the parlor, where bric-a-brac and the offending newspaper lay scattered on the floor.

"Will is possibly dying, Judge. I hope we have another twenty-four hours to save him. The digitalis is all I have to strengthen his heart, which appears incapable of circulating the blood. It needs to be strengthened as much and as rapidly as possible."

"Might his heart be overstimulated and beating too rapidly, Charles? Too much digitalis, perhaps."

The silence between them became almost tangible.

"I'm sending for Dr. Ester in the morning."

The two men studied one another and shifted their weight. Judge Matthews went to the window and pulled aside the curtain, dropped it, reached down, and picked up the newspaper. He laid its headline up on the table. Charles dug the heel of his boot into the Oriental rug and spoke.

"Judge, I was with Will before this episode, at the time it began, and in all that has transpired since then. Do you not trust that I have a close and accurate reading of the necessary treatment?"

Judge Matthews took a step toward Charles.

"If you wish me to stop treatment, Judge Matthews, I will—on your orders. But I will also tell you bluntly, sir, that I believe the only hope for his recovery lies in continued stimulation of the heart. It is your decision, sir."

The judge stepped around Charles as he walked to the door, where he stopped and spoke with his back to Charles.

"You will stop the digitalis now."

Charles stood, swaying from side to side. He slammed his palm against the door before following.

As Charles entered the bedroom, Adeline took his arm and spoke quietly to her son. He appeared to reply, then shook his head. Belinda was distraught and frantic with weeping. Charles lifted her to her feet and held her against his chest. When she had gathered herself, Charles spoke gently to her.

"We are stopping the digitalis, Belinda."

"Why? He's no better, Charles."

"This is my decision, Belinda," Judge Matthews said. "There is every possibility that the problem may be too much digitalis."

Belinda's face paled and she looked from Charles to the judge and back.

"How can you do that?" She advanced on Judge Matthews, her fists clenched. "You would let him die. You would. I won't have it. I am his wife. I am the one to say."

Will stirred, opening his eyes, and Belinda turned toward the bed. She ran to him and took his hand. He muttered something unintelligible and she lowered her ear. Judge Matthews came close and leaned toward his son. Adeline watched in silence.

"Let them save me," Will said feebly.

"Do what you have to do," Belinda said to her brother. She glared at Judge Matthews. "How could you?" she said.

Charles reached for his bag. He motioned to Emily to hold Will's head steady as he emptied another dropper of the tincture into his mouth.

Will died in the night, toward dawn, not long before he should have risen to start a new day. Belinda lay across him, her tangled hair spread like dark wings across his chest. Charles pressed two fingers against the side of Will's neck, laid his stethoscope aside, looked up, and shook his head.

Emily rose and went to her father. The warm light from the hearth made his hollow face more stark, his eyes gleaming like the live coals in the grate. She laid her cheek against his chest, her hands trembling on his shoulders. Without looking in her father's face, Emily returned to the bedside. She did not touch Charles as she knelt beside the bed to take Will's cold hand. It struck her how sudden, how stark the difference between life and not life. Like that.

Emily was the first to speak. "I will make coffee," she said. "And we will need to eat. We will need our strength." She stood in the center of the room. Charles was staring out the window into the gray dawn. Emily studied her husband. She slipped behind him and started toward the door. Charles caught hold of her arm as she passed.

"I am sorry, Emily." His voice was hoarse.

She nodded, walked past Adeline, and left the room.

Will was buried beside his first wife, Fran, and their unnamed baby boy, just below his mother on the incline of the family plot. The church had been almost full. A throng of assembled friends and slaves accompanied the family to the grave. Belinda, supported on one side by Hammond and on the other by Adeline, wept throughout. Judge Matthews had no words of his own, but his voice resonated with a scripture known by heart:

> *For I am persuaded that neither death, nor life, nor angels, nor principalities, nor powers, nor things present, nor things to come, nor height, nor depth, nor any other creature, shall be able to separate us from the love of God. . . .*

As the casket lowered, Judge Matthews crumbled a handful of earth and let it fall into the depths of his son's grave. He brushed at his hand, but Emily grasped it as it was and led him toward the waiting buggy, leaving Charles to walk alone.

In the ensuing days of grief, Rosa Claire Slate was born at three o'clock in the morning on April 18, 1860. Only Ginny and Adeline were in attendance. They laid the newborn on Emily's bare skin to deliver the afterbirth and cut the umbilical cord. Nothing could have prepared Emily for the warmth that pervaded her from this tiny body. Charles was away, on a call, he had told his mother. Emily fretted and complained at his absence, but by the time she handed him their first child, Emily had forgotten her fears and the pain of the birth. This infant girl enthralled her, captured her in an elation and warmth that pervaded life. This love amazed her. She was not prepared for it, had not expected it. Her rapture did not extend itself to Charles. Rosa Claire was some months old before Emily's awareness included an unfocused wariness of her husband. He had not saved Will. He had broken with her father. He had been somewhere not with her when Rosa Claire entered the world. He had not shared this moment with her. Nor was he part of the ripening love she shared with this child. Will's death had set them apart and she had no way to find the bridge, if one existed.

CHAPTER 13

The Indian summer heat rose off the fields in waves of liquid mirage. Benjamin shielded his eyes against the midday sun and pulled at the prickly rope. The bell clanged out across the place, summoning the slaves near the house to dinner. Bent figures straightened in a rippling surge across the fields, speckled with leftover bolls of cotton like the dirty remains of a rare Southern snow. A group of field hands trudged toward the main house. They mopped their brows, with nodded greetings to those passing in the other direction, carrying loads of food to the outer fields. A few stopped briefly, exchanging news or a hearty laugh before trudging on.

On the summer kitchen porch, Ginny set whiteware and a pile of utensils on the table. She was proud of the dinnerware on the long table, spotless from her scrubbing. Mismatched glasses stood on a side table, beside two white pitchers of fresh water. All these things were something of a rarity, indeed a luxury, among Southern slaveholders. She shook her head to think how many here had never eaten at a proper table before the judge purchased them.

The laborers lined up at the well to wash, the women wiping their faces with the corners of their aprons, the men shaking their hands dry in the air. Benjamin mounted the steps and took his place at the head of the table. The others followed, adults leading, followed by the older adolescents. The judge did not work children. No one made room for Samantha, who remained aloof and had not yet made a place for herself among the slaves.

Ginny set a skillet of crisp cornbread at each end of the table. Samantha laid a plate of freshly molded butter beside Benjamin. She did not speak, but she knew he was looking. She felt his gaze on her as she retreated to the far end of the table and pulled an extra chair to the corner. As she sat, she glared at two or three of the women. Then she raised her eyes to meet Benjamin's. He nodded. Benjamin raised his glass and took a long draft, still gazing at her. Beside him, Nathan glanced back and forth between the two of them.

"Thank you, Samantha," Benjamin said. "You serve a right fine dish of butter."

A soft smile turned up the corners of Samantha's rounded lips. Nathan, watching, let out a hoot. The others at the table looked askance, but Nathan laughed on. Samantha lowered her head, shook it side to side until she, too, burst into laughter.

As the contagious merriment died down, the talk around the table turned to the weather, the morning's work, and which fishing hole seemed most likely for a good mess of crappie. Benjamin caught Samantha glancing his direction and smiled down into his bowl of peas and cornbread, soaked in pot liquor, the melted butter floating in golden puddles on the surface. When he finished, Benjamin excused himself. As he passed Samantha's chair, his hand brushed her shoulder. She did not look up, but stilled as if a butterfly had landed in her hair.

* * *

"Afternoon, Mason. What can I help you with today?" Judge Matthews stood and extended his hand across the desk as the sheriff entered his office "Tangled in a legal knot?"

"No, sir. Though if the struggle over Kansas gets much worse, we're all likely to be tangled in worse than legal knots. World is headed toward bloodshed."

Judge Matthews pulled a sheet of paper over a book on his desk, but not quickly enough to keep it from the sheriff's keen eye: *The Impending Crisis of the South*. The subtitle following was long and unwieldy, but Mason knew it instantly. He had read Hilton Helper's treatise on the moral failure of a slave-holding society. He found Helper's economic arguments more rational than his moral ones: that slavery inhibited the progress of the South and worked to the detriment of the non-slave-holding Southerners. He needed little convincing that on a moral basis slavery was an abomination, and yet he found himself obliged to uphold laws that were an offense to him. Why he stayed in office was a constant struggle for him. But he had little land, did not know commerce or any trade, for that matter, and most of his work was upholding the law as he construed it. And like Judge Matthews, he found he could intervene and ameliorate where possible with injustice at the individual level.

"Might get yourself in a knot with that book, Judge. You know they're locking folks up just for its possession. You might ought to be more careful."

"I know, Mason, but seeing as you are the sheriff and I'm the judge, I don't reckon there is too much danger here in chambers. Do you?"

"No, sir." Mason chuckled. "But you might want to be careful who else sees it. Folks are mighty scared of that book, and you know scared folks is dangerous folks." Mason bit his lip. "Well, enough about all that. Mainly I came by to see how you are since Will's death."

Judge Matthews averted his face, then sat down and motioned Mason to do the same. The judge swiveled in his chair to stare out the window.

"I idolized that boy, Mason," he said at last, back still turned.

"He was your firstborn, Judge. Your primary heir." The sheriff sat back and crossed his knees. "How is Belinda holding up?"

The judge hesitated. "Not well, Mason, not well at all. She's erratic at best, you know. So is Jeremiah. The curse of inheritance at work."

"Yes, sir. All that girl's life, seems to me. Never quite levelheaded, that one. Been knowing her a good part of her life and never could tell what she might do or say next."

"More true now." The judge cleared his throat. "Speaking of heirs, Mason, I have made a grave mistake."

"Hard to imagine, Judge."

"No, I have. Distracted by these slavery issues. Spending my mental energies on all this damned secession malarkey. And how to get around the law to free my Negroes."

"Yes, sir, I am aware how close you came to losing your office." Mason shifted and crossed the other leg. "You calling that a mistake?"

"Well, likely it is, Mason. Likely to answer for that choice when I meet my Maker. Priorities and such. Kinds of mistakes we will all answer gravely for in this country, but not what I was referring to." The judge stood, came around, propped himself on his desk. "I made an agreement with Will about the land and inheritance. All verbal. I was distracted. Had my mind on all this conflict. Distraught about Kansas and where this country's headed. Bloody Kansas. Rightly termed. On our way to being the bloody States." He waved his hand in an impotent gesture, as if to rid himself of something vile. "Kansas and that damned Hamilton. Can't get myself past it even after all this time. Going on two years now. The Marais des Cygnes massacre. Hell of a peaceful name for such despicable violence.

One of the dead in that massacre was an old childhood friend of mine." The judge pushed away from his desk and paced across the office. "What kind of man captures peaceable Free-State men who knew him? Trusted him and went with him willingly, for God's sake—takes them down in some damn ravine and starts shooting. Portends of what's to come, I'm afraid, and—" The judge stopped, shook his head. "Well, I digress. Distracted. You see." He tugged at his beard and scratched his cheek. "I never expected to outlive my son, Mason. Foolish, foolish. People outlive their children all the time."

Mason waited.

"Sorry." Judge Matthews shook his head as if to clear it. "I was headed somewhere. Ah, yes, the absence of a written document on inheritance. Pure negligence, I'm afraid. And now Belinda is beside herself. Goes on incessantly about the land. Jeremiah too. He can't even deal with the thought that Emily should inherit land from me. Only the males in his head. And looks like Charles is taking on Belinda's cause. She vacillates between cloying dependency and hysterical anger."

"At you, Judge?"

"Hell if I know, Mason. One minute she hates me; next, she adores me. Depends on the day and what time the clock says. I try to contain myself, but I blame her for Will's death. Her and Charles. And Jeremiah is fit to be tied. No containing him. Never has been. I don't want Emily to have to deal with my feelings toward Charles, but I know she does. I try to reason with myself. I know in the end it's possible no blame exists at all. But in my heart, it's there. Maybe Belinda's irrationality about the land is just a diversion for her. Easier to deal with than Will's absence. Better to be angry with me than with death. At least it gives her someone to blame. Same with me."

Judge Matthews stood. He seemed to return to the room from somewhere else.

"I beg your pardon, Mason. You came to extend friendship,

not to hear my woes." He sighed. "I bear this loss so poorly and I haven't anyone to discuss it with. I took advantage." He extended his hand.

"I came to see a friend, Judge. No advantage taken."

The Mississippi heat descended early and shimmered over the fields of young cotton as Charles rode toward Greensboro. He unbuttoned his coat to the artificial breeze he and his sorrel gelding stirred up. As he passed a few white pedestrians, he tipped his hat. He ignored the slaves along the way, his gaze concentrated past the horse's ears. He began to whistle tunelessly as the horse trotted into town.

A drab, heavyset man with red suspenders, known about town for loafing his time away, ambled out into the street and waylaid the doctor. "Been having some problems with my stomach, Doc."

"Well, now, why don't you come on out to the office and we'll see what we can do for you?"

"Well, I seen you trotting in here and thought maybe I could just ask? Figured you could script me some sort of remedy."

"Now, you know I don't practice medicine from the saddle in the middle of the dusty street. But offhand, my first prescription would be to spend a few less hours a day at Jenkins Saloon and a few more in the open air."

"Coolest place in town, Doc. Heat's no good for a body. You coming in the saloon?"

"Seeing a patient."

"One that don't have to come out to the office?"

"I don't have all day to stand here chatting. You think about what I told you."

The man ambled into the shade of the overhang at Jenkins Saloon and watched Charles tie his horse, walk away, then circle back in the direction of the town brothel. Instead of going into the saloon, the man thought for once he might take the good doctor's advice, stay in the open for a while. But after half an hour, he wandered inside, anyway, ordered a whiskey, but unusual for him, didn't have much to say. When he exited, Charles's horse was still tied at the same post.

"Hmff," he said under his breath, "can't do his doctoring in the street, but looks like the whorehouse is a different proposition."

From the second-floor window of the courthouse, Judge Matthews checked to see Charles's horse still tied where it had been the better part of the afternoon, same as every Thursday. Marriage had changed nothing. He lowered the shade. And then he lowered his head, wiping at his eyes. *What have I let happen,* he thought. He dropped into his chair, rested his forehead in his hands, massaging the bridge of his nose with his fingertips. He nudged his spectacles up on his nose, lay back against the smooth leather, turning his head from side to side. *I should get up now,* he thought. *I should be waiting for him when he comes for his horse.* He raised the shade again. A deep inertia overwhelmed him. What use would a confrontation be? Out there in the street for people to see, to add to their gossip, to reach his already sad daughter. No, he hoped in spite of the small rifts in the marriage he noticed that Emily did not suspect her husband's whoring. Making it plain would not protect her. Nor did he think it would bring James to the cross. His only true choice to care for her and her child was his silence.

Judge Matthews rose and tidied his desk, straightened the corners of papers and books, brought order to what he could. He took his hat from the coatrack and locked the door. Somehow the subtle clank of the keys as he pocketed them brought him comfort. For all the rest, he would wait.

CHAPTER 14

"You didn't save him, Charles," Belinda said. She was sitting in a dim corner of the parlor, staring. Charles sat down beside her on the blue-striped divan and took her limp hand. Her eyes looked almost bruised, but her dark gaze was direct and unreadable. The velvet-trimmed widow's garb hung loose on her thin body and her pallor shook him. He put a hand against her forehead, then against her throat.

"What are you saying, Belinda?"

The autumn heat hung in a brilliant stillness in the house and across the surrounding fields. It was Sunday afternoon. Charles had left Emily visiting with her father and had ridden to Belinda's.

"I trusted you." She gripped her hands in her lap. "You said you could save him and you didn't. It makes me crazy. I know you couldn't help it, Charles. Well, I think I know you couldn't, but then sometimes I don't. I see Will's face and his fear, and I see Judge Matthews and your mother asking if the medicine was wrong and if Will could die if you kept it up and you did and he died."

He walked to the fireplace and grasped the mantel, waited before he spoke. He did not remind her that the decision to continue the digitalis had been essentially hers.

"Yes, Will died," he said.

Belinda threw up her hands and stood. "You could have listened, Charles. You could have told me I was wrong. I needed Will to live."

They both sat back down, at opposite ends of the divan. Neither spoke until he said, "Hiram Blakeny came by this week. About you. And the settlement of Will's estate."

"That scoundrel lawyer? He came to you?" Belinda rallied somewhat.

"He apparently accosted you with questions on the acreage Will had been farming." Charles pressed his hands on his knees, studied his fingernails, raising one finger and then another.

"Well, I have a right to it," Belinda said, looking away from him. "But I can't imagine how I would manage that land if I had it, all by myself. Even with slaves." She wiped at her cheek with the back of her hand, pushed the disheveled curls from her forehead. "Besides, it's not even the land I care about. I belonged to Will's family. And now he's dead and I don't."

"Belinda, you belonged to a family well before you even knew there was a Will." Charles gripped her shoulder. He felt its bony thinness through the crisp silk of her sleeve.

"Well, yes, of course I had a family. I don't need you to tell me that." She threw a dismissive hand in his direction. "But Pa was—well, I don't need to talk to you about Pa. And Mama was good. She stayed by me when I was weak." She rose and took two steps away, her back to him. "Well, truth be told, I don't even know that. Pa says she would have let me die when I was born. But Pa says what he wants. He'll say anything. And there's you and Hammond, of course. It's family, I reckon, but something was different being a Matthews. Something substantial. I am still a Matthews. I am Belinda Matthews. But now the judge, who I thought cared for me—I did believe that, Charles—he treats me like it's my fault Will is dead." She sobbed into her cupped hands.

Charles came to her, took her by the arms, lifted her chin with his forefinger. "I could help you manage the land, Belinda. Maybe even Pa. If he hadn't lost the farm in Ohio, he might be a different man. Maybe if he could help you with this farm—"

"Oh, Charles," she said, shaking herself free of him. "Talk sense. You don't have time to manage any land, and Pa can't do one thing unless it's wrong. Mama has to follow around in his tracks rectifying everything he's spoiled—that is, when he puts some drunken effort into doing anything at all. You know that."

"Well, try to imagine him sober."

"Oh, Charles, for pity's sake!"

"Yes, for pity's sake." He was shouting. "You never knew him then, but he was a different man and a good daddy to me." He quieted himself and walked to the window, gazing out across the half-picked cotton in the field. "He just lost himself when he lost his farm."

"You make it sound as if you want that land for him, not me. Maybe for yourself. Is that it, Charles? Was I your path to Will's land? Maybe you think I still am."

"Belinda, get hold of yourself."

"Well, it's being a Matthews I care about. And that land would show that I am a Matthews." Belinda flicked the hem of her skirt. "Anyhow, I expect one day very soon, when his grief eases up a bit, the judge will invite me to come live with him, as his daughter. Of course, he will. He just needs to get past some grief. He's all alone, just like me. It's taking time, that's all."

"Belinda, now you talk some sense. It's long past saying it will just take time." Charles glared at his sister. "You are right about that land. It belongs to you and I intend to see that it is yours. It's long overdue for this to be settled and for you to buck up. I mean to see this finished and finished differently. That land is rightfully Slate land now."

Belinda glared in return. Her voice grew flat. "Slate land? It is not Slate land. It is Matthews land and I am a Matthews. This is not about you, Charles. It is about me. I used to be so scared and mealymouthed and more than a little crazy, truth be told. But being Will's wife changed me. Being a Matthews made me somebody. It gave me a life of my own. My own, do you hear?"

"Let's not argue, Belinda. I'm going now. We'll talk again when you are less agitated."

"Yes, you go," Belinda said. "And when we talk again, I hope it is not about this."

Indeed, talk everywhere in the fall of 1860 turned to conflicts far larger in scope than the perceived wrongs of Belinda's inheritance. November came and with it the election of Abraham Lincoln to the Presidency. On December 17, the First Secession Convention gathered in the Baptist Church of Columbia, South Carolina. Because of a smallpox outbreak, the Convention adjourned to Charleston, where three days later that state declared itself free of the Union. January of 1861 arrived and with it the Mississippi Ordinance of Secession, the grounds for secession being the economic basis of slavery. Mississippi had been a state of the Union less than forty-four years. Judge William Matthews had been seven years old when Mississippi became a state, old enough to remember the celebrations.

Now he paced the floor of his study in front of his daughter. "I am sick to death over this," he said to Emily, who had come the moment she heard the news, knowing how distraught her father would be. "Second to secede. Without Mississippi falling into South Carolina's misguided footsteps, perhaps this insanity would collapse of its own weight, or lack thereof. But now it is done and the South will go down like a row of dominoes."

"What will we do, Papa?" Emily said. On the edge of her chair, she fidgeted with the pleats of her skirt. One of the rosettes at her sleeve hung loose. As she fiddled with it, the stitching gave way. She tucked the tiny flower into her pocket.

"Nothing," her father said. "Nothing but wait. The Union will prevail. Peace will prevail, I believe. Anything else is insanity. The South hasn't force enough to go against the United States Army. Nor do we have the righteous cause. And yet they are claiming the righteous ground, calling this vile institution 'the greatest material interest in the world.' Pronouncing officially that we are engaged in 'the most important commerce in the world.' I pray this may lead to the end of slavery, but God help us, if it should come at too high a price. The wages of sin, perhaps."

"Is there really nothing to do?"

"Only to wait, my dear. This won't last long. It isn't feasible. Months, I expect. The Union's too strong."

Emily pulled at her ear. Judge Matthews thought how typical that gesture was, since her early childhood, whenever she felt insecure, adopted when she was no longer allowed to suck her thumb. He smiled.

"What if you are called up, Papa?"

"Highly unlikely, Emily. We have not come to arms yet and if we do, I am too old. This will be done with before they get desperate enough for the likes of me."

"And Charles and Jeremiah?"

"Don't get ahead of your horse now, Emily. Time will take care of this without you. Before you can worry yourself too much, we will have a new peace. And the freedom this country was founded upon."

"Do we have a country now, Papa?"

"I don't know how to answer that, Emily. You just see to Rosa Claire and leave the peacemaking to the experts."

"Well, I will do that, Papa, but not without the strength and intelligence to do it well. Do not think, because I am a woman, that I am oblivious to the world around me."

Judge Matthews kissed his daughter on the forehead and bid her goodbye. By late spring, Abraham Lincoln would be the president of the country to which she held allegiance, but in which she no longer lived. The Confederate States of America would have unleashed a war of unprecedented proportions. And Emily would be overwrought about bringing a second child into an uncertain world. She would still be waiting without an answer—belonging to no country to which she could give a name.

On March 4, 1861, Lincoln would be inaugurated as president of a country divided, whether or not against itself to be decided on the battlefield with unparalleled bloodshed and horror. The newly formed Confederate States would fire on Fort Sumter, and Emily would announce her second pregnancy to her husband. Other small or large or seemingly insignificant details would have been either noticed or passed over. The seeds of fate would begin to sprout into a deadly and poisonous growth. The harvest would be unprecedented.

CHAPTER 15

In the quiet dark of the barn, Benjamin rose from milking the cows and nodded to his son. Lucian took the steaming buckets of milk up to the kitchen, where Ginny covered them with cheesecloth. She rested her hands on the sides of the buckets, soaking up the residual warmth. Mopping his forehead, Benjamin appeared in the doorway. Without a word, Ginny handed him a glass of the warm milk. He turned it up and took the whole in one draught.

"Where's Samantha?" Benjamin asked.

"She be along," Ginny said. "She gone to deliver a basket to Miss Belinda. Some early things. Carrots, radishes, lettuce, and peas and such. Can't you keep up with your woman?" Ginny eyed Benjamin.

"All right," he said. "All right now." He shook his head and laughed.

Today, Benjamin and Samantha would wed, sure and legal with Judge Matthews presiding, though they would jump the broom after. And in spite of general disapproval among the slaves. Samantha's demeanor from previous abuse had softened little, and her gratitude at her rescue was mostly absent. She carried her past like a hundred-pound sack of cotton.

Before dinner, Samantha returned from Miss Belinda's. Her broad face glistened in the sunlight. She fanned her face with her apron and sat heavily on the cane chair beside the hearth. Handing her a cup of tea and a bowl of peas to hull, Ginny stood with her arms folded.

"How come you all tuckered out?" Ginny said.

"That woman is touched in the head." Samantha continued fanning and scooted the chair away from the hearth. "Plain-out touched. Something wrong with her other than a dead husband. Just being a widow woman don't make a body that crazy."

"What she say?" Ginny said.

"Don't ask me what she say. Ask me what she do," Samantha said. She stretched her feet across the floor. "I'm at her door with my basket of goods, nice and polite, like Miss Emily say, and some young slave I don't know, she open the door when I knock and say thank you and how you folks over to the big house and here come Miss Belinda, that wild hair a flying everywhere and she say, what that nigger woman want with us. That gal show Miss Belinda the basket and Miss Belinda go to yanking, say what that for, so a widow woman won't starve? I ain't no charity case. I's a Matthews. She say, you get on out a here, nigger, but you tell Miss Emily I say thank you, anyway. You just tell her that and don't you say no more, you hear me, nigger? Me, I'm backing down the steps and I hightail out of there, but I hear something *clunk, clunk,* and I turn round and that crazy woman throwing chunks of lettuce and carrots after me. Throwing everything right out that basket. Yelling, I don't need no nigger woman coming 'round here with no vegetables. I got a garden of my own. I's a Matthews. What I need with this garbage? You hear me, nigger?"

"Yeah, I know she touched," Ginny said. For once she was in agreement with Samantha. "I seen it plenty times before, but sound like she's got worse. Right now I got my mind on a bride. You gone wear that no-good dress to your wedding? You get on out of here, like Miss Belinda said."

Ginny pulled a black iron stew pot from the hearth, stirred the contents, and lifted the spoon to her lips. She added salt, tasted, and rotated the pot back into the fireplace. Later in the day, she delivered a message of thanks from Miss Belinda to Emily, but there must have been a hint of something not convincing in her voice or face. Emily looked at her askance, but Ginny did not elaborate, just asked if Emily needed anything else before she went on down to the quarters.

Any special event called for great anticipation in the quarters. Although Samantha was not greatly liked, Benjamin's wedding elicited an eruption of celebration. Uncle Corinth struck up his fiddle, Tolbert his banjo, and Lucian a mouth harp, with various odds and ends of percussion. Not only was this a day of joy and much oblique jesting at Benjamin's expense, but a gathering of kin and friends from surrounding plantations, most of them as glad for a day of rest as for a night of carousing. The women wore their finest shirtwaists and wide-brimmed bonnets, ornamented with varicolored ribbons. Samantha was stoutly glorious in a green and yellow checked dress, a makeover from Miss Emily with extra fabric taken from the skirt to round it out more than a bit. For her straw bonnet, she had broken the rules of style, adding the natural black and white polka dots of guinea feathers instead of more ladylike ribbon trim. Some fine gallantries commenced among the men in their frock coats and Sunday hats, testing whose fried chicken was crispiest, and whose bread and butter pickles wanted for a bit more sugar.

"Ain't so spare yet in this war, we can't have a spoonful of sugar in the pickles," Aunt Lucie chided. "Next thing we'll be leaving the butter in the milk and just pour the cream on the biscuits."

"And right on after that, them Yankee soldiers gone come

through here and get the cows, won't nobody have to take the butter out the cream, nor the cream out the milk, nor the milk out the cows," Uncle Clive said. "Won't make no nevermind about sugaring them pickles neither. We be following after them Yankees. Say they gone take good care us."

"Yeah, Clive, you believe all that?" An old slave spoke in the husky voice of age. "I ain't following nobody nowhere. You believing that talk. I don't believe nothing white folks tells. Mayhap they believe it when they tell it, but next time they tell it, they done gone to believing something else. I don't trust nobody I don't know real good, and the ones I do know, I don't hardly trust neither."

The wedding ceremony had all the dignity Judge Matthews brought to any such event. The vows were solemn, with words some of these slaves had never heard before. Deep feelings of worth and seriousness pervaded those gathered. When the service ended, Benjamin and Samantha jumped the broom Lucian laid in their path. A great shout of celebration rose from the crowd and the music fired up. Spontaneous dancing surrounded the couple and drew them into the center of festivity.

From the edge of the crowd, Emily watched, humming low to herself and patting her feet and hands. She did not realize when exactly she began clapping in time to the music. Her father had given her a kiss and gone back up to the big house. She could not pull herself away. The music and the dance surged from one tune to another without faltering. Her feet under her wide hoops moved on their own. It took some moments for Emily to become conscious of Ginny beside her, matching her steps. At Emily's recognition, both women laughed with joy.

"Well, Miss Emily, you got rhythm, honey. Natural rhythm. Come on now and dance. Show these folks how to do it. You come with me."

"Oh, no, Ginny, I couldn't. I wouldn't want to intrude. And I don't know the steps."

"Steps? Honey, you don't need no steps. Your body know its own steps. I see you over here dancing. You know all the steps you need to know." Ginny offered her hand.

"Really, Ginny, you know I couldn't. I would draw attention and this is their time."

"All right, then. You and me just dance right here. Right where you dancing anyway, seemly or not." Ginny took her hand and slipped into an open space just beyond the trees and the undulating crowd.

Laughing out loud, Emily lifted her skirts and let her feet and body have their way.

Chapter 16

June 10 of 1861 brought the first land battle of the war at Big Bethel. Given another ten days, West Virginia would secede from Virginia to side with the Union. July arrived and with it what should have been a celebration of unity and freedom. Instead, there was celebration of secession and the new union of the Confederacy. Charles insisted on taking Emily with him into the streets of town. He cheered the secession and waved a makeshift Confederate flag. There were loyalist protesters and some of the celebration went ugly, some bawdy, some verging on evil, and in a case or two, verging on deadly, though responsibility in either direction never solidified. Emily cringed at the fighting and insults, some hurled her direction. At last, Charles, half-drunk, relented and let Benjamin take her home. The day of the Fourth passed, as did the night. Emily hid in her bedroom in tears. Two days later, Charles returned home, looking scrappy.

"Lots of injuries to see after," he said. "Pretty wild celebration there."

Emily did not answer.

"Are you upset?" Charles asked. She had decided to cook breakfast herself in the house kitchen. At his entrance she had dropped the spatula, picked it up with impatience, only to drop it again. Emily stood with her back to him, her hands pushing against the counter, elbows locked. He wrapped his hands around her stiffened wrists. His freckled hands affected her like the sight of dirty snow.

"Angry?"

"No," Emily said, pulling away from him, plunging her hands into the dishpan, scrubbing at the already clean surface of a platter, a ring of soap around her wrists. "Yes. Yes, I am," she said. She whirled to face him. "Where have you been, Charles? Not just these two days. Where have you been all these other times? How do you spend so much time away, Charles?"

Charles put his hands on her shoulders and pulled her toward him, disregarding the greasy water dripping on them both.

"People get sick, Emily. You know that. You knew that when we married."

"Apparently there were a lot fewer sick then than there are now, Charles."

"Or perhaps my practice has grown that much. What is the matter with you?"

"I saw Mrs. Bellingham in town and said how glad I was to see her feeling better. She had no idea what I was talking about. Said fortunately she hadn't been sick in a year. I said I was glad to know she was doing so well and I didn't ask why you were at her house half the night last week."

"Maybe you just confused her name with Mrs. Melton, Emily." He dropped his hands and stepped away. "Maybe you're confused about a lot of things. You haven't been yourself lately."

"Perhaps," Emily said, returning to the dishpan, where her hands went limp. "And perhaps I'm not confused at all. Maybe it is you who think you can confuse the truth."

"Goddammit, Emily. I'm getting tired of this. How would you even know the truth?"

"The truth, Charles? All right, here's the truth." Her breath caught in her throat. "The truth is I'm afraid, Charles. I'm terrified."

Charles came back, stood close beside her. "Afraid of what, Emily? Just what do you have to be afraid of?"

"Of war. Of life. Of death. Of bringing another child into such a world as this. I was afraid with Rosa Claire," she said. "Of course I was. How could I not be afraid? But with this new one on the way, I don't know. It feels like madness."

He held her shoulders steady, her wet hands draped around his arms, soaking the blue stripes of his shirt.

"After Will—" She dropped her head, shook it twice. "Oh God, Charles, he never harmed one living soul. So young, so kind, so alive. If Will could die like that, then so could I, like my mother. And so could you, for that matter. This war terrifies me. So many people will die so horribly. So many of us, Charles."

"Yes, people will die, Emily. I see it every day. It's what I do. But most of us live. And I'm here."

"Are you here, Charles?" Emily stared him in the face. "Did your being here save Will? Or prevent my father from blaming you? Here is not where you are most of the time. And now this war at our doorstep. And Belinda acting so strange, not just grief, but something I don't understand. Maybe she blames herself. Maybe she knows my father—Oh, Charles, everything is flying apart. I don't know how to hold on."

Charles picked up a towel, wiped her hands and arms with it, ignoring his sleeves, stained with gravy and dishwater. He waited while Emily caught her breath, then led her to the porch.

"Don't be afraid," he said quietly. Brushing her brown work skirt aside, he settled in the swing beside her and pushed back.

The chains creaked as he let go. "You wear too many petticoats, Mrs. Slate," he said, but Emily did not smile.

"The baby will be fine, Emily, and so will we," he said. "We will prevail. Our life will not change. The war will be done soon. It cannot last. The Union doesn't have the will and commitment of the South. They haven't the economic motivation to pursue this very far. We will see a return of prosperity and freedom to conduct our commerce as we see fit. Life will go on as is."

"But, Charles, it must not go on as it is," Emily said. She half turned in shock. "That is the point. This culture is not fit. Everything is so wrong. The country is coming apart. And you are never here. We have no right—"

"No right?"

"We have no right to enslave—" she said.

"The Bible disagrees with you, my dear." He pushed the swing back with his feet, let it go again. "Even your father, in the end, for all his exalted ideals and rhetoric, has not freed his slaves. He prefers to keep his Judgeship and his high position." The chains of the swing creaked. He took her hand. "And, besides, he won't buck the law, at least not far, and freeing slaves is illegal. He won't go further than teaching them to read and write. Which is also illegal. Or reading that Helper book. That's crime enough for him."

"My father despises slavery. And the breakup of our nation is—"

"Breakup of what nation, Emily? We are citizens of a new nation, or have you yet to realize that? And as for you, Emily, how many slaves do you own?" Charles said.

"I am ashamed to say." She withdrew her hand.

"But they work your land, and cook your food, and tend your crops, wash your clothes, and feed your chickens. And how much else?" He stared across the fields. His jaw was set. "Well, be that as it may, Emily, we now have a country that will maintain our ideals and our way of life. We will see the preservation of the South, of the land, and good things to come."

"In a land soaked with blood?"

"For God's sake, Emily, will you stop? What do you want? Poverty? Poverty for this new baby, for us? Or do you really just want what you have, disguised in high-minded rhetoric, like your father?"

The swing jerked erratically when Emily stood. There was a long silence.

"There is poverty, Charles, and there is poverty." She brushed his shoulder as she left him there. He did not look up.

The day passed. The sun set and night came. Ginny tucked Rosa Claire in bed. Emily did not know when, or if, Charles came to bed, when or if he rose. At daybreak, she stretched her hand into the empty place beside her.

At her dressing table, Emily paused with the hairbrush in her hand, laid it on the lace dresser cloth, and stared into her reflection. *I am plain,* she thought, *but I am not unattractive.* She picked up the brush again, gave her hair a few more strokes. With her comb, she straightened the center part, then pulled the weight of the hair behind her into a twist, pinned it, and pulled a fine net around the knot. As she stood, she let the embroidered batiste gown fall to the floor and examined her body. The rounding belly that had never fully flattened since her pregnancy, the breasts that had remained more full since nursing, the curve of her back into the width of her hips. She had no comparison for herself, no knowledge of how other women looked, no concept of how she was supposed to look. But in her reflection, critical as she might be, she saw nothing unattractive.

Emily picked up the nightdress and slipped on her clothes for the day just as a soft knock came at the door and Ginny peaked in.

"Wanting this day to get started, are you, Miss Emily?"

"Or wanting it already over, Ginny." She came and let herself be held in Ginny's arms, felt the reassuring caress of these familiar fingers between her shoulder blades.

"What's got hold of you now, honey?" When no answer came, Ginny leaned back, her fingers under Emily's chin. "You want to say it or not?"

"No, I don't want to say it. I don't want to make it real." Emily half turned, stared out the window, where the pasture was coming into full daylight. "I don't know if I am amiss or my husband is amiss. Well, there it is, Ginny."

Ginny dropped her hands, picked up the edge of her apron, and studied it. "Well, Miss Emily, I'm not going to say that he is amiss. I don't have no proof of that. But I am going to say this. It ain't you who is amiss. And that's all I'm going to say."

Emily brought her head upright and nodded.

"You want your breakfast now?" Ginny nodded and turned for the door.

Chapter 17

At the end of a week in which little was said between Charles and Emily, she left with Rosa Claire to spend a few days with her father. She settled into her old room with an ambivalence that vacillated between familiar comfort and a sense of displacement. The rosewood bed with its carved half canopy felt massive to her, the rose damask drapes at the window oppressive.

On the second night of her visit, with Rosa Claire tucked in, Emily sat after dinner by the fire with her father. If she had been some other woman, her hands would have been busy with a needle. But even now her stitches, like those of the motherless young girl she had been, remained clumsy and uneven, despite Ginny's coaching. Instead, Emily sat with a book from her father's study, open facedown, across her lap. The title had intrigued her, bold words about slavery as the economic and moral crisis of the South, but the text had proved very dense and somewhat inaccessible. She would take it home and attempt to focus more.

Emily stared at her father, his sloped shoulders outlined by the light from the flames. His silence at supper had been uncharacteristic. A deft conversationalist, her father generally prompted lively talk at the evening meal. Tonight, there had been only the two of them, in an uneasy quiet. Emily guessed that the reality of war had settled over him. Now alone, the two of them by the fire, Judge Matthews began to talk.

"This war will change us all," he said. He rose from his chair, grasped the iron poker, stooping to nudge at the embers. "For the good, I pray, change who we are. Though for all the high rhetoric on both sides, Emily, the whole affair in the end is likely to be nothing but a living hell of blood and power and gain."

"What are you implying, Papa?" Emily asked.

"I am not implying, Emily. I am trying to be plain." Reaching into the woodbox, he threw another log on the fire. Sparks flew up the chimney.

"Then I must ask you to be more so."

"There are so many things, Emily, that we imagine benefit us: intellect, position, wealth. At this stage in life, I have begun to wonder if we ever truly recognize those things for which we have real need, apart from survival. Things that can't be quantified and possessed." Small flames flickered as the log began to catch.

"I believe you, Papa."

More sparks rose as he probed at the ashes. After a moment he straightened and continued, "We live our lives on second-best replacements, substitutes. We miss the sunlight looking for gold. I only see this in hindsight, mind you. I hadn't such thoughts when I was as young as you."

Emily nodded, pulled at her ear, unsure how to respond.

"I'm rambling." Judge Matthews took his pipe from the mantel and tapped it against the bottom of his boot. "But you know, Emily, I had such grand ambitions. When I was young, I wanted to have honor, prestige, and recognition."

"You have."

"By some standards," Judge Matthews said.

"Certainly by mine." Emily smiled at him. "What was it you wanted that you failed at, Papa?"

He sighed, cradled the bowl of the empty pipe in his palm. His backlit white hair and beard took on a golden tinge.

"I wanted to be good," he said. "I was the seventh child of nine, six of us who lived."

"Yes, I know. You have told us those stories." She brushed at some nonexistent lint on her skirt.

"My father farmed his land with a vengeance." He continued as if he had not heard. "In Virginia. Not so long ago, but it seems another age. Mississippi was not even a state. We had land and slaves, a fair number of them. My father was not good to them, though he was not cruel. Indifferent is what he was. He used them like he used the mule and the plow. You take good care of plows and mules. And my father took care of his Negroes, fed them, brought the doctor in when one was sick, kept the mothers home to nurse their babies for several months. But who those people were? That was not in his realm of thinking, Emily. Any more than who the mule might be."

"But you are better than that, Papa. You are a good man."

"What good is being better? Because I know and care for our people? Even that phrase, the use of the possessive, is offensive. These people are not ours to possess. Or because I entered into a conspiracy with your tutor to teach them to read and write in spite of it being illegal? Because of my thwarted attempt at manumission, also illegal? The very concept that setting a man free should be illegal, should be a crime, is an abomination. More than that, that any man could be denied his innate freedom. And yet I succumbed." The judge stamped at some embers fallen on the hearth.

"It is strikingly different from most of what I see around here," Emily said.

"Perhaps. But I doubt myself. My disguise is simply more subtle. Slavery is slavery, and my pitiful attempt to free these people has come to a shabby end."

"You were prevented by the law, Papa." She brushed again at her skirt.

"I was a coward, Emily. I hadn't the power—no, that isn't true. Maybe not legally, but somewhere I had the power. And perhaps I had some courage, but not enough to use it against the tide of greed and fear." He ground his foot on the hearth. "Even that's not true. I made a choice. I thought I could do good. I thought there was time. And I was afraid."

"Afraid of what, Papa? Of war?"

"Not so much of what, as for whom. I am still afraid—for you, for me, for all of us."

"So am I, Papa," Emily said. "I am very afraid." Agitated, she rose from her chair, her hands spread wide.

"None of us knows how this conflict will go, Emily. No more than we know our true nature. Not one of us knows who we really are. There is too much overlaid." He pulled his white hair back away from his forehead. "This Confederacy is like an ornate plantation house with all its framing and brick and millwork and finery—that could go up in flames. All built on a foundation dug from the earth like a grave."

"Papa, your hope seems to have evaporated. What dire talk. You leave me—" She dropped into her chair, staring at him.

"I'm sorry. I don't know what has made me say these things. Will's death. This bloody war I thought could not sustain itself goes on and on. So much more ghastly than anyone foresaw. Our boys coming home, if they come at all, without legs or arms, with half their faces gone. For what? To defend this other horror here at home?" Judge Matthews lifted his head to face her, as if only then aware of his daughter's presence. "Forgive me, Emily. I've only added to your fears. I'm sorry. I want you happy. I have tried to protect you from life, ever since your mother died. I know now that was both impossible and foolish. It may have been a grave mistake." He looked her in the eye. "I thought it was love."

The judge laid his dead pipe on the mantel. At the edge of her chair, Emily struggled with the impulse to go to him, to hold him. She knew it would silence him, and whatever else he had to say would go back into hiding, like a salamander slipping beneath a rotten log. Her father was attempting to rearrange his mind, she knew. But the foundation would not change. His face was hidden, the fire illuminating the bush of his brow and the length of his beard as if from within.

"I blame myself, you know, for your mother's death," he said at last. "Sometimes I believe that I killed her. No, more than sometimes. It lies beneath me like her grave."

Emily started from her chair, the book dropping to the floor, but his outstretched hand stayed her.

"I need to say this, Emily. And I believe you have the courage to hear me through. You are very like her, you know?" He turned his head toward Emily. She could not read his face in the backlit dark.

"It is worse for Jeremiah. Both of us carry the guilt of her death, and I cannot take his away with mine. Perhaps, we compete for our guilt. He believes he should not be alive. He believes I didn't want him because I wanted her." He hesitated, turning his face back to the fire. "He was right, Emily. I didn't. I am deeply shamed by that. It has always lain between us. You see the results, Emily: his inability or unwillingness—I never know which—to see anything through; his obsession with land; the violence of his temper; and nothing ever enough to fill his emptiness."

"Papa—" Emily leaned toward him, but he continued to hold up his hand.

"No, Emily. I bear the blame. I am not good, you see. And I

have forfeited the love of my son. I forfeited Will. I should have taken control that day. And I am afraid that I have forfeited you."

"Forfeited me, Papa?" she said.

He rubbed his eyes. "Emily, are you happy? Or should I say, at least content?"

She hesitated. "I am afraid," she said.

"There is a great deal to fear." He turned. "Emily, does Charles treat you well?"

"He—I suppose he does. I have no comparison. He is hardly ever at home and we disagree on certain basic things. Important things."

"Things like slavery?"

"Yes, and the Union."

"I believe Will had the same difficulties, plus Belinda's wild moods. Such differing views on major issues make marriage difficult, in spite of love. I should have been more vocal to you both. I should have warned you what I thought—no, what I knew to be true."

"I don't want you to worry for me, Papa."

"Well, I do worry for you. I always have." He rubbed his eyes again, faced away from her. "You know that our family has been somewhat shunned because of my attempt to free my slaves and for my stance on slavery. Perhaps, you are not as keenly aware of that as I am. I think Will was. Perhaps, I have managed to protect you there, if nowhere else." The judge locked his gaze on her. She could feel it, though she could not see it for the backlit fire. "You hadn't any suitors, Emily. Oh, a few who soon disappeared. I held myself to blame for that. Certainly not you, so beautiful and kind. So intelligent and sweet." A log fell in the dwindling flames. Her father shifted his weight and pushed it back with the toe of his boot. "So like your mother, really."

The judge reached into the woodbox and dropped another

piece of wood onto the fire. He stoked the embers. "When Charles came courting and you brightened and seemed to bloom, I went against my judgment and gave my blessing. I felt myself to be a primary obstacle to your happiness. You and Will both. I wonder that I was not more careful with your life. I am afraid I failed you, Emily. I ignored my reservations. I thought because of me there might be no one else. If I had been stronger for you both, perhaps he'd be alive."

He saw her quiet crying and paused. Then he said, "Now that I've commenced this rambling, saying things better left unsaid, I can't seem to stop without saying it all."

Emily wiped away her tears.

"Maybe that is all." He took her hands. "Well, such rambling," he said. "I'm very tired. Belinda's endless haggling over the land exhausts me." He cleared his throat. "That was unkind. Everything I have said tonight is unkind. You see what I mean about who I have become."

Emily put her arms around him, feeling the residual heat of the fire on his back.

"Don't be sorry," she said. "I made my own choice. I had a chance at a family of my own. My own children to adore. You are not at fault. You have been my mother's gift to me."

His body sagged.

"Let's go to bed now, Papa. Maybe tomorrow you will feel less burdened. Maybe I will, too." She kissed his forehead, reached for his hand, and pressed it between hers. "I'll bank the fire. Rest well."

At the door, he looked back. Emily had not moved. He nodded and disappeared into the dark hall.

In the weeks following her stay with her father, Emily struggled with his confession to her; she could think of it as nothing else. She felt undone that he had approved Charles as a suitor without approving of him. His fear that there would be no one else because of his stance on slavery was a shock to her. That he felt he had sold her out triggered every insecurity she had lived with nearly all her life. Or at least since her mother's death: her lack of real friendships, her hesitance at knowing the right fork to use on rare social outings, the feeling of something wrong in the way townsfolk looked at her, the distance some kept or the cold formality with which they spoke to her. She had been an outsider and would always be, she thought. She would not have burdened her father more by confessing the strain in her marriage since the Fourth of July. She was even more wary of her husband now, less at ease in the house that no longer felt like home, the house in which she was pervasively aware either of his presence or his absence. Sad as she had often been in her father's house, she had felt at ease, accepted, safe—except for Jeremiah's heedless taunts—and at rest without even realizing. Now she perpetually reminded herself to stop moving, to stop tapping, to stop drumming her fingers, to stop ruminating. Falling asleep had become an effort, and often she woke in the morning drained and fatigued.

With resolve to divert herself and focus on the cause against slavery, Emily picked up the book she had brought from her father's, intent on reading, only to lay it down again. The book fell from its careless placement at the edge of the table and Emily stooped to retrieve it. She roamed from room to room, rearranging bric-a-brac one-handed, the book clutched to her breast with the other.

In the parlor Emily happened upon Ginny. On impulse Emily asked for help in improving her stitches. "Well," said Ginny, "I reckon you gone have to put that book down somewhere." Emily handed it over and Ginny laid it on the side table by the window. Even with her fresh intention, Emily's work on new dresses for Rosa Claire and the baby was as uneven as ever, perhaps more so.

Charles came and went, sometimes without speaking, often in the night.

Emily did not sleep well and her fatigue showed in unusual crossness with Rosa Claire and sometimes with the slaves. It occurred to her that she had absorbed her father's guilt and his lack of faith in her.

CHAPTER 18

Summer settled over the land like the lid on a pot of boiling greens. In the fog of her pregnancy, Emily took to napping with her daughter in the heat of the day. One afternoon, she awoke to hoofbeats, as Charles's voice penetrated her exhaustion. She rose, leaving the little girl asleep.

From the muffled voices through the window, she realized that Charles had gone into the cutting garden with Benjamin. By the time Emily reached the back door, he was walking toward her with a bouquet of foxglove in his hand.

"Look what's blooming," Charles said, holding the flowers out to her.

Almost by reflex, Emily received them, along with a kiss on her cheek. Digitalis. After Will's death and the conflict in the family. Her stomach knotted. How could he walk in like this and expect her to receive them?

"They will go to seed right quick now, so don't let them spread near the henhouse. Remember?" he said.

Emily nodded, arranging and rearranging the tall, unwieldy stems in a blue vase Charles had ordered for her the Christmas before, an ineffectual attempt at replacing her mother's broken one. She tried to shake off her reaction. It was only a bouquet. She would not die from touching them.

"I remember," she said. "I will collect them and save them for the fall. No foul gloves for evil fairies around our fowl!"

Charles laughed, put his arms around her waist. Emily was so rarely lighthearted these days.

"Perfect!" Charles said, fingering the hanging blooms. "We need those chickens fried up for Sunday dinner! Let's not have any slaughter here that isn't our own. And our glorious and victorious slaughter of the Union forces at Manassas. Scattered those cowardly bastards off in a goddamned bloody panic. The ones we didn't bury."

Emily pushed away. "Men are dying, Charles. And you rejoice? You make me shudder."

"It's life, Emily. And it's war. We are in the business of slaughter. Or haven't you noticed how we are slaughtering the damned Union? Like we slaughter those Sunday chickens." Each insistent reiteration of the word *slaughter* fell on her like a blow. "Or haven't you paid attention? So protected by your dear papa that you don't see the niggers slaughtering your chickens for Sunday dinner? Or care to know the slaughter it takes for them to take care of your messy business?"

She turned away. "You promised not to use that word, Charles."

"Nigger? Or slaughter? The chicken slaughter? Sunday dinner slaughter? Open your eyes, Emily. Haven't you seen the Sunday slaughter?"

"I've seen a little—by accident. It makes me sick. I just haven't ever . . ."

"Well, it doesn't seem to make you sick to eat chicken. To repeat myself, Emily, this is life. This is survival. We kill the chickens. And we will sure as hell kill the goddamned invading Yankees. We are at war. To preserve the life you live thanks to your niggers, madam. The ones who kill your chickens for you. The chickens you love to feed and gather their nice, warm eggs. Love holding those little soft biddies, don't you? But you also love fried chicken come Sunday. And that means slaughter, Mrs. Slate. So better us than the foxes, eh?"

Emily walked into the house kitchen. Charles followed her and pulled her to him. She resisted and pushed away, picking up a dirty bowl. The bowl clanged against the bottom of the chipped enamel dishpan. Emily plunged her hands into the cloudy water. Her fingers circled 'round and 'round the smooth edge of china as though it would never come clean. She felt Charles watching, but she could not stop herself.

"Thank you for the flowers, Charles," Emily said over her shoulder, her voice barely audible.

The sound of Charles's boots as he walked away hammered into Emily's head. The bowl sank in the murky water as she wiped her hands on a clean linen towel. She followed him to the door, the towel hanging like a dead thing in her hand.

Halfway across the yard Charles turned his head and spotted her staring after him. She felt unable to do otherwise. Several chickens pecked around his feet. Charles kicked at them, sending them scattering. He whipped around, closing the space between them. Emily backed away, but Charles was at the top of the steps, his fingers curled around her wrist, shaking the towel loose from her fingers. His laugh at her shock was harsh and empty.

"You think I'm cruel? To speak the truth? About you and me?" he said. "Let me show you who we are, my dear."

Charles yanked her stumbling down the steps. His intensity terrified her. Emily pulled against him, struggling, but her wrist might as well have been cuffed.

"Grab that rooster," Charles commanded Jessie, who was sweeping by the shed.

When he let go of Emily's wrist, she lost her balance and almost fell. He strode across the yard while Jessie chased the squawking bird, pitched after it, caught its tail, and tucked it under her arm, holding its neck in her hand.

"Put that thing on the stump and bring me an ax." His voice softened. In a gesture resembling tenderness, Charles took Emily's hand. "Here, now, come stroke the feathers. Beautiful, aren't they? Not quite the fashion for high-minded ladies, but a few might look right fine on your Sunday bonnet. Here, these long ones from the tail." He jerked several out. The bird shrieked. Charles dragged the luminous feathers across her cheek. "Ah, they frame your face so fine. Perhaps a bit bawdy for you, though? Give me that, Jessie." Charles grabbed the ax from her.

"Now, Emily, you just hold this bird down. Like this." He forced her hands around the struggling body. The bird's wild heartbeat hammered at her hands like the throbbing in her own chest. She could not tell the difference. "Don't move," he said. Charles raised the ax over his head. "Open your eyes, Emily."

The glittering blade came down. The bird's round eye stared at her, unblinking. The beak gaped open, the tongue sharp and grotesque between the hard parallel curves. Blood spurted from the severed neck.

Emily screamed and jerked like the slain bird. The headless cock leaped from the stump, its wings battering the blood-spumed air. Red spatters stained Emily's hands as she covered her eyes. The bird's frantic body flopped against her skirt. Vomit spewed from Emily's mouth and nose. She fled toward the outhouse. Terrified, Jessie flew after her. Emily's boot tangled in her crinoline and she plunged face-first onto the hard-packed earth.

Charles pushed Jessie aside. "See to that rooster," he said, low and impassive.

Vomit clung to Emily's lashes and her hair, the smell and sight of it gagging him, despite his exposure to illness and wounds and death. An oozing abrasion followed the curve of her cheek. Her right eye was beginning to swell. A fine spray of blood from the rooster darkened her forehead. By the time Charles reached the porch, Emily stirred in his arms, moaning. He pulled at the door with his little finger, forced his boot into the opening, and shouldered his way through, twisting to protect her head. In the parlor, Charles lay Emily on the divan, cradling her head with his hastily folded jacket. Its bloodstained sleeve lay limp on the floor.

Ginny stood in the door, her face dark and flat as well water for which there is no bucket. Charles turned sideways to shoulder past her. She blocked his way.

"I seen what you done," she said.

"I—" He stopped. "I didn't mean her harm."

Her eyes were on Emily and he looked down, seeing her now as Ginny was seeing.

"Help me, Ginny," he said.

"Help you?" Ginny turned her back. "Yes, sir, I'm gone help."

Ginny set his medical bag beside him, a wet towel and calendula oil in hand. He swabbed the clotting blood and applied a sparing portion of the oil to Emily's bruising cheek. Emily opened her eyes and Charles saw her effort to focus.

"You are in the living room," he said, quiet and professional. "You fell. I am putting calendula oil on your cheek. Ginny is here."

Emily's unfocused eyes wandered from his face to Ginny's. She raised her hand and Ginny took it.

"You gone be all right, honey child."

Ginny set aside her scuffed boots, as Charles checked Emily's ankles and wrists.

"I don't find any other injury," Charles said, placing Emily's hand across her ribs. "I want you to lie still for a spell. I am going to talk to Ginny and bring you a cup of tea. No sitting up now. Don't even try. Just be still."

Emily's eyes followed his face, rolling upward, going out of focus as he kissed her forehead and lifted his hand from hers. She watched him walk away. On the ceiling, her eyes traced a web of cracks that split the plastered ceiling.

In the kitchen, a teakettle steamed. As Ginny sifted a spoonful of crushed tea into a blue china teapot, she surveyed him.

"I never meant to hurt her."

"Meant or don't mean, I seen what you did. I seen how cruel."

"I only meant—" Charles stopped. "How does a woman grow up on a goddamned farm and not know she has shit on the sole of her boot? My sister, Belinda, wrings chicken necks all the time—guts them, plucks them, cooks them, and eats them."

"She ain't Miss Belinda."

"No, Miss Belinda never had slaves to do her every bidding," he said.

"She do now. Don't reckon she's out killing Sunday chickens these days," said Ginny.

Charles plunged his hands in the dishpan, wiped them with a half-clean towel, and ran his fingers through his hair.

"She tell you she got a baby in her?" Ginny said.

"Of course she did." Charles whirled on her. Ginny did not move.

"I'm gone tell you a story. About Miss Emily, when she was just a baby child, not much past walking good, maybe almost three. Right soon after I first come here, me still a child myself. Maybe ten, eleven, I don't know. Ain't never knowed how old I am. We's out back playing chase and her laughing like to lose her breath. Old Sarabel out there chasing up a hen and Miss Emily, she think we all just playing some game. She think that chicken playing chase, too. Well, Sarabel, she got hold of that hen, whop it on the stump, and ax that head in half a breath. Jump back out the way. Chicken flop straight into that baby's face with its old bloody, headless neck. Knock her down, wings flapping in her face, blood flying, claws scrambling on her skin, and her screaming and screaming. I'm yanking that baby out from that old hen and flying in the house. Mistress come running out, grab that girl away from me. What you doing to my girl? she say. Sarabel, she running behind me, crying and trying to explain, but she bawling too hard. Mamie, she running from the kitchen, fetching water, grabbing towels. She seen it from the window and she can talk, not like me and Sarabel, and she tell Mistress the whole tale. Mistress rocking that baby, smoothing her hair and patting at her little back."

Charles pushed his hands against the worktable, shaking his head. He took one deep breath, exhaled, his shoulders going slack.

"That little girl, she go still then. Real still. Don't make one sound for nigh on the whole day, just a little whimpering, sucking her thumb. Mistress say fry that chicken, Sarabel. Crisp. And salt it up good. And don't never let my baby see you kill no chicken ever again, you hear. And we didn't. Not then. Not now. 'Specially not after she see her mama die and all that blood everywhere. She be eating chicken ever since, but chicken fried up crisp on the table don't look like chickens running round out there, laying eggs she love to gather, pecking up the feed she throw. Her mama give her a little yellow biddy for her own right after that, let her keep it on the porch in a crate till it get too big, so she don't be afraid. And she never was, till now." Ginny reached across Charles for the sugar bowl. "Wasn't long after that she see her mama die."

Ginny poured boiling water into the blue teapot, set a cup and saucer on the tray. "Beg pardon, sir." Ginny brushed past Charles, whose face was hidden in one hand, the other still gripping the edge of the worktable. "Jessie and me'll get her to bed." She disappeared down the hall.

After several minutes, Charles went out the back door. In the shed, he took down the crosscut saw and motioned to Benjamin and Lucian. At the stump, Charles studied the dark stains. He handed the saw to Benjamin and watched as the two men bent over the blemished surface of the wood. When the stump was smooth and clean again, Charles returned to the kitchen. On the worktable he saw Ginny's tray, Emily's cup of tea untouched.

Sometime before dawn Emily stirred, her nightgown a sticky wad around her. She struggled, exhausted, between waking and sleep. She tugged at the gown and half rolled toward Charles's side of the bed. A jolt of dizziness disoriented her. The rocker creaked and Emily raised her head, pain shooting through the side of her face. Charles sat close to the bed with his face averted. He looked spent and haggard. Emily watched his Adam's apple move. Charles stood and disappeared without looking in her direction. Emily puzzled at the pattern of yellow spots on the ceiling above her. When she closed her eyes, the spots shifted to the interior of her lids. She watched them sway as her closed eyes moved, back and forth.

Ginny brought in a tray with toast and tea.

"Ginny, what's wrong with me? And Charles? Ginny, he—I think he was weeping. Did I lose my baby?"

"No, honey, you just had you a little spill. Hit your head real hard. Might near dove through the ground. Dr. Charles been here all night. Wouldn't budge. You eat now. That tea gone be cold." Ginny pulled the rocker closer and sat.

"I'm gone tell you a story now, Miss Emily. Seem like I'm full of stories about you that you don't recollect." Ginny recounted her tale, including the terrible nightmares that ensued and how Emily began to wet herself and her bed afterward. Emily remembered her humiliation. It had lasted a long time.

Especially after her mother's death. Then Ginny told her the details of yesterday. She softened the account as much as she knew how. Both women were silent, the rocker creaking as Ginny swayed.

When Charles returned, Emily touched his face and, out of habit, smiled.

CHAPTER 19

Emily had come to Charles a virgin. Charles had come to her full of knowledge and had intermittently taught her pleasure. She had not questioned his desires nor his skills, assuming them to be the innate gift of a being man. Though he had often simply used her, Charles had frequently enflamed her, had taken her innocence and kindled a burning desire with his mouth and his hands and his body. Then had come pregnancy and fear and sleepless nights and worries at his often long absences. Still, there were moments when he delighted her. And since the shock of this discordant summer, he had taken her often, saying how a pregnant woman had the greatest pleasure since she needn't worry about getting pregnant.

Outside the window, the dew lay like a thin sheet of summer snow across the ground. Emily lay satiated across the bed, staring out at its pale shimmer. She smiled when Charles pulled her to her feet and told her to cover her body and ride into town with him.

Old Mrs. Gossard, a widow, living alone, had fallen on her porch. A neighbor found her lying on her side, her leg apparently broken. A slave boy had come to fetch the doctor. Charles needed Emily to help in binding a splint. Emily and Charles found her moaning in pain. No one had dared to move her.

The old lady had broken a hip, not a leg. Now, she lay whimpering in her bed, where the slave boy had helped Charles settle her. He gave a note to the boy, who went running to the pharmacy. Charles shook his head at Emily. The widow was still in her nightclothes, a blessing because moving her had caused excruciating pain. Emily lifted the covers and loosened their weight around the old woman's gnarled feet. She followed Charles into the hall.

"I have laudanum coming, or at least, I hope I do. There is almost none to come by with it all gone to the troops. There is nothing I can do other than possibly diminish the pain. She will never leave this bed. I doubt she will live more than a few weeks at best. A broken hip in the elderly is a death sentence. She will need a companion and—"

"My father can spare someone. I am sure of it. I will go and ask him now. He should be at his office after morning court."

Emily found her father in his office, as expected, and open-armed for her. He sent a boy from the rear of the courthouse for one of the house slaves to go at once, prepared to stay. When Emily returned, Widow Gossard had quieted in a laudanum fog.

"I must speak to Horace at the pharmacy before we go," said Charles. "He'll need specific instructions on dispensing the drug. I don't want her in pain and he may be hesitant about the quantity without my say-so. Especially with the shortage now."

Charles helped Emily into the buggy. As they passed up the street, various townsfolk nodded or waved. Emily remained in the buggy while Charles entered the pharmacy.

The sun was soft and warm on Emily's back. She was feeling

soft herself, thinking about her husband: the way folks greeted him, the way he handled Widow Gossard's frail body, so concentrated to spare her pain. Emily settled back against the leather and closed her eyes. When she opened them, Charles was coming out of the pharmacy. Beside him, holding his arm, was a laughing woman she had seen before but did not know, a woman whose bodice was cut too low, whose laugh was too loud, whose familiarity in tapping Charles on the sleeve with her fan was too bold. The woman looked her way and went silent. She dropped Charles's arm and smiled up at him, tipping her folded fan against her cheek.

"Well, Dr. Charles, you have a good day now," the woman said. She lifted her skirts unnecessarily high, exposing her slim ankles as she swirled away. He tipped his hat and climbed silently up into the buggy.

"Who was that woman?" Emily said.

"A whore."

Emily's stomach wrenched at the scene and at her husband's glib manner.

"You know her, obviously."

"Yes, I know her," Charles said. "Or were you referring to the scriptural sense." He laughed, almost to himself.

Emily reddened, her hands gripped tight in her lap.

"Whores get sick like the rest of us, Emily. The practice of medicine is not just for the good and the godly."

Emily tried to think of something to say. Nothing came. Her head swirled with her mounting awareness of inconsistencies in his excuses as to his whereabouts. He had such a way of brushing them off, making them quirks of her memory, as he had done when she confronted him about her encounter with Mrs. Bellingham, who had not in fact been ill. Even at the time Emily was certain that she had not confused the name, but had no way to refute his insistence that she had. There were constant reasons he offered for his increasing absences, including a mounting number of patients. Either that or no excuse at all, just a silence she felt an intense dread to break. She had been raised to avoid confrontation and it paralyzed her. Without evidence and without becoming the kind of needling sort of person she could not envision becoming—no, in truth, feared becoming—she had no real means of challenging what she believed to be his untruths. Somehow she had not considered whores. The idea was too far beyond her cultural sense of decency. Yet here it was. She opened her fan, closed it again, and laid it in her lap, her hands folded.

"Hope the rain comes soon," Charles said. "Fields are drying up. Guess it's a good thing, after all, that I'm not dependent on the land for my well-being—our well-being, that is. At least not directly."

"Yes." Emily kept her eyes straight ahead on the road. Her body was stiff. "I'm sure that Papa would be glad of some rain."

"Good of him to send some assistance." Charles took her hand. It was unyielding.

"Yes, I'm glad he could spare Clara. He would have sent her even if he could not, you know."

"Yes, I expect he would." Charles released her hand and flicked the reins.

Nothing more was said, but when Charles reached for her that night and laid his kisses down along her spine, his tongue warm and wet in the small of her back, his hand cupping her buttock, Emily stiffened. Though she embraced him, drew him into her, though she blamed her lack of response on the pregnancy, something within her had crept into hiding, something Charles could not coax out.

When his breathing slowed into a light snore beside her, she turned her back and wrapped her hands beneath her rounding belly. With the edge of the tangled sheet, she wiped between her legs. Her breath caught in her chest and she covered her mouth with her hands to muffle the sound that threatened to escape. Tears trickled through her tight lids as her body shook with silent weeping. In the night, she woke to find her face still wet, the tears continuing even in her sleep. She wiped her eyes, turned the damp pillow over, and stretched her body as near the edge as she dared.

After breakfast, Emily held Charles's plate, staring at the biscuit crumbs caught in a dark stain of molasses. She half turned toward him, then changed her mind. Holding the plate before her like a sacrament, Emily went to the door and brushed the crumbs onto the swept dirt of the yard. The chickens materialized in a lopsided run, a blur of white, rust, and yellow, squawking, pecking, beating against one another. Emily watched as if she had never seen chickens fight over crumbs, or did not see them now. Plate in hand, she returned to the kitchen, her hands sticky brown with molasses. Charles was gone.

September heat blanketed the house like so much wet cotton. Emily swatted at flies and stared out the window. In the late morning, she put a pot of water on the stove to brew coffee, in case Charles came back from the office. He preferred black coffee to tea, no matter the extra time it required Ginny to roast the beans over the fire, stirring constantly to prevent them scorching. Charles ambled in just as Emily removed the beans from the grinder and dropped them into the boiling water.

"Only a couple of minutes now," Emily said.

"I've been thinking on your fear," Charles said without preamble, "and frankly, I haven't the patience for it. You are alone far too much. Gives you too much time to stew over things. Your fears and your anxieties are a real burden to me, Emily. Between you and Belinda I can't concentrate on my work. I have decided you should stay with my mother until you deliver. You'll have all the help and support you need. My mother is a sure hand at birthing, and you can take Ginny with you."

Emily stared at him, the pot growing heavy in her hands. He ignored her.

"Maybe you could even be of some comfort to Belinda," he added. "Maybe, she to you. Maybe you can help each other lighten up your grief a bit. It's been long enough. Benjamin and Ginny can go back and forth to look after my needs and the house. I will come by as often as practical, aside of course, for emergencies—check on you on my way to and from the office."

Emily set the pot on the stove. "I don't know what to say, Charles. I'm trying. I really am. Could you just put your arms around me, hold me for a moment?"

He patted her shoulder stiffly. "For God's sake, Emily. I have work to do." He reached past her for the coffeepot.

There was nothing to say. She walked out of the room. In the minutes that followed she heard him pouring his coffee and his careful slurp at the hot liquid. In the parlor, she sat immobile. This room, her house, her life had become unfamiliar to her, would now be taken from her. Over what? Not her fear. No, something else without a name had torn between them, flapping its silent way through the house.

Outside the window, two small sparrows nipped at mealworms and blown thistle seeds. On the floor, a tiny mother-of-pearl button shone pale in a slanted ray of sun. Emily picked it up, stroked it with her fingers, and lowered it into her pocket. It must have fallen from Rosa Claire's petticoat. Something that could be fixed with needle and thread.

Emily was still aimlessly fingering the button, when Jessie came in to say the doctor was on his way to the Kitchens' place to stitch up a gash across the old man's leg. He would not return at noon for his dinner.

"Talk like it bad, a accident with the plow," Jessie said. "Too bad to be jolting him all the way over here in the wagon. You all right, Miss Emily? You looking kind of peaked."

"Is Rosa Claire with Ginny?"

"Yes'm. Ginny's dusting the doctor's office while he gone."

"I think I will lie down for a spell. I haven't much appetite, anyway."

"Yes'm. Maybe you don't want me ringing that dinner bell, Miss Emily. Your head hurting you?"

"No, ring the bell. I just need to rest."

"We take care of Rosa Claire, Miss Emily. You just go and rest yourself."

"Thank you, Jessie." Emily felt a great surge of gratitude toward these women who helped her now in her inadequacy. She crawled up onto the bed.

The stillness in which she lay was akin to paralysis. Her mind emptied as did her emotions. She could not apprehend what had hold of her. She longed for something larger than herself, something to envelop her, to anchor her to her life. She had no tether.

She must have slept, and for a good while. It was Rosa Claire's bright laughter from the garden that woke her. She raised herself on one elbow, brushed back the loose strands of hair against her cheek. Standing, she smoothed her skirt and realized she had never removed her apron. She draped it over the end of the bed. Pulling at the pins in her hair, she sat down at the mirror, watching with disinterested curiosity as her hair fell in wide loops from her temples. She swung her head from side to side, watching the long waves widen. Emily picked up her mother's monogrammed silver brush and pulled at the tangles. She twisted her hair into a knotty bun, pushed the loose ends into place, and jammed in a last pin.

From the hot shade of the porch, Emily watched Ginny toss beans to Rosa Claire, whose laughter spilled into the air at every bean she missed, which was every one. Ginny looked up at her standing there.

"You all right?"

"Yes, Ginny. I must have been more tired than I knew."

"Honey, you with child. 'Course you tired." She tossed a bean to Emily, who instinctively stepped forward to catch it.

Emily came down the steps. "Rosa Claire," she said. "Here, catch."

The child toddled forward, scooped up the fallen bean, and threw it straight overhead. It landed on the ground behind her, where her mother scooped it up and began a game of keep-away, swapping the bean between hands behind her back, swaying from one foot to the other. Rosa Claire clapped her hands and threw her head back in laughter. *Is there any more beautiful sound,* Emily thought. Her children would be her consolation.

"Is Dr. Slate back from the Kitchens?" she said, scooping Rosa Claire into her arms.

"Yes'm. Told me not to wake you. Said when you got up, tell you come on up to the office."

"Thank you, Ginny. Rosa Claire, want to come with me?"

The little girl held out her hand as Emily lowered her to the ground.

At the steps to the office, Rosa Claire let go, tucking herself into a squat, hands between her knees, squealing at a beetle scurrying in the dirt. Emily sat on the steps, watching.

"Emily?" Charles's face emerged from the dimness of the office. He glanced down at Rosa Claire, poking her finger at the bug. He came down the step to Emily and extended his hand. She took it and stood. He put his arms around her. After a moment, she surrendered. What else was she to do? He was her husband, the husband she had chosen for better or for worse. She had been too innocent to consider it might be always for the worse. Now there was Rosa Claire and this new one on the way. She would make the best she could of the choice she had made.

In the days that followed, Emily would move to Adeline's. Her pregnancy would advance. Charles appeared and disappeared sporadically. Belinda grew more agitated about the land. On November 22, in the afternoon, Hammond would ride off with Charles to Belinda's, and Emily's life would be torn asunder.

Book Two: Death

November 1861

Chapter 20

It should have been an ordinary night: the late cicadas whirring in the chilling air, three women by the fire, waiting for the men to return—Adeline knitting, Emily jabbing a needle in an awkward attempt to embroider a red rose on a linen towel, Ginny darning a sock for a man none of them knew was dead.

No one had spoken for the last half hour. All three turned in their chairs at the creak of wagon wheels and thudding steps on the porch. Adeline pushed the green wool back on her knitting needles and held up a hand to stop Ginny from rising. Adeline was already halfway to the door when the knock came, tentative, then insistent. Emily was quick behind her, in spite of the late pregnancy that made her awkward. Ginny held her mistress's elbow to steady her.

At the open door, Benjamin stood clutching his worn jacket around his throat, his face contorted in grief. He nodded. "Miss Adeline, I got real bad news for Miss Emily. You too, ma'am."

Adeline took a step back. Emily reached her hand toward Benjamin's familiar strength.

"Miss Emily, Dr. Charles done shot your daddy. He's dead."

The world slid into silence. Emily stared at him. In the distance a hoot owl called.

"Charles?" she said at last. "My father? Dead?"

Adeline covered her mouth as if to stop herself from vomiting. Emily clutched at her bulging middle and her body went slack. Benjamin bent to help Ginny ease her mistress into a hall chair.

Benjamin righted himself and spoke to Adeline. "I'm real sorry, ma'am."

"Oh, God, Benjamin, where?" Adeline said, her hands moving in the air as if searching for something to grasp. "What happened?"

"Over to Miss Belinda's place. Some of the judge's slaves seen it. Sheriff Johnson got Hammond and Dr. Charles in the jail."

Emily stumbled up, pushing at whoever was near. "I have to go," she said. "Benjamin, take me home."

"No, Miss Emily." He took a step back. "You don't need to be there now. Not tonight."

"Then take me to the jail." Emily's words caught in her throat. She was speaking through sobs that merged into a wild wail.

"You're in no condition to go." Adeline nodded at Ginny to calm her mistress. "There is nothing you can do."

Adeline motioned Benjamin back into the night, where the wagon waited. Adeline refused his hand as she mounted the wagon and took the reins he handed up, familiar as her own palms, seasoned by her sweat and the oil of her skin. Her arms trembled. Emily's cries pursued her into the night. Adeline refused to heed those cries, nor could she cry for her own sons, for the life she had struggled so long, so hard to attain. She left Benjamin standing, his arms hanging at his sides, and turned the wagon toward the jail.

Adeline was a good horsewoman. Her father had given her

that, if little else, even if the price of the gift had left her flesh and her spirit scarred. "Adeline," he'd shout, from where he stood with a stick in his hand, "you hold them horses. And don't you sit. You stand that wagon, you hear me, girl." Though she tried, when she had failed, had sat, her brother had paid the price for her with his life. She stood the wagon now, her father's vicious tones in her ears, steering the horses toward Greensboro, forcing her mind to go still and empty. She could not fail. The drone of the cicadas clotted the air above her head, their thrum echoing the shock inside her. By instinct, she stretched toward the sound, toward some remnant of ordinary life. She forced herself into a numb focus on the horses, their breath swirling into the deepening chill. A faint click of her tongue pressed the horses on. There was no lurch. She rode like that, standing, across the field.

In the shadows of a lone oak left in felling of trees for the town, Adeline dropped the reins, her hands loose at her sides, and stared at the jail. Its weight, the very structure itself paralyzed her: the ponderous logs, the untold ax blows it had taken to fell them, the knotted muscles of men lifting them into place, and a sudden realization that nothing short of fire would undo them now. She gathered her skirts and dismounted the wagon, bracing herself against its side as her foot sought ground. At the step she stumbled and sat hard on the stoop. For a moment she did not move. The definition between earth and sky receded in the fading light. She struggled to her feet. A shooting pain pierced her knuckles as she rapped on the heavy door.

A narrow, barred window in the door opened onto the sheriff's half-lit face. Adeline knew this stark, lined face far too well from countless trips to fetch her husband home after some drunken brawl. Over time the humiliation of such dealings waned. Tonight Adeline's mission had nothing to do with drink. Men recovered from drink, sobered up, nursed their hangovers, and made peace with one another or not. Tonight was about death, spread around her like brambles in an endless swamp. *And there is no recovering from death,* she thought.

"Mrs. Slate." Adeline absorbed his formality, the way he fortified their distance. "I can't let you in. Nobody here to sober up."

The darkness surrounded her.

"I got rules," he said. "You go on home now. Go do whatever you can for Emily. She's bound to be needing you."

The memory of Emily's desolate wail poured through Adeline's head, as it had poured from Emily's mouth at the news. Adeline tore herself clear of that memory and concentrated on the shadowed face in the barred window.

"I've come a ways, Sheriff. You know how far. I won't be long. I can't."

"It ain't safe, Mrs. Slate. Now, just you go on home. You come back in the daylight."

"Mason," Adeline said, cutting through his formality, "you've got sons, some good, some not. If one of yours, let alone two, was locked up here, not safe as you say, would you be bound to see them?"

Adeline could hear Mason fidget. Resolute, she locked his eyes in the dim rectangle that framed his face.

"Adeline," Mason said, "you are one hard woman. I may be responsible for your sons, but I can't be responsible for you. I told you now. Don't push me no more."

The steady chant of cicadas saturated the quiet as Adeline's voice came clear. "And will you be responsible for my grief if—" She stopped. "Will you?"

Adeline breathed deep when Mason did not close the shuttered window and walk away. She heard the clinking of his key ring, saw in the faint light how he stared down at it. At last he fumbled a key into the latch and the door opened. Adeline slipped inside. And so the thing was done, with no undoing now. Behind her Mason extended his lantern into the darkness outside, and in her mind Adeline chided him for seeking some nonexistent comfort in its impotent flicker. The wooden bolt slammed across the door like a gunshot.

Adeline set her boot on the unpainted tread of the first step. She shivered. Her sons would be chilly in the big cell at the top of the stairs. She knew Mason would not have separated them. Adeline stepped aside for the sheriff to pass. Inside the murmur of Charles's voice became apparent. Wordless she followed Mason up the stairs and heard Charles go quiet at their footsteps. She kept her eyes on the key as Mason opened the cell, and started when the door clanged shut behind her. The key scraped as Mason removed it. He returned the ring to his pocket, the keys hanging loose and jangling as his boots echoed down the stairs.

Adeline saw Hammond first, his clothes stained dark with blood. He stumbled against the far wall and covered his eyes with his forearm. His low moan mingled in her head with the memory of Emily's anguished cry. Adeline reached for him, lost in those sounds. She felt Charles's grip on her arm. She stared up at him as if at a stranger and pulled Hammond into her arms, his face buried against her.

"Did you kill Judge Matthews?" she said at last.

Charles did not answer.

"Emily knows. Benjamin came to the house. He said the slaves saw it all." Adeline bit down on the far side of her hand.

"And you think those niggers know what they saw?"

Adeline turned aside. "And Hammond? You dragged my boy into—"

"God, no, Mama." Charles's fist pulled at the air. "He was just there. That's all. You know damned well he wouldn't—I wouldn't . . ." Charles shuffled his feet. "Well," he said, "you ought to know a lot of things." He waved the back of his hand away from her. "Hammond tried to revive him. I had to pull him off. Make him mount up and ride into the thickets. But he kept trying to go back. So they got us."

"And now he's here," Adeline said.

"I didn't leave him, Mama. I could've gone, but I didn't."

"And if you'd left him, would they have only come after you?" She searched his face, wanting to reach for him, wanting a way around the abyss.

The silence was too heavy for either to hold.

"Why, Charles? God help us. Emily's father?" She wiped the side of her free hand up her cheek. "Your kin?"

"Goddammit, Mama. Emily's kin doesn't make him mine. Not the way he's done Belinda. Withholding her goddamned inheritance. Nothing settled right by her. Hell, Mama, Belinda's your daughter. Am I the only one who gives a damn?"

Adeline looked down at Hammond, moaning in her arms like a fevered child. "What was the judge doing at Belinda's?"

"She wanted him to come talk it out, get it settled."

"And you, why were you there?"

"I said I'd help her." He dropped his head. "I owed it to her."

The space between them grew heavier.

"You know that land ought to be Belinda's, Mama," Charles said at last. Adeline watched his lips move, thought she saw words spill from his mouth, thought if her hands were free, she would pick them up and fling them across the cell. "Nothing but greed. Judge saying Belinda wasn't entitled. Saying the land wasn't hers to inherit. Only Jeremiah." He hesitated. "Said even mine didn't belong to me. Just to Emily."

She turned away, bracing Hammond's weight against the wall to free the hand with which she pointed, not at Charles, but somewhere visible only to her. "It is not your land," she said. "Nor Belinda's. Belinda has what she has—her house and her slaves and her garden. That's it. That's more than she ever had before. And Emily's farm does not belong to you."

Charles's chin whipped up. "What's hers is mine."

Adeline studied his unshaven stubble. "She didn't come with a dowry, boy."

"She's still my wife."

"And you believe your wife, your pregnant wife, will ever let you touch her again, touch your children—with hands that killed her father over land that never belonged to Belinda? Nor to you. And you shot him over that?"

"Mama, I didn't—" There was a wild pleading in his voice. "Now listen to me, Mama. It got into an argument. And a scuffle. And I had the gun. And then—"

"And then you shot him?"

"No, Mama. Listen now. You have to believe me. Things just happened—I didn't kill him."

"Then who did?"

From the streets below, jagged shouts and smashing glass shattered the night. A tumult of running feet rolled in like a distant storm. A flickering light of branch-shredded torches slashed across the ceiling of the cell. Adeline stiffened as an ominous pounding commenced at the door below. She stared at Charles while the jail shook with thud after thud, until the door crashed in, its bolt splintered and broken. Above the babble and scuffle of feet, Adeline heard Mason yelling one name and then another in an attempt to halt the flow of the mob. A crack of pistol fire pierced the tumult. Then another.

Hammond slid to a crouch, toppling Adeline with him. She reached out to Charles, fear for her sons overcoming all discord. The shouting below rose like smoke, absorbing the air in the cell. The men shoved up the stairs, their heavy boots trampling on the bare wood, scuffling for purchase against the bars of the cell. Adeline stared up at the rage-disfigured faces, the fists rattling the bars of the cell. In her panic, these familiar faces blurred into a panorama of frenzied craze. She felt, more than saw, how she knew these men. At the door of the cell, the face of Jeremiah Matthews emerged from the throng. It was his hand that came into focus then, as the barrel of his pistol slid between the bars, catching the dull gleam of a lantern along its length. That dim reflection paralyzed her, imprinted itself in her mind. She would never not see it again. Her empty hand shot out into the air. Her eyes tore from one son to the other. Charles turned between her and Jeremiah, his feet anchored where he stood. She reached into the empty space between them. Hammond hunched low against the wall, an unintelligible sound caught in his throat. Adeline turned and cradled his face in her hands, lifted his chin, locked his stricken gaze to hers. A shot rang out. Above her powerless fingertips she saw the bullet as it pierced the temple and entered Hammond's brain.

Adeline folded over him, cradled his wounded head in her lap and rocked. Charles stood abandoned, sequestered, his face and clothes spattered with a web of blood and brains. He knelt and laid his hand over the obscene, intimate opening in Hammond's skull. Flickering through Adeline's memory, a faint image: Hammond's head at birth, her several babies' heads, the blood, the mucus, the soft spot in the newborn skull unclosed and vulnerable.

The chaos dissolved into stunned silence as the men took in Adeline's presence. She turned toward them, her face stained with Hammond's blood, recognizing neighbors, townsmen, Conklin—all Jeremiah's cronies. She knew their names, their faces, altered by carnage. While she stared, Charles offered his body as a flawed and impotent shield against her seeing. She wrapped her arm around him, her face buried against his shoulder. She held him as if she could.

"Break it up now." Mason's voice cut through the crowd. "Adeline? I've got to get you out of here."

She searched for his face. The crowd shifted and the sheriff broke through, his eyes on her and not on her gruesome burden. "I've got a son alive in here," she said.

Mason was unarmed, his gun snatched from him in the mêlée. She saw, however, that his authority exerted a force of its own, establishing a momentary island of sanity.

"Where'd you pull this mob together, Jeremiah?" Mason said to the men. "You fools let him rile you into this? You'd follow him straight into hell, would you? Maybe that's what you've just done. Think he's going to take care of you when you hang for killing an innocent?" Mason pushed his way among them. "Get out of my way, Willy, you're drunk. Now, go on home and sober up. Jonas, get him out of here. Conklin, what are you doing here, anyway? Haven't earned your way to hell on your own? Truman, hand me back my gun. Come on now, son, give it to me." Mason held out his hand and the boy was on the verge of giving up the gun when someone knocked it to the floor. The boy backed away and fled down the stairs. Conklin scooped up the gun. The men jostled, muttering. Mason turned to face Jeremiah. Above his head, Jeremiah jangled Mason's keys, pilfered in the confusion. Jeremiah's long body twitched, his hand opening and closing on the ring of keys. The other held his pistol. The men struggled to see as the cell door clanged open, its hinge creaking. Adeline lurched, but failed to rise.

"Hand over the gun," Mason said. "Enough. You've got one killing on your head. You're a dead man if Hammond was innocent, which I feel sure he was. That's one cold murder, Jeremiah. Don't add another one."

"Innocent, my ass. These two bastards gunned down my father. Hell, you can see his blood all over them. My slaves saw it all."

Charles twisted from Adeline, though she held to his coat. "Your niggers were clear off on the other side of the yard. You think they know what they saw?" Adeline pulled at his jacket, threw him off-balance. His knee hit the floor beside her.

"Yeah, my niggers, Slate." Jeremiah slammed open the door. "Matthews' niggers."

"They couldn't see, you bastard. Hammond was innocent." Charles struggled against Adeline's hold.

"Innocent? With my daddy's blood all over him?" Adeline cringed as Jeremiah pointed the gun at the body she held. "You bastards. Set my father up at Belinda's and ambushed him."

"Nobody ambushed anybody. And I didn't shoot—"

"So who did? One of the slaves? You son of a bitch. You trying to whip it up we got us a slave uprising. Hell, it was the slaves brought him to me."

In relief, Adeline saw Mason struggle in behind him. "Give me the gun, Jeremiah. Leave Charles to the law. If he's guilty, he'll hang. Judge Simpson'll be here tomorrow. Think about Emily, goddammit. He was her father, too." Mason glanced at Charles. "She's got enough to deal with already."

Jeremiah twirled the key into his palm. He eyed the men around him. "I reckon she'll live with what she has to. But I intend to see her shit of a husband dead this night."

Charles wrenched himself from his mother's grip. Her hands grasped at the air as he whirled up and around, in a single motion, his fist slamming into Jeremiah's jaw. The closest man grabbed Charles's arm and twisted. Jeremiah jerked him across the cell. Mason lunged after, but someone shoved him back.

"You're a dead man, Charles Slate," Jeremiah said. He raised his gun, inches from Charles's head.

"For God's sake. You don't know what you're doing." Charles struggled, but his arms were pinned. "Don't make my mother see any more. Are you sane, man? Have some mercy." He lunged his shoulder at Jeremiah, but his captors jerked him back, his hands imprisoned behind him. Adeline grabbed at the nearest pant leg, but the man's swift kick loosened her grip.

"Mercy?" Jeremiah said. "Like the mercy you and your halfwit brother had for my father? And you want mercy?" Jeremiah shoved him again.

Mason inserted his body between the two men. "You're putting more blood on your hands, Jeremiah," Mason said. "You're as good as putting a noose around your own neck. And you," he said, raising his voice at the quieted mob, "get on out of here and get yourselves home. Jeremiah's leading you into the pit. Leave Charles to the judge. If he's guilty, he'll hang by the law."

"Not me who's going to swing, Mason. I don't give a shit for tomorrow or a new judge," said Jeremiah. "My father was the judge and he's dead." He waved his pistol. "Tonight I'm the judge and I'm the law. And Charles Slate is swinging." Jeremiah wrestled Charles toward the door. "Bring the sheriff along. As to his mother, she can witness it or not. I don't give a damn. Now move."

Adeline raised her eyes to Charles. She struggled to stand without losing her hold on Hammond. She cried out, one hand stretched in the empty air. Charles turned toward his mother as Jeremiah heaved him toward the stairs. She saw the pleading in his eyes as he opened his mouth to speak, then closed it. Weeping, she laid her forehead against the bloody remains of Hammond's face.

The mob parted. Jeremiah rammed his prisoner down the stairs. Someone shoved Mason ahead, struggling and shouting uselessly above the crowd. An outbreak of gunshots ripped the night. Adeline heard Mason's voice cry out in pain. The noise of boots and breakage dulled as the men spilled onto the packed earth outside. She strained to hear what she could no longer see. A wavering light from the torches below flickered up through the window of the cell. She stared up at it, rocking her dead son. From below, the sounds registered in distorted familiarity: men's shouts, the stamp of a horse's hooves, a terse command for Charles to mount. A moment later the crack of a whip sliced the night. Adeline imagined a hesitation in the horse before its burden lifted. Its hoofbeats halted and her body stiffened like the already dead. She imagined she heard the horse exhale. Someone cleared his throat and coughed. Muffled voices reemerged. Then no one spoke. Eventually, the tread of boots and hooves faded, leaving the cicadas shrilling in the night. Alone with Hammond in the dark, Adeline watched the darker bloom of his blood soaking through her skirts to the flesh from which he had come.

Adeline struggled to her feet and pulled Hammond toward the stairs. Descending backward, she dragged his body down, his head shrouded in her skirts. At the base of the stairs, she stopped, her breath ragged, her heartbeat thrumming in her ears. There remained the door, and outside in the night, three steps down and then the high bed of the wagon.

A gurgled cough punctured the dark.

"Adeline?" Mason's voice splashed into the darkness.

She waited, nausea rising in her throat.

"I tried to make you go." The sentence was garbled. Another wet cough.

"Don't you die here, Mason," she said. "Just don't you die."

A jagged piece of wood from the splintered door tore at Adeline's hand as she struggled past the threshold. Two steps now to the ground. Adeline stared at the high bed of the wagon. Beyond it, hanging from the oak, Charles's body twisted against the sky.

"Mrs. Slate?" There was kindness or something like it in Michael Lambert's unexpected voice behind her. "Let me help you."

Numb, Adeline nodded.

Lambert had happened into town to fetch his neighbor's young son home from a saloon on the outskirts of town and had heard the mêlée. His horse panted from Lambert's charge toward the scene, but it was done, and he was sick to see the size of it. Nothing to offer but his impotent assistance. Lambert was lithe and uncommonly strong for his age, from his long years as a farmer. He lifted Hammond to his shoulder like a child and rolled the body onto the wagon bed, arranging the arms and legs as if he might yet make Hammond comfortable. He stepped back and Adeline mounted the wagon. He offered a hand. She did not take it, but reached for the reins. Lambert handed up the hitching line.

"Let me help you with Charles."

"No," she said.

At her soft click, the horses moved and she turned the wagon. The heavy branch swayed with Charles's weight. Adeline halted under the tree, feeling beneath the seat for her knife, which would never again be an innocent tool for her chores. She whispered to the horses as she climbed onto the seat and grasped the rope. The long knot did not give easily. At the third slash, the rope separated and the body dropped askew over Hammond's. Adeline cringed, but she knew it made no difference to the dead.

"Lambert?" Her voice was thick, like a dreamer rousing from sleep. A gust of wind whirled the name away.

"Yes, ma'am."

"The sheriff is in there in the jail," she said. "Trying to die. Don't let him."

She flicked the reins and rode away, standing as she had come, her sodden petticoat stuck chill against her legs. Her body weighed her down, but she dared not sit. Her grief would crush her now and she might never rise. The wagon rolled out of the emptied town and she entered the deeper darkness of the woods. She held the reins high as if they supported her and not the reverse.

A faint light emerged ahead and the wagon rolled into the bare yard. As the horses stamped and whinnied, Adeline's torso curled over the blackness drying in her skirts. If she fell, she would not get up, and she was falling now. Adeline gripped the side of the wagon and held, breathing hard. She groped her way to the ground. Ginny stepped down from the porch, a lamp in her hand.

"Oh, God, Miss Adeline." Ginny's voice reached Adeline in a muffled rasp, her hand over her mouth. The lamp trembled. Adeline took it and set it on the raw wood of the step.

"Go find my husband," she said. "Tell him I've brought his sons home. Tell him they're dead."

Ginny's hand still covered her mouth.

"Go, Ginny," she said. "I'll be with Miss Emily. Don't let him come in there. You just fetch me. I'll come out and speak to him."

Ginny took a deep breath. "Mr. Thomas in the shed with a bottle. Since 'fore you got gone."

"Just go find him, Ginny. Emily must know. So must he."

Late in the night Adeline piled her dress in her arms, Hammond's blood against her breast. She stood in the cold kitchen beside Ginny, her fingers stroking the fabric.

"Is the fire lit?" Adeline said.

"Yes'm. Not big, like you said. But burning hot, leaping up like it want to lick the sky."

"Thank you, Ginny. Now go and see to whoever needs you." Adeline closed the door as she went out into the night.

Alone in the dark, Adeline studied the fire. In a slow arc she suspended the dress above it. The hem flared. Flame rent its way like reverse lightning up the skirt. She refused to release the dress as the blaze leaped up the bodice. Her right hand beat against the air, but the left would not surrender its hold. The flames licked at her skin and she opened her hand, the blazing fabric flowing downward to the earth. She stood with the heat on her face until the flames went out and only cinders glimmered in the night.

Ginny waited in the doorway.

"Leave it till morning," Adeline said, as she passed through the door.

In the kitchen, Ginny soothed cool lard over Adeline's burnt hand and wrapped it in torn white muslin. Adeline was as silent as if she were alone.

"Put the ashes in Hammond's coffin," Adeline said at last. She left the kitchen and went through the yard toward the house.

CHAPTER 21

In the dining room, Ginny braced her back against the table. The intermittent sounds of hammer and saw in the shop rang out into the dark. Ginny imagined Benjamin and his Lucian at work on the two coffins. She could almost hear the sizzle of great brown moths drawn to the light of their lanterns. The bodies lay side by side on wide planks atop the trestle table against which she leaned. She flapped open a pillowslip to wrap Hammond's head. It proved too small. She lay it loose over his ruined face. As she pulled fresh sheets over the bodies, a slight sound in the hallway startled her.

Adeline appeared in the doorway.

"I must wash them," Adeline said to no one in the room. She reached for the corner of the sheet, but Ginny caught her hand.

"You ain't doing this, Miss Adeline."

Adeline raised her head. "You forget yourself, Ginny."

"I ain't never forgot myself, Miss Adeline. But you ain't doing this. You don't need no more in your memory. It's enough. I'm gone wash them like they was my own. You go on out of here now. You got tomorrow coming."

Adeline's tears came at last. Ginny guided her to bed, where she lay curled, face to the wall, her burned hand cupped in the other. Ginny loosened the dark, heavy hair, just graying, and smoothed it away from her face. Adeline relaxed her hands against her breast, and Ginny turned back toward the task of the night.

Ginny had prepared any number of bodies for burial, but none like these. Benjamin and Lucian had cut away the fouled clothing, but the odors of death—blood and urine and feces—assailed her and she gagged. For close on half an hour, Ginny sat motionless. Her nausea subsided. She could not wait any longer. Even in the chill of the night, the stiffness would soon set in. Ginny raised the pillowslip and washed what was left of Hammond's beautiful face, his muscular body, and covered him with a fresh sheet.

On the other side of the table, Ginny held her breath. Heavy saliva and the bitter taste of bile filled her mouth. She sloshed her rag in the bucket, wrung it, and began to wash Charles's body by feel, not looking at the rope-ruined face. When she was done patting the bodies dry, she took her bucket out back, flung the fouled water across the hard ground, and threw the washrag into the trash pit to be burned.

Back inside, Ginny struggled to maneuver fresh clothing onto the bodies. But the weight of death was more than she could manage. With Adeline's scissors, she cut through the shirt collars, ripped the fabric down the center back, and slipped the stiffening arms into the sleeves. She slit the trousers and laid them over the bodies, tucking the raw edges underneath. Like making a bed, she thought. She could not cut the boots. She left them under the table. Ginny laid Adeline's handkerchief, embroidered with violets, atop the pillowslip over Hammond's face. No matter how she adjusted it, the neat blue-striped shirt collar failed to hide the bloody furrow on Charles's neck, his face a strange dark hue, a bizarre almost black, blotched in a coagulated web of broken blood vessels. Ginny had never seen a white man lynched. She dropped the sheet onto the floor and padded away to her narrow room.

Bars of colorless late-morning sun slanted through the narrow pines. The coffins jolted in the wagon, banging against one another. Thomas Slate held the reins slack, hunched forward, making no effort to avoid the ruts. The meager procession of mourners followed on foot.

Behind the wagon, Adeline supported her bandaged left hand in her right, as the group trudged toward the graveyard. She carried nothing, no Bible, no prayer book. Steps behind her, Emily held the weight of her womb under her heavy skirts, her feet sluggish, dream-like. At the rear of the group, a fine cloud of red dust rose around Ginny's dogged footsteps, made heavier by the weight of the little girl in her arms. Rosa Claire's stockinged legs protruded from under the blue woolen shawl Ginny had wrapped around them both. She hummed, her dark hand stroking the girl's pale curls. Ginny's tears were silent.

The coarse cawing of a blackbird broke the air. The sky darkened with the harsh flapping of a hundred unexpected wings. No one raised an eye except the child. She rubbed her eyes and buried her startled face back into Ginny's shoulder. The wagon turned from the uneven lane onto more level ground, punctuated by fallen leaves piled against an array of angled headstones and rough crosses.

"Whoa, you devils, whoa." Slate's snarl was broken by a rasping cough. His flick of the reins confused the horses. They halted, stamping and restless. The wagon lurched. Slate pulled on the reins. Behind him, only the horses caught a faint click from Adeline's lips. They snorted and held.

"Goddamned, stupid beasts," Slate muttered, as he slung himself from the wagon. He grasped at the footboard to maintain his balance. He cursed again and slapped his hat against his thigh, raising dust that brought on another bout of coughing. He hunkered against the spasm. The hat dangled at his knee. The women watched while Slate staggered upright. He wiped his mouth on his sleeve and pulled the hat low on his head.

"Where's them goddamn niggers?" he said, and coughed again.

Adeline gazed across the cemetery at the newly dug graves, two at hand and one far across the field.

"Benjamin is here," she said.

The little group stood like that, huddled, yet each one alone, waiting. At the edge of the woods a twig snapped and Benjamin stepped out, tall and easy gaited, his skin glistening with sweat from digging, his white hair catching the sun. Lucian followed, a younger version of his father, though a shade lighter. Benjamin tugged at his beard and nodded to Adeline.

"Miss Adeline," he said. Then again, "Miss Emily." He nodded a second time.

Benjamin focused on the wagon, gauging its contents. He did not speak to Thomas Slate, but nodded. He did not remove his hat. As he reached to take hold of the ropes, the welted scars of two different brand marks showed on the backs of his wrists. Without warning, Slate's sallow hand coiled around Benjamin's wrist, while the other knocked Benjamin's hat to the ground.

"Goddamned nigger," he said. No one moved. Slate's wracking cough crippled him again. Benjamin picked up his hat, dusted it off, and resumed his task, unwinding Slate's inept knots, coiling the ropes in orderly piles.

"Excuse me, ma'am." Benjamin's voice was subdued and husky. He lifted a corner of the nearest coffin, testing its weight. "Lucian," he said.

Adeline backed away, her bandaged hand on Emily's arm. Lucian applied his shoulder to the coffin as Benjamin slid it from the wagon. Emily flinched at the raw scrape of wood on wood. Benjamin paused to assure himself his son was secure before readjusting the load. As the full weight of the coffin slipped free of the wagon, Lucian staggered, then righted himself. The two moved slowly toward the nearest open grave.

Slate, standing apart, coughed again as Benjamin and Lucian revolved in a strange dance beneath the coffin. In a singular movement, they shifted its burden from their backs and lowered the casket into a cradle of ropes secured by yellow pine stakes. The father and son stood back, their breath heavy, as Adeline guided Emily, stumbling and pale, into the space between the open graves. With the grace of habitual labor, the slaves anchored a rope cradle in the other grave. In minutes, the second casket lay in it, rocking. The two men stepped back.

Ginny readjusted Rosa Claire on her hip, put her hand on Emily's elbow, nudged her mistress forward. Adeline looked back at her husband. He shook his head, his feet planted where he stood. She regarded the faces of the women near her.

"These were my sons," she said. "I loved them."

That was all.

Benjamin cleared his throat. Lucian loosed a coil of rope, holding it tight against the stake, its fibers cutting into his palms. Benjamin braced his outspread legs and together father and son coiled and uncoiled the ropes. The coffin descended in small jolts until it hit the earth below. When the second coffin lay in the earth, Benjamin straightened his back and waited.

Adeline filled her hand with dirt. She dropped most into Hammond's grave, the remainder into Charles's, brushing her hands against one another over his grave. The sound of the dirt falling onto his coffin was insignificant. Adeline nodded to Emily, took Rosa Claire from Ginny, and motioned across the field.

"Come on, Miss Emily," said Ginny. "Let's us go."

Emily's eyes were on the ground. The path round and among the headstones was a maze, and her feet caught on thick clumps of uncut grass. As she neared the other side of the cemetery, she raised her eyes and the assembly gathered there came into focus: numerous slaves, their faces familiar, some grim, some weeping openly; a band of people from the town, mostly business associates; and Preacher Morton, surrounded by a cadre of parishioners. Apart to one side, Michael Lambert removed his hat. Beside the grave lay an elegant oak casket.

One of the elderly slaves came to meet the two women. Emily concentrated on his leathery hand as Old Benton led her to the open casket. An irrational fear seized her that the heavy cover might suddenly fall shut. She did not stoop. Benton waited as she studied the face in the casket, the cheeks sunken in death and devoid of color.

Emily backed away, stumbling. Benton steadied her, then leaned forward to close the coffin. The ropes slid through the men's hands as it lowered into the earth. The businessmen stood apart. No one from the church came near her, not even Preacher Morton. Emily nodded to the dark, familiar faces around her and turned away. Through her grief, she felt Michael Lambert's gentle strength steadying her as he brought her back to the waiting women. Ginny followed.

"Mr. Lambert," she heard Adeline say as they approached. "Yet again."

Thomas Slate crouched retching at the far side of the wagon.

Book Three: Endurance

1861–1863

CHAPTER 22

Ginny jammed a stick of wood into the steadying fire. Her angular shoulders drooped above the long sag of her body. She closed the firebox, letting it clang. Her exhaustion mired her; she could not recover from the too-long night preparing Charles's and Hammond's ruined bodies. There had followed, without respite, the equally long day of wretched burials. Most nights since, she had slept in heavy unrest, waking more tired than when she lay down. She was steeped in death. To rouse herself, Ginny hummed, low and soft at first. Her voice swelled as she straightened to roll out the biscuits. Her humming and the rolling melded. The rhythm was comfort.

"Gin?" Rosa Claire stood in the doorway, a stuffed rag doll hanging at her side, feet bare, her nightgown askew.

"How you get out here to this kitchen all by yourself?" Ginny said.

No answer.

Ginny lay down the rolling pin and knelt, her aching arms outstretched. Glum, Rosa Claire twisted her feet.

"Come on, honey. Ginny got you."

Rosa Claire rose on tiptoe. The still-baby face brightened as she flew across the floor.

"Where your mama, child?"

No answer. Rosa Claire nestled her head on Ginny's shoulder. She tucked her doll tight under her arm and sucked her thumb. Ginny snuggled the little girl in one elbow while she stamped out rounds of biscuit.

"You all right, baby. Ginny got you now."

With her free hand, Ginny laid the raw biscuits one after another in orderly rows on a buttered baking sheet. She folded the scraps of dough, patted them, rolled them again. Rocking the child on her hip, Ginny stamped out three more biscuits and added them to the pan. She offered a pinch of raw dough to Rosa Claire. The little girl shook her head. Ginny popped the fragment of dough into her own mouth, sucking at its savory-sweet flavor.

"Ginny gone put you down now, baby. Got to slide these biscuits in. You stand way out behind me now so you don't get burnt. That's a good girl."

Adeline appeared and scooped up the child. Observing the breakfast progress, she laid her hand on Ginny's shoulder.

"Emily hasn't moved," Adeline said, and left the room.

Breakfast done, Ginny sat by the kitchen fire, gathering herself for the task ahead. After a while she stood and made her way into the house.

The hinges creaked as Ginny opened the bedroom door. The press of the room assailed her: stale air, disheveled bedding, lank strands of matted hair across the coarse ticking of the pillow. The pillowcase, with its incongruous flowered embroidery, lay wadded on the floor. Ginny hardly responded to the tug on her skirts, then twisted and knelt, shielding Rosa Claire from seeing her mother. Ginny wrapped her arms around the girl, nuzzled her cheek, and whispered, "You go on out to the porch now, honey. And don't make no noise doing it. Mama's asleep."

Ginny smoothed the collar of Rosa Claire's jacket. She stood and propelled the child toward the porch, monitoring her faltering steps. Rosa Claire turned back, a silent plea on her little face, but Ginny shooed her on. "Go on now, child. You go rock your baby doll in the sunshine. That baby need some sunshine."

Though it was now December, the front door stood ajar. The warmth of the winter day was unremarkable so deep in the South, though recent extremes of weather had created a certain desperation among the farmers. Today, however, was balmy, and the child collapsed in a folded knot on the porch floor, the doll akimbo under her elbow, thumb in her mouth. Ginny slipped back into the room where Emily lay.

"Miss Emily," she said. There was no response. "Miss Emily," firmer now, "you got to get up. You got a baby needs you out there. And another one gone need you soon enough. If you gone live, and I expects you is, then living's what you got to do. And this ain't no kind of living." Still no shift, no response at all.

Ginny propped up the window sash, tied back the muslin curtain, untied and retied it. Something in arranging the curtain pulled aside a barrier in herself. She sat down on the side of the bed, her narrow back upright. She adjusted her hips, took a deep breath, and spoke into the thin air.

"I'm gone talk to you, Miss Emily. I got something to say. You can listen or not." She raised her chin, leaned a bit straighter. "You got to give up this bed, honey. You can't do this no more, not to that baby out there on that porch, sucking her thumb, and not to me." Had she said that? "What happened to you ought not happen to nobody on earth and that's the Lord's truth. But you ain't by yourself. Not by a heap. This slavery, this war—well, never mind about that right now. That's too much for either one of us. I'm gone talk about me. What happened to me ought not happen to nobody neither."

Emily did not move. Nor give any sign of hearing.

"I ain't unhappy amongst you. Better here than anywhere else." Ginny's voice was hoarse with tension, her tall back supported by her hands on her knees. "I got no complaints. Your daddy always treat me good. Taught me to read and write. You and me had us a talk on that. Your daddy tried to set us free. Didn't happen. Now he's gone. You been good to me, too. All you been good to me. Not like where I come from. They's things that happened there I don't talk about. Whippings, lashings, all kinds of other things." She paused. "They took my mama, Miss Emily. Me no more than four or five years old, and not much bigger than your baby child out there."

Ginny rubbed her hands over her knees; her eyes scanned the room.

"I don't know nothing 'bout my daddy. Trader took him was all my mama ever say. Might of just been some breeding buck. Don't have one thing to remember him, not even a name. But I remember my mama. Standing on that block half-naked. Some man snatch me right out of her arms and her reaching for me, screaming, crying. Driver lash her then, but she don't stop crying. Load her off in a wagon, chained up. Still crying, holding out her arms after me, chains clanking. Won't never get over her crying. Won't never get over remembering her. Nor wanting her. Don't nobody get past wanting their mama. Like you, so little, when I first come here. Like Rosa Claire out there on that porch. Curled up, trying to hold on to herself by a thumb, wanting her mama. Wanting you."

Ginny shifted her weight, took a deep breath, let it out.

"I know you be wanting them others. Your daddy, maybe your husband. I know you be wanting your mama, too. They ain't here. They gone. And they ain't coming back. But, Rosa Claire, she's here. Out there wanting you, like you wanting them, like me wanting my mama forever. They ain't no end to such wanting, Miss Emily. You just got to live with the wanting." She stood and walked away from the bed.

Ginny steadied herself on the doorframe. Down the hall

through the open front door, she could see Rosa Claire on the porch, folded in on herself, seeming to sleep. Ginny arched her back and dragged herself to the back porch, her eyes roving the ragged fields beyond. At the churn, she rubbed her palms up and down the cool sides of the blue and gray pottery, took the dasher in her hand, hummed herself into the rhythm of the coming butter.

Emily lay in the dimness of the room. In the air around her, Ginny's words hovered fine as spider webs, catching bits of light. From somewhere beyond her, the faint sounds of the farm mingled with Ginny's humming and the steady heartbeat of the churn. Emily surrendered to the sounds of the day. The cadence of the churn hushed. The cooing of a dove caught in the web of Ginny's words, rending a small tear in the stillness. Emily opened her eyes, rolled her face to the window, where the edge of the muslin wavered in a breath of air. Outside, the bare branches of a low-growing crepe myrtle fractured the light. Emily's paralysis lifted. Here and there her hollow emptiness absorbed bits of commonplace life: the scrape of Ginny's stool across the floor, the slosh of the buttermilk into a pail, the low mooing of a cow in the far pasture, the faraway clang of a gate. Under the porch a kitten mewed and its mother answered. Something maternal in the sound propelled Emily to rise.

The slanted sun through the window warmed Emily as she put her foot on the cool floor. Holding the wall for support, she inched along the hallway to the porch toward the crumpled form of her daughter. When Emily neared, Rosa Claire's little body twitched and she stuck her thumb back in her mouth. Emily lowered herself around the child's body, cocooning it with the bulge of her abdomen on the hard floorboards. Emily inhaled the milky scent of her daughter, brushed the pale, slightly sour hair back from her face. The unborn infant turned inside Emily, as Rosa Claire stirred in her arms. They lay there, all of them: fatherless, husbandless, together, alone.

* * *

"What's his name, Mama?" Rosa Claire whispered, leaning over the baby's wrinkled face. The window was open to the ongoing warmth of December; a breeze ruffled the curtain, still tied as Ginny had left it days ago.

"I don't know, sweetheart." Emily tugged at the strands of hair caught on the pillow behind her, pulled on her ear. Rosa Claire laid her hand over the baby's, which curled around the edge of a worn blanket that had only recently been hers.

"He got to have a name. Don't he, Mama?"

"Doesn't he," Emily corrected. "Of course, and he will when I rightly know what it is. You wouldn't want Mama to go giving him the wrong name, now would you?"

"I have a name. How you know, Mama?"

"You told it to me."

"I talk?" Rosa Claire stared up at her mother's face, letting go of the baby's hand.

"No, you told me with your heart. Rosa Claire. Like a sweet little coral rose that blooms and blooms. And that's how I knew who you were."

Rosa Claire was silent. She looked down at the baby's 'old man' face. "Daddy know his name?"

When Emily did not answer, the child looked up to see if her mama was still with her. Emily caught her breath and spoke.

"No, honey. I don't think he would. I'd like to think so. But I don't."

"Where Daddy? Won't he never come back?"

"Ever," Emily corrected. "No, Rosa Claire, he won't ever come back."

"Mama, you come back. Auntie Gin bring you back for me."

Emily brushed the soft curls away from her daughter's face, away from the innocence of the gray-green eyes with their too-long lashes.

"Yes, I did," Emily said at last. She remembered the hard boards of the porch floor against her hip and shoulder, the warm curve of her daughter's body in the morning sunlight. Yes, she thought, she had, incomprehensibly, come back.

The birth had gone easy. Emily, moved beyond her fear, had cared little what might come to her or of her. So much had overcome her now. She let it happen as it would, listless with exhaustion between contractions. It was only the head, in the end, that split her, riveted her into nowhere that was not pain. And then he slithered out, leaving his mother behind him. He dropped into the waiting hands of Adeline and Ginny, both of them crooning, their motion blending, though their voices did not, while Emily reached for the hardly human little body, all blood and mucus, this child that was hers alone.

Emily stilled herself in that memory. And then she spoke to Rosa Claire.

"His name is Alonso, but that's too old a name for him just now. So, Lonso, meet your sister." Emily pulled the blanket from his wrinkled face.

"He tell you?" Rosa Claire's little voice was all awe.

"Yes, baby girl. He told me a secret. About being alone and then I knew his name."

"No, Mama. He got me! Got you, Mama. Got Gran and Ginny."

"I know, honey. But no matter how many folks we've got, in the truth of it all, we are alone."

"I not alone, Mama."

"Not that you know of, baby. Not that you know of yet."

Satisfied, the child lay her head beside the sleeping bundle in her mother's lap. Her fingers caressed the soft, frayed edge of the blanket that still felt like hers. She thrust her thumb into her mouth. Her breathing slowed as she comforted herself into sleep.

They were there like that, the three of them joined in their separate slumber, when Adeline came in. Before she eased the door shut again, she stood for a moment, beset by this momentary respite from grief.

"I'm afraid you've come for naught," Adeline said, returning to her parlor, where Michael Lambert stood, curling the brim of his hat. "Emily is still in bed and they are all sleeping. I'll tell her you came to ask after her."

"Thank you, ma'am." Lambert seemed not to know where to put his eyes or his feet. "Fact is, I brought something she might need. Then again she might not, having Rosa Claire already. So, you can tell me straight out if it is going to be in the way and I'll just take it on back home." He shifted his lanky body from foot to foot, ducked his head and lifted it. "It's my mama's rocking chair," he said. "Been out in the shed a while now. Didn't Asa or me either need it, two old bachelors getting by with one another, and it didn't fit either one of us. It was in some disrepair, from the years, you know. But I cleaned it up, glued it, laid a new finish on. I tried it out, and even with my big frame, not a squeak in the joints. But she might not need it. Might just be in the way."

From the porch, Lambert returned with a spindled lady's rocker. Adeline's throat constricted as she walked around it, flooded with memories of rocking her baby boys. The chair tilted back as she ran her fingers over its surface, absorbing the care he had given to its restoration.

"We do have a rocking chair, Mr. Lambert," Adeline said at last. "But we can use another now that there are two to soothe. Rosa Claire's hardly more than a baby herself. This will help her not to feel left out." Adeline's palm roamed the smooth edge. "You've put a lot of work in this. I'm sure Emily will be grateful."

He nodded and turned for the door.

"Mr. Lambert." Adeline's voice wavered.

He pivoted, lowered the hat, clenched it in his hands again.

Adeline took a deep breath and gathered herself. "I understand you took Sheriff Johnson home with you. That you and your brother have been taking care of him."

"Well, mostly it would be Asa deserves the credit there, I expect. It was Asa dug out the bullet. Stuck in a rib. After that, I guess it was just Mason's own healing did most of the work."

"I expect it took a bit more than that. Healing is never so simple."

"Yes, ma'am." He cleared his throat.

"Mr. Lambert—" Adeline hesitated. "We are in your debt. Both myself and Emily." She sucked in a sharp breath. "I am not sure how I would have—"

Lambert bowed his head and stared at the floor.

"And then . . ." Adeline's voice trailed off. At last she said, "I walked out to the graveyard the other day. I saw the crosses." He waited. "They are well crafted."

Lambert raised his dark eyes and cleared his throat again.

Adeline stared through his painful awkwardness and said, "It's only gratitude, Mr. Lambert."

"Yes, ma'am." He clutched and unclutched the brim of his hat, raised it to his head, and reached for the door. Bumping the rocker, he reached out to steady its clumsy, unoccupied tilt.

Chapter 23

Lambert stabled the mule, pulled his coat around his neck, and headed toward the house he shared with his brother, Asa. When their parents died months apart after more than forty years of marriage, the two maintained the farm and house together. Asa was the elder. Even now, he took a protective stance toward his younger brother, amusing most days, but considerably annoying on others. Michael Lambert, who had come to be called by his last name, tended the chickens and collected the eggs, but it was Asa on whom it fell to kill them. Lambert fried them up, crisp and salty. Though Lambert was always at hand in October to help slaughter the hogs, he had a tenderness toward the chickens, almost as much as for the tricolor shepherd, who followed him most everywhere he went. The Lambert boys had become two old bachelors, taking care of life and of each other: companionable, incisive, industrious, respected in the community and beyond.

Asa was the primary cook, except for the Sunday chicken, and had quite a way with ham and vegetables. Good at crisping cornbread, too. During the sheriff's convalescence, the brothers brought the supper plates into the bedroom until Mason could join them at the table. When he was on his feet again, the three lingered over supper by the fire, long silences interspersing their comments. The war news from the upper east confounded them.

"Well, we may have us a president," Asa said. He folded his napkin, pressed his fingernail along the crease, and laid it beside his place, ready for next morning. "Leastways, this Confederacy does, but looks to me like he's presiding over doom—all these defeats. An unworthy cause. Union is looking strong."

"How many now?" asked Mason. "Fort Henry, Roanoke Island, Fort Donelson. Lost three key defenses—gives the Union an open door on the Tennessee, the Cumberland, and a good part of the coast."

"And Grant driving for unconditional surrender. Hear that's the nickname his initials stand for these days."

"Not looking hopeful," said Asa. "I don't understand this war."

"Nor I," said Lambert. "The will to maim and kill confounds me."

"The will to violence doesn't require war," said Mason. "Jeremiah Matthews, prime example."

"You are right about that," said Asa. "And you victim to it, too. Goddamned coward, running off to the Confederates. Right in the face of his daddy's memory and all he stood for. Can't you send some bounties?"

"Now, Asa, you know damn well I can't do that. Illegal, first of all, and crazy as hell to boot. You figure I go creeping 'round those troops to find him and they just turn over a rich, slave-owning planter to some jackleg sheriff like me? The man's got more protection now than Jeff Davis himself. They'd have me scripted before I got my mouth open."

"I know, I know. Just wrong, is what it is. Man getting away with murder. Maybe he'll get him a Yankee bullet. War just seems like such a separate thing, alienated from life someway."

"Well, for the moment, it also seems distant," said Mason. "It's all happening a hell of a ways from us to be so absolutely about us. Like a bad dream come real somehow. Like you want to just wake up from it. Of course I feel that way about a lot that goes on right here in town. Good folks and wild folks all drawn to frontier promise. Including me, I reckon."

"You mighty quiet, Michael," Asa said, probably the only person to call Lambert by his given name.

"I'm just listening."

"You take Mama's chair to the widow?"

"I did."

"She like it? All that work you put in it?"

"I don't know. She's not doing well, I gather. Just gave it to Adeline."

"Don't know anyone who could do well after such violence as that," said Mason. "How was Adeline?"

"Seemed sturdy enough; holding up, I reckon. Asked about you, Mason."

Asa maneuvered a toothpick between his back teeth. He studied both men without speaking and grinned. Lambert shook his head, slapped the tabletop, and rose.

"I'm turning in," he said. "Asa, make sure your patient there gets some sleep."

The always irregular post arrived. Adeline did not recognize the slave who brought the letter to Emily, nor the handwriting. But she recognized the fear and the sick blanching of Emily's face at the sight of the soiled envelope. Adeline bent to take the baby and left Emily, the letter trembling in her fingers.

Vicksburg
January 3, 1862

Sister,

I am enlisted in the Confederate Army, fortunately stationed near Vicksburg, where I reckon myself to be safe, though we move at inconsistent command. We are well positioned and our forces set at all costs to defend control of the Mississippi River, and we shall most certainly not fail. Vicksburg is unconquerable.

The weather is exceedingly cold and miserable. I have never known our South to be so wretched. As I departed in more haste than convenient, having avenged our father's death and at the risk of my life, my two heaviest coats must be posted at once. Use the address on the envelope. The rains have been terrible and the sloughs are now frozen over, so that movement of the troops is treacherous both from the ice itself and from its breakage.

I must reconfirm to you that it is I who am primary heir to our father's land and estate. Do not take my absence as your personal opportunity to misuse my property nor to misadminister it. It is your duty to obey my wishes, and you will answer to me for full responsibility of my property's care.

See that you do not fail.

Jeremiah Matthews
Proprietor

Emily's breath came short and fast. The letter lay precariously on her lap as her fingers gripped the arms of the chair. Jeremiah, the brother for whom her mother had died. A boy and now a man for whom no one should die. Jeremiah, who had taunted her all his life, made her wretched with his slights and outright insults, so unlike sweet Will. Jeremiah, still alive, and the brother she had loved so dearly gone, along with half her life. Now he goaded her from afar and insulted their father by joining Confederate forces, fighting against their father's undying allegiance to the Union. Bragging to her that he had avenged their father's death with this violence and tragedy and injustice. And now to pose himself in their father's place? *His treachery is complete,* she thought, *and has no limits.* Her body filled with a wounded hatred she made no attempt to abate.

Emily ripped the letter in half. She tapped the pieces against her fingers, then tossed them into the fire. The paper caught, the torn edges charring, flaming. Fragments of the blazing words lifted in the draft and floated, directionless, onto the hearth. Emily kicked at them with the side of her foot, then stamped at those remaining, the sole of her boot hard against the brick. When her breathing had slowed, Emily went to Ginny with instructions for Benjamin regarding coats and blankets and provisions. And then she went to fetch her baby from Adeline.

A feeble January sun labored to lift the heavy fog, but failed to burn it off. The week had come and gone, and with it a tense continuation of life. It was Monday. The fire under the wash pot had reduced to embers, as Ginny slipped clothespins over the last of the sheets, diapers, and Emily's pads, each discreetly covered by a diaper. They would all smell of smoke, she thought. Ginny retrieved the turning stick and propped it against the house. She ran her hands down the smooth wetness of a petticoat as she turned to the kitchen chores and dinner cooking. She was alarmed to find Adeline distraught and pacing. *Ain't like her,* Ginny thought. Then she saw the knife from under the seat of the wagon. Adeline's hands curled and uncurled around it, blood spreading from the dark blade across her roughened skin.

"Here, Miss Adeline." Ginny held out her hand. "You give that to me."

"What on God's earth was he doing with it?" Adeline rubbed at her forehead with the back of her bleeding hand, the knife dangling loosely from her curled fingers. "He just cut some damned old thing and handed it off to me like it was nothing. Like it was nothing at all. How in God's name could he do that?"

Ginny understood immediately that Adeline meant Thomas, who must have pulled the knife from the wagon seat, unaware, uncaring, or both.

"I have to be shed of this thing, Ginny." Adeline's eyes pleaded, her face distorted with grief, but she continued to grip the knife.

"I got it, Miss Adeline."

Ginny took hold of the knife with one hand. With the other, she tucked a few graying hairs from Adeline's face. Adeline whirled, the knife clattering to the floor. She kicked at it and it spun away, its heavy handle leading. Ginny stood very still.

"Bury that thing, Ginny." Adeline grasped at the table for balance. "Take it somewhere I won't ever come near. Somewhere I won't ever know. Just get it gone."

The knife was old and worn, sharpened untold times, with a nick in the blade near the handle. Ginny felt the burden, the shocking heft of it. She walked into the yard past the laundry, holding the weight of what Mr. Thomas had done. Out past the lower field, deep in a grove of long pines adjacent to an ancient oak, Ginny dug into a dense bed of moss. The smell of damp earth rose around her fingers. She placed the knife in the depression, stood back, evaluating, then bent and retrieved it. Deeper, then deeper, Ginny dug. *Could be setting a fencepost,* she thought. Blade down, she thrust the knife into the ground. Dirt and moss replaced, Ginny studied the spot. She raised her eyes to the surrounding trees and the sky beyond, visible now that the fog had finally burned off. A bit of light shone through the trees. Ginny laid a flat rock over the disturbed earth, wiped her hands, and returned to her chores, as Adeline had to hers.

The days passed. The children slept, woke, ate. Soiled clothes got washed and dried and soiled again. Ginny observed a cycle of precarious tolerance set in, held together on the spare framework of habitual civility. Moments of temporary delight broke through the darkness that encompassed Adeline: Ginny watched her respond to Rosa Claire's laughter, saw Adeline's disconnection lift as she caught a kicking baby foot in the palm of her hand, recognized the blending of connection and loss as Adeline handed the baby back into his mother's arms. She saw how the touch of these women's hands in that exchange only separated them more. *A matter of time,* Ginny thought. *And it ain't long coming.*

Mason, recovered well enough to ride, brought the second letter. Its envelope was muddy and the address smeared, but legible. The weather was bleak.

"You know there's nothing I can do," he said. Adeline watched as he put it in her hand and turned back into the wind, his collar pulled high over his uncovered head.

The spindled rocker creaked slightly where Emily sat by the window, staring into the gray world as she nursed the baby. On the floor Rosa Claire devised a game of hide-and-seek, flipping the edge of her mother's skirt back and forth over her head. When Adeline entered, the little girl scooted under the skirts, waiting to be found, but Adeline only handed the envelope to Emily and left the room. Rosa Claire climbed out of her disappointment and hid herself behind the curtain.

Lonso's hand went limp against Emily's breast. She managed the letter into her pocket and disengaged her damp nipple. The baby's lips sucked at themselves in his sleep. Emily rose and propped him between the pillows on the bed. With her back to Rosa Claire, she said, "Please don't muss the curtains."

The child pouted to come out of her hiding place, but neither did she want to stay. She wanted to give that baby back to somebody. Lonso should be her name. Maybe Mama had heard it wrong. Her mother shooed her off to find Ginny. The child dragged her feet down the hall toward the light of the parlor fire, where Auntie Gin would smile at her. She glanced back to see her mother leaning against the wall with her hand in her pocket.

The mud on the envelope left grit on Emily's fingers. Alone now, she sat down in the rocker and dangled the letter at her side. Her fingers shook and she was tempted to toss it in the fire, a gesture of riddance to this brother who had forever been hateful. But he was her brother.

Near Port Gibson
January 18, 1862

Sister,

Again I take up my pen because your assistance is critical. My slave Ballard has succumbed to the fever, which is rampant in the camp. Consequently I lack the care of a man from home and suffer exhaustingly from it. Being that I remain primary heir to Father's estate, as I have reminded you already, and continue to have such rights thereof, I ask, even though I might demand, for you to send me a new man from among the slaves. I have no particular preference which among the inventory, other than that he be young, of reliable character, and strong. The food supply is abominable. There is much rot and mold, and the cold is excessive. One of my coats that just arrived has already been commandeered. Therefore, send a blanket as well. Or two. Whatever the man can handle. I need a ham and other such nonperishable foodstuff as he can carry, wrapped under careful concealment in clothing and the blankets. You will need to equip him with rations for a minimum of three days, a set of shirts and new underclothing from my goods, and papers of permission for him to travel. You will find a seal for the documents in Father's library.

I am encamped a few miles to the east of the town and whatever buck you send will have no difficulty locating me, although he will require the utmost care in travel and must beware of inquiries as he nears our embattled position so as not to jeopardize my provisions.

Jeremiah Matthews
Proprietor

CHAPTER 24

As the days dragged past, Emily and Adeline had little to say to one another, each in her own isolation, with nothing to speak of beyond the artificial. One evening, Emily noticed a hole in Rosa Claire's sock. Her darning stitches had not improved. She jabbed at the needle until at last she wadded the sock and threw it into the fire. The time had come to leave.

Their parting was strained: Emily and Adeline left unspoken the web of causes and blame. Emily loaded her children and traveled home to the vacancy of her life.

As the weeks passed and winter surrendered its cold, she caught her reflection one afternoon in the window. She took a deep breath. The habit of life. She sat down by the window, fingering the drape and blinking at the light. The world was there. It would continue to be there, with or without her. If she were to live, it must be beyond the habitual.

Half an hour passed before she went to find Ginny in the library.

"I am going to town," she said. "Tell Lucian to hitch the buggy."

Ginny busied herself with the feather duster as if she had not heard.

"Did you hear me?" Emily said.

"You ain't got no business out there by yourself," Ginny said at last. "There's a war on, even if it ain't hereabouts. They's gangs roaming the country, hunting runaways and such. It ain't like it used to be, case you ain't noticed. And I guess you ain't had call to notice."

"Ginny, you talk to me as if I were your child," Emily said.

"Just about, Miss Emily. Especially if you take leave of your senses."

"I am going, Ginny. We are fortunate enough to have a warm spell and I cannot remain closed in this house the rest of my life. You are the very one who told me I must choose to live. The longer I put it off, the more difficult it becomes."

Tapping the feather duster against her apron, Ginny studied her mistress.

"You sure about this? You ain't got to do it this way." Ginny took a book from the table and slipped it into the shelves.

"I'm sure, Ginny," Emily said. She took the duster from Ginny and laid it on the table where the book had been. "Now give me a list: thread, black silk yardage, if it's to be had, what else? And how much silk? Oh, and buttons, or were you able to find some in the trunk among Mama's things?"

"I found them. All you need is yardage and thread. And some muslin for lining. For sure, you do need a spare black dress. I can make another set of cuffs and a collar for that one you wearing. Spruce it up. But that ain't lasting a year." Ginny untied her apron. "I'm going with you. Don't be looking like that. You can drive if you want."

The creak of the buggy and the jangling traces soothed Emily's anxiety as they rode, the familiar sounds lulling her into the ride itself and away from its destination. Beside her, Ginny hummed. Overhead, pale-leafed trees interlaced along the drive. Near the edge of the farm, several fence posts tilted, tugging each other toward the ground. *One brings down the other,* Emily thought. Repairs to make note of. Cows grazed in the pasture, its green dotted with yellow dandelion, the bucolic scene as indifferent to the war as to her pain.

Along the way, men and women bent over their work in the fields, their color blending into the new, plowed earth. A blush of early leaves—green, pale yellow, and melon—softened the treetops along the boundary lines. Houses appeared, set close, like friends stopped on an outing to gossip. On the wide porch of a faded white house, a woman knitted from a ball of purple yarn, a small dog at her feet. As the buggy neared, the dog commenced yapping. The woman looked up, gathered her work, and disappeared into the house, calling the dog. Farther along, a thin black woman in yellow calico tidied a front walk. She leaned on her broom and peered over the gate. A male slave left off trimming a hedge and lounged beside her, staring. From porches and gardens, as the buggy passed, a rolling hush accentuated the rasp of the wheels and trailed the two women into the town and along the boardwalks, where townspeople stopped to stare or darted into storefronts.

Though her hands trembled, Emily nodded at the spectators. She stopped the buggy in front of Chaney's Mercantile and stepped down. Ginny followed.

In the dim interior of the store, a handful of women, two of whom Emily recognized from church, broke off their transactions and disappeared. A young woman dropped a handful of Confederate dollars on the counter and left without her change. The blacksmith's wife whispered hasty instructions for her purchase to be charged and was gone. Within minutes, Emily found herself the sole customer. Mrs. Chaney vanished behind the brown plaid curtain at the rear of the store, while Chaney himself cut nine yards of black silk serge and four of cotton bodice lining. Ginny reminded Emily of a packet of needles and three spools of thread, cotton in the absence of silk. Chaney took the fifty-dollar Confederate bill from Emily, returning her four. When she thanked him by name, he raised his eyes and nodded.

"I'm real sorry, Mrs. Slate," he said. She returned the nod.

All three turned as the bell on the door tinkled and a man's footsteps echoed across the wooden floor.

"Nice day," Lambert said. "We can use an early spring." He removed his hat and nodded to Emily. "Mrs. Slate. Ginny."

"How you do, Mr. Lambert," Ginny said, a gentle smile playing across her narrow face.

"I'm well, thank you, especially this nice day." He turned to Chaney. "Needing some shirt buttons, please, sir. Howdy, Mrs. Chaney." He nodded toward a crack in the plaid curtain, which promptly fell closed. "Asa is a hard man on buttons. If they were seeds, we'd have us an orchard of button trees by now." He laid some coins on the counter and Chaney produced a card of buttons. "You ladies leaving? I'll walk you out, if you don't mind the company."

Emily's uncertainty was apparent, but she felt immense gratitude as Lambert took her arm and escorted her toward the door. He assisted her into the buggy and handed up the reins. As Emily pulled away, Ginny was aware of him standing alone in the empty street.

"Funny thing to think of two old bachelors sewing lost buttons back on their shirts," Emily said as they turned the corner. "I never thought about such a thing."

"Reckon somebody got to do it." Ginny had seen Mr. Lambert about to mount his horse as they entered the town. She knew he had seen the townspeople scatter. She had watched him hesitate and loop the horse's reins at the post again. "Reckon a man who sews on his brother's buttons might be a handy kind of man to have around."

As she turned off the main street, Emily regarded the empty

boardwalks. She had not considered how any one of these townsmen might have been in the mob that night. And if not, they would know who had been. An unknown number of these men had seen Hammond shot and her husband hanged. They knew the name of the man who had put the noose around Charles's neck: a name she was more and more sure was Jeremiah.

"Mama?"

Adeline heard the door and sighed. *Why*, she thought. *Why*? She lifted her soapy hands from the dishpan and dried them on her apron. Adeline was keenly aware of the click of Belinda's boots in the hall. She was lugging a picnic basket covered with a hemstitched linen napkin. Adeline shook her head, the motion almost imperceptible. She picked up a frayed tablecloth and followed her daughter outside, spread the cloth on the ground under the arching branches of a nearby pecan. Belinda's attempts to help simply got in the way.

"I'll do it, Belinda."

Above them pale wisps of cloud shredded the sky.

The two ate little, spoke of the weather and planting time, touched with restraint on the difficulties of Belinda managing her farm on her own. They fell silent and stared away from one another.

Finally, Adeline uttered the unspoken question that hung in the air between them. "Where were you, Belinda?"

"Where was I?" Belinda's voice was almost a shriek. "What do you mean, where was I? I was there. How dare you ask that?"

Adeline steadied herself. "You were there, Belinda?"

"Of course, I was there. You know I saw it. All of it. Blood everywhere. You had to know, Mama. Benjamin had to tell you so." Belinda put her hand over her mouth and caught her breath. She looked at her mother as if afraid. "Charles had to tell you."

Now Adeline's breath caught in her throat. Time stopped. Charles? Charles had been in his coffin. "I was asking why you weren't at the cemetery, Belinda," she said at last.

"Oh—oh, the cemetery. Oh, yes, of course. The cemetery." Belinda sat back, her voice steadying. Belinda did not answer. She twisted the corner of the napkin.

"I was there," Belinda said at last. "In the woods. By the cemetery. Watching. I couldn't bear to see it and hear it after what I—" Belinda pulled at the grass. "I couldn't. So, I just walked off in the woods."

Adeline kept still.

"I walked around and around. Just walked. I couldn't get it all out of my head and I didn't know what to do. I kicked things—twigs and acorns and pinecones."

Adeline waited. She had seen Belinda kick things. Sometimes they were alive.

"I kicked a tree. I kicked a lot of things." Her voice was rising. "I bruised my foot and ruined my boot. I got myself lost and somewhere out there I wrapped my arms around a tree and the bark was all rough and it scratched my cheek. It hurt, but I didn't care. It was too much, too much. The judge and then my brothers. God. I had to hold on to something, do you see?"

Adeline nodded. *But it was not you who lost all you had*, she thought.

"I must have cried. Well, yes, of course, I cried. How could I not have cried? I cried for a long time. It seemed like my fault. And then I went home." Belinda plucked a clover blossom and began to pick at the petals, dropping them one by one into her lap.

Adeline studied the horizon. "Was it, Belinda? Your fault?"

Belinda ignored the question. "Later, sometime, I don't know—just later—I went out to the graves. I stood there forever. It was so horrible. That dirt all raw and red like a bloody wound and mounded up, except for Will's."

"Stop it, Belinda." There were tears on Adeline's cheek. Her voice cracked. "Just stop."

"Oh, Mama, I don't know what I'm doing here." Belinda began snatching at the picnic things. "I shouldn't have come. I don't know why I did. I needed to know if you would still see me. I just needed after—"

"Belinda, I can't hear these things."

"But I need you to hear me." Belinda's voice took on an air of desperation. She hesitated, then plunged ahead. "I stayed there a good long time. Not too long, though. And not good, either. Then, I came to see you, Mama. You were sitting in your rocker. You looked up at me when I came in, but you did not open your mouth. You did not get up and hold me. I stood so long in front of the fire, and after you never said a word to me, I left." She waited. "And now I have come back."

Belinda covered her face and sobbed. Adeline let her.

CHAPTER 25

Emily twisted the key in the latch. The door swung open on its own. It had not been locked. Inside, everything was dark. She waited for her eyes to adjust to the gloom. Her husband's desk, his chair, his books, his examining table engulfed her in their undertow. The weight of the room pulled her down into his chair with its squeaking spring, the leather molded to his shape. She, too, had molded herself to him, Emily thought.

The leather of the chair was cool against her back, and the emptiness of the office matched her own. She sat, feeling the shape of him. Outside, Ginny called to Rosa Claire, and Emily roused, uncertain how long she had been lost in apathy.

Behind the desk, bookshelves overflowed, but with a sense of purpose and order. Volumes of medical texts and professional materials lay on the floor in neat piles, separated by category. Above the shelves hung his diploma, its elegant script declaring: *Charles Harvey Slate, Doctor of Medicine.* The desk was wide and cumbersome. Across its surface, the wood grain rippled like the markings of an untamed animal. In the window, a delicate circular pull dangled from the partially closed shade.

She had tatted it herself, under the tutelage of Adeline. Emily stood up, walked to the window, and yanked at it. The shade clattered to the top of the window, the pull swinging wildly. Sunlight glared into the room.

From the bookshelves behind her, Emily removed one volume after another, glancing at titles and an occasional inscription. Once or twice she recognized Adeline's hand and lay the book aside. Benjamin had assembled three wooden crates for her. They would not suffice. Charles's library was more extensive than she had thought. She would ship the books to his college in some feeble impulse toward redemption.

Somewhere near mid-morning, she stood and stretched, hands pressed hard into the small of her throbbing back. The remainder could wait. Why had she refused Benjamin's offer to spare her this chore?

As she walked the path back toward the house, she caught sight of Ginny hanging wash and Rosa Claire frolicking under the dripping laundry. The child halted beneath a clean petticoat, head back, mouth open, trying to catch the drops from its ruffled hem. When a dribble landed on her forehead and ran down the side of her nose, Rosa Claire squealed, threw her arms around Ginny's leg, ducked her head into Ginny's skirts. As two little hands lifted the skirts in the rear, Ginny shimmied and twisted. She spread her long legs, as a halo of soft blond curls peeked from under the front of her apron. When Rosa Claire emerged, she spied her mother and came racing, arms outspread. *He will never see her like this*, Emily thought, as she swooped the child aloft. *Nor will my father.* Rosa Claire pouted at the suddenness with which her mother set her back on the ground.

"Would you like some buttermilk?" Emily asked, taking the child's hand. Rosa Claire nodded, scurrying to keep up with her mother. Jessie had finished churning and a blue pitcher of buttermilk sat on the porch table. Emily poured two small glasses and carried them outside, where Rosa Claire was conversing with a make-believe prince. As Rosa Claire finished her drink, Emily was struck by her innocence, by their mutual vulnerability. Emily rose and shooed her back to the yard, where Ginny stood stretching. The milky glasses were slippery in Emily's fingers. She left them on the edge of the porch and walked back to her task.

Reentering the office, Emily had an impression the air had thinned in the intensified light. She was exhausted. The buttermilk and the moments with Rosa Claire had not refreshed, but oppressed her. Benjamin had been here in her absence. Additional crates were stacked, empty and waiting. Emily worked on into the long afternoon, now and then pulling at her ear or biting a fingernail. Collecting the last of the heavy medical books, she picked up a text on botanical remedies. *How like him*, she thought. The volume opened to a thin white envelope, its seal broken, the end folded twice. The marked page bore an etching of foxglove.

Emily unfolded the envelope, releasing a cascade of tiny seeds into her palm. Holding the dark seeds in her open hand, she sank into the chair. Digitalis. Such memories of Charles, her first naïve impressions of him. Her memories of Will. Emily focused her eyes and began to read. She skimmed the folklore of wicked fairies. Her breathing shallowed. Feeling faint, she pushed the book away, then pulled it back. Her fist closed around the seeds. Pressing the pages back, she continued reading:

> *Although all parts of the plant are toxic, it has a use in modern medicine for heart conditions. . . .*

Emily half rose, rubbed her closed hand across her brow, spilling dark seeds across the page. She brushed at them. What seeds did not scatter invisibly across the dark surface of the desk cascaded into a thin black line in the galley of the book. Emily read on.

Digitalis must be administered by someone qualified in its use. Overdose or accumulation of digitalis leads to nausea, vertigo, depression, anxiety, visual hallucinations, coma, convulsions, followed by death . . .

Emily's mind emptied into a dark void between her ribs.

The blizzard of March 4, 1862, came on fast, covering the wet ground and the vulnerable growth of premature spring in a sludge of snow. Above the blanket of white, tips of early daffodils peeked out in iced casings like blown glass. Nothing moved about the place for days, except the hands, their homespun wool coats pulled high, struggling to keep the animals fed. In the house, Emily sat alone in her room, the door shut. She heard Rosa Claire laughing with Ginny, but she did not respond. She accepted the plates of food that Ginny placed in her hands. She ate, but did not taste. She watched Ginny stoke and feed the fire, but did not reply to her random comments. On the warm day the snow melted, Emily rose, took her shawl, and left the house.

Mud from the thaw sucked at her boots. She trudged on, eyes raw from the wind. She pulled her woolen scarf across her face. Broom sedge tugged at her skirts. Her ankle turned and Emily bit her lip. But she did not slow her pace. By the time the Slate house came into sight, her thighs burned and she had a stitch in her side. She stooped and waited to get her breath.

There was no sign of life about the place. That meant nothing. Thomas Slate would be drunk somewhere, Belinda gone, Adeline somewhere at work. Wherever she was, Adeline would not be at rest. Emily straightened, wiped her palms down her skirt, and mounted the steps. She knocked. Waited. The door opened against the darkness of the house, and Adeline stepped into the light.

"Come in, Emily." No greeting, no surprise. "I'll make some tea."

Adeline did not wait for a response. Nor ask Emily why she had come. Perhaps she had expected this visit. Neither woman spoke as Adeline put the kettle on, added a stick of wood to the stove, and arranged a pair of cups and saucers on the worktable between them.

Emily's finger circled the chipped rim of the cup. She watched Adeline open the tin and scoop out the tea. She noted how little there was. She hesitated, felt the impulse to leave straightaway, but stopped, a brutal hardness bearing down in her.

"Did you know, Adeline?" Emily asked.

Adeline put the spoon on the table, hands on each side as if the table might hold her up. "Did I know what, Emily?" she said.

"Did you know what he did? Even before—"

Adeline looked up. The corner of Emily's mouth twitched.

"What he did at what point, Emily?"

"Did you?" Emily said again.

"I ask myself daily if I know anything at all. If I will ever know—"Adeline pushed the heels of her hands onto the edge of the worktable and shook her head. "I know that he tried."

"Tried what?"

Adeline picked up the kettle, set it down again. "He tried to take care of his sister," she said at last, her voice barely audible.

"And what about my brother?" Emily turned strident. "You were there. You knew. You could have stopped them."

"Hush, Emily. Stop now. These are my children. Charles was so full of remorse."

"For what? For killing Will?"

Adeline stared at Emily as if startled awake from a nightmare. "No, Emily. For failing to save him. For inexperience, incompetence even. For letting Belinda decide."

"For causing his death? Say it, Adeline."

"I can't say what I don't know, Emily."

"And you won't say what you do."

"Neither of us can ever know." Adeline reached out, her fingers wrapping Emily's wrist, but Emily wrenched from her grasp.

"Don't touch me," Emily said. "You are as well as dead to me. I will not mourn. I have had enough of mourning."

"And so have I," said Adeline, withdrawing her hand, "and all of it because of you."

Emily ran from the house and stumbled onto the road. Benjamin sat in the cart, waiting. He spoke to the mule and stepped down, his hand extended.

"I seen you leaving the house, Miss Emily. Ain't much reason for a stroll in this weather. I got hitched up and followed back behind."

Emily took his hand. Her strength withered and Benjamin pulled her up. From under the seat, he handed her an old wool blanket, gave the reins a flick, and turned, the wind behind them now.

Though the kitchen was warm, the world had gone cold. Adeline held on to the doorframe and slid to the floor. The boards were ungiving. She did not cry. No more than she had cried as a child, when her father whipped her for tears, when he shot her dog and turned on her, hand on his belt, saying, "Don't you cry." She remembered her terror that he might shoot her, too. She wished that he had.

It was Thomas who, after a while, found her, helped her to bed, where she lay unmoving. Sometime up in the afternoon, Belinda arrived. He must have sent for her. Why else would she be there? Adeline said she felt ill was all, same as she had told Thomas—but Belinda knew better. Belinda knew how he had found her after Emily left. Belinda went straight out the door, swearing. Adeline had never heard her so like Thomas. She heard the clank of the chains as the buckboard pulled away. Belinda was gone. Adeline turned on her side and curled the pillow under her arm.

The fine cotton filament from last fall's meager harvest spun out from Emily's unsteady hand. Tiny moats of fiber floated in the sunlight. She followed them with her eyes. The whirring of the wheel soothed her, stilled her thoughts. The repeating sound and motion lulled her mind. On the floor beside her lay two baskets lofted with finely carded cotton. Emily pulled one closer and pressed the pedal on the wheel.

The slamming door reverberated through the house. Emily rose and peered into the dim hall.

"Hello?" she called. "Who is it?"

Belinda was upon her, gripping her, shaking her.

"What in God's hell do you think you are doing?" Belinda screamed. "What have you been saying to my mama?"

Shock paralyzed Emily. She stared at the woman clutching her. Her cheek stung like hornets from Belinda's sudden blow.

"How dare you, you hateful slut!" Belinda shouted. "You witch! You wicked whore. What lies did you say to her?"

Emily crumbled in confusion, her eyes riveted on Belinda's contorted face. Emily slumped to the floor, propped up on one hand. With the other, she covered her burning face. Belinda crouched, her face so close that Emily could not focus her eyes.

"What did you say to my mother?" Belinda spoke each word as if it were a separate thing. She seized Emily by the shoulder and shoved her farther down. "You stay away from my mother, do you hear? You and your evil, twisted lies."

Belinda stood over her. "She is *my* mother. Mine!" Each word drove like a nail, driven into the room, into the house, into Emily. "You leave her alone. Do you hear me? I'm all she has left. You keep away from us, you evil, lying bitch."

She was gone.

Emily lay immobilized. She did not even weep. She pushed herself upright and stared around the room. *Where is my basket?* she thought. *I must finish my spinning. Two basketsful left to do. We will want to be weaving soon.*

Ginny found her at the spinning wheel, humming, when she entered later with an apron full of brown eggs. Emily did not look at her or speak, but continued to hum with the whir of the wheel, her eyes on the fine cotton filament as it flowed from her hand.

CHAPTER 26

The late spring, if it could be called that, brought with it news of Confederate defeats as the Union collected strategic control of vital strongholds: Pea Ridge and partial control of the Missouri and Mississippi rivers; Shiloh and the death of General Albert Sidney Johnston, one of the Confederacy's finest; and most crucial, control of the mouth of the Mississippi and the surrender of New Orleans. Only one victory enhanced the strength of the Confederacy: the routing of Union forces from Winchester, Virginia, and a victorious culmination to "Stonewall" Jackson's Shenandoah Valley Campaign. The weather was miserable, unseasonably cold and very wet, as if the land itself exuded the vast residue of death covering its surface.

In time the weather broke. Peals of laughter spilled in through the open window. Emily, tired of struggling with her stitches, tucked the needle into her sewing and stood. She pulled the curtain back to see Rosa Claire and Aimee lying on the ground, heads almost touching, the color of their skin barely distinguishable. Two toddlers squealing with delight. Their glee was contagious and Emily laughed, not knowing at what. By the time she went down the hall and out the front steps, Rosa Claire was sitting up, one arm outstretched, the other hand jiggling against it. Emily watched from a little distance as Aimee rose and fingered the back of Rosa Claire's hand.

"What do you have there, children?" Emily said after a few moments.

The children answered with wild giggles and pointing fingers. Kneeling beside Rosa Claire, Emily spotted the object of their hilarity. The caterpillar was black with fine pinstripes along its back and a bright yellow underbelly. Both tips were black and marked with white dots that looked like huge eyes.

"Look, Mama, it has two heads," Rosa Claire said, pointing. She could hardly get the words out between giggles.

"Well, now, just look at that," Emily said. "How do you think he knows which way to go?" She held her fingers against the top of Rosa Claire's hand while the caterpillar wriggled onto her hand. "Well, looks as if this head has the lead for now," she said. "Do you think he'll go the other way? Put your finger there, Aimee. Maybe he'll go the other way." When Aimee touched the opposite end, the caterpillar sped its way up Emily's wrist. "Well, now, he seems to like me, don't you think?" she said.

"But, Miss Emily," Aimee whispered, "don't he like me, too?"

"Of course, he does. How could he not? Here, put your finger here." Emily guided the child's finger so that the little creature crawled onto her hand.

"Make him go this way, Mama," Rosa Claire cried. She put her finger at the other end, but the caterpillar did not change direction. "Don't he like me, too, Mama?"

"Put your hand the way he is going," her mother said.

"But I want him to use his other head. See, Mama"—Rosa Claire pointed—"he's got two heads."

"What if it's only there to fool you?"

"Fool me? Why?"

"Well, maybe it isn't you he wants to fool, Rosa Claire. Maybe to fool something that might want to hurt him. Like a bird, perhaps."

"A bird?" Rosa Claire took the caterpillar back and dropped it into her hand. Aimee hovered over her, stuck out her finger to make a bridge. The caterpillar crossed between them.

"Well, you know the saying 'the early bird gets the worm.' Birds eat little bugs and caterpillars, but if they get the wrong end, or if they get confused by those big, false eyes, this one just might get away."

The caterpillar wriggled up Aimee's arm. Rosa Claire turned peevish at not having a turn and Aimee relinquished it into her hand, then ran to the edge of the yard and returned with a bit of moss and a handful of leaves. "The caterpillar needs a nest," she announced, and proceeded to create a circle of overlapping leaves centered with moss. Rosa Claire approved and was willing to give the caterpillar up to its "nest." She pulled at Aimee's hand and the two went running off to the other side of the house, leaving Emily and the caterpillar to each other's company. Emily watched them disappear. She looked down at the circle of leaves, the soft moss, and smiled. *If only I had another head,* she thought. *If I knew which way to go.*

Jessie lay between clean sheets on the four-poster bed Nathan had built anew for her. Aimee lay beside Jessie, her pale nose tight against her mother's skin. She loved her mother's rich scent, like yeast rolls set to rise. Across the room, Ginny pressed her hands to the window in the growing light, her soft pink nails luminous against the chocolate of her fingers. She rotated her wrist, comparing the blush of her palm to her nails in the colorless dawn. Behind her, Ginny heard the child stirring.

As she turned, Ginny was struck by the image: the dark

mother with her childlike appearance, and the pale child, her little hand curled into her mother's hair. Ginny tiptoed to the bed. Aimee looked up, curious, but Jessie did not wake. Aimee turned her face back to her mother's neck, inhaled, and surrendered herself to Ginny. Quietly, Ginny carried the child into the other room and nestled with her in the rocking chair by the fire.

"Your mama need rest now, baby." Aimee snuggled her head into Ginny's angular shoulder. "Mama gone sleep all day, I expect. So we gots to be real quiet. Your pappy coming before long. Gone take you up to Miss Emily's. Maybe she take you on a picnic with her—you and Lavinia and her childrens. You like that, baby?"

Aimee nodded without lifting her head.

The door of the cabin creaked and Nathan ducked into the warm room.

"How she doing, Ginny?"

"Quiet. Sleeping. Bleeding done stopped for now. Baby's gone, Nathan. Would have been a boy. Benjamin out working on a box and Lucian got a little grave dug. Out beside your arm. Jessie gone be all right."

Nathan rubbed his chilly hand against his pant leg and squatted by the fire. He stirred the embers with the iron poker. Standing up, he tousled Aimee's coppery hair. She twisted her face toward him and slid from Ginny's lap into his one-armed embrace. He began a little jig, humming and tapping his feet. Leaning back, Aimee giggled, ruffling his beard with both hands.

"You gone be a good girl for your pappy?"

A silent nod.

"All right, then. I expect we better get you fixed up. Ginny, put some yellow ribbon in this gal's hair, please, ma'am."

As he set Aimee down, Ginny studied Nathan's drawn face, the anguished look he hid from the little girl.

"Ain't gone be no more, is there, Ginny?" he said. "Why God give me a white slave daughter and there ain't gone be no more?"

"She gone be all right, Nathan." Ginny began to twist little strands of Aimee's hair.

Aimee, assuming the remark to be about her, said, "I be good, Pappy. Aimee a good girl."

"I know that, my honey bee. For sure, I do know that."

They watched Aimee down the steps, then skipping toward the lane, where she turned to wait for Ginny. Nathan moved back into the house. Ginny caught hold of his arm.

"She ain't gone be your last child, Nathan. I'm sorry about your boy, but Aimee ain't gone be your last. Jessie gone be all right and you gone have more babies of your own."

Emily drew aside the heavy curtain in the parlor, only to drop it again. Her mind darted in confusion as she paced the room. She sat and rose again. Every thought had its counter. She could no more still her mind than her feet. Emily turned from the window to see Ginny, watching from the doorway.

"What's got you going, Miss Emily?"

Emily merely shook her head and leaned against the window.

"How about some tea? Maybe some talking?"

When there was no response, Ginny went to fetch tea, leaving Emily to struggle with herself while the kettle heated. When Ginny returned with the tray, Emily was sitting on the divan. Ginny settled the tray on the table between them, took her own cup, and sat down.

"All right," Ginny said, and took a sip. "All right, now."

Emily sat back without touching the cup. "Ginny," she said, "I want Aimee to come and live in the house. I want to raise her."

"She ain't yours to raise, Miss Emily."

"I know that, Ginny. But she's almost totally white. I can give her a life she won't otherwise have."

"New Orleans full of white slaves. Lots of other places, too. What kind of gumption got into you?"

"The picnic, Ginny. The picnic last week. Watching Aimee with the children, seeing how like them she is."

"All God's childrens like that, Miss Emily. Ain't you seen that for yourself? You and me, playing together little."

"Oh, Ginny, of course. That isn't what I meant. I meant how she looks." She picked up the cup, set it back down. "Except for her hair, she could be one of my children."

"But she ain't one of your children. She's Jessie's child. Jessie losing this baby, what might be last. Conklin's harm ain't over, by far. And you thinking about taking another child from her. And all this time, I thought I knew you."

"Oh, Ginny, it's not to take her away. Of course not. It's to give her a life. Don't you see that?"

"What I see is—well, you asked me and I'm gone say it. What I see is privilege. White slaving privilege. You thinking you can do what you please with somebody else's child. That's a slaving mind, Miss Emily."

Emily stared into Ginny's eyes, the words and the truth penetrating. She did not look away when she nodded. There was a long silence before Ginny spoke again.

"Well, you could ask, Miss Emily. Ain't no harm asking."

Jessie and Nathan entered by the back door. Ginny brought them into the parlor and motioned for them to sit down. The two looked at one another and continued to stand. Ginny repeated the invitation to sit. As they settled uneasily on the edge of the fine chairs, Ginny served them tea from the silver service. No one looked in Emily's direction.

"I done told Jessie and Nathan your thoughts, Miss Emily. So no need to explain that part. You all just got to talk to one another." Ginny sat down and sipped her tea.

For long minutes the only sounds were the clink of cups and saucers, and the tinkling of spoons. At last, Nathan cleared his throat.

"I don't much know what to say, Miss Emily."

"No, Nathan, neither do I," said Emily. She waited. "Perhaps I should never have—however, I did. And now we must deal with this in the open."

"Yes'm."

Emily regarded Jessie, who had not raised her eyes from her cup. "I have no intention of taking your child from you, Jessie. Can you look up at me and believe that?"

Jessie looked up and, after a moment, nodded.

"I don't know what I thought, Jessie. It's all so complicated and strange. But I watched her with the children picnicking last week and I just felt how wrong it is that Aimee shouldn't have every opportunity my children have."

"Ain't that something every child should have?" Ginny said.

"Yes." Emily looked from one to the other. "Yes, it is. But you and I know we can't, I can't, change the world. That's why we are at war. I can only do the things that come to me to do, however small they may be."

"Changing our girl's life ain't nothing small, Miss Emily." Nathan's words struck hard. Emily nodded her head.

"They's too many things don't nobody know, Miss Emily. Not till too long after to make it right again. Every choice, we take a road we don't know. That girl love her mama like she love the air she breathe. She love me, too." Nathan saw that Emily heard him. "And ain't no assurance she ever be accepted among white folk. Especially not 'round here. Might be a lot worse life than the one she got already." Nathan rubbed his knee, then folded his hand over the stump of his arm. "Ain't no assurance she be accepted much among black folk, either. Maybe she won't have no place on earth where she belong."

Emily rose and walked to the back of the divan.

"All right," she said, "what about this? What if she comes to the house during the day? Jessie, you will be here with her. You are already in the house and she simply joins you. She studies with my children. She spends her days with us instead of at Auntie Mag's. She eats her primary meals here and learns her table etiquette. She will have all the advantages of the same training as my own children."

"But she gone live with us?" These were Jessie's first words.

"As long as she reasonably would in any case."

"Mayhap she get herself refined, she won't want to be with us." Nathan looked down at Jessie and she at him.

"All right," Jessie said. "Us gone ponder this and then we talk some more. May not be right soon, Miss Emily."

Three weeks passed before Jessie searched Emily out in her father's library. She stood inside the door, her eyes roving the shelves of books. She rested her gaze at Emily's questioning face, nodded, and left without a word.

Aimee took her place in the children's schoolroom and at the table with Emily's children. Jessie's presence was constant, and often Aimee, tired of studying, ran to play in her mother's shadow. No one coerced her one direction or another. The transition was almost unnoticeable, so easily did her time with the other children extend. In the evenings, she walked home with her mother, chattering about whatever had interested her most during the day. At the cabin, she regaled a tired Nathan with a running flow of fascinating new information and, in spite of fatigue, he absorbed it like a sponge.

Under her spade, the earthworm wriggled up through the disturbed surface and over a clod of dirt. Emily wiped her forehead and stood back. The worm was just slipping back into the sod when she bent to pick it up. She dropped her gloves on the ground, careful not to lose the worm. Its gentle twisting motion tickled her palm. For a moment she was a child again, her hand thrust into a small, rough bag full of worms, searching among the squirming bodies to capture one. She could hear her father's laughter and Benjamin's, could almost smell the scent of pipe tobacco as her father bent to examine the prize she held up to him. "Benjamin's taking me fishing," she had said. And Benjamin had.

Emily had been too squeamish to put her worm on the hook. She couldn't bear to hurt it, and Benjamin had to bait her line for her. She remembered looking away as he slipped it on the hook, but she had been elated, dancing and clapping, when a bit later, he pulled a flashing silver fish from the water. The skill of his thick fingers unhooking the fish fascinated her, as did the contrast of its metallic skin to the warm brown of his. She remembered with chagrin how she had asked in childish innocence if his fingers tasted like chocolate when he licked them. Laughing, he had rehooked the fish on a big ring submerged at the water's edge. Entranced by the fish and the sparkling water as it floundered about in the shallows, Emily had stepped into the creek and squatted beside it. Benjamin had made a big hullabaloo and lifted her dripping and kicking out of the creek. He had left the pole on the bank, grabbed up the fish and the bag of worms in one hand, her by the other, and taken her straight home. She remembered how her father had laughed and then, in relief, Benjamin also.

But after Benjamin had gone and Ginny had helped her into dry clothes and shoes, her father had sat with her in the parlor. She could see his stern face even now, warning her against entering the creek, or any water other than the bath. But as he talked, she also felt the freedom of the water washing over her body, its delightful cold, the tingling jolt of it splashing on her face. Emily had tried to honor her father's warning, which she interpreted as more dutiful than sincere. The water and the worms drew her like a magnet. She begged to go again, then again, until at last she tagged along with Benjamin whenever he went to fish, even if it meant an escape from the tutor. She learned to dig for the worms, bait her own hook, snag the bite when it came, and pull in her own catch. She learned to remove her shoes and stockings, tuck her skirts into her sash, and regale her father with tales that did not include wading in the shallows. And she learned that Benjamin would not tell a tale that differed from hers.

Now, dropping the worm into her apron pocket, Emily lugged the spade along toward the shed, where Benjamin was at work sharpening a plow blade. When he looked up, she jiggled an earthworm in the air, laughing. "I'd forgotten the fun we had," she said. "Put down that file and come with me to fetch the children."

Rosa Claire and Aimee were fascinated. Rosa Claire thrust it right under Aimee's nose, making her shriek, then giggle. Emily did not scold her.

The little group trooped off toward the creek. At the edge of the woods, Emily stopped and took the spade in spite of Ginny's protests. She thrust it into the rich earth. With only two jabs, a trove of worms appeared, and other bugs as well. Rosa Claire and Aimee vied with one another as they tallied up the worms they let fall into a coarse bag Benjamin had filled with a scoop of moist dirt. Emily joined the children in bagging the worms and relinquished the spade to him. When the supply was adequate, they trooped down to the waterside for the children's first fishing adventure.

They returned with five fish for supper, one for each of them, four caught by Benjamin and one by Ginny, but alternately pulled to shore by each of the children as they waded barefoot in the shallows. Two fish had gotten away, to Rosa Claire's immense disappointment. Aimee was indifferent, but happy out in the fresh air. Tired, thoroughly soaked, and overwrought with excitement, the children poked at one another and fussed as the group trudged home. The wet hem of Emily's skirts dragged heavily across the ground. She had not even attempted to resist the temptation of the shallows. *I am happy,* she thought in surprise. *How long since I have been happy?*

CHAPTER 27

The summer of 1862 brought with it unprecedented drought, following the equally unprecedented floods and snow that had characterized the winter and spring. The arbor gate of the cutting garden needed repair. Three overhead slats hung at precarious angles. Emily looked over her shoulder at Benjamin. He pursed his full lips and shook his head. Her mother's wild climbing rose, which had scrambled untended through the years, was wretched, long canes of it bare. Here and there, an odd plant with a wilted blossom struggled to grow, and hollyhocks flagged against the back fence. In one corner, a handful of foxglove had seeded. Emily cried out and wrenched them from the earth, roots dangling, as she crushed them and flung them away. Benjamin stooped to retrieve the pile of them.

"Get these poisonous things out of my ground," Emily said. "Don't you ever let one sprout here. Never, do you hear me?"

Benjamin nodded and threw them onto a pile of weeds to be burned.

Emily shaded her eyes against the afternoon sun. The undisturbed blue of the sky dispirited her. Weeks had gone by since the last rain and the ground was hard in spite of desperate hauls from the well. Jessie's older children helped, hauling three buckets to Emily's two, balancing an extra on their heads. She must give this up as a waste of time and water.

"Benjamin," Emily said, "let this garden go. What we need is food. Just leave it be. We'll put our energy into getting water to things we can eat."

Resolute, Emily turned her back to the garden. Jessie's older children scuffed their bare feet in the dust nearby. Aimee clung to her big sister's arm. Clearing his throat, Benjamin scratched his beard. From behind the smokehouse, Nathan approached in long, easy strides. He nodded to Emily, but spoke to Benjamin.

"I been pondering this here garden," Nathan said, "and all this water hauling. I's laying in bed a night or two ago and it come to me, just out of the dark there. I'm thinking, how about us dredge up a ditch here, not real deep, from the well to this garden. Then cut little gullies between the beds and dump water right out from the well, without no hauling, chunk the water over and let it run in amongst the flowers there, just by dumping, see? What you think, Ben? Sure would save some hauling."

"Nathan," Emily said, "I believe you have a plan."

"Well, yes'm." Nathan looked at her direct now. "I reckon."

"But to the vegetable patch, not here," Emily said. "Nasturtiums and roses and whatnot won't keep any fat on our bones, even if they are edible. We need to focus our efforts on vegetables and corn."

"Well, Miss Emily"—Nathan turned his shoulder, inserting himself a bit in front of Benjamin—"I been pondering that one, too. It's a lot longer way to the vegetable patch than here. Heap more dredging and dumping. I'm thinking we could take that fence down cross the back here and till up a plot right back yonder." He pointed with his remaining hand. "It ain't too late to plant, get us a fair crop. We could still mix a bit of flowers with the vegetables. Plant beans and cuke on the fence all 'round, squash blooming in with everything else. It'd cut the work, for sure. Wouldn't take half a day to till it up." He turned to Benjamin. "We got plenty manure in the pile, cured and not too hot. Excuse me, ma'am. I kind of forgot myself."

"Never mind that, Nathan," Emily said. "I'm in charge of this farm now and I can't be delicate about surviving."

"We could be planting by tomorrow." It was almost a question. "I reckon the corn'll have to do what it can by itself. Ain't nothing but prayer and the weather gone help that corn now."

"Nathan," Emily said, "we're behind the season as it is. But you give me hope that we could make it. And maybe—" She paused, caught her breath. "Maybe this bloody war will end before we lose ourselves completely."

As the mist burned off, Nathan's mellow voice filtered through the morning air, talking to the mule, Old Joy—singing really, coaxing, praising. Emily had never heard such carrying on with a mule. How many years Old Joy had worked this hard earth for them. Emily did not recollect why she had named that mule Joy.

Never heard anyone sing to a mule, Emily thought. *And that mule is about the only joy around.* Her dish towel discarded, she stepped out to the porch door, entranced. A pile of rescued cypress posts lay to the side of the present fence. Benjamin and Lucian were rimming the expanded garden. Old Joy, hitched to the straight stock, plodded clean and straight under Nathan's one-handed guidance, the dark earth rolling out from the blade. The mule's heavy body swayed on her narrow legs, her long ears flicking. The mule stepped in time to Nathan's voice. Or perhaps it was he who adapted his impromptu song to the slow staccato of her hooves.

By late morning, Emily sat churning yesterday's milk, on which the rich cream floated. The rhythm soothed her, quieted her, as she anticipated the weight of the butter to come. Outside, she heard the clink of the chains as the mule pulled the slider, spreading manure across the fresh-turned earth. Emily inhaled the edge of its raw scent, the comfort of the cycles of the farm. She smiled to herself as she skimmed the butter from the top of the churn, rinsed and patted it out on a plate, absorbing the excess liquid in a clean towel. As she tapped the butter into corn-shaped ceramic molds, Emily heard Old Joy's clomp again, pulling the turning plough. The plot was too small to warrant a section harrow or a middle buster. The little field would soon be ready. Emily turned the last mold over, loving the shape as the butter slid out. *We will live,* she thought.

Emily licked the butter from her fingers, pulling them one at a time through her mouth with her eyes closed. She heard a horse approaching. Wiping her hands on her apron, she stepped onto the porch to see Mason Johnson dismounting.

"Sheriff," she said, her throat constricted, her muscles gone tight.

"Morning, Miss Emily," he said, his discomfort as poorly disguised as hers. "Just making my way around to keep the folks outside of town apprised of the war."

"Neighborly," Emily said, an edge to her voice, "if you can call war news neighborly."

"I know folks need to keep themselves prepared," he said, "physically and mentally, though things change so fast these days I'm not right sure that's a possibility."

"And what is the situation then, Sheriff?"

"Memphis is defeated and fallen into Union hands. That puts the fate of the river at Vicksburg now. Only thing left in the way of the Union. Well, not the only thing, but maybe the key thing." Mason brushed his hat against his leg and looked across the field. "Look like you got a pretty good crop making, given this drought."

"We've set up a system from the well to deliver water. Nathan's ingenuity to thank."

A long silence ensued.

"I know Jeremiah's somewhere 'round Vicksburg. I thought I'd best tell you the war was headed his way. Got a lot more folk to bring up to date."

Emily did not speak for several minutes. Mason was remounting his horse when she said, "Perhaps Vicksburg will topple and we will have this whole insane enterprise done with. And perhaps the war will bring its own justice."

The black dirt spread open in front of Adeline, the plow grating against rock now and then. The mule trudged before her, leading her even as she guided, his head dipping and rising in a hypnotic rhythm. She raised her eyes and muttered, "Whoa." The mule stopped and Adeline stared at Lucian standing at the end of the turn row, waiting. She flicked the reins and proceeded toward him, her pace unchanged. He stepped aside as she turned the mule and the plow, and halted.

"Morning, Lucian." She raised the corner of her apron and wiped her forehead.

"Morning, Miss Adeline."

"What can I do for you? Not bad news, I hope."

"No, ma'am. Good news, I hope. Daddy and me been talking over what we might can do for you, Miss Adeline."

She studied the long lines of his narrow face. "Well, Lucian, that's mighty kind of you, but far from practical, it seems to me."

Lucian scuffed his feet and seemed to be speaking to the ground. "We got to thinking I could come and lend a hand now and then, whenever we got caught up. Do a little plowing, seeding, picking—whatever be needed when."

"Lucian, you are needed at your own place. I assume Miss Emily can hardly be aware of this plan you and Benjamin have hatched?"

"No, ma'am. We just come upon it by ourselves. We got plenty hands at the place and we letting a fair mite of land go untended now. Ain't gone be hard to find a bit of time to slip off over here. Me or one of the other hands. Might be somebody you don't know, but they every one good for trust."

"Lucian, you and Benjamin are fine men and I am most appreciative, but this is an offer, no matter how kind, that I am not going to accept."

"But, Miss Adeline—"

"I will not have you here without Miss Emily knowing. And approving. Now move aside so I can finish this field before dinnertime, Lucian. You just head on home now."

Lucian lowered his head and turned away. Adeline took up the reins and the mule jerked forward, the plow cutting into the hard dirt.

Over her shoulder, Adeline said, "Tell your daddy thank you, Lucian."

The mule took up his plodding gait, head nodding. Adeline's face set in blank determination toward the opposite end of the field.

Sometime in the night a week or so later, Adeline heard the old hound barking. With the desperation wrought of fatigue and interrupted sleep, she rose and went to the window. Moon shadows lay across the floor. Nothing moved in the yard but a brief sway of the trees and their long shadows across the ground. The hound barked once more. Then only the familiar sounds of cicadas and tree frogs filled the semidark. *Must be Thomas,* she thought. *God knows what he's up to.* Adeline returned to her bed and fell straight asleep.

As dawn spread evenly through the room, Adeline rose and slipped into yesterday's dress. She lifted a clean apron to her face and breathed in the scent of fresh air before she tied it around her. She loosened the thick braid of her hair and twisted its heavy mass atop her head without looking in the mirror. She readjusted a pin in her bun as she went out to the kitchen and loaded wood into the fireplace. Once she had her biscuits in the Dutch oven and ham warming in the skillet, she wiped her hands and walked out toward the shed to find Thomas. The Lord only knew what he was up to in the night, but she had long since ceased to care.

She turned the corner of the kitchen and halted, her mind working to assimilate what she saw. A narrow trench sloped from the well halfway to the edge of her vegetable garden. What crazy thing had Thomas been at in the night, she thought. As she opened the shed door, the reek of whiskey halted her as if the air had substance. She stood at the edge of the odor and studied him, his body tangled in the quilt, arm hanging from the edge of the mattress, one hand hanging limp above the whiskey bottle, its partial contents spilled and drying on the floor. She took another breath, turned, and shut the door, harder than she intended. She was hungry and the biscuits would be done.

When she had eaten and the kitchen was clean enough to satisfy her, Adeline walked back out to examine the trench. Her mind was filled with resentment at Thomas's wasted and crazy drunken exertions when what she needed was real work. *I'll just have to fill it in again,* she thought. More wasted effort. But not today.

For days Adeline studied the trench. Her puzzled resentment grew. When he was half sober one morning, Thomas asked her what the hell she thought she was doing, wasting time digging that nothing business out there. She assumed he had been too drunk to remember doing it. "Just don't fall in it," she said. For a brief, irrational moment, she imagined him lying in that trench, imagined his having dug his own grave, imagined tossing the heavy dirt back over him. "I don't have time to nurse a broken leg," she said. "I'll fill it when I have the crop laid by." Wasted time and energy was right, she thought. Leave it be till then.

Adeline had two fields plowed and planted late: one for corn, one for hay. The vegetables were in the ground and working hard to survive—beans, cucumbers, okra. The potatoes had sent up straggling shoots, and she was waiting daily for the turnips and carrots. Adeline was also watching the hard blue sky for signs of rain that did not appear. She hauled two buckets at a time from the well, balanced across her shoulders on a pole, one trip after another to wet the struggling plants.

At night she boiled water and sat by the fire wringing hot water from a towel to lay across her aching shoulders. *This is how Thomas saved Belinda,* she thought, *wrapping her in those hot towels, breathing into her frail lungs, saving her when I walked away, so sure that she would die.* Adeline dropped the towel back into the water and lifted it to wring again. *Belinda had not died. How different would it be if she had? Would I still have living sons?* She shook her head, shamed at the question, and arched her neck. Belinda had lived, though delicate and ever unstable. Adeline muttered under her breath as she laid the hot towel across her shoulders again. She had not seen Belinda since that terrible day with Emily. So typical, she thought, the wild dramatics, then nothing from her daughter. Adeline sighed and spread the towel on the hearth to dry. This was her nightly ritual now. She banked the fire and eased herself onto her bed. Outside the frogs and katydids trilled their lullaby.

As dawn cast its light across the land, Adeline rose to her morning routine: the fire, the biscuits, the salted ham, the trip to the shed to check on her husband. When she rounded the corner of the kitchen, the ever-present trench stretched now to the edge of the garden and down along its edge. Its center was mud, though the earth around was dry. Adeline followed the trench, step by step, puzzling over it as she followed its careful length. At the edge of the garden, she saw small tributaries among the rows. Her plants had been watered in the night. Lucian, she thought, with a realization that she no longer needed to bear the heavy buckets on her shoulders. She put her face in her hands and pressed her eyes. She dared not cry.

She said nothing to Thomas as he ate the eggs she fried on this rare morning he had managed to come inside. He returned the plate without speaking, but grabbed her wrist and growled, "You renting niggers? Who dug that ditch out there?"

Whirling 'round, Adeline studied the cragged face of her husband. "I don't know," she said. "I had a crazy notion it was you."

Thomas swayed to his feet. "Somebody dug a ditch to the garden and you don't know who? How the hell you don't know a thing like that?"

"Because someone chose to help me in secret."

"In secret? You hanging on some man I don't know about?" He shuffled toward her, but his face was menacing.

"No, Thomas. I'm suspecting someone else's slave did it out of charity for me."

"Charity? Goddam it, woman! Goddamn! From some goddamn nigger? Sneaking around my place at night. I'll shoot the fucking bastard." Thomas stabilized himself with one tight-knuckled hand, shook his fist at her. "I'll kill his black ass, do you hear me?"

She backed away, erect, and walked out the kitchen door, her eyes on the barn. She would make it that far. She must.

"I'll kill him. Do you hear me?" Thomas hurled the words like stones. "And I'll collect the bounty on his goddamn nappy head. Then we'll see how much charity you need."

Thomas lurched away toward the back field. Adeline patted the mule on his muzzle and walked past him. "You have a day of rest," she said to the mule. She led her horse from his stall and hitched the wagon. When she drove out, Thomas was lying propped against the shed door, his head hanging loose to one side.

Town was crowded, but Adeline maneuvered the wagon

through the streets and stopped just past the jail. She stood for a time, breathing hard and slow. She waited. Her breath quieted and she dropped to the ground. Hesitating at the door, she put her hand out and pushed it open. Mason looked up and then was on his feet. She stood without entering and he came toward her.

"Would you walk with me, Sheriff?" she said.

He nodded, retrieved his keys from the desk, and closed the door. He leaped from the stoop and held up his hand to her. She ignored the gesture, picked up her skirts, negotiated those three gut-wrenching steps down which she had dragged her dead son. On the ground, her gait was swift, and he matched her until they reached the edge of town.

"How can I help you, Adeline?"

"I need you to make a trip for me. Something I cannot do for myself."

"That would be a rare thing, Adeline, but all right. Whatever you need."

"I need you to go to Emily's place and find Lucian."

"Lucian?"

"Yes, I need you to tell him he must never again set foot on my place if he plans to live."

"You've got me right puzzled, Adeline."

"This is crucial. I would try to go myself. But I can't go hunting after Lucian."

"Lucian been bothering you, Adeline?"

"No, Mason. The very opposite. He's been coming in the night to help me. Dug a trench from the well to water my garden, part one night, part another. Thomas is fit to be tied, even drunk. He doesn't know who, but he went into a wild rage to think some black slave had pity on me. Says he'll kill him if he can. Who knows? Says he'll send for bounty hunters and collect on a runaway. He has to hold on to something just to stand up most of the time, but it is not worth the risk. There are times he might be able to shoot. And he would. I need you to forbid

Lucian to come again. What he's done is more than enough. It will spare my shoulders through this drought. I won't have Lucian's blood on my conscience, too." She turned toward her wagon, leaving Mason staring after. "You tell him, Mason."

Adeline mounted her wagon and passed him without looking down.

CHAPTER 28

Bethesda Church needed a coat of paint, but even whitewash would be an extravagance while congregants tendered their collective offerings to their newly declared country and its military, their Biblical nation of slaves and masters. The church would not fall for lack of paint.

Emily felt as naked as the exposed wood of the church steps. Why had she come? Her longing for sanctuary, for the balm of human, and the arrival of a new minister had won over her reticence and her fear. She made the trip into town this morning despite a foreboding that she had been stripped of the comfort of fellowship. It was not God that she sought. She dared not think much of God. Not the God of her childhood, the God of her brideship, her birthings. The only God she knew now was a god of death or of absence. If not that, then a God of impotence. Her longing was for a God she was not yet prepared to know. Her longing for God as a longing for life.

Emily hoped to slip into a back pew, perhaps unnoticed. But her hesitation had betrayed her. The church, almost full, was a blur of diffused motion, filled with the murmur of voices, the rustling whisper of wide skirts. Though there were plenty of open seats scattered through the church, only the family pew, far to the front left, was available without others. Emily focused on the polished wooden cross at the altar. As she walked forward, Emily registered in her peripheral vision the swivel of men's heads and women's bonnets, as if attached to puppet strings. Silence trailed her down the aisle to her father's pew. She sat alone.

She did not hear the sermon. Her mind refused to focus. But the tunes of the old hymns sank deep into her. Though Emily did not sing, she felt embraced by the music. A great release opened her, liberated her, as if a tight corset had been unfastened. At the final hymn, the pastor stepped down and whispered to Mrs. Gladstone at the piano. The old lady, who had played at this piano since the church was built, flipped the pages of her hymnal and shifted on the piano bench. Preacher Johnson announced a change in the last hymn and the sound of rustling pages whispered through the church. The voices of the congregants rose in robust union, then disentangled as the words came clear:

Crimes of such horror to forgive, Such guilty, daring worms to spare;
This is Thy grand prerogative, And none shall in the honor share,

Emily could hear the reverberations of a few hasty departures behind her. As the hymn neared its conclusion, only the piano continued. Before the last "amen," Emily slipped from the pew out onto the side stoop. Ben Aiken materialized around the corner. Startled, he dropped his eyes and skirted around her. Emily stepped into the churchyard. Sarah Benson and old Mrs. Claiborne approached, arm in arm. Their unabashed stare unnerved her. Men disappeared in various directions. Her old playmate Elsa Stanford nodded to Emily and stretched out a hand to detain Sarah and Mrs. Claiborne. The three lowered their heads and spoke in low voices, but Emily could not fail to notice the almost imperceptible gesture of Elsa's shoulder raised in her direction. *Why did I come?* she thought.

Emily's horse lifted his head as she approached, then continued to graze at the bare edge of the yard. The trio of women stood between her and the buckboard. Emily inhaled, raised her narrow chin, and walked past them without turning her head. But she saw that they turned theirs. As Emily passed, she heard Sarah's scathing platitude, "There but for the grace of God . . ." Her voice trailed off.

Michael Lambert stepped away from the back of the church. He lifted his hat to the women without looking their way and took Emily's arm. The buggy was only steps away, but she was grateful for his support. She did not look at Lambert until she had mounted the buggy. His smile was gentle and sad. Emily took the reins, lifted her head, and turned toward, rather than away from, the little cluster. The huddled women in their awkward hoops scurried out of the path of the oncoming horse.

"Beware how you speak of God's grace," Emily said as she passed them. "You may find yourself in need of it." She did not look their way and had no idea if they heard her. It did not matter. It only mattered that she had the courage to say it out loud.

Ginny watched through the window as Emily dismounted the buggy. She was already at the door when Emily came up the steps. Emily brushed past without a word and Ginny followed. She did not ask. She simply waited.

"Ready for your dinner?" Ginny said at last.

Emily seemed to wake from a trance and nodded. As Ginny turned to leave the room, Emily detained her. "Sit with me, Ginny."

"All right. Dinner can wait."

"No, sit with me to eat, Ginny."

"Miss Emily, I—"

"Please, Ginny. Just please."

Ginny nodded.

Emily played at the food with her fork as she had done as a child with carrots or broccoli. Ginny ate little herself.

"What do you make of the church, Ginny?"

"The church, Miss Emily? Which church?"

Emily looked up, surprised. "Well, any church: Methodist, Baptist, Episcopal, Catholic. Any Christian Church."

"In the South?"

"Well, yes, of course, Ginny."

"The ones always preaching obedience to us slaves?"

Emily looked into Ginny's dark, wide-set eyes.

"That ain't no Christian Church, Miss Emily."

"Not Christian, Ginny?"

"Your daddy taught me to read. That's Christian. Give me a Bible and I read it. Mostly about Jesus. You know what he say first time he speak out?" She saw that Emily had abandoned the fork. "He didn't come to no rich white folks, Miss Emily. He come to the poor and he say, 'I come to set the captive free.' Now, who you think that is? That be us, Miss Emily. That be us slaves. We the captive, we the bruised reed he come to free, like Moses to the pharaoh. Now I grant they's Christian folk amongst the rich white. Poor white, too. Plenty of good Christian folk. More than we might know for sure. And they's good Christians who don't cotton to the church; don't never darken the door. But if that church was true Christian, wouldn't be no slaves, wouldn't be no lashings from the good Christian masters and mistresses, and there wouldn't be no war. Wouldn't be folks like your daddy going against the church and the law to treat us right, 'cause right would be the way of things. Like Jesus said, every little thing you do, you do to him." Ginny picked up both plates. “I wished you hadn’t asked me that, Miss Emily. But you did and now you got your answer. Maybe not the one you wanted.” She paused to study Emily’s face. “Then again, maybe it is.”

In the dim autumn chill of her father’s study, Emily shivered. The Union had come out victorious at Antietam, but slavery was not yet the primary issue of Lincoln’s agenda. Pulling back the heavy green brocade of the drapes, Emily felt the warm sun on her fingers. The room was as she remembered, of course, but its dark walnut paneling wore the hush of her father’s absence. The deep-wine Persian carpet absorbed her footsteps. At the desk, Emily fingered a neat stack of papers, secured with a red glass paperweight she remembered giving her father long ago. Its surface was cool and smooth to her touch, the red fold deep in the glass inaccessible.

The drawer was locked. After a bit of searching, she found the key in an inlaid box. Inside the drawer, as she had expected, was the embossed black ledger, with its gilt-edged pages. Tracing the lined sheets with her little finger, she found the names of every slave her father had inherited or bought, grouped in families, along with a record of births, marriages, and deaths. There were no sales.

Beneath the ledger lay a thick envelope, bearing the judge’s seal in red wax. Cautious, so as not to tear the paper, Emily pried the closure loose with a silver letter opener, engraved with her father’s monogram. Tarnished, she noted. The wax left a red stain on the cream paper of the envelope. Inside lay a stack of documents, certificates of emancipation or of manumission, one for every slave, dated from September 2, 1859, forward, bearing her father’s signature and seal. Scanning a handful, Emily noted with irony that a few of the detailed physical descriptions no longer matched the appearance of the intended recipients, who had grown up or grown older, gained weight or lost hair.

One had died, and several more had arrived since the certificates were filled out. She placed the papers on the desk and lay her forehead on the papers. When Ginny came to find her, Emily was asleep.

Ginny withdrew and closed the door, but her momentary presence wakened Emily. She stirred and gathered herself. Using her father's form as example and checking against his precise inventory, Emily wrote certificates of manumission for every slave for whom papers were missing. She studied the letter for the one slave who had died and placed it at the top of the pile to give to the woman's son. He could carry her in his memory as a free woman. Emily gathered the stack of papers and went to ring the bell for the hands to come. This was her father's long-wished heritage. Legal or not, at the end of the day, she would own no slaves. Their freedom had waited long enough. Several months would pass before Abraham Lincoln would issue the Emancipation Proclamation in January of 1863.

CHAPTER 29

"Mason, what brings you way out here?" Adeline pushed back her bonnet and shaded her eyes against the sun. "Come in. I'm done here." She picked up the empty laundry basket, adjusted a clothespin or two on the line, and brushed her hand down a wet sheet that had folded back on itself in the breeze.

"Just scouring the country round about. Keeping my eye out for skulkers. Of several varieties."

"And do you find them?" He caught the edge in her voice.

"No, but I find a lot of rumors about them. Folks that are scared will believe any old tale, even if they made it up themselves."

Adeline smiled, a rarity in her life these days. She opened the door and motioned the sheriff in.

"Mainly I thought I'd put your mind at ease that I delivered your ultimatum to Lucian. Where's Thomas?" he said.

Adeline hesitated, looking Mason in the face.

"I expect he's propped against a tree somewhere out back with his bottle, Sheriff," she said. "Do you need him?"

"No, ma'am. But I imagine you do."

Adeline slid the basket onto the table, holding hard to its sides, her shoulders rising as she took in a deep breath.

"I'm sorry, Adeline. I don't know what took hold of me to say that. I stepped clean over the line on that one and I'm begging pardon. I reckon I better keep scouting."

"No, no pardon to be given, Mason. You just stepped on the truth, not the line. Have a seat. I was about to have my tea anyway. Or what passes for tea these days. You might as well join me."

He touched her elbow. "Adeline, there's something I've wanted to tell you for a long time now."

Adeline hesitated before looking up. "Perhaps there is something I should tell you first, Sheriff." She stood very still. "Belinda is getting married again. To George Gattaway." She studied his face for reaction. "Yes, I see you know him. She wants me at the church tomorrow morning. I am loath to be there, Sheriff. The man is a snake. Ill-treats his slaves."

"May ill-treat her, Adeline."

"She chooses for herself, Sheriff. I have no sway with her at all since—" Adeline grasped at the edge of the door. "I am searching for the words here. There is something that she doesn't say and I cannot be around her now."

"What are you thinking?" he asked.

"How different," she said. "How very different from Will."

"Will was a man of integrity."

"Yes," she said. "His death so—" She paused, seemed to have difficulty speaking. Then, "So here is this man who bought his way out of service. Paid for young Graham to take his place. Now, that boy is dead."

"So is Will," Mason said.

"Yes, Will is dead. So are they all. All dead, Mason. And what have you done about it?"

"I can't go to the front and bring Jeremiah back, Adeline, hard as I want to. I can only pray the war will do my job instead."

A long silence ensued before Mason positioned his hat on his head and stepped from the porch.

"Mason."

He stopped.

"What was it you wanted to tell me?"

"Nothing that won't wait. Maybe another time." He looked back once to see Adeline standing in the sun, her bonnet hanging down her back, her hand shading her eyes.

A slow drizzle commenced after dawn the next day and continued through the morning, with brief glimpses of sky that assured better, then broke their promise. Another disastrous spring seemed on its way, the weather as erratic as Belinda herself. The air was cool and barren, the ceremony brief. Adeline watched as Belinda, now Mrs. Gattaway, gathered the rose silk of her skirts and bestowed her new husband with her gloved hand and her smile. A light-skinned slave held an umbrella over the bride. Belinda did not look back, even to wave, but leaned toward George's bald head, whispering. The couple's laughter rolled over Adeline as the carriage pulled away.

The rain stopped and a fine, evaporating mist swayed up into the forsythia blooming in the churchyard. Adeline gazed around. The whole empty horizon glowed in the damp air. No one was there. Adeline was struck both by its beauty and by her aloneness. By her losses: a husband drowning in drink, her two sons both horribly dead, the daughter with whom she had never connected gone into a life with no place for her and with which she disagreed—sickeningly so. And Emily, gone in ways for which she had no words, the one who had become the daughter of her soul. What had she left of her life? And then her breath came deep, her shoulders straightened. There were the children. The children were Emily's, but the children were themselves. The children were not Emily. What had she been thinking? How had she surrendered so to Belinda's and Emily's power? Rosa Claire and Lonso were her grandchildren, Charles's children. She would see them. She would enlist Ginny. These children would know her. She was their blood.

The parson and his wife came out of the church and brushed by her, turning to murmur their farewells.

"Is there anything I can do for you, Mrs. Slate?" the parson said. Adeline realized she could not recall his name.

"No. No, thank you, sir." She smiled at the wife, whose name perhaps she had never known, and extended her hand.

"You're all right, then. Are you sure?" the woman said.

"Yes, thank you. I shall be quite fine. Quite."

Adeline mounted the wagon and turned it, standing, in the direction of Emily's house.

CHAPTER 30

News of the war came spasmodically and the post was unreliable. Another letter arrived and Emily tucked it into her pocket, where it stayed until dark had descended. She lit her lamp and opened the envelope with grave reluctance.

Near Vicksburg
March 23, 1863

Sister Emily,

I have succumbed to one of the fevers that assails this hell of a camp, as you will note now returned toward Vicksburg. My remaining coat is in tatters. I am grateful for the blanket but never sure when it may be stolen from me even by one of my comrades, many of whom have forsaken their Southern honor and become no better than animals themselves.

Since I am quite ill and appear now not much more than a skeleton wearing my skin, which I thankfully still have, who knows someone might steal that next, I thought I should reveal a small ugliness I did against you before you are in too much need of it for the spring shearing, which season must surely arrive sometime in the not too distant future. Though you may have missed it last year, the fever seems to bring it to my mind and give me no rest. On gathering things at my departure, I concealed two pair of Father's best shears. It was petty and impulsive, but you will find them in the shed on one of the high shelves above where the axes hang.

Perhaps you will forgive me that, if not much else.

Your brother,

Jeremiah Matthews
Proprietor

As the days progressed and the spring of 1863 wrapped its warm cloak across the farm, Emily walked out to the edge of the fields. Taking hold of her heavy petticoat, she lifted her skirts. The soft chirring of insects surrounded her. Her black dress magnetized the sun's heat onto her shoulders. Raising her head to the sky, Emily turned in a slow circle, then faster until she spun like a child. Her skirts swirled against the high grass. Above her, the clouds whirled and blurred like spun sugar. Overwhelmed by dizziness, she tumbled to the ground, with a fleeting vision of her mother's laughing face, the sound of it lost in the whirr of startled insects. Nausea rose at the drunken whirling of the white-flecked sky. She blinked hard to stop the reeling world and groped through the bruised grass to steady herself. She sat up. The spinning diminished.

She stared at the edges of her apron pockets, frayed by the habit of thrusting her roughened hands into them. Her fingers were raw, and not only from work; she was chewing them again, tearing them bloody with her teeth as she had after her mother died. She remembered a bitter compound someone had put on her fingers to prevent her chewing, but she had chewed them, anyway, had chewed the bitterness and stripped the skin raw until they were infected and two nails fell off. The nails had grown back slightly crooked and remained so. Now her palms were rough and chaffed from plowing, and from other chores she was learning alongside the hands: to keep the place from falling apart, to survive the war, to slow the steady disintegration of her life.

Lying back, Emily stared into the depths of the sky. Above her the clouds had stilled, but her stomach continued to lurch. With her fingertips, she grasped the insubstantial edges of the grass. Plucking a blade, Emily pressed it between her thumbs and blew, producing a thin, reedy screech much like the whistling she could never master, however patiently her father tried to teach her. Emily remembered his full, deep tone, but the tune somehow escaped her. Already, she was losing him, the daily reality of his presence draining out of her like the last drops of water through a sieve. Soon, he would be only her fading memory of him, with blood stuck to the edges.

Emily struggled to her feet and ran. Below the barn, her boots slipped in the fetid muck. Stumbling, equilibrium gone, she caught her fall with one hand, plunging into the tool shed where she spun, oblivious to the alarm her flight had generated among several servants at work nearby. Desperate, she rifled after her father's mislaid shears. She had no way to reach the high shelves. The intensity of her anger multiplied. On the worktable lay Benjamin's crate of carefully organized tools.

Emily's chaos rebelled against its order. She shoved the box onto the floor, scattering the hoard of nails and screws and bolts. Grasping at neatly hung hammers and files, her hand fell on an ax. She jerked it from the wall, capitulating to the horror it evoked, the memory of the warm chicken in her hands, its thudding heart, and Charles's face as the ax came down. Reeling under its weight, she twisted, its momentum spinning her round. It slipped from her hands and flew sideways into the heavy muscle of Benjamin's thigh. He did not make a sound, but she heard the chunk of the blade before it fell to the ground. Lucian, who had been running behind Benjamin, lurched through the door. He gathered his crumpling father in his arms and lowered him onto the dirt floor.

"What you did, Miss Emily? What you done did?" Lucian said.

Emily dropped onto the dirt and crawled toward them, staring as the blood soaked through Benjamin's breeches. Lucian jerked the kerchief from his neck and tried frantically to wrap the wound. Emily's flailing hands were in his way, the kerchief too short. Emily knelt back, caught the trailing hem of her petticoat and tried to tear.

Breathless, Ginny appeared, Jessie and Nathan at her heels. Stepping over the two huddled men, Ginny snatched the fabric from Emily's hands. Lengths and lengths, she ripped, throwing them toward Lucian. Emily heard the tearing, the rustle of the faded pant leg as it disappeared beneath the winding strips of petticoat. No one asked anything. No one said a word. Lucian and two other men helped Benjamin up and took him away.

Outside the cabin door, Emily sat with her back against the rough wall, knees pulled up under her crossed arms, her face hidden. Her anguish destroyed all etiquette and Emily reverted to childhood. When she heard footsteps at her side, she did not move.

"He gone live, Miss Emily, and he ain't even gone be cripple," Ginny said.

Emily did not raise her head.

"He's gone have a tale to tell his great-great-grandbabies. Yes'm, he's gone have some kind of tale," Ginny said.

Her steps faded back into the house. After a while, they came again. Without moving, Emily could see the toe of Ginny's boot.

"You know, honey child, one of these days you gone have to stop getting froze up over things. It don't serve nobody. Now, come on, let's go home."

Emily watched the toe of the boot.

"You ain't budging?" Ginny said. "Well, all right. I be back."

Ginny's voice echoed from inside the cabin, talking loud, assuring Lucian and Samantha that the chamomile would help, especially with a slug or two of the brandy she had brought from the house; that she would be close by in the night if needed; that she would be there again at first light. The women's voices sank into a murmur, then rose.

"You get that woman off my porch," Samantha said. "She think she got the only crop of suffering 'round here?"

An inaudible response.

"She got grief, do she?" Samantha's deep voice rose over the sounds of the night. "Well, ain't I got grief? Ain't we all got grief? We just ain't got room for it 'round here. We got slave grief. And all her fine freedom papers don't make that go away. Now get that woman out of here."

The toe of the boot reappeared. It touched Emily's, then tapped it, three times, hard. Emily's head snapped up.

"You will show me some respect!"

"I believe that's what I'm doing." Ginny half squatted, one hand propped on her knee. "You gone keep wearing them petticoats?" she said.

"What?"

"Them tore up petticoats? You gone keep on wearing them?

Because if you ain't, I'm gone be needing the rest for fresh bandages, and I'd just as soon they be clean next time."

Emily stared at Ginny's pink palms, the dried bloodstains on her cuff.

"No. I mean, yes. No, I won't use them. And yes, of course you can have them."

"Then, you better stand on up here and let me take you to the house so I can get them washed and get some supper in you."

"I don't want any supper."

"All right. I'll fix you some buttermilk and cornbread. They's some left over from dinner. It ain't much, but still might be more'n you'll eat. Now let's you and me go."

Ginny extended her hand and Emily took it. She braced herself against the wall to rise, standing immobile as the sharp needles of blood returned to her legs.

"You got tomorrow, honey," Ginny said. "And a good heap of days after that, I expect. He ain't going nowhere soon."

The sleepless night passed and the first edge of dawn pushed gray through the interweaving of pecan and oak along the path through the quarter. Grateful for the light, Emily made her way to Benjamin and Samantha's cabin. The slaves emerging in the morning gloom nodded and gave her space. Emily nodded, but did not raise her eyes. Samantha opened the door to Emily's knock and turned a silent back. Approaching the bed, Emily waited. The cover of quilted scraps was neatly tidied and folded back. Benjamin opened his eyes and tilted his head, pushing up on his elbows. Raising her hand, Emily shook her head. Benjamin lay back, his eyes closed. Emily waited.

"Forgive me, Benjamin," she said at last. "I am terribly sorry."

"Yes'm. I knowed that from the start." He did not open his eyes until she had gone.

* * *

In the shade of the side porch Ginny, churning the morning's butter, alternately hummed and regaled Rosa Claire with bits of folklore. The girl was entranced. Emily appeared at the door and motioned for Rosa Claire to come and tidy up. Ginny smiled down at her and nodded. "You gone hear the rest. Don't you bother. Never knew the end of a story to run off by itself," she said. "Go mind your mama now." Rosa Claire hugged Ginny's arm before following her mother into the house.

Samantha sauntered across the yard, fanning herself with an old palmetto fan.

"Hot enough?" she said. "Where's that devil ax woman?"

"Always hot enough. She's inside. And you best watch your mouth," Ginny said. "Could get a lot hotter."

Samantha frowned and fanned. "I hear men's dying out on the march, falling out from the heat. Never heard of no slaves in the field dying from the heat. Them white men ain't got stamina."

"You got news or opinions, Samantha? Here, take this dasher. I got something in the house to finish."

"Hmhh." Samantha started down the steps, but changed her mind and took up the churning.

Inside Rosa Claire yelped as Emily pulled at a tangle in her hair. Ginny took the brush from her and jerked her head for Emily to find something else that needed doing. While she wound new ribbons into the blond curls, Ginny finished the tale she had begun about a messenger raven who taught people how to fly. She patted Rosa Claire's shoulder and sent her out to play, with instructions not to get herself dirty.

In the parlor, she found Emily stirring up dust with the feather duster. "Now what you doing?" she said.

"I am cleaning my own parlor, Ginny. What does it appear I am doing?"

"Truth? Looks like you just shifting dust from one place to another."

"Well, it just comes right back in, anyway. In this heat with the windows open. Is this how it is, Ginny? Nothing ever really done?"

"That's it, Miss Emily. Nothing is ever done. Not in this life."

Emily flicked the duster over the tops of the window frames. A cascade of dust floated in the air, accentuating the rays of morning sunlight through the open window.

"Hand me that thing," Ginny said, as she coughed and reached for the duster. "Come on now, Miss Emily, hand it to me."

"Stop it, Ginny." Emily yanked the duster behind her.

"Stop trying to get that thing from you before you stir up a dust storm?"

"No." Emily gazed up into Ginny's face. "Stop calling me Miss Emily."

Ginny shook her head.

"I mean it, Ginny. You are a free woman and so am I. You have been the closest person to me in my life, more than my mother. So this is my last command to you. You will call me Emily."

Ginny turned sideways and stared out the window. She pulled the curtain back, fingered the lace, and cleared her throat.

"All right, Emily. There, I done it. And you heard it. You remember now you heard it, because you ain't never gone hear it again." Ginny dropped the curtain edge and faced Emily. "Now you gone hear the rest of what I got to say. You don't know what you talking about. You got these grand ideas—and I'm not saying they ain't good. Or they ain't right. But you don't know any more about life than you know about this dust you stirring up in here. You go on like that and you gone stir up something you can't settle like this dust. You gone get me killed, or worse. You gone get me raped or burned and then killed." Ginny snatched the duster from Emily's hand.

"You think ending slavery gone put things right? You forget

we living amongst them that's fighting to the gates of hell and right on in to keep us down? They's gone be some flesh to pay for this war, however it come out. And most of it gone be black. We gone be to blame whoever win this thing. You think because Mr. Lincoln say we free now, everything gone be like it ought. Well, it ain't. Just like life, it ain't never gone be done with till it's done. And ain't neither one of us gone live to see it, Miss Emily." Ginny waved the duster in the air and left the room.

CHAPTER 31

"Miss Emily. Wake up." Ginny shook her, then shook her again. Emily opened her eyes, started up from the sofa, her focus on Ginny's face coming slowly. "You all right, honey. Just you wake up now."

Emily sat, her hands against her temples, shaking her head.

"What you dreaming, child? You moaning like somebody dead. I can't hardly wake you up."

"Oh, Ginny." Emily lay back against the sofa, her arms limp at her sides. "I—yes, it felt like death. It was, Ginny. It was death."

Emily stared at Ginny, laid her head against her bony shoulder.

"I was wading in the swamp, following a snake like a brilliant underwater rainbow. The water got all stinking and foul. And there was a bird, like a fragile peacock made of lace and filigree, dying in the water. Everywhere I touched, it fell apart. I loved it so, Ginny. But it was dying and decaying, making the water deadly. And I saw a young blue heron there behind it, so dull, but vulnerable and alive, and I knew it would die in this putrid water. When I touched it, it was soft, and I clung to it, staring at the color of the dying bird I could not save. And though I loved it so deeply, I had to let it die to save that young blue heron. It was such a grief, Ginny, like the grief—" She stopped, choking on her breath.

Ginny stroked her hair and hummed some tune that sunk into Emily with familiar comfort. They sat like that, the mistress and her servant, the servant with her sister-child.

"Miss Emily, I got something to say. You know the Bible talking about Eden, how Eve and Adam sinned, eating that apple or whatever it was, and God run them out and set that angel with the fiery sword to punish them?"

Emily nodded against Ginny's shoulder.

"You know what that fruit really was? It was the Truth. The knowledge of good and evil. Those two just got a wild longing for truth." Ginny shifted her weight. "Now I got another story for you. About yourself. You been trying all your life to get back into Eden. You think that's what life's supposed to be about, finding Paradise again. But it ain't. You been spending your whole life headed the wrong direction, looking over your shoulder wishful for that garden, like Lot's wife looking back. Mercy you ain't turned to a pillar of salt. Now, you got to look the other way, look toward life the way it is. And life the way it is may not be so fine, but it's life. God didn't put that angel with the flaming sword at the gate for punishment. No, God put that angel there for protection. That's a strange grace, I know. But God knowed it was way too dangerous for us to go around pretending life could ever be Eden in a world so broken as this one."

Chapter 32

In the early morning, Lucian hitched Old Joy to run a section harrow on the north field. He also hitched a newly acquired, however ancient, mule to the plow. Emily caressed the gray muzzle of the mule, Remnant, so named because he had been the last creature sold when her neighbor gave up trying to survive the war and the weather without her man, packed up her brood of children, and left for Alabama. Emily did not mind that the mule was old, and he did not seem to mind his new name. She tugged at his bridle and set her hand to the plow. This would be her first field on her own. She did not stop until she had turned a small plot for sweet corn.

At the edge of the field, she surveyed the tantalizing furrows, like a beginner's quilt with an awkward pattern. She had done it. A plot of her own. She and Remnant, with Benjamin's spotty dog trotting at her heels, lying down panting at the end of each row while she turned the mule and the plow. Now, he lay at her feet, eyeing her, resting and waiting. Her legs trembled, but she dared not sit to rest. A sudden desire to drop seed corn into the furrows caught hold of her. The ground was broken. But far from ready to plant.

The field was of insignificant size, a learning field. From the turn row, Benjamin limped out and surveyed her work. Emily was intensely aware of his whitening beard, his frayed shirt, and her deep regret.

"Well, I reckon now this ground is broke, you wanting to plant something," he said.

"How do you know that?" she said, tilting her head toward him.

"Oh, been there myself. Remember the first field I plowed by myself. It was even crookeder than yours."

Emily smiled. "How old were you?"

"Now that I don't rightly remember. Real young. Skinny, little old thing. But I seen the dirt open under that plow and I wanted me nothing but some seed corn to drop in." Benjamin wiped his eyes with a handkerchief. "Yes'm. Didn't give a hoot that field wasn't near ready yet. No turning plow, no section harrow, nothing. Just wanted to see the corn drop in that open ground." Benjamin chuckled, deep and throaty.

"And did you?" Emily laughed with him, stretching her aching arms and back.

"Well, my Uncle Dothan—he wasn't my uncle, but that's what us kids called him. We didn't have no daddy, you see. Well, we did, but he got sold, somewhere off down the river we heard, but we never did really know."

Emily studied the crooked furrows, the image of her father flooding her. Benjamin cleared his throat. He bent awkwardly, favoring the injured leg, and picked up a clod of dark earth, working it with his fingers, sifting it down into the furrow below. Watching his hand, Emily thought how like the earth he was, as if he had sprung from it whole, warm and dark.

"Well, anyhow, Uncle Dothan come hunting me 'round dinnertime. I was that took up with my field, I didn't even hear the dinner bell. He's real quiet a while, just looking at me and my work. I hadn't never done any work you could look at and see what you had done, right in front of your eyes. After a spell, he say, 'Come on, boy, ain't you hungry after all that work?' But I couldn't stop looking. Finally he say, 'You wanting something to go in that dirt, ain't you, boy?' and I nodded."

Benjamin scrutinized Emily's profile.

"So Uncle Dothan, he say, 'Now, boy, they ain't no way from here to there, except from here to there. You go shortcutting and your work gone be lost. You and your corn, too. Ground ain't ready yet. Got three, four more passes to go. But I know what you wanting. You wanting life to grow. Here, now, go put this in there somewhere.' And he reach in his pocket and put something in my hand I can't see. Then he say, 'Get on now, boy, before I starve.' "

Benjamin reached in his pocket and held his hand out to Emily. She opened her palm. Both of them laughed, Benjamin's broad face rounding out.

"Now, you go put that somewhere in that broke-up ground, Miss Emily. Then you best come eat," he said.

In Emily's palm lay a single hard kernel of corn. For a full five minutes, she stood with her fingers closed around Benjamin's offering. With her eye on the center of the field, she followed the crooks and turns of the rows and slipped the hard, slight seed into the earth.

"Ah, child, now that's an onion, sweet and juicy. Makes your Ginny want to cry. You want a slice of that onion. You might like it, baby. It only takes tasting. Looky here." Ginny took the onion, put it to her lips, and bit it like an apple.

Rosa Claire pushed back, shaking her head, ready to cry.

"Don't want none, do you, honey child? Sure make them butter beans tasty. Ain't you gone eat nothing? How about some cornbread, baby? With fresh butter? And some pot liquor? You ain't got to taste no old onion."

Rosa Claire scooted closer, her chin resting on the table edge, watching.

"How 'bout some sweet milk with your cornbread, baby?"

Perched on a thick dictionary, the little girl raised her head and nodded, reaching for the handle of her dented silver cup.

A noise at the back door caught Ginny's attention. Adeline scraped her feet on the step, a basket on her arm loaded with early peas, carrots, beets, and radishes. There was no telling when she might appear and disappear just as quickly. Once she had brought a rag doll small enough to fit into Rosa Claire's pocket. Ginny uncoiled her long, lean body and bolted toward the door.

"Don't be perturbed, Ginny," Adeline said. "I won't be staying and I won't even ask if Emily is at home. I assume she's not around." She stepped inside. "Here, take these. Once they're fixed and on the table, they will taste like she might have planted them herself."

"Well, Miss Adeline, she out working the field. She don't never rest."

"Seems that is what women all over are learning to do for themselves these days, Ginny."

The dictionary tumbled to the floor as Rosa Claire clambered from her seat and tugged at the corner of Adeline's basket. Adeline handed the basket to Ginny and stooped level with the child. She fingered Rosa Claire's blond curls, winding an unruly lock around her finger. Dancing on tiptoe, Rosa Claire threw her arms around Adeline's neck.

"Grammy—" Her voice was hardly a murmur.

"Are you being a good girl for Ginny? Eating your dinner?" Adeline saw the untouched food.

"She ain't too hungry today, Miss Adeline. We about to have us some cornbread and sweet milk, though." Ginny smiled and nodded at the child for affirmation. "You hungry, Miss Adeline? I fix you a plate."

"No, Ginny, thank you, though. This will have to do me for now. It's not worth the risk for me to want too much." She touched the top of Rosa Claire's hand and waved. "Let Grammy go. I'll see you again soon."

Rosa Claire blew a kiss from her wrist, rather than her fingertips.

"Bye-bye, Grammy. I see you, too."

Ginny resettled the child back on the dictionary and pushed aside the plate of food. In an empty saucer, she broke up the buttered cornbread, spooned pot liquor over it, and handed the child a small silver spoon. Rosa Claire spilt the juices on the table and on her bib, but she ate.

Ginny sat beside her for a moment, her eyes out the window. Then, putting her hands on her knees for leverage, she rose and emptied the fresh vegetables into larger baskets on the porch, tucking Adeline's basket under a corner table. Stepping back, she assessed its visibility. The table wobbled as she held its edge. Another chore to put on Nathan's list. Ginny tucked the basket farther back with her toe. When she straightened, Rosa Claire was finishing her milk, head tilted back to catch the last drop from the cup.

Ginny wiped the child's face with the corner of her apron and took her upstairs for her nap. Though they still frightened her, Ginny was becoming accustomed to these visits. Almost always Adeline brought something. Now it was early produce from the garden: vegetables, wild strawberries, new potatoes. She made sure to bring enough to help, but not enough to attract attention. Ginny cooked it all as if she had plucked it herself. And Emily ate.

If Rosa Claire spoke of Grammy, Emily ignored her, and so the child gradually stopped, as if she understood how to carry the secret.

Chapter 33

Steam from the boiling pot mingled with the heat of the cooking shed as Emily waited for Ginny to return from the root cellar with turnips for supper. Supplies were adequate, if only just. Emily pulled the edge of a second knife over the sharpening stone. The rapid sound of horse's hooves and a muffled scream from Ginny broke into her reverie. Dropping the knives into the deep pockets of her work apron, Emily stepped into the open.

Three Union soldiers rode into the yard. Reined in so close that Emily stumbled back, their bony horses pawed at the dirt. Their dusty blue frock coats hung loose across their thighs, and each man carried some variety of small arm. The sergeant in the lead, shorter than the other men, but clearly in command, wore a side pistol and light saber engraved with oak leaves. Across his left shoulder hung a repeating Spencer carbine.

Ginny attracted scant attention from the soldiers, other than the glance they threw her when she uttered her stifled scream. They had ridden past her as if she mattered not at all.

Emily's mouth went dry as cotton as the soldiers towered

over her in the late-morning sun. The children had taken their pails and gone with Samantha in search of wild berries at the edge of the woods. They would not return for at least another hour. Emily fingered the knives in her apron pocket. Ginny stole past the men and stood close to her.

The commander rose in his stirrups and slung himself onto the dusty earth almost in Emily's face. She retreated a step and slid a finger along the blade of one of the knives.

"Well, ma'am," the sergeant said with a mocking courtesy, "we find ourselves in need of extra rations. Looks like your cook had an apron full before she scampered back here to your protection." He waved in Ginny's direction without taking his eyes from Emily's pale face. "Perhaps she'll be good enough to cook something for us. We'll see to the rest of your cellar after we've been satisfied."

Emily did not stir. She lifted her head and fingered the knife again. Ginny shifted her weight and backed away.

"I'm assuming that you heard me," the man said, "and that you both speak English. These men are hungry. Now get to work." He turned to Ginny. "I'm talking to you, nigger!"

"Nigger, is it? Ain't you supposed to be the ones here to emancipate us? Bring freedom and respect to us darkies?"

"I'm risking my life to liberate you and you had best act as if that matters."

"You ain't liberating me. You way behind on that. I been freed before you come along, thanks to this lady and her abolitionist father."

"Abolitionist?"

"Yeah, you look surprised as you want, but we got us some Mississippi abolitionists. Judge bought up every slave he could. Over a hundred. Educated us against illegal and tried to make us free." Ginny looked from one soldier to the other. "Yeah, I see your faces, all three your faces. They's things you know and things you don't."

"Nonetheless, we are risking our lives to liberate slaves. Free or not free, you know why we're here in this godforsaken place." The sergeant's voice was vehement. Over his shoulder, the third scout glared at her.

"I tell you what I know. I *know*," Ginny emphasized the word, "you here to steal our food. Now how I'm gone be liberated if I can't eat?"

The sergeant had lived a principled life, had entered the nightmare of this war on good intentions. In his mind he carried nothing but ideas of white cruelty, lashings, beatings, and an inhumanity that must be destroyed if it cost him his life. And he had seen firsthand the proof of those evils. He had seen the abomination of slavery. Now, here was this ignorant black woman, confronting him and his motives. A curious group of hands had gathered, staring. The sergeant was aghast, his anger fueled by the witness of his men.

"Shut your mouth, woman," he snapped. "Now, you get my men and me some water. And not from the well, from the cistern over there. And you make sure that water is clean!"

"You thirsty?" Ginny said. "I expect them horses thirsty, too. I'm watering them first. They don't care about no clean water. You"—she pointed at the one still mounted, young, boy-faced, and at a loss—"get down."

"I didn't give you orders to dismount!" the sergeant snapped. "The horses can wait."

"And, so can you," Ginny said, reaching for the closest set of reins.

The sergeant grabbed her wrist. "We'll keep charge of our own horses. Now, get that water." He pushed her aside.

Emily leaped in front of the man. She stood very still for a moment and took a deep breath. "I believe you gentlemen should leave," she said to the soldiers. "And as for food," she continued, "we haven't much. And what we have is to feed those you have come here so courageously to liberate. What we have would do you little good and would deprive these free blacks."

"Ma'am, I find myself at a loss." The sergeant fidgeted.

"We will give you water, not because of your orders, sir, but because you are thirsty. We will water your horses for the same reason. And we will give you some turnips for your supper. The same as we are having. There is no need to steal them. However, if you steal from us, you clearly see the faces of the people from whom you steal."

Benjamin and Lucian led the horses to the trough. Samantha went to the cellar and returned with the turnips Ginny had dropped in her fright. Ginny brought a bucket of fresh water from the cistern. As the men wiped their faces on their coat sleeves, Ginny retrieved the gourd dipper from the boy-faced soldier and handed him the turnips.

"Get your horse, Stapleton," said the sergeant. "Stop staring and put those turnips in the saddle bag. Mount up, Jamison." The sergeant tipped his cap to Emily and turned his horse. "Madam, you may expect a good number more like me. They will not be intimidated nor so docile in accepting your turnips. Captain Beckwith of Colonel Grierson's division is close behind us. And you, madam, will soon be hostess to both Captain Beckwith and his men. I assume you have turnips and more to spare."

The captain arrived within half an hour. Alongside him rode the three scouts. Emily stood at the gate, waiting. She licked her dry lips and nodded.

"Madam, I am Captain Warren Beckwith, in charge of the 4th Iowa Cavalry of the Union Army of the United States. My men require food, water, bandages, and other such supplies as you may have in your possession. Sergeant Digby here tells me you have generously offered us turnips for supper. I fear that will not do, madam, in spite of information that you and your family are Southern abolitionists. I have encountered such sympathies before. I assume you would also then be a Unionist and eager to provide for these men who are risking their lives to bring that abolition and Union into permanent reality."

Emily looked out across the array of bedraggled troops, studying the captain's small, tight face.

"Sir, we are doing our best in hard times. There is little extra. I entreat you to spare us."

"We are also doing our best in hard times, madam. My men have been in the saddle two full days and a night without rest. No one is spared in this conflict." He motioned to the officer nearest him. "Sergeant, prepare the men to pitch camp. Set out a watch. Designate six men to take inventory of this property. You can be sure the cache will be ample. See to the horses. Enlist whatever help you need from the hands on this place. Conscript the men themselves if you see fit and find them willing."

Captain Beckwith regarded Emily, who had not moved from the gate.

"Madam," he said, "I shall require an invitation to dine at your table this evening. On something other than turnips. Perhaps one of those chickens I hear cackling. I shall expect you to sit at the table with me. We will dine at eight o'clock. Thank you for your kind invitation. I accept."

In the field, tents were already flapping in the wind. Emily could not imagine how many. The air pulsated with the shouting men and the pounding of stakes into the ground. The rank smell of their accumulated sweat and grinding filth gagged her. She stood transfixed as the transformation in the field took place. Ignoring her, the captain passed by and stooped to enter a large tent already nearby. The flap dropped behind him.

"Ginny," Emily said, "bring me the ax and catch the smallest chicken you can. Set some water on to scald."

Ginny did as she was told. With the exception of giving Emily an ax. She and Jessie chased down a small hen. Propping the ax beside the stump, Ginny laid the chicken's neck across it. Emily jerked up the ax. Ginny straightened.

"What you doing, Miss Emily?"

"I am killing a chicken for that Yankee, Ginny. You heard the menu, chicken and turnips."

"Yes'm, I did. Now hand me that ax."

"And to that," said Emily, "we will add a cake of cornbread and pot liquor. Do we have any greens?"

"Got some collards. Maybe tough, but they'll do."

"All right. Put that chicken's head back on the stump, Ginny."

"Miss Emily—"

"On the stump, Ginny. And get your hand out of my way."

The ax came down. The chicken's head fell to the earth. Ginny fought to hold the jerking body, aiming the spurting blood away from Emily, who dropped the ax and covered her face.

"You be ready," Ginny said to Benjamin, who had slipped into the scene.

He stood behind Emily. She lifted her face, standing still. Her breath came in violent shudders.

"Get this chicken out my hands, Benjamin. What's wrong with you?" Ginny handed off the still-twitching body and came up behind Emily. "Tell Jessie get that thing scalded and plucked."

She turned Emily around.

"Why you do that, honey?"

Emily wiped the back of her hand across the front of the apron. Slowly, she withdrew the knives hidden in her pockets. "I expect you will need these," she said, between breaths.

"Yes'm." Ginny studied Emily's white face.

"You can go on now, Ginny. I am not going to faint or go crazy."

Ginny turned. Emily reached out and caught her hand. Ginny stood for a moment, their hands holding one another. Then she walked away, a knife in each hand.

* * *

"A fine table for turnips and chicken." Captain Beckwith gave Emily a slight bow. "I appreciate this dinner, Mrs. Slate. And your help in provision for my men, who are much fatigued."

"I find myself unable to say that you are welcome, Captain Beckwith."

Beckwith examined the room with its sparse, well-made essentials. The table, the chairs, the china and silver Emily had hesitated to use, silver that had been her mother's. He saw her look.

"My commander, Colonel Grierson, is a gentleman, Mrs. Slate. A music teacher, actually. It is a matter of some puzzlement that he became a soldier, let alone the cavalry, let alone the leader that he has become. He is also a just man. We are under firm orders that there be no violence against civilians, no looting, no thievery—although you may consider our conscription of food and necessary supplies to be just that. Your silver is safe in my presence and that of my men. Our focus is on the preservation of the Union and the liberation of slaves. To that end, we are only interested in the destruction of railways, depots, armories, and strategic weakening of rebel forces."

The captain drew the chair for her to be seated.

"Now, Mrs. Slate," he said, settling himself opposite her, "in spite of discovering you in the midst of preparing turnips, which I expect you do to preserve supplies, you would not expect me to believe that you do not have ample reserves. This is a rather large plantation, and I presume your servants are experienced hands at husbandry and farming."

"We have suffered ill weather for crops, sir, as I understand you have suffered ill weather for war."

Captain Beckwith noted the twitch at the corners of her mouth. He took a sip of water. Jessie entered with the platter of chicken, four pieces fried to perfection, and set it before him. Ginny followed: in one hand, a bowl of turnips with greens, dotted with shining drops of bacon grease, in the other, a plate of fried corn pone. She set the dishes in front of the captain. He did not seem to know what to do.

"Please serve yourself, Captain."

The forks clinking against the china sounded startlingly loud. Emily cut a leg and thigh apart. With her fingers, she raised the drumstick to her lips. Beckwith looked up in surprise, his knife and fork poised over the chicken breast. He hesitated, laid the silver on the plate, and picked up his piece of chicken. Emily was aware of his scrutiny. He would have cut every bite, she knew, forked it morsel by morsel to his mouth, as she would have in other days.

"Did you volunteer?" she said.

"Yes, ma'am. I did."

"Why?"

"You are very straightforward, Mrs. Slate." Beckwith cleared his throat. "I believe in the Union. And the freedom of all men under our Constitution."

Silence. Emily did not divert her eyes.

"I was young," he said at last. "I was idealistic. I believed in a number of lofty ideals. I still do. And I had no notion of the grim realities of war."

"Are you married, sir?"

Beckwith returned the directness of her gaze.

"Yes, I am. Less than a year now."

"And where is your wife?"

"At home with her mother."

"And her father? Is he fighting also?"

"Yes, he is," Beckwith said.

"And what will she do, sir, in case you do not return?"

"I intend to return, Mrs. Slate."

"We all intend something, Captain." Emily put her napkin alongside her plate and sat back.

"And your husband, ma'am, is he—"

"Dead. My husband is dead. My father is dead. My brothers are dead." Emily halted. "Except one whom you may wind up killing if you reach Vicksburg. He is there fighting against my father's cause."

"I'm sorry, Mrs. Slate. This war—"

"They did not die in this war, sir. They died in a much more Biblical way. Cain and Abel and greed. They died at war with themselves."

Beckwith shifted in his chair and pushed back from the table.

"Ginny will wrap the rest of the chicken in paper," Emily said. "You will want it tomorrow."

"Mrs. Slate, I wondered at something today and feel I might not be too bold to ask. You are so exceptionally forthright."

"What do you want to know?" she said.

"I was watching today when you killed the chicken."

"Oh," said Emily. "And you want to know about that."

"Your servant seemed in distress. And afterward I saw why. It has troubled me and I must say, it has been difficult to eat this meal."

"I had an unfortunate experience as a child with the killing of a chicken, Captain. It left me scarred inside. I was falsely protected from a great deal after that. It was all a great delusion. My life has consisted of a number of great delusions. The time has arrived for me to move past them, sir. You have witnessed my first killing."

He regarded her and then stared out the window.

"You have much in common with my commander, Colonel Grierson, Mrs. Slate. As a child, the colonel was kicked in the head by a horse. He lived, but was blind for some time and grew up with a terrible fear of horses. Now he commands seventeen hundred men of the 6th and 7th Illinois and the 2nd Iowa Cavalry regiments. He lives on a horse."

"Well, Captain, I hope I shall not have to live on my chickens, although they do their part." Emily rose and extended her hand.

"There are many kinds of courage, Mrs. Slate. I salute you." He clicked his heels and bowed.

She withdrew her hand. "Good night, sir. I hope your young wife will see you come home."

Before dawn, the Union forces broke camp. Some confusion rose at an apparent desertion by one of the scouts, overshadowed by the urgency of Beckwith's mission. Left behind was the stink of unwashed bodies, vomit, and worse. Lucian stared at the open latrine, slick with excrement. Flies already swarmed around it; the putrid soil jumped with fleas left behind from the troops. He considered their deprivations, the filth and disease they suffered. Lucian wondered what made men endure the march they were on and the fight to come. He leaned on the shovel and closed his eyes. *Supposed to be about us,* he thought, and shook his head. *Men is men,* he thought. *Just 'cause they trying to do good, don't mean they's good.* His head swirled with the brutal memory of the night before.

Nathan touched his elbow. "You ready?"

Lucian turned away and spat. He gazed into Nathan's face, a face he could trust, all blinders gone. "Yeah," he said.

The two men set to digging, Nathan with a longer shovel and the lopsided stance he had adapted for his one arm. Neither spoke. As the trench of the latrine grew deeper, Nathan stopped to readjust his leverage. Lucian glimpsed in the face of this man beside him, a mirror for the unexpected alterations that had befallen them both. Here was another man who forever might or might not recognize himself. *Life can do that to you*, Lucian thought. *You just don't see it coming at you till it's too late*. He lifted another load of the muck and studied the deepening hole. The earth sucked against the shovel as he dug.

"That's enough," Nathan said.

Lucian jabbed at the side of the hole and threw another shovelful to the side.

"Come on now, Lucian," Nathan said. "It's time. Gone soon be too light. Folks'll be coming."

Lucian thrust the shovel into the mound of earth and led the way into the barn. The two men reemerged, dragging between them a heavy load wrapped in a length of homespun, taking on the color of the earth as the mud slathered onto it. They dropped it into the gaping latrine. Without speaking, they shoveled the muck back over their mysterious load. The task done, they leaned on their shovels to catch their breath and watched the dawn soften the sky. By the time a few more hands joined them in the field, there remained only the rest of the latrine to cover. Talk among the men focused on the soldiers who had come and gone out of their lives, on the visceral realities of the military and their mission, on who among themselves had followed after the troops. They speculated as to what these men, whatever their cause, actually felt about the coloreds they encountered. Lucian walked toward his cabin. A few of the men stared after him. The latrine was closed, the stench barely diminished.

A skillet, half full of bacon fat, sizzled on the back burner. With a piece of scorched quilting, Ginny clanged open the fire door and shoved in a stick of wood, jabbing at the coals. As she backed up, Ginny stumbled against Rosa Claire, who straddled a small pan, stirring some make-believe concoction with a piece of kindling.

"Rosa Claire, what you doing in my way? You gone get us both burnt up." Ginny exhaled as she hiked the child onto her hip. Her apron strap drooped. She yanked it back with her thumb. As she turned toward the door, the sizzling grease stopped her. She yanked the skillet off the burner. Rosa Claire squirmed, whimpering and then wailing, as Ginny jerked her away from the stove.

"Jessie," Ginny shouted across the empty porch to the yard where she spotted the other woman, lugging an armload of kindling to the wash pot. "Get this child off me. And see she don't harm herself. And nobody else neither. I got okra to fry and she all over my kitchen underfoot. Gone trip me up sure." Ginny tugged Rosa Claire from her hip. "Where your young'uns', Jessie?"

"Gone with they daddy."

"Gone? Gone where? You know it ain't safe 'round here."

"I don't know. Said he had something he had to do and the childrens could go and play along the crick."

"You don't know where he gone? With them children? And you let him? All them Yankees round about? And who knows what Seceshes spying for runaways? And what about playing at the crick by themselves? Ain't you got one lick of sense, Jessie?" She handed down Rosa Claire. "Somebody gone wind up dead."

"Nathan just say he had to go. Said it was time and he be back."

"Well, don't be letting this one go off nowhere. I got work to do."

The inventory of foodstuff seized by Beckwith's troops from the hidden reserves trailed three pages in Emily's ledger. Freedom felt scant now. Ginny was withdrawn and sullen. The quarters teemed with disgruntled complaint and gossip: Who'd gone missing to follow the Union troops? Who had headed North? What was to be had from abandoned cabins? How to make crop, short-handed? In all thirty-eight people from the Matthews place had disappeared in one direction or the other.

Three days after Beckwith's unit marched off to the west, the sheriff rode into Emily's yard. She gripped the porch railing as she watched him approach. Though she knew this man's integrity, the sight of him evoked unbounded agony in her. She steeled herself to stand still. As Mason dismounted, he surveyed the place and nodded, almost imperceptibly. He stood at the foot of the steps, holding the reins loosely in his hand.

"I've got news, Miss Emily," he said. "For you and your man Nathan."

Puzzled, Emily motioned him onto the porch and sent Ginny to fetch Nathan. Mason declined a chair and stood.

"Mrs. Slate," he said, in his slow, deliberate way. "I've been wanting to speak to you plainly for some time now. I just didn't quite have the gumption. I didn't know how you might receive it." He hesitated. "I know it's nothing you need, just the opposite, most likely, but it's something I need right badly. I failed you, ma'am. I'm sorry and I need you to know that." Mason stared at a fragment of brown leaf caught in a crack between the floorboards. "More than sorry. I'm full-out grieved." He waited to find his voice. "I couldn't stop your brother's mob, and I couldn't go off to arrest him in the middle of the Confederate Army. Couldn't ever pin anything direct on Conklin, either, but maybe justice has a route of its own. I know in reason I couldn't have made it different, but knowing it don't help. My failure haunts me. Lots of nights I don't sleep much and when I do, I'm pestered with nightmares. Wake up in a sweat. But you don't need to know all that, Mrs. Slate." Mason raised his face to hers. "I just need to tell you straight out how deep my regret goes."

Emily bowed her head. She did not respond. She wanted to, but nothing came.

"Sheriff," Nathan said, running up the path. His eyes narrowed. "Ginny say you need me, sir."

"I got some news, Nathan. Not sure quite how you may take this, but I figured it was important for both of you to know. Holbert Conklin is dead. Old slave found him hanging from the rafters in his barn yesterday." He watched Nathan as he waited for Emily to absorb the shock. "He'd been hoarding contraband cotton, against regulations. Useless to the troops when what they need is rations. Appears they headed over there when they left here. He wasn't the only one hereabouts. Been smuggling it over to Bankston to the cotton mill. All gone now. Looks like Grierson set fire to the future on his way through. Damned near burned Bankston to the ground in the night. All but a handful of Conklin's slaves loaded up and tailed the Yankees. Only ones stayed are too old. Conklin's wife took their boy and a pair of slaves last week before the Yankees came and headed for Winona. Seems she's got people there. Maybe she'd had enough of Conklin and the war both. Anyway, one of the old slaves left behind found Conklin yesterday morning. Had some kind of injury to the head, bad blow, looked like, maybe from the troops, maybe not, but looks like suicide, so that's what I'm calling it."

"Suicide?" Emily said. "What about the Yanks?"

"Could've been the Yanks. Could have been somebody else. Could've been someone we'd least expect. Head injury's right bad, bad enough to've killed him, but I'm calling it suicide. Wouldn't want to call it anything else. Justice, maybe. Man should've been hung a long time ago." Mason slapped his hat against his leg. "Anyway, I thought you both should know. Especially you, Nathan."

Mason mounted his horse and nodded. "Oh, and keep a sharp eye for a Union deserter. Probably long gone by now. But just in case. Can't be too cautious."

Chapter 34

By the time the last two letters arrived, gloom had fallen over Greensboro, even for those who longed for this rebellion to end in failure and the preservation of the Union. Deprivation touched every house and cabin. Emily recognized her brother's hand, though only just, scratched and blotched as it was.

Vicksburg
July 8, 1863

Sister,

As you must surely know, as all God's hell must surely know, Vicksburg is four days surrendered to the Yankee devils and I am taken captive. We shall have no need of hell hereafter, except to punish these damned Yankees. The conditions here are hell itself. No food, filthy water, filthy clothes, fleas, lice, men in filth from every sort of horrible disease and sickness. Men are dying everywhere and not from wounds. The rain and mud make the stench itself enough to kill a man.

I am in urgent need of rations and clothing. The blanket you sent is long gone to rags. I had as soon pitch it except it is now my only bed. There is no protection from this excessive heat. Men are dying from that alone. I am in an agony of discomfort. There is no remedy for my current debilitation.

Your brother,

Jeremiah

The handwriting on the second envelope was unfamiliar, the paper ragged on the edges and dirty. Emily stared at it for some minutes before she opened it. She squinted to decipher the scrawl.

Nigh onto Vicksburg
July 1863 to the best of my knowing

Dear Mrs. Slate,

Your brother Jeremiah Slate is dead. We got captured together at Vicksburg and suffered prison alongside one another and got released the other day. I'm not sure what day that was. We have lost all sense of time in there. Your brother took the fever again and he did not make it far. He was mighty weak and I am shamed to say, though I woke to see it in the night, it was one of our own cut him with his own little knife and made off with the grab or two of goods your brother still held on to. We found some wood from a nigger shack close by and laid him on it. We didn't have no hammer or nails, but we laid a ragged blanket over him that he said one time come from you and we buried him deep enough so you shouldn't worry.

I know it would be right of me to say I'd help you find him, but I am not yet 20 years old and have a wound in my leg, but it is not so bad I can't walk with a stick. I am going home to find my Mama now and I am not ever going back near Vicksburg again.

Very truly,
Gilbert Adamson

Outside across the field where Emily fled, heavy clouds hung above the horizon like the smoke of a fire gone out of control. The grass was seared. Brambles tore at Emily's skirts and ripped her hands. She sank to her knees. Her mother lay bloody in her vision, the women turned away with the baby, her mother unmoving and white except for the blood, Jeremiah wailing. And this was what had come of it all. Emily clutched her ribs as she rocked, her cries piercing the semidarkness, ripping her, gutting her. Surely she must die; she was bewildered that she was unable to. Emily rocked more slowly. Her forehead touched the ground. She felt her hands go blind.

From down the side row, a man approached. He leaned toward her. His strong hands gripped her arms and raised her to her feet. Through her tears she recognized Michael Lambert. She stumbled toward home, his arm around her waist for support.

Lambert waited on the front step until Jessie came to say that

Emily was calmed. Putting on his hat, he nodded and walked away. A week later, he came again. Emily sat on the porch beside him.

"What were you doing there, Mr. Lambert? How did you find me?"

"I was out helping Asa hunt a new hound he just got from old man Everett over off the Bellefontaine Road. Just a pup. Not more than six month old. I reckon he was headed back to where he thought was home. I was up the field there and saw you go into the woods way off. So far off, I wasn't for sure it was you. You didn't come out and then I heard you crying." Lambert hesitated. "Well, a little more than just crying, maybe. I thought you'd run up on a cat. I started running. Seemed like the crying got worse; then it just stopped. Felt like I was in one of those dreams where you get to running and your legs get slower and slower till you're not going anywhere at all." Lambert scratched his head where his dark hair was thinning at the temples. He pulled at his collar as if he needed more air. "Got real quiet then. Without the sound, I couldn't tell where to find you. I got right scared and I was running again, keeping my eyes on the woods, listening, and I saw a speck of blue cloth. Flapped just once on a puff of air. I reckon you must of tore your dress."

"Yes, I did." Emily stared along the horizon. The sun was beginning to set. "Did you find the dog?" she said.

"No, ma'am. Hound turned up next day back where he came from. Asa went and got him. He's on a tie now till he gets used to thinking of us as home. Looks to be a good dog."

Emily stood. Lambert rose, his tall, angular body blocking the sun from her eyes.

"I was just there, Miss Emily. That's all," he said.

"Mr. Lambert, I want to thank you." She faced him, her head tilted up to his height.

"Yes, ma'am. I know—"

"I don't believe you do, Mr. Lambert. Not for bringing me home. I am thanking you for being there."

"Well, that's a comfort to me, ma'am. I felt kind of like I'd trespassed holy ground."

"I appreciate that, Mr. Lambert. I'm not sure this ground is holy, but it is private."

"I'm sorry. I regret—" he said.

"There is nothing to regret, Mr. Lambert. You brought me home. And strangely, I am surprised at the comfort in having someone witness how I really am."

Emily went into the house and left him standing on the porch, staring at the door.

"Miss Emily, we got us a stuck calf." Ginny was breathless. "Out of Bliss. Well, not exactly out, and there lies the problem. You got to decide, do we save the calf or the cow? May not can save either one. But you got to say."

The fringe of Emily's shawl caught in the chair spindles as she whirled and dropped a bowl of peas half-shelled.

"Where you going, Miss Emily?" Ginny said.

"To the barn."

"That ain't no place for you. Just answer me. I ain't got time to fool with you."

Emily jerked at the shawl as Ginny tried to free it, their frenzied hands at odds, peas crunching underfoot.

"We can't afford to lose that cow!"

"Then we'll save the cow," Ginny said.

"And we have to have that calf! We have to last this war."

"Well, now, that ain't no answer."

"Send Jessie to fetch Granny Sonja. She's birthed enough babies. A cow can't be so different."

Emily unsnagged the shawl and kicked at the peas.

"You don't know what you getting into," said Ginny, her mind back to Miss Liza's death, the screaming baby, the blood, and Emily watching. She stood full height, her eyes penetrating. She breathed deep. "Then again," she said, "mayhap you do."

In the filtered light of the barn, Lucian knelt in the second stall. The fetid air was dense and stank of blood and urine. Around him, the hay was soiled with blood. Bliss lay exhausted, her breath erratic. From her rear, a single leg protruded.

"Coming backward," said Lucian. Then he saw Emily, her hand over her mouth. "This ain't no place for you, ma'am."

"Is it breech?" Emily managed to say.

"I don't know about no breech," Lucian said. "It just trying to come foot-first, one foot stuck. Bliss done give out and I can't get this calf turned. I can kill it and get it on out real quick like, once you say and go on back to the house. Coming like that, they don't hardly live nohow. Save us a good cow. What you want, Miss Emily?"

"Get out the way." Granny Sonja's voice startled them. "What she doing here?" The old woman elbowed her way past Emily, who struggled not to vomit. "If she gone stay, she got to get out the way."

Emily stumbled over the cow's legs and knelt at Bliss's head. She ran her hand up the white crest, folded an ear forward, and traced the soft eyelid with her fingertip. Bliss opened her eye. The exhausted resignation in the heifer's gaze stabilized Emily.

Granny Sonja scowled. "Look like her labor stopped," she said. "What else you tried sides turning?"

"Thought about a horse and rope," Samuel said. "But that other hoof still stuck and I don't aim to tear her. She dead for shore, do she start bleeding."

"Fetch me some soap and water. Lucian, get me some lard. And be quick."

The midwife slathered on the grease and thrust her arms into Bliss, her elderly body weaving as she crouched on her haunches. The cow's eyes widened and its huge head lifted. Emily concentrated on those eyes, attached herself to the life in them. She murmured, trance-like, to the animal. The old woman's shoulder muscles tightened and the calf disappeared into the depths of its terrified mother.

Granny Sonja's leathery hand reentered the cow. She maneuvered the offending hoof back into the birth canal, aligning it with the other, and pulled them both out. "Can't turn it," Granny Sonja said. "We gone take it backside first. Get that horse and hitch him up here."

Lucian grabbed a piece of torn stable blanket, swaddled the calf's hooves, and bound them with rope. Taking the bridle, he led the horse out slow. The calf dropped onto the hay.

"Well, now, alive and breathing," Granny Sonja said. "Gone stand right on up. How's Bliss?"

"I don't know." Emily's voice was a hoarse whisper.

"You ain't gone faint, now, is you?" Granny Sonja peered at Emily's white face, while she cleaned the placenta and smoothed its bloody folds. "Where's Ginny? Tell her to see to this woman."

From the corner of the stall, Ginny studied Emily. She did not go to her.

"Bliss ain't standing up," said Benjamin, who had returned.

"Bliss done got herself cripple," Granny Sonja said, wiping her arms on her apron. "She don't supposed to be lying down for this. All right, Benjamin, you gone get this cow up?"

"I'll make a sling, Granny. I can get her up. But might be days before she can stand by herself."

Granny Sonja scrubbed at the calf with fresh hay. "Benjamin," she said, "get this baby up to its mama's nose. See what that do."

Benjamin arranged the wet calf against its mother's nose. Bliss extended her tongue to lick at the baby. She did not raise her head. With eyes closed, she continued her feeble efforts to nuzzle the calf.

The men maneuvered a canvas sling under the cow's inert body and heaved the rope over a rafter. Knots secured, Lucian led the horse forward and the cow's prone body rose. Simultaneously, the calf struggled to her feet, rump first. She swayed against her mother's leg. Held upright by the sling, Bliss worked the calf with her great tongue. Within the hour, the calf was nuzzling her mother's swollen udder.

It would take a good three days for Bliss to regain movement in her legs. According to Benjamin, that was "mighty quick like." It would be another four before he risked letting Bliss stand without support. When the sling came off, Lucian led Bliss out of the barn. Ginny stood by the fence with Emily, watching as the calf followed, flicking its paintbrush tail, blinking against the glare of the sunlight.

Chapter 35

The walnut wardrobe creaked on its hinges. Emily had not opened it since that day three years before when she wrapped her soft batiste nightdress, with its tiny rows of tucks and finely stitched embroidered vines, in tissue and lay it on the upper shelf beside the folded stack of delicate underthings she had abandoned in favor of plain shifts and homespun cotton drawers.

As her fingers traced the undulating pattern of wood grain, Emily stared at her hardened, sunburned hands. She tucked them into her apron pockets and turned her back on the wardrobe. In the kitchen, she picked up the jar of cold bacon grease and rubbed some on the back of her hand.

In the doorway, Ginny stood watching. Without speaking, she broke a leaf of aloe from the old plant by the window. Reaching into the cupboard, Ginny took out a blue patterned saucer. She squeezed the sticky gel from the leaf and stirred in a spoonful of lard, slowly, then with vigor, until a thick cream had formed. Ginny wiped the spoon between her fingers and dropped it into the dishpan.

"Let me see them hands now," she said, reaching out.

Emily did not move.

"Come on, honey. Let's see them. They ain't no secret, you know. Not in this house."

Emily raised her hands. Ginny's touch was quiet, but her stroke was firm. The cream felt cool, soothing. Emily laid her cheek against the top of Ginny's head.

In the warm autumn sun Emily lay back on the grass, her palms moving over the tips, feeling the soft itch of it. The trees shed their many colors like Joseph robbed of his bloodstained coat. Emily peered into the opening canopy of interlocking branches. Life had become her work now, one that brought a satisfaction and an occasional joy wrapped in the hands of her children. Or in the warm strength of Ginny's arm. She was surprised now to be surprised, taken unaware that life could touch her so, that joy, however small or fleeting, could find her.

Emily stared at the astonishing blue of the sky, studied the interlocking pieces of it where the bare branches meandered. What she saw were not the branches, but the random pieces of the sky. Fitting together like an intricate puzzle, like a shattered bowl of half-shelled peas, carefully mended, each broken piece in place. *The scars of brokenness,* she thought, *are bold, yet the sky still astonishes. There is beauty in the broken.*

At the sound of voices Emily turned her head and raised on her elbow. Ginny sauntered toward her with Lonso on her hip, Rosa Claire running ahead, her voice shrill with excitement, waving sheets of paper in the air.

"Look, Mama, look." As Rosa Claire neared, one of the papers floated out, offering a glimpse of color in the air like a last leaf falling from the overhanging trees. She stooped to retrieve it and stepped on it in her excitement. Her face fell and she held it up to Ginny with an eruption of tears.

Ginny knelt with Lonso. "It's just a little smudge there now. Ginny gone wipe that right off for her gal." Ginny rubbed at the spot with the corner of her apron. "Don't cry now, honey. Go show your mama what we found."

Rosa Claire held the papers out to her mother. Emily sorted through them, unsure what she was seeing. It soaked into her that here was her mother. Rosa Claire knelt beside her, watching with fascination. Her little hands stroked her mother's arm, her cheek against the worn fabric of the work dress. Emily raised her eyes. Ginny stood against the sky, Lonso still on her hip.

"Where did you find these?" Emily said.

"Over to the big house. I got some women cleaning up there. Hannah found this old chest in the attic. Full of these. I told Lucian to bring it on over here."

"What all is in it, Ginny?"

"Miss Liza's paintings. You children's paintings, you and Will, marked on the back in your mama's hand: your name, date, sometimes a little note. And some paints and paper, left over. Reckon your daddy had them stored away after she died. Don't reckon he could manage seeing them."

"My mother's paintings. I used to sneak into his office and stare at his collection of them hanging there when I was a child. I thought that was all of them."

"They's a whole chest full. Stacks of them. She must have had you children painting alongside her when you was mighty little. Seems like I remember some of that."

Emily pulled Rosa Claire into her lap. "See this," she said. The image was one of wobbly circles converging on one another in varying colors, bleeding into one another. On the back were Emily's name and a date that had been smeared. "I did this, Rosa Claire, when I was a little girl like you."

"Can I do that, Mama?" Rosa Claire traced the image with her finger.

"Of course you can."

Emily studied the images. Will had painted a man, it seemed: a circle of sorts for the head, lines that appeared to be arms and legs extending out of the head, no body, all in a brilliant yellow. Emily's pictures consisted generally of multiple circles in a wild array of colors. But one with her name showed a similar figure to Will's and beside it, another in brown, the lines connected as if the two might be holding hands. On the back was written in delicate script, *"Emily and Ginny."*

"Did you see this?" Emily held the paper up to Ginny.

"Yes'm. I seen it."

"What a long time we have been together, Ginny, you and I."

Ginny handed her a small book, a sketch pad bound in worn leather. Opening it, she found page after page of loose depictions of slaves: at work in the kitchen and fields, sitting on porch steps visiting, playing fiddle and dancing, walking the quarter path with a child in hand. A loose page slipped out.

She lifted the image: a little girl in a blue dress reaching for something out of sight. *Me,* she thought. An unexpected sense of being loved enveloped her, a moment of stillness, a stoppage of time.

Book Four: Love

1864–1866

CHAPTER 36

Through the tangled limbs, the sky formed a canopy of blue stained glass. How could she have forgotten? How could color astonish her so? Emily lived in shadow and she knew it. Her back to the sun, she leaned into the great old sycamore tree, cradling herself in the split of its trunk. She fingered the bark in the crevice where the tree took two equal directions toward the light. She turned her cheek to one side and stared at the curling gray bark. She pulled a piece away, like a child picking at a scab on a partly healed gash. Under it curled another dark piece, and another. But under that, there was no more peeling, only a glimpse of the pale meat of the tree, like skin of whatever color the instant before it bleeds. Above the wound, a single green leaf grew from the hard trunk. Not a branch, but one solitary leaf.

A bunting's rapid song came clear to her, the distant bark of a dog, and the sound of wagon wheels on the road. She surveyed the scene around her, the hills, with their magnitude of greens and the earthy, new-planted fields. Clearly this green and these woods and the birds had gone on without her, gone on without Charles and her father, without Will or Hammond, gone on in spite of the war. They would go on without her, too, when she was gone. Emily withdrew her fingers from the tree and walked into the field.

Small, and bluer by far than the sky, a feather lay at Emily's feet among the clover and the milkweed in the ungrazed pasture. The cows had been in the back fields for weeks, and the buntings had come and gone in their migratory passing. Entranced, Emily had watched as a multitude of small birds rose and fell, wave on wave, like hovering blue jewels, cresting and plummeting, cascading over the fields. Their iridescence flashed and glimmered in the sunlight. She picked up the feather and brushed it against her cheek.

Holding the blue feather, Emily felt the intensity of all she could never know, what had been done and not done, and by whom, all of it buried in various graves. Her life hung over her like a wavering mirage of summer. Emily closed her eyes and leaned against the fence. A slight rustling made her blink. In front of her a lone blue bunting darted up. It mounted the air, then dove into the clover, up and down, seen, then not seen. Emily held out her hand. She yearned after this bird. She was a pillar of yearning in a field of green clover. The bird darted and swooped, a brilliance of unreachable, impossible blue in the sunlight; then he was gone. Still holding the single blue feather, Emily lowered her hand.

The length of wood was rough to Lambert's touch, much like his own hands. He laid down the saw and righted the plank. The board would come smooth with sanding. Not so with his hands, no matter how much fat he rubbed into his skin. Rough hands were not a thing Lambert had ever cared about before, but now he thought of Emily, how soft the skin beneath her simple dress must be, how many years he had in age beyond her. In his hands, this board would become as smooth as he imagined her to be.

Lambert took a plane and a sanding block from a low shelf in the shed. He stretched his back, one hand on his lower spine as he returned to the stack of evenly cut boards. Laying one across the sawhorses, he took a few strokes, then paused to readjust the balance. Satisfied, Lambert addressed the board again, following the grain of the wood in firm, long strokes. This walnut would make a fine new cupboard.

When the sun was overhead, Lambert sat against the shady side of the barn and took out the cornbread and bacon Asa had wrapped in a clean handkerchief. Brushing crumbs from his breeches leg, he leaned back dozing in the warm spring air.

A great bellow from the south field woke Lambert, brought him to his feet in an instinctive sprint. He could see the bull, its horns trapped between two poles of the fence, its massive head jerking, its body braced with its powerful legs. He sprang over the fence, loping toward the enraged animal, visually assessing both danger and damage. His concern was for the bull. The fence could be mended. There seemed to be no injury, but the bull had yet to come to the same conclusion. It bellowed frantically, pulling against the fence pole. Asa had heard the ruckus and came running from the other end of the fence, ax in hand.

"You just back off now, Lambert. I got this one."

The ax hovered in the air for a second and then sliced into the pole near the head of the frantic beast. The pole bent and split. The great animal lumbered backward, caught its balance, and charged at nothing, its hot breath smoking in the air. The brothers chuckled as the bull halted in confusion.

"Well, Lambert, reckon that's what love'll do for you," said Asa. "Eh, boy! We'll have to move him over to the other corral till that heifer's out of heat."

Asa slapped Lambert on the shoulder, chuckling, and strode

back toward the barn. Lambert studied the bewildered bull, laughed, and spoke to the air.

"Well," Lambert said to himself, "what are you waiting for?"

Great fork loads of hay dropped over Benjamin's shoulder from the loft to the mounting wagonload below. The scent of earth emanated from the hay as it fell through shafts of sunlight, shifting from fodder to gold, back to fodder again. The sun outlined Benjamin's face, his warm features intensified, his white froth of hair haloed in the golden light.

Across the open field, Benjamin spotted a man approaching on horseback. The man's body adjusted easily to the horse's gait so that his movement suited that of the animal. Benjamin wiped the sweat from his brow and leaned against the fork, watching, anxiety consuming him, as it did every day now since the Union scouts had appeared and Lucian had gone silent. Below him, in the yard, Benjamin heard the laughter of the children, Aimee and Rosa Claire, playing ring-around-the-rosy with Lonso, who threaded in and out between them. Ginny's laughter, now returned, rang out with the mirth of the children.

Presently, the man's form grew familiar. Benjamin relaxed and readjusted his grip on the fork. Below him, the dust of the hay still eddied in the light. Benjamin wiped his forehead again and pocketed his handkerchief. He resumed his task, though his fear for Lucian felt like the empty space below him. By the time Benjamin dropped the last fork of hay into the wagon, the rider and his horse had entered the yard. It was Mr. Lambert.

At the porch steps, Lambert removed his hat and peered up at Emily, working at her churn. He cleared his throat and propped his work boot on the lower step.

"Mr. Lambert." Emily's voice was cordial. "Would you care to come up and have a seat?"

Lambert settled on the edge of a cane chair next to hers. He twirled his hat in his hands, appeared uncertain what to do with it, then laid it on the floor.

"Nice day," he said, looking around.

"Yes," Emily said. She waited. He cleared his throat. "Well, Mr. Lambert," she said, "what brings you here mid-afternoon on a workday?"

Lambert twisted his rough hands. "Well, Miss Emily, here it is. I have some things to say to you, but there's some other things I need to say first, so I guess that's where I should start." He hesitated. "I was there that night, you see."

Emily looked puzzled. Then her face blanched. She rose, reaching out to the back of the chair for support. She took a few halting steps and stood at the edge of the porch, her back to Lambert.

"I didn't think you'd know that," he said. "I don't reckon Adeline would have ever talked about that night. But I was there. I was coming on foot toward town. On my way to Jenkins Saloon to fetch Logan Mackey's boy home for his ma. If I'd been a mite earlier—well, no use talking like that. I wasn't. Nothing changes what's already done. It troubles me something awful. But I'm off the target now." Lambert pressed his open hands against his thighs.

"Well, here's the point, or thereabouts. I helped Adeline load Hammond in the wagon. He was like a baby. I laid him down comfortable as I could, as if that mattered—and I guess somehow it did. She wouldn't let me help her after that. Sent me off to try to keep the sheriff alive."

Lambert rubbed at the worn knee of his breeches.

"Point is, Emily, I don't need as much imagination as another man might to put myself into your mind and heart. I know that can't be done. But anyhow, maybe something akin."

He rose and took a step toward her, where she gripped the porch railing.

"Strange way to go about this, Emily. Maybe I am a bit strange, or so folks think—some folks, leastways. Here I am more than twenty-three years your senior. By rights, you should still be a girl, and I could be your father. But you've had a share of hell not many folks could walk through. Though this war is making lots of them do just that. I reckon that makes the difference in our age not count for much."

Lambert walked to the railing. His hand was close but not touching hers.

"My brother, Asa, and me been living together all these years, taking care of one another, not that he needed it, but I needed to care for something and he was there. Never courted, either one of us. I don't guess I'm courting now." Lambert half turned. "I'm just asking you to marry me."

Emily considered his face, the weathered lines somehow softening it. She studied the kindness in his hazel eyes. Very slightly, she nodded. Lambert laid his coarse palm against her cheek. She turned her head in his hand and kissed his palm, then raised her lips to his. He held her to him, rocking. She leaned back, a smile on her lips and tears in her eyes.

When Lambert departed, kissing her hands, the part in her hair, her lips, Emily wandered through the last of the day, thinking. Lambert would not take away her suffering. She knew that. But that he had been witness to her anguish gave her peculiar comfort. There was no need to explain herself, no need to tell her story, or to hide it. Lambert's story lay alongside hers, wove itself into hers without fixing it. With him, she was simply whoever she was. There was nothing different he wanted.

She would sleep on this, hold it through the night, like the pillow in her arms. Tomorrow, she and Ginny would turn her least worn dress inside out, spruce it as they could, and Lambert would come for her.

* * *

They were married by Jason Trumble, in the parsonage of the newly come pastor of Grace Methodist Church. The day was warm, with a cool breeze that forestalled the coming heat of summer. Asa served as witness for Lambert. The pastor's wife, Nellie Anne, stood up for Emily. The children were at home with Ginny. No one else was present.

How different, Emily thought. How utterly different, in her simple cotton dress, trimmed with salvaged scraps from three other dresses that had succumbed to various rips and tears over years of wear. She felt authentic, beyond pretension now, with a simplicity that fit.

Lambert stood beside her, tall, lanky, his long beard newly cropped, his butternut frock coat hanging loose on his frame. He wrapped an arm around Emily's shoulders, his other hand, warm and damp, cupping hers. She felt his gaze on her and smiled. His face was as steady as his hands.

When they returned from the parsonage, Ginny brought the children out to greet them. Lambert was not a stranger, but somehow both children sensed that today was different. While Rosa Claire flew to them both with arms outstretched, Lonso hid his face in Ginny's skirts. When Ginny knelt to give him encouragement, he began to cry and buried his face in her neck.

"Shush now, baby," Ginny crooned. "Ain't everyday a little boy gets a new pappy." She patted his back and smiled up at Lambert, who lifted Rosa Claire high in the air and settled her giggling on his shoulders. He bent toward Emily, into whose arms the little girl dropped in abandon, then immediately held out her hands to Lambert for another ride. As Rosa Claire played, Ginny shifted just enough for Lonso to see. He peeked over her shoulder.

"You want to go ride on your new pappy's shoulder?" Ginny's voice in the boy's ear was a half-whisper. She transferred him to her knee and jiggled him as she spoke.

Lambert knelt with Rosa Claire perched on his shoulder, his other arm widespread toward the boy. "It's all right, Lonso," he said. "It's just me coming by again. Only difference is this time, I'm not leaving."

The boy disentangled himself from Ginny's neck and squatted beside her. He stared up at his mother, who was peeking 'round at him from behind this man. She winked at the child, waving and crooking her finger. Dodging Lambert's outstretched arm, Lonso ran to her. Emily wound her fingers into his soft curls, holding him close. From her vantage point on Lambert's shoulder, Rosa Claire dissolved into laughter and twisted back and forth, her hands over his forehead. Lonso let go of Emily's skirt and stood in front of Lambert, solemnly studying him.

"Well, Lonso, what do you think now?" Lambert studied the boy in return. Giggling, Rosa Claire hid her face behind Lambert's head and Lonso slipped into his embrace.

Lambert pulled Rosa Claire's hands from over his eye and spotted Aimee watching at the edge of the little gathering. "You, too, honey," he said, and she came and stood beside Emily, still just watching. Rosa Claire jumped down from his shoulder and the two girls ran off, hand in hand, whispering and giggling.

On the sideboard, a wedding supper awaited the new family. Ginny and Jessie had spent the afternoon making it something festive. The meal was not lavish, given the war and the blockades, but generous and homey: a slow-cooked stew of beef and onions; green tomato pie with potato crust, minus the called-for lemon zest; layers of sliced turnips and potatoes baked with cheese; Indian bread; and rice pudding with molasses, flavored with a bit of brandy and the carefully hoarded nutmeg. Amidst repeated compliments to the cooks, who smiled as they had not done of late, Lambert did most of the talking. Emily concentrated on the children's manners. Asa, a naturally quiet man, had a gentle way with children, and Emily noted them looking to him often for approval. He was aware of their curiosity and smiled at them, or winked and made little faces. Asa would make a fine uncle.

After supper, Ginny took the children to wash up and ready themselves for bed. The three adults sat by the fire. When the children came down for good-night hugs, neither was shy with Lambert or Asa. The adults rose to watch the children back up the stairs, catching blown kisses from the landing. No one sat again. Asa wished them well and said good night, going home to live, for the first time, alone.

"You got anything else for me, Miss Emily?" Ginny said, descending the stairs. "Jessie done cleaned the table."

"No, Ginny. You go on home and get some rest. Jessie, too. Anything still to do tonight will be still to do in the morning. Not a single dirty pan has ever run away from home that I know of."

Like sisters, the two women embraced, holding each other. Ginny stroked Emily's back, then pushed away and ducked her head. Emily watched her go. When she turned to Lambert, he folded her in his arms. They stood beside the fire, rocking slightly, both of them soaking in the presence of the other.

"Lambert, I—" Emily spoke into the fabric of his shirt.

"Shh, now, love." He stroked the back of her head and spoke into the air above her netted hair. "I have something to tell you."

How kind and knowing his face is, Emily thought. Reaching up, she cupped his cheek in the palms of her hands. In the firelight, his eyes were dark pools, moist and vulnerable. Vulnerability stirred her always, beyond the scope of language. She trailed her fingers over his lips, across his undefended lids. She embraced the square turn of his bearded jaw in her hand and he pressed his lips into her palm.

"Emily, I—" Lambert paused. "I have loved you for a long time. Seems like I've been loving you all my life. I hardly remember not loving you. But by the time you were grown, I was already old. You were so young. I watched you from a ways off. At church. In town sometimes. At gatherings. I saw how sad you were. And shy. I saw you on the edges of a dance one night. I had it in my mind to speak to you when I saw Charles come sit beside you."

Emily felt the memory, the strangeness to think that Lambert had been aware, had seen. She remembered his solemn face in the crowd.

"I knew you would be his. And I loved you without any hope you would ever be mine. I made up my mind I would stay 'round the edges of your life. I vowed never to interfere. And someday when I was truly old and you had aged yourself, when we both got so old it wouldn't matter anymore, I told myself that I would find a way before I died to tell you, to make you know how dear you were to me. I'm not so good with words, but this love in me for you has held my life together, rooted me, made my life have meaning, even in your absence."

Raising herself to meet him, Emily pulled his lips down to meet her own. She lay her cheek against his chest, where she could feel his heart.

"I never did let myself think on a night like this," he said. "I'm so sorry for your pain, Emily. Terribly so. I would give you up all over again if I could spare you that. I reckon your suffering has broken all through me, and I hate to think that it is how you finally came to me. But, God forgive me, I'm grateful to have you mine." As Lambert rocked her, his tears fell warm on her forehead. Emily rose on her toes and kissed the dampness of his cheeks.

"Oh, Lambert," she said, "I never suspected."

"And you never would have, apart from—" He paused. "I'm sorry."

"I am sorry, too, Lambert, for everything that has come and gone. I'm glad I never knew and grateful that you spared me. But I am with you now, whatever the case, and that is all I need."

They stood in the firelight, neither knowing more to say. Lambert bent and without releasing her hand, shoveled the ashes to bank the fire. Still holding hands, together they slid the fire screen into place. Lambert led her toward the stair.

Emily woke early. The air was clear and fresh. She stretched. Her body felt alive, fulfilled. Lambert had already risen, dressed, and was standing next to the bed, adjusting his suspenders.

"Good morning." He leaned in and kissed her forehead. "Go back to sleep, Emme." He had given her this endearment, along with his name. Emme Lambert. She rolled the easy sound of it in the roof of her mouth.

"I'll get up and start the fire," she said.

"Ginny's way ahead of you, Mrs. Lambert. She's bustling around down there already. I saw the light from her lamp as she came across the yard earlier."

"How long have you been up?"

"Not long—but long enough. I've been watching you sleep."

Emily smiled, stretched again.

"You are beautiful, Emme. I don't know how to speak of how I feel. To know that you are here beside me." He stroked the curve of her cheek, where a slight scar remained. "I love you, Emme. I will never harm you if I know."

As he slipped his arms under her, she covered his mouth with her fingertips.

"Go on now," she said, kicking at the covers. Then aware of her nakedness, she recovered herself, fumbling for her night-dress.

Lambert watched, his face tender. He laughed and retrieved it from the floor, tossing it lightly over her face.

"I'll see you at breakfast," he said.

Emily listened to his lopsided steps descending the stair, one boot on, the other still dangling by the laces in his hand. She burrowed back into the covers, hugging the nightdress against her. She dared not think in comparisons.

CHAPTER 37

Lucian bent over the nest boxes in the chicken coop, gathering fresh eggs. His long fingers moved knowingly under the red hen, catching the warm egg almost before she knew she had laid it. When he had five in the basket, he pulled his shoulders back and walked toward the cabin, where his father would be boiling water for coffee. Lucian had always been quiet, but of recent, he'd closed off inside himself. He couldn't even talk about the weather, only brief muddled words necessary to some task at hand. He and Nathan had exchanged only rudimentary greetings since their night of digging at the trench. He knew his father was waiting for him to speak, waiting to know what ailed his son. He knew this barrier between them was an agony for Benjamin, and he shared it.

He laid the basket on the table in Benjamin's cabin and watched his father's hands: the way they handled the fragile eggs, the way they washed the thin shells clean, the way everything was sterling in his father's fingers. Lucian deliberated how to speak. In the end there was no way except to say it plain.

"Daddy," he said.

Benjamin looked up. He heard the reluctant determination of his son's voice. He dreaded what would come, but felt a deep relief that it would. "What you got to say, boy? It's time."

"Daddy, I done killed a man."

Benjamin moved the eggs aside. One rolled from the tabletop onto the floor. He ignored the broken yolk spreading across the planks. He shifted his weight to his uninjured leg and wiped his hands over his eyes. "I been waiting, son, but not for this." He reached for the cane chair, steadied himself, and lowered himself into it. Lucian grasped at his father's arm to help him settle, but Benjamin shrugged away. "How you come to kill a man, Lucian? Who you kill?"

Lucian pulled his hand back. He shook his head, took a deep breath, and spoke into the brittle air that filled the room now. "It was the night of the soldiers, Daddy. I didn't go to do it. It just happened."

Benjamin lowered his head and wiped the heel of his hand over his brow.

"I couldn't sleep, Daddy. All them strange men out there. I just wandered around. Keeping watch, I guess you'd say. Along 'fore daylight I heard a commotion amongst the cows and went toward the barn. Couple of them stomping and snorting. Thought Ginny must have started the milking early. I heard a muffled kind of scream and when I got in the barn, I seen one of them scouts, one of the three that come here first, his hand over Ginny's mouth—couldn't mistake it was Ginny, that long body, taller than him—and her struggling against him and him struggling to get his pants down. She was fighting. Seen me coming and her eyes got wide, but nothing else to give me away. Man's pants half down and his pistol tangled in the leg. Wasn't hard to snatch it. And I killed him."

Benjamin looked his son in the face. Then he lay his forehead on the table. His hands folded in his lap.

Presently, he raised himself.

"She told me she holds the blame. Ain't no blame but mine, Daddy. And I reckon I'd do it again. He'd have killed us both if he saw he was caught."

"But you saved her."

"Yes, sir. I reckon I did."

"Don't nobody know you did this?"

"Nathan knows. He helped me bury him in the latrine. Pistol, too. Now, I'm telling you. Don't know as I'll ever be the same again, Daddy. Doing evil to ward off evil. Don't know who that makes me now."

"You my son. That's who you is. No way you could be other."

"Yes, sir."

"He in the latrine?"

"Yes, sir."

"So stench just mingled and wasn't nobody looking under their nose for that deserter."

"No, sir."

"What you planning on, son?"

"I don't know, Daddy. Maybe go North. Get away from this."

"You think you be any safer that away. Killing a Union man?"

"Don't know as I can tell that, Daddy."

"No, son, life ain't laid out so one can tell the next curve one way or the other."

Lucian knelt beside his father. "You gone be able to love a killer, Daddy?"

Benjamin took Lucian's wide jaw in both his hands, fingered the high bones of his cheeks. Benjamin raised Lucian's chin, locking his gaze, knowing he looked into the dark eyes of a man who no longer knew himself.

"Who I love," Benjamin said, "is my son."

CHAPTER 38

Adeline loved the dark of the early morning, rising from the warmth of her covers to reignite the embers of the banked fire. The chill of the room energized her while she watched the wakening flame. She lit a straw from the hearth broom and guarded the tiny flame as she crossed the room to light the lantern. She'd had this lantern most all her married life, and it comforted her now on her way across the yard to the kitchen. She set the lamp aside and bent to light the kindling. It caught and the stove readied itself for her eggs. Her ham was long gone, but the scent of yesterday's cornbread warmed the room.

Lifting her lantern, Adeline stepped down from the kitchen and crossed to the shed, where Thomas would be sprawled, cradling a bottle, or curled round it like a baby. On the floor lay other bottles from other nights. She was never sure how he managed to get them, though egg money was often missing. She studied him, this husband of hers, this man she no longer knew as a man. *He is gone,* she thought. *His children are gone. Perhaps I am gone.* She extinguished the lantern and returned to her kitchen. The almost light of early dawn guided her feet. She could have walked this worn pathway blind.

Settled in the light of the stove, Adeline rested her hand on the journal. Benjamin had found it in Charles's office and brought it to her after the confrontation with Emily. Without the courage to open it, Adeline had dropped the slim volume into a drawer. The book had remained in its hiding place all this time, until last week when, imprisoned in the house by the rains, she had resolved to read it. And she had. Now she struggled with what to do. She ruffled the pages and pushed the book aside.

Adeline sipped her coffee, played at the eggs with her fork, lifted them butter-soft to her tongue. She swallowed. Grief flooded her, penetrated her bones. She lay her head on her folded arms and let it come.

From a great distance, the low mooing of a cow penetrated the vast pain of her awareness. Daylight had slipped into the room. Adeline stirred. She raised her head. The coffee was cold. She rose and threw the dregs out the door. She would not die. She would live her life alone.

Alone is not lost, she thought. *Alone is still alive, and I am alive.* She poured another cup of coffee, dipped the remaining cornbread into it, and held the bitter crumbs against her tongue. Yes, alone would have to do. There was no remedy for alone.

The egg was still warm from the nest, straw stuck to its side as Lambert placed it in Emily's hand. It was neither brown nor white, but a luminous blue, and clear as the morning sky. She held it as if a jewel had materialized in her palm.

"See that nothing-looking hen over there with the bluish feet?" Lambert said. "Looks like she forgot to come in out of the cold. It's from her. She'll give you a fresh one every day near about. They're not blue inside, of course. Looks just like any other old egg. But you can have blue eggs for breakfast, a blue egg for a new day, like Easter all year long."

The chickens became Emily's calling, as they had been in her childhood. She delighted in them—how they squawked and scratched around the gate, their heads bobbing, eyeing her sideways as she tossed out corn she brought bundled in her apron. Emily knew each one and named them—Lucy, Juliana, Sylvie, Greta—the way her father had named his cows. She loved their gawky feet, the array of colors to those skinny, scary feet: yellow, brownish, almost white, and the blues from that one strange hen Lambert had made considerable effort to find for her. With those wintry-looking feet came the gift of spring-hued eggs, which he presented to her fresh boiled and warm every morning for breakfast, a daily reminder that life goes on.

Wood sizzled in the firebox, and bright coals flickered in its dark interior. With a scrap of blue quilt, Emily lifted the coffeepot and poured. Outside on the step, she studied Lambert's profile against the emerging light. He had the plow on its side, filing at the back edge. As she approached, Lambert rose without turning. She stood beside him, her feet bare against the chill earth. The steaming cup warmed her palms. Emily handed it to him; his fingers were chilled from filing the plow. They stood in the cool air, looking out over the land as the horizon cleared with the rising sun.

"I love this time of day," Lambert said as he sipped the coffee. "Something about the light. And the smell of the earth. Like everything comes around new."

Emily smiled and touched his bare forearm, tucked up the fold of his shirtsleeve.

"Having the plow in my hand settles me inside," he said, rolling the cup in his hands. "Something about the sound of the file shushing away the dull edge. I know it just goes back in the dirt, but it has a rhythm, like life, the plow does. It keeps you walking slow enough to see the world."

Emily held out her hands for the empty cup. She saw he was studying her.

"I am with child," she said.

"Ah," he said, and she felt his coffee-warmed hand on her belly.

Emily leaned her head into his shoulder, letting her belly slide into the assurance and comfort of his palm. With her arm around his neck, the still-warm cup dangled against his spine. This man, she thought. This man will be a father, this man who thought to live out his life alone, this man who has loved me from afar in all these years of grief and sorrow, longer even, through my girlhood. *Had I known*, she thought, *would I have chosen differently?* Would this have been my life instead of that? No use to go there. None at all. It had been what it had been. Now she was here with Lambert beside the plow with its gleaming edge, his arm around her, his hand on her belly where their child together waited. She was not afraid.

Chapter 39

Lambert relished the sight of Emily holding their son. He was charmed at every new aspect of his wife: the way she dug worms, played with the children, chased lightning bugs, and handled a plow. He experienced joy just watching her. Joy in the life that had become his, and the baby she placed in his arms when the time arrived. They agreed to name him Will, after the brother for whom she still grieved. Rosa Claire wanted to know how the baby had told them his name.

The farm went on as always. Lambert rested his saw on the ground and looked up. Emily stood at the edge of the yard, an old blue-checked dress hanging loosely about her. Without petticoats, she appeared insubstantial, even in the leftover swelling of her pregnancy. Lambert removed his hat, brushed his brow with his forearm, and started toward her. Sweat trickled from his temples into the corners of his eyes. There was sawdust in his eyelashes. Emily raised her hand. Overhead, a breeze unsettled the leaves of the sapling Lambert was cutting. Both of them shaded their eyes from a glint of sun on the saw blade. Lambert reached for her.

"What is it, Emme?"

"I am just low today," she said.

"Not the children? Or the baby?"

"No, Rosa Claire and Lonso fuss over him like a mama hen with one chick. He's as much sibling to them as they are to each other. I should be rejoicing, Lambert."

"But something's amiss."

"I don't have a name for it." Emily paused, examined his face, lined with sawdust plastered in the rivulets of sweat. "It's so strong."

"So are you, Emme."

"So many people suffering here about. Especially the women. I should be grateful." She twirled a loose thread from his frayed cuff between her fingers. She must remember to turn those cuffs.

"Maybe you're afraid of things seeming too good," he said.

"That has words to it."

"Are you afraid because of the rift with—"

"Don't say it, Lambert. I don't want to hear it." Emily turned her back to his chest, letting his arms fold around her; her head tilted to the side, as he kissed her neck. She could feel the grit of the sawdust. The tree would be down with a few more strokes. She had interrupted his work.

"All right," Lambert said. "But that has words, too, even if you don't want to hear them."

She pushed away from him. He held on to her and she stopped.

"Come to dinner when you get that tree down," she said. "Ginny has made a pot of corn-cob soup. I'll be all right."

Lambert watched her walk away, knowing she would not—not so long as the rupture remained unhealed between her and Adeline.

CHAPTER 40

Within a few weeks the countryside would erupt first with the news of General Lee's surrender at Appomattox Court House and only six days later, on Holy Saturday, hordes of drunken men would spill out into the streets of Greensboro, cheering the assassination of Abraham Lincoln. The face of the country and the face of Reconstruction would be forever changed.

Beyond the porch overhang, the clouds stretched near to tearing. The rocker creaked as Ginny eased her back into it. The respite was fleeting. As Ginny rolled her head to stretch her aching neck, she spied the pot of nasturtiums, spindly orange and yellow, too dry even for nasturtiums. Ginny had nursed them in that pot all winter, trying to provide enough sun to keep a little joy in her cabin. In her fatigue, she tried to ignore them, but duty and the habits of a lifetime won. She rose and headed for the well.

As the bucket sloshed its way up, Ginny turned at the sound of an approaching horse. She recognized Shaver, a slim, nervous man, the color of almonds, who had appeared one day from unknown origin or history and settled in to help Adeline. He rode Adeline's blue roan.

"You thirsty?" Ginny said, reaching for the gourd.

"I am, thank ye," Shaver said, dismounting.

"What you need, Shaver?"

"Nothing. Got news. Can't say good or bad. Old Man Slate finally drunk himself to death. Miss Adeline told me to come on over and give the news to you, Ginny. Found him this morning in the shed."

Ginny nodded, puzzling on how, or even if, to break this news to Emily. "Miss Adeline all right?"

"She's all right. Not much different from any other day."

"Tell Miss Adeline I'll ponder the news." Ginny untied and retied her apron strings. "You be careful riding hereabouts. Got your papers?"

"Hell, yeah. War's over and I'm a free nigger, woman." Shaver remounted.

"Free nigger don't mean you a safe nigger, now do it?" she said.

The bucket teetered on the rim of the well. Ginny hauled it to the porch and poured a stream of water on the nasturtiums. News or no news, life demanded her.

A torrential rain came in the night. Benjamin's tin roof had been alive with it, the air charged with the electrical energy of lightning. The morning dawned soggy and gray, the earth pulpy and scattered with debris.

Sleep had been fleeting. The nightmare had shaken him like a hound killing a rat. In the dream, lightning had entered the room. Its flickering touched nothing, but held him prisoner, knowing that to put his foot out was to enter a river of lightning. He sat up, thinking he could wake himself enough to end the dream. *Ain't nothing but a dream*, he thought. But as his eyelids sagged again, the swirling currents recommenced. So he asked out loud, "What you want from me?" The answer he heard was that something must die. In the middle of the floor stood a man with long dark hair and beard. He held out a hand and beckoned. Benjamin stepped into the river of lightning, astonished to find himself alive and free. The man disappeared. Benjamin was alone with his disbelieving hope.

In the wake of the dream, Benjamin had slept, a hard sleep that left him exhausted. When he heard Lucian stir in the early dark, he had difficulty rising. The bed, the sheet, his nightclothes all felt laden with the storm. As he followed the sounds of Lucian's preparations, Benjamin pulled at his lower lip with his fingers. He rubbed at his thigh, aching now with the wet weather.

He stood watching his son thrust his few possessions into a damp croker sack.

"Morning, Daddy," Lucian said, tying the sack and depositing it by the steps. He braced himself against the post and faced his father. "You gone be all right, Daddy. Samantha got you now." His voice was hoarse.

Benjamin did not answer. He searched the dim outlines of Lucian's features, seeking the soft face of the boy who no longer existed. "Where you gone go, son?"

"North. I don't know, just north."

"Got your papers?"

"Don't know as I need them, but I got them. Miss Emily give them to me yesterday. Look all official, by the judge's hand and signature. Reckon he fix them a long time ago. Papers for a boy. Description don't match me no more, but I don't reckon it matters. War over and we all free, anyway, thanks to Mr. Lincoln, even if he dead. Miss Emily give me some Federal dollars. Don't know where she got them or if they worth the paper they on. Don't reckon she had many, but she give me what she had. She say, 'You take care.' Bout all she say. Seem like she want to cry and she went on back in the house."

"North is a big place," said Benjamin, pulling at his beard.

"I know."

"Long way from home, boy."

"Ginny fix me eight days' ration. I got it all in the sack."

Benjamin walked to the edge of the porch. He took his clay pipe and handed it sideways to his son. Lucian took it.

"Judge give me that when he first bought me. Brought me here with a load of scars, just a good-size boy. He say, 'Benjamin, a man needs a good pipe.'"

Lucian put the pipe in his pocket and picked up the coarse sack. One step down, he turned and put his free arm around his father. Benjamin's arms hung slack at his sides.

"You know where home is," Benjamin said. "You ain't no prodigal son."

Lucian nodded. He lifted the sack to his shoulder and stepped out onto the wet road, the pools of the night's deluge mirroring his reflection and the indiscriminate light of a colorless sky.

Chapter 41

From the porch, Emily surveyed the patchwork of wild color and bloom that covered her yard now. The transplants from the woods that had survived filled the space in unregulated drifts. The paths through them created a living puzzle for the children, and for her. She loved to wander among them, see what they might do next to surprise her. Perhaps it was time to add some domesticated flowers. She remembered marigolds and nasturtiums growing in profusion around Ginny's cabin and other slave cabins along the row at the end of the fields. She had loved their brilliance, loved going to Ginny's, holding her hand, smelling the smoke and lamp oil in the house, the greens cooking on the fire. In spring Ginny might present her with violets or pansies, their intriguing faces wet and dipped in sugar, for a treat. In the summer, oxalis, lemony and acidic, leaves and stems and blooms equally seductive to the tongue. Sometimes Ginny gave her lettuce from the slave garden with nasturtium blossoms wrapped inside, a peppery lettuce sandwich, the color of jewels. The flowers were always at Ginny's or one of the other slave cabins, never at home. The women would have gladly planted around her house, but the judge would not have it. After her mother's death, there were things he could no longer bear, despite his inherent goodness and a burning love for his children. The riot of flowers his wife had loved was beyond him. Emily determined to ask Ginny for nasturtiums, for pansies, oxalis, and daisies.

Easter arrived and with it, a picnic by the creek for the children. Emily lay against the moss, which was lush and damp. Through the canopy of leafing branches, she could see the alternating color of the sky: blue and white and blue again, brisk winds sweeping the clouds across the wide expanse. She closed her eyes, the air on her cheek like the touch of a child. The children's laughter mingled with the murmur of the water running its familiar way across the stones.

I belong, Emily thought. *I am here.* She turned her head and watched the children from this strange perspective: their chase, Lambert with them, dodging. Aimee tripped and Emily started up, but Lambert caught the girl in his arms and lifted her high in the air. She joined in his spontaneous laughter. Lambert set her down, dodging Lonso's tag. Lambert caught his breath, patted Rosa Claire's curls, and smiled over at Emily. He removed his hat, slapped it against his pant leg, and tossed it onto the moss beside her.

"I'm about out of wind, children," Lambert said, and sat down beside Emily. The children protested, pulling at his arms and shirt. "No," he said, "you all know how to play tag without me. Nothing I can teach you about that. I'm going to make sure this pretty lady lying here in the shade is all right. She just might be in need of resurrecting."

"You are my resurrection," she said.

Lambert sat facing Emily, one arm around his knee. He peered up at the sky. Pushing his hat aside, he lifted her hand from the moss, kissed her palm, and lay it across his knee. Her roughened fingers caressed his. "You are your own resurrection, Emme. No one can do that for you."

She smiled, his words sinking deep into her. "I always liked Easter," Emily said. "Maybe it's the time of the year—the first new leaves. So fragile, yet so alive, all at once."

"They do make these old woods light," Lambert said. Indeed the world had taken on a celestial kind of glow.

"You can feel the wind breathing," she said, "blowing on things, like the fluff of a ripe dandelion."

A gale of laughter broke from the children, the sound rippling across the creek. Emily turned her head as Lambert lifted his.

"Lambert," she said, "I want to make a child. I want a child to start its life this very day."

"Well, in that case, Emme," he said, rising, "we'd best get these children home and fed and settled down."

"I can't imagine they need feeding," Emily said. "But they can peel their eggs. They've had enough fried chicken today to be laying eggs themselves!"

Protests rose as Ginny gathered the boiled blue eggs the children had discovered along the creek, putting them into the various baskets, not all of which Emily recognized. The children mustered quickly, clamoring over whose blue egg was whose, but with a sense of fairness, Emily noted, handing off extras to those who had less. No one went wanting today. Their young world had been so altered by war, so shattered by events of which they had little awareness, but the children were exulting in this good day.

"Yes," Emily said, walking ahead of Lambert, reaching back for his hand, "let's us be at home. You and me at home."

"What you doing, Samantha?' Benjamin hardly limped now when he walked, but going up the steps into the cabin was still difficult.

"I'm going," she said. A croker sack bulged with her few possessions. He could see the corner of the Bible she couldn't yet read where it poked at the fabric. "You going with me?"

"Going?" Benjamin took hold of her shoulders, and she lowered her bundle to the floor beside the bed. "Where you think you gone go?"

"I'm going where I ain't never been a slave, Benjamin. I'm going to another life."

He dropped his hands, clasping her elbows. "I ain't never had another life, Samantha. This is my home. Judge rescued me when I was just a boy. Been here ever since. Been growing old right here. Growing old with you."

Samantha surveyed the room.

"I ain't never had a life of my own," she said. "Never had a life that didn't belong to somebody else."

"But you free now, Samantha. And you got a home. You got me. What you thinking?"

She faced him. "I'm thinking I want to be somebody I ain't never been. I been sold and bought, and sold again. I been beat and I had the lash. And I got you. And yes, a home. What I ain't never had was me. Without all that hanging on me. I'm going north and find me a place where don't nobody know me this way. And I want you to come."

Benjamin sighed and slumped onto the bed. He rubbed his forehead, shook his head. When he raised his face, his cheeks were wet with tears.

"I'm old," he said. He wiped at his face with the back of his hand. "Ain't no way to tell what's waiting out there. You seen all them hungry folks tagging out after them Yanks. Seem like it's supposed to be so much better, but I don't know that. I ain't sure them Yankees care so much about us colored, for all they fine talk and valor. Maybe some do, all they dead in this war. Sometimes I'm not sure we're what this war's all about." He straightened his back. "I can't hardly let you leave, Samantha."

She came and sat beside him, took his hand, lay her cheek against the back of it. He put his arms around her.

"Closest thing I've come to being a person is here with you, Benjamin. But I got too much yearning for something more, for being somebody without no history. That's freedom and I want it. And I want it with you."

"Now my boy's gone, you all I got, Samantha. You my home now." He tilted his head. "You got a plan?"

"Some of Conklin's people going north, 'stead of following after the troops. It's about six of us."

"Just like that?" he said. "No goodbyes?"

"Just like that. You try saying goodbye and you be too torn up inside to go. All them folks you love gone be all right. They ain't your people, Benjamin. I am." She handed him a sack and began to help him gather bits and pieces of his meager life. "And you and me, we gone be all right."

He kissed the small scar at her temple, where some mistress from her tangled history had hit her with a walking stick.

"I can't hardly let go," he said.

Samantha hesitated, then held out her hand. He smiled at her and took it.

The shovel clanged against the barn as Mason dropped it and eased himself to the ground. Gauging by the height of the sun, it must have been nearly noon and the trench only half done. Mason was tired and slower than he had been before the Slate lynching. More than the gunshot wound, the lynching itself and Hammond's murder clutched at him. He knew the men in that mob, the men of his town. Some he saw daily. But there was nothing to charge them with. They knew as well as he whose gun took aim at Hammond's head, whose finger pulled the trigger. And in the mêlée, whose hand had almost killed him, too. He had not witnessed whose hands had made the knot, slipped it over Charles's head, whose horse had held him so briefly at the end of the rope. He was sure it had been Jeremiah. Maybe Conklin's horse. He would never be certain, though his instincts felt it. He'd been in a pool of his own blood by then. But the men who had been there knew. So he held himself distant. And they, in their guilty knowledge, skirted him wide. With the war, a good number had gone elsewhere to kill and be killed. Jeremiah had fled into the Confederate army, into his false safety and ironic justice. Those slaves who'd brought Judge Matthews's body home were all trustworthy men, but each one had seen a slightly different thing. Putting it all together, Charles had outright ambushed a good man and deserved to hang, but not like that. No, not like that. Mason sighed and braced himself with the shovel to get to his feet. He stood there, thinking not of his garden, but of guns, bone and gut, visceral secrets not meant to be exposed.

However, this was the life he had chosen. Greensboro was still frontier, with all its hope for new life and its escape from the unforgiven past. Respectability and goodness mingled with drunkenness, thievery, fistfights, and whores. And Mason was the sheriff, chosen to settle violence, if it could be settled. If not, he delivered word to the widow or the mother, should there be one. He officiated hangings, except this one that so haunted him. He had grown tired. Tired of quarrels and squabbles, hostility and conflict. Tired of bearing cruel news.

Among the memories was Adeline's face framed in the window of the jail door. He had unlocked it and let her in. He had seen her face when the bullet shattered Hammond's brain. That face haunted his nights, when he woke sweating and fighting for breath. He had not seen Adeline cut Charles from the tree, but he dreamed it, over and over. In the dream, Charles would still be alive, his face black, his tongue protruding, but alive. Mason would hand Adeline the knife and watch her hack at the rope. He would be too paralyzed to help. The body would plummet, Charles's hollow eyes fixed on Mason.

He might have spared her. He could have kept the bolt in place. He could have said no and she might have gone home.

Adeline had known what could happen. She'd had a choice and she took it. He'd had a choice and he made it. If he had forced her to go, had brought her dead sons home to her, the face in his memory would still be terrible, only in a different way. Instead, Mason carried the sight of her face with Hammond's head exploding in her hands.

That vision fixed itself to Adeline's face every time he saw her, which was frequent now that Thomas had died. She seemed to accept him when he could not accept himself. She welcomed him when he came. He worked alongside Shaver, mending fences and sharpening tools. Sometimes, he scrounged the woods for wild strawberries, which the three of them ate with a bit of cream from her one remaining cow. Whatever he did there, Mason was plagued by the absence of her sons. Belinda, too, was gone now, holding on to her delusions of the past.

Mason studied his half-dug trench. The location was good. The ground sloped out from the barn and so would be fertile from the residue of manure. The southwest sun would be good. A rain barrel stood handy at the corner. Below the slope Mason would mound a row for potatoes, put in tomato seeds, preserved from last year. He had not decided where to plant peas and he had no seeds for okra, unless some neighbor gifted him. Not likely with the war. He would nail twine to the siding to hold pole beans, and between them he would plant sunflowers, for beauty and for the seeds he would roast on the hearth come winter. He imagined the crunch between his teeth, the arc of the shell as he spit it into the fire.

Mason wiped his brow on his sleeve and resumed digging. Tomorrow, the seeds would be in the ground. He would haul water along the two long rows before he saddled his horse and rode to the jail. He would leave his badge on the desk; then he would go to Adeline. He would beg her forgiveness.

* * *

Adeline balanced herself on the handle of her hoe, working at a speckled gray stone lodged in the sole of her boot. When it did not budge, she let the hoe fall and sat on the ground. She pried a small, pointed rock out of the plowed dirt and used it to gouge the stone from her boot. She lay back on the cool earth, fitting her long body into the furrow. Loose hair dangled in her face. Digging a kerchief out of her pocket, she wiped her forehead and pushed the hair from her eyes. Using her fingers like a comb, she readjusted her hair and lay with her forearm shading her eyes.

From her sanctuary between the rows, she could see the tips of the picket fence, the angle of the weathered plow handles, the golden tops of seed corn poking from her basket, and a few fallen grains on the dark earth. She fingered the handle of the hoe lying beside her, the smooth wood seasoned by the work of her hands. Adeline inhaled the heavy, promising scent of the soil. Above her head lay her trove of seed packets, ordered over winter from Ferry-Morse. The soft-colored illustrations on the packets pleased her: baskets of squash, red beets, and little blond girls with aprons full of flowers. She pasted those images inside her chifferobe and her cupboard doors, so that when she dressed and when she made biscuits, they greeted her. She loved the names as much as the drawings: Scarlet Runner, Bluebell, Four O'Clock, Ruby Chard, Snap Dragon, Yellow Crookneck, Rutabaga, Lupine. Beyond the Ferry-Morse packets in the furrow lay her own thin envelopes of saved seed from last year's harvest: tomato, lettuce, mustard and turnips, dried Kentucky Wonder, and lady peas. Late-morning sun glinted off the blade of the hoe, reflected bits of sky glimmering on its sharpened edge. *No jewel I ever saw that bright*, she thought.

After another peaceful minute, Adeline reached for the hoe. Her back arched, her eyes closed against the sun, her hands pushed hard against the loose earth. And then she settled, her body fitting itself to the earth. Mason found her there, a packet of mustard seed beside her stiff fingers. It was he who brought the news.

Lambert massaged the back of his weathered neck, kneading the stiff muscles. Looking over his shoulder, he noticed a rake left with the tines up. He took a deep breath, held it, let it out. Shaking his head, he pulled the latch. At the threshold he scraped the dirt from the soles of his boots and entered the house.

"Lambert?" Emily called from the front room. Her voice was bright.

"It's me, Emme." His feet felt leaden.

As she came through the hallway, Lambert half turned away.

"Are you all right, Lambert? It's early. Are you ill?"

He took Emily by the hand and led her through the house to a chair beside the fireplace. He pulled up another chair and adjusted its leg on an uneven floorboard.

"What is it?" Her voice became tight and fearful.

"Emme," he said, taking time to find his voice. "Adeline is dead."

Emily's face blanched, her hands clenched the arms of the chair.

"She died this morning. Mason found her a while ago lying between two furrows in a fresh-plowed row. He sent Shaver to Belinda's and came to find me out in the field."

The struggle to absorb the news, to believe it even, played across Emily's face.

"I am sorry, Emme. I cannot imagine how this—"

Emily rose. She raised her hands as if to ward off his words. Lambert gripped her arms, as her body went slack. A painful cry escaped her and then she wept, her head against his shoulder. He held her through the tears and the choking breaths until they finally stopped.

As Emily's last sobs subsided, Lambert saw Ginny in the

doorway, waiting, her dark face glistening with tears. He knew that his throbbing inadequacy was plain to her. His voice failed him. Together, the two of them guided Emily to the bed in the back room. Lambert lifted her feet and unlaced her boots. He could hear Ginny humming as she stroked Emily's hair. When he stood, Ginny pulled the rocking chair close to the bed for him. She patted his shoulder as she turned to leave the room.

When Emily opened her eyes, Lambert was sitting like that, watching her, waiting for her life to transcend yet another death. Hers and the new life within her.

On a Friday morning in late April 1865, in the wake of a doomed cause and a slain president, Adeline was buried next to Hammond. From the quiet cover of the woods, Emily cried without a sound, Lambert beside her, his arm around her. In the distance, Belinda wept beside the grave, held up by her husband, George, as three black men, one young and two older, lowered the coffin of finely varnished oak into the ground. On the other side of the grave, separated from Belinda by its chasm, Ginny stood with Rosa Claire and Lonso. Each child held one of her hands. Belinda ignored them. She turned to George without speaking. He took her arm and walked her to the carriage waiting in the pathway. One of the black men held the horse while George helped Belinda up and mounted after her. The servant took the reins and flicked them. The sleek black horse tossed its head and snorted.

Ginny stood with the children. When the carriage pulled away, she bent and spoke softly, glancing from one child to the other. Rosa Claire leaned over the grave and released her grip on the handful of flowers she carried. Lonso hid his face in Ginny's skirts. She lifted him onto her hip and held out her other hand to Rosa Claire. The girl's narrow shoulders shook, though the sobs were inaudible to her mother until the little group reentered the edge of the woods.

Emily reached for Rosa Claire's hand, but she shrugged away. Together, the five of them trudged back through the undergrowth to the road, where their mule and wagon waited. No one spoke during the ride home. Emily rode in the rear between her children, an arm around each. Rosa Claire sat stiff and unbending under her mother's embrace.

Arriving home, it was to Ginny that Rosa Claire reached for assistance from the wagon. She did not look at her mother. At dinner, the girl ate half her piece of cornbread and drank her milk, then asked to be excused. Ginny helped the child unlace her boots and climb up onto her big bed, the one that had been Emily's, built and carved by her great-grandfather Matthews before the family migrated South. There the little girl stayed until long past her normal naptime. When Emily looked in, she was sure Rosa Claire was pretending to sleep.

Later, Emily returned to find the bed empty. She wandered through the house searching and found her daughter on the edge of the porch, legs dangling, propped against the wall, her back to the door. Emily sat on the ledge beside her and reached for her hand. Rosa Claire stuck it in her pocket.

"I'm so sorry," Emily said. "I know—"

"No, you're not. And you don't know!"

"I know you are upset, but it is not acceptable to—"

"Don't talk to me, Mama. Don't tell me 'not acceptable.'"

"Rosa Claire, what has taken hold of you? Being upset that your grandmother Adeline died does not account for your speaking to me like this."

"She was my grammy. My grammy. You don't know anything!"

"I know a great deal about death and losing someone—"

"You don't even know who Grammy was! You wouldn't even let me see her!"

"There are reasons—"

"But she came anyway! And you didn't know it. Ever. She loved us!"

"She came?"

"Yes, she came. A lot! She brought us stuff from her garden and jelly and fig preserves and little dolls she made herself. And you never noticed. You thought it was Ginny all the time, but it was Grammy and I loved her. And you didn't!"

Emily turned away, stunned. It took her some minutes to speak again. Rosa Claire was crying.

"No, Rosa Claire, I loved her dearly once. She was a second mother to me. She supported me, took care of me, when I could not take care of myself or of you or Lonso. No, Rosa Claire, you are wrong. I have loved her very much."

"Then why did you be mad at her and not let her visit and not let me go see her? Why did it have to be secret when she came?"

Emily lay back on the hard boards of the porch floor, her hands above her head.

"I don't know how to tell you. I don't know how to explain so that you could understand. When you are older—"

"No, Mama. Now. Tell me now!"

"Sometimes, grown-ups make mistakes. We don't mean to, just like you don't mean to, but sometimes we do. And when we do, sometimes they are very big." Emily rolled her head toward the child. "When did Grammy come?"

"I don't know. All the time. And sometimes she didn't. And I would miss her." The little girl stared out across the field, but her narrow shoulders softened.

"Where was I?"

"Gone. I don't know. In the field, I reckon."

"Why didn't you tell me?"

"I thought you would be mad at me. Or mad at Grammy."

"I might have been."

"Why, Mama?"

"Your grammy and I had a misunderstanding. I thought she knew—some things that maybe she didn't really know. Things I couldn't—"

"What things, Mama?"

"Things maybe none of us can know. But whether she did or not, the uncertainty of it all was too hard for me. I blamed her."

Rosa Claire turned toward her mother, who was crying now. "Are you sad, too, Mama?"

"So very sad."

"Can we be sad together?" Rosa Claire laid her head in Emily's lap, her fierce little hands brushing at the wrinkles in her mother's skirt. The girl shifted her body into a ball and pushed her feet against the side of the house. Emily remembered that day when she had decided to live, remembered how she had found Rosa Claire on Adeline's porch, in a ball like this, and had wrapped herself around this child. She wrapped her arms around her now.

When the children settled for the night, Emily found Ginny out back, gathering kindling for the next morning. Ginny deposited her load and brushed her hands.

"Ain't you plumb wore out now, honey?"

"Yes, Ginny. I'm 'wore out' with too many things."

"Yes'm. I expect you is."

"Come sit with me and talk, please. There seems to be a great deal I do not know."

Together in the gathering dark, the women sat on the back steps, their history holding them close. Emily asked, and Ginny answered: how Adeline had come, whenever possible, with vegetables and Black-eyed Susans, and tiny dolls or bears made from scraps, stuffed with scavenged cotton and wood shavings, small enough for Rosa Claire's pocketed hand. Ginny confessed to sending Adeline word by Lucian when she knew Emily would be gone into town for the day. She told Emily how she had helped plan secret picnics and berry pickings. Ginny knew she'd taken chances, feared that both Belinda and Emily would be furious had they suspected. When Emily shook her head, Ginny confessed that she knew it was Belinda who would be most furious, knew it was Belinda whom both Adeline and Emily feared. In truth, whom even Ginny feared.

"I suppose it is time I paid Belinda a visit, Ginny. Tomorrow. I have a lot to think about tonight." Emily held Ginny's hand.

"You sure you want to go seeing Miss Belinda? I mean, real sure?"

Emily nodded.

"You don't know what you getting into, honey. Ain't no telling. That woman is unexpected. She unhinged."

"I know how unexpected, Ginny. Now go to bed. I am not the only one here who is 'plumb wore out.'"

The house was dark. Lambert had banked the fire, secured it with the screen, and was standing by the mantel when she entered. A momentary vision of her father there assailed her. She went straight to Lambert and put her arms around him. With one hand he stroked the even part in her hair, twirled his finger around her ear, and bent to kiss her. She pressed herself against his warm chest. In his hand, as he drew it down from the mantel, was a book. She felt it against her back as he embraced her.

"There is something you need to see," he said, holding the slender volume, one finger marking a place. "You'll need a lamp."

Puzzled, she ignited a broom straw in the embers and lit the lamp. He opened the book, handed it to her, and motioned for her to sit. He resumed his stance at the hearth, watching her.

Emily stared at Charles's orderly handwriting. She began to read, puzzling over the journal: a trip into town, brief comments on the day's patients, a purchase list of medications, a reminder to himself to speak to Benjamin about repairs to the shed door. Then a break. A smudge of ink spilled on the page. A growing unsteadiness to the writing. And the words:

My inexperience has betrayed me. No, more to the point—my arrogance. I have failed my wife and my sister. Belinda is left with almost nothing. Not quite true, a hell of a lot more than we had coming up, but not as much as she should have as Will's widow. I must make amends to her. The judge blames me for his death, thinks I poisoned him, and in a way, I did. I should have stopped. Should have been less proud, less cocksure of myself. Had I at least listened to Mama. I should have defied Belinda. Will might have died, regardless. But at least not by my doing, not by digitalis poison. Then I would be the one to blame myself—not Emily, not her father. I want so much to lay it all on Belinda. So tempting, but I dare not. She was so furious. Insisted. But she didn't know. Hell, I didn't, either, though I should have. Such a fragile balance. She said what I wanted to hear. I wanted to be the hero. Wanted the judge's approval. No, more than that. I wanted praise and gratitude and reward. Like Belinda, I wanted belonging. Now I must make this up to her. I must convince the judge to give her the land.

Emily folded the book in her lap; her fingers gripped its edges.

Lambert squatted beside her and took her hand. "At least now you can be sure," he said.

Morning came after the long exhaustion of the night. She had slept briefly and had dreamed. Adeline was there, had smiled at her and handed her a knife. Above them Charles's body twisted from the tree. They held the knife together and cut him down, his body falling into her arms. She struggled against the weight of it and gagged at the blood pouring from invisible wounds. Her mouth was full of it and she strangled. Somehow she swallowed and as she did, a miraculous peace fell upon her. A disembodied voice said one word: *Communion.*

As Emily left the house, she also left behind her the hilarity of the boys as Rosa Claire and Aimee teased them with waving spoonfuls of grits. Emily clasped the ties of her bonnet as she descended into the unexpected chill of the wind. She thought how the weather these past years was as unreliable as life. Lambert waited at the foot of the steps, his face restrained and grave, his head bare.

"Emme," he said. His voice blew toward her in the wind, quiet, intimate. Her name was like a prayer, the kind offered when knowing how to pray is lost.

The green bonnet took flight in a gust of wind and Lambert leaped to retrieve it. He slipped it over her head, grappling with the wind, holding the brim while Emily tied the bow. When it was secure, he put his arms around her, feeling the swelling of her waist against him. He rocked her side to side.

"I am going with you, Emme. I'll stop whenever you say and let you walk the rest. And then I'll wait."

Emme pressed her hand to Remnant's muzzle as she passed. The old mule turned his nose into her palm and snuffled. After Lambert settled her in the wagon, he opened a worn, gray blanket across her lap and tucked it under the sides of her skirts. They rode in silence, his hand over hers. When they neared the Gattaway place, he helped her down. Without speaking, Emily walked away. She did not look back.

The road crunched in precarious ruts, dried hard after the early-spring deluge. Emily struggled along the uneven ground, her side vision limited by the brim of her hat. *Like blinders on a horse,* she thought. *Like invisible blinders that have hampered me all my life.*

Around a curve, the cedar-lined allée to the house rose up. Emily was unprepared. She studied the brick Greek revival that

George and Belinda Gattaway shared, its imposing height and entablature supported by enormous Doric columns. She walked up the immaculate brick path and onto the wide verandah. Allowing her finger to trace the faux marble surface, Emily half-circled one of the enameled columns. Behind her the wind whirled a few orphaned leaves, left behind from the other side of winter, across the path.

Before her stood the door with its tall inserted panels, its knocker a grim lion's head, holding the heavy ring in its mouth. No one came to the clang when she lifted the ring and let it fall. She scanned the unplowed fields, scraggly still with bits of last year's harvest. Inside her the baby moved and Emily lay her hand across her abdomen. She lifted the heavy knocker again. The door opened and there was Belinda. Neither woman spoke. Belinda made as if to close the door, but then stepped out, pulling it partially shut behind her.

"How dare you come to my house," Belinda said. Her voice was low, harsh, almost secretive.

Emily did not waver. Belinda opened the door wider.

"You're letting in the chill," she said, and backed inside.

Emily followed.

The center hall was lofty, spacious, and chill. A massive arch divided the front portion from the rear. On either side, expansive double doors opened: on the left, to an elegant muraled dining room; on the right, to a parlor where a small fire burned beneath a *faux bois* mantel. An expensive paper of red poppies in an intricately latticed pattern covered the walls. Over the sheen of the floors lay carpets in a design of bold imperial circles in contrasting red and gold.

Even in her extravagant silk of gray and gold stripes, Belinda appeared unchanged. She still wore the face of a hard child on a woman's thin body. Dark wisps of curl escaped, as always, from her netted hair. Belinda's green eyes flicked everywhere except at Emily.

"I have learned," Emily said without preamble, "that Adeline visited my children, her grandchildren, without my finding out. Did you know this?"

The women stared at one another, unaware how, with every breath, each inhaled the other's wary exhale.

"Did you know that I loved her?" Emily said at last.

"Loved her? Like you loved me? Like you loved Charles?" Belinda sliced the air with the edge of her hand.

"Belinda, I never—"

"Never what? Never meant to break my mother's heart? To make my brother out a killer? You and your fine family with your godawful genteel greed? Is that what you never meant?"

"To harm—"

"Harm? Well, isn't that a fine word on your tongue! Harm! You, who threw away everything good in my brother? And my mother?"

"I loved her like—"

"Stop it! I won't hear it. Don't you say you loved her like a mother. She was not your mother! You didn't have a mother!"

The blow of Belinda's words was physical. Emily caught her breath.

"She was mine! Do you hear me? Mine. And now she is gone and you have the gall to come here?"

"I need the truth, Belinda. I have so much regret—"

"Regret? For all the filthy, hateful things you did to us?" Belinda took a step toward Emily.

"Stop now, Belinda. Before you have your own regrets."

"Regrets?" Belinda was screaming now. "You think I haven't had regrets? You get out of here. I'm done with you."

"Belinda, please—"

"Belinda, please," Belinda mimicked, her mockery bitter.

She was too close now. Emily crossed her hands over her abdomen and backed away.

"Please what? Please share your mother? Please share your

brother? Please, share your toys?" She stepped closer to Emily. "And while we are at it, Emily, why don't you share with me? You share your brother and your father, and all that land he owned, and all those slaves he didn't free!"

Unintended, Emily reached out. Belinda slapped her hand away.

"What did you imagine this was all about, Emily? Didn't you care that your dear, beloved father refused to settle Will's land on me? Refused me as a daughter when he died? And that Charles tried to help me? Didn't you know your father's glorious rejection was at the heart of this? Holding on to Will's land for those precious children of yours my mother came to see?"

"You are not sane, Belinda. I don't know what—"

"The trouble with you, Emily, is you don't know anything," Belinda snarled. "You never have. You were nothing but a child playing dress-up. A child in a family of landed men." Belinda backed away, her manicured fingers reaching for a threshold to support herself. She found the doorframe and grasped it. "Land, land, and more land, for God's sake. That's all they care about, these men. Land and power. They think it can do everything. That's all it has ever been about. All this bloodshed and death. And God help us, this godawful war."

Belinda collapsed against the doorframe and sank to the floor, knees bent, her hoops awry beneath the silk ruffles, her dainty buttoned boots and white stockings exposed. She covered her head with her hands. "What do you want from me, Emily? Truth? You want truth? I'll tell you the truth." Belinda paused. "I had no idea," she said into the space between her palms. "I didn't know what could—what could happen."

"What are you talking about, Belinda?" Emily moved closer, leaned down to hear Belinda's muffled words.

"About them coming here—no, not here—that other place, Will's place, our place—that stupid old log house your father built. Charles said we could talk and it would all be over. I sent for them—no, him—to come. Your father. Charles told me to. To try to settle the estate. Be done with it, he said. I was so tired. So tired." Belinda leaned her head against the door, rolled it side to side. "I still am," she said.

The clock ticking on the mantel was the only sound. Emily leaned against the doorjamb on the opposite side of the hall. She rocked her body, her hand at her abdomen, waiting. Into the tension, she said, "You sent for my father? And he came? Trusting you both."

"I didn't know. I couldn't. No one could. Not even Charles. It just—happened."

The clock ticked away the time, louder than sound should be, and chimed a quarter hour.

"What happened, Belinda? What exactly—"

"I don't know what exactly. Don't you see? I don't know. I thought he was my father, too. It wasn't land I wanted. It was being a Matthews. And I wanted a father. But he didn't want me. He said there had to be a child. All he wanted was a child and I didn't have one and I hit him, I was so hurt and angry and Charles grabbed me and then it got into a fight. They were pushing and shoving and there was the gun and I snatched it and Hammond tried to get it from me and—" Belinda pressed her white fingers into her stricken face.

Emily rocked, her eyes closed.

"And then there was blood everywhere and blood all over me. How could I have all that blood on me? Oh, God." Belinda vomited into the folds of gray silk between her knees.

In the silence that followed, Emily no longer heard the clock. Her hands tightened over her abdomen. "You killed him? It was you. You let Charles, let Hammond—let them be taken? Hammond died for you? And Charles? You never told the truth? You just went and got another life and let us all believe—" Fingers spread, Emily pushed at the air between. "Even your mother."

Belinda wiped her mouth on the velvet trim of her sleeve and said without looking up, "I want you out of my house."

Emily pushed away from the doorjamb, her balance imperfect. She fumbled with the latch. The door caught in a blast of cold air and slammed open.

Outside, the wind whipped at Emily's skirts as she fled across the verandah and down the steps. At the bottom, she stumbled on her petticoats. Her vision blurred, but she caught herself. The green bonnet flew from her head, hanging from her neck by its ties. When Emily bolted into the road, Lambert was waiting.

Chapter 42

When the baby came, Rosa Claire was all questions as to her name, a name Emily thought she knew, but could not be sure. Weeks passed and the child was simply called Baby Girl. A quiet, strong infant, she nursed well, kneading at her mother's breast, pushing away hard with her little hands when she was full. She rarely cried and woke only once in the night to be fed.

"I'm taking the baby on an outing this afternoon," Emily said one day at dinner. "I may be a while."

"Where to, Mama?" the boys asked in unison.

"Just out."

"Can I go with you, Mama? I don't need a nap and I'll be safe. The war is over now," Rosa Claire said, her demeanor straightforward, as if she sensed the coming of something important.

"May I," Emily corrected. She studied her daughter's face, the unguarded openness of the very young. "Yes, you will be safe," she said. "Here, hold the baby while I get your things."

"All by myself?"

"All by yourself."

Emily propped the baby in Rosa Claire's arms while she

reached for a shawl, but Ginny was ready with it. She wrapped it around Emily's shoulders and her arms around Emily. Aimee leaned over and fingered the infant cheeks. Arm in arm the two women stood watching the girls: Aimee beside Rosa Claire, cradling her sister, tucking the soft yellow receiving blanket around her again and again.

Emily retrieved the baby and the three of them went out together. She studied her daughters closely, the one in her arms, the one holding her hand. *Moments like these are drops in a sieve,* she thought. *They will drain away or evaporate. As will sorrow.*

Near the cemetery, Emily stopped and adjusted the baby in one arm. She put her other arm around Rosa Claire's shoulder. When the little girl realized their destination, she raised her clear gray eyes and nodded.

"Would you like to pick some flowers?" Emily asked, and Rosa Claire nodded again, running toward a row of wild forsythia. She returned, arms draped with cascading branches of yellow forsythia. They negotiated their way among the stones and makeshift wooden crosses. There were so many now. The field was crowded with them, for those whose remains had made it home. Emily thought of the war-torn fields filled with young bodies across the land, the dead crowding the dead. She threaded her way through the graves to a plot marked with four wooden crosses, three quite simple, bearing the names of Charles, Hammond, and Thomas, with corresponding dates painted on the plain façades.

"This is your daddy's grave, Rosa Claire. He was a better man than any of us knew," Emily said, her hand on the little girl's head. "Would you like to put some of your flowers on his grave?"

The child nodded and arranged a handful of the blooming twigs on the ground in a small circle.

The fourth cross had been carved from a tree stump and retained the appearance of its origin. The roots remained intact, though clipped so that it sat level, semiburied in the earth. Two intricately carved branches, equally truncated, formed the arms of the cross. Along the back rose a natural, unbroken branch, bearing no leaves. Carvings of ivy wrapped the primary trunk of the cross, on which Adeline's name appeared. Below the name was a single word: *Beloved.* And above it the phrase: *At Rest.* Surely the work of Mason Johnson.

When Rosa Claire looked up, she saw her mother's cheeks were wet with tears. As Emily lowered herself and patted the ground, Rosa Claire laid the remaining forsythia against the stump and curled against her mother. They sat like that, together, in the quiet, until the baby woke and stirred. Emily pulled back the shawl, freeing the infant, who rubbed her clear eyes and stretched.

"Has she told you her name yet, Mama?" Rosa Claire said.

"Yes, her name is Addie Grace."

A READING GROUP GUIDE

THE ABOLITIONIST'S DAUGHTER

ABOUT THIS GUIDE

The suggested questions are included to enhance your group's reading of Diane C. McPhail's *The Abolitionist's Daughter*!

Suggested Questions for Discussion:

1. How familiar are you with instances of opposition to slavery in the South? Were you surprised to learn about Southern abolitionism? Do you know any stories of other areas of resistance to slavery in the South? How do you understand the underlying foundations of such opposition?

2. Were you aware that by the 1820s, manumission—freeing slaves—had become nearly impossible and ultimately illegal? What are your thoughts on the moral dilemma of a man opposed to slavery being himself a slave owner? What other options could he have considered? What might the repercussions have been to those options? How do you view the route Judge Matthews chose?

3. We often think of the "frontier" as the expansion out into the West of the United States. Were you surprised at the idea that Mississippi was, indeed, considered "frontier" in the early to mid-1800s? Since this novel is based on actual history, how does life in Greensboro fit with your concepts of the frontier? How do you see the qualities that motivated people to move toward the frontier in the town of Greensboro?

4. As legends often do, the story of the Greensboro "feud" in reality has taken on a dual tone of "good guys/bad guys," based solely on the motivation of land greed. Yet these families had enough in common that two siblings from each family married siblings from the other. What are your thoughts on the relationship of these two families? What were your initial ideas on reading of the murder and mob lynching?

5. We all have certain unconscious assumptions based on our cultural background. Where and how do you see

such assumptions playing out among the characters in the novel? Did you find yourself affected by your own assumptions as you read?

6. Today we are all familiar with the concept of PTSD, especially in military conflict. The novel examines numerous traumas of a non-military nature and the long-range effects on various characters. How do you see this playing out in the book? Were you surprised to learn that those effects can be lifelong? What about the effect of repeated trauma? How do you see the courage of various characters to overcome their trauma?

7. The Civil War marked the beginning of a major shift in the role of women in the United States, leading to the suffragist movement around the turn of the century. What factors do you see contributing to that shift? How do you see the shift in Emily as a woman as a parallel to this historic shift for women in general? How do you perceive Emily: for example, strong, weak, changeable, likable, unlikable, realistic, idealized, simple, or complex? What qualities in her did you relate to personally?

8. Which of the masculine characters did you identify with? What qualities appealed to you? Frustrated you? Which did you admire, find courageous?

9. Were you surprised by ambiguities and conflicts in various characters? Did you identify with any of them? Where did you find qualities to admire?

10. In general, which characters or scenes might have made you think about your own pre-judgments? Were you surprised? Has that changed your thinking on any issues or on the tendency we all have toward premature judgment of others without knowing their full story?